KATE MOSES

Kate Moses was born in San Francisco in 1962 to a British father and an American mother, and grew up in various parts of the United States before returning to California to attend university. She subsequently worked as an editor in publishing and as literary director at San Francisco's Intersection for the Arts, and in 1997 became one of the two founding editors of Salon.com's *Mothers Who Think* website, which led to the American Book Award-winning anthology *Mothers Who Think*, co-edited with Camille Peri. She lives in San Francisco with her husband and their two children. *Wintering* is her first novel.

'It's generally not advisable for a first time novelist to imagine herself into the mind of a famous poet, particularly one as famously complicated and adored as Sylvia Plath. But if the writer is as discerning and talented as Kate Moses then what should be an impossible project is not only viable but significant . . . *Wintering* is beautiful and moving . . . This is a novel about ambition, motherhood, identity and love. The real story, though, is that of a woman finally finding her muse.' Kate Bolick, *New York Times*

'Moses sets out brilliantly Ted and Sylvia's compulsive incompatibility . . . [and] produces an extraordinarily perceptive pathology of a dying marriage . . . One of the strengths of *Wintering* lies in how Frieda and Nicholas stay wonderfully present throughout the novel, anchoring their mother to reality and to Hughes . . . the final effect [is] never less than admirable and occasionally breathtaking in the audacity of its achievement.' Ranti Williams, *Glasgow Herald*

'A heartfelt book, penetrative, original and thoroughly researched . . . Her Plath is devastated, resourceful, needy and wilfully domestic. And s[...]ible.' Joanne Hayden, *Sunday Business Post*

D1396148

'It's with an astounding sense of empathy that Moses recreates the final few months of [Plath's] life and succeeds in providing real insight.' Marissa Burgess, *Big Issue*

'It is striking that so lyrical a novel can be so unsentimental about artistic production . . . moving and beautifully sustained . . . a heroic tale about writing in the face of despair, about art as the most cunning weapon one can bring to a marriage.' Regina Marler, *Los Angeles Times*

'Written in lush, luminous prose, *Wintering* made me feel that Moses was channeling Plath herself. The big familiar drama of Plath's story is missing, giving way to all things daily and domestic, which creates an altogether new portrait I found revelatory . . . While the novel is primarily Plath's, Hughes is here, too, revealed not as the villain driving Plath to her death, but as the flawed man whose departure leads Plath to her greatest work . . . A remarkable novel.' Caroline Leavitt, *Boston Globe*

'A valuable, searing addition to the Plath canon.' *Washington Times*

'What *Wintering* suggests is that perhaps what kept Plath going as long as she did was the conviction, however fallible, that she was invincible. Without it, no artist can create, and it's an aspect of the poet that has long been overlooked . . . In uncovering it, Moses does Plath a great service.' Melanie Rehak, *Newsday*

'I resisted this book. Presumptuous, I thought, an author inserting herself into the imagined mind of Sylvia Plath and making a novel out of it . . . But Kate Moses got to me . . . It's the ebb and flow in Plath's mind that Moses performs with such high-wire daring. While we do get the sense that "fixed stars/Govern a life", as Plath wrote in *Words*, we also understand, on every page, that things might have turned out differently.' Cath Kenneally, *Weekend Australian*

'A convincing, beautifully modulated prayer for life.' Dorothy Johnson, *Canberra Times*

For my children, my roses

Contents

I

Morning Song

Gold seeping under her eyelids. Sleeping pills worn off, effortlessly obsolete as breath, their expiration reeling her fast from the silty floor of sleep to the surface, awake. It's morning, or almost: a slow December sun rises through her curtainless bedroom windows, snagging on her rumpled bedcovers, dragging its faint eastern light across her face. Her borrowed single bed is thoroughly churned, coverlet bunched and askew, leaving her exposed in nothing but a nightgown on one unblanketed side, the flannel stiff with cold. She has grown accustomed to tense, motionless drug-sleeps these last months, bedclothes still tucked with hospital precision between mattress and box spring when she wakes. Pinning her still as a crated statue to her bed, binding her in taut cotton like a mummy, like a dangerous patient. Like a patient, more accurately, paralyzed with fear. Trapped in her bedding: it's a feeling that's been not entirely uncomfortable. Not much else has held her since summer.

But something today is changed. More than her untroubled night, her turning in sleep as easily as a fish. Could one call what she's beginning to feel, coming awake just now, ruby light radiating through the fine tissue of her

1

closed eyes, *happiness?* Not that, but something close, though more hollow, tentative, and just faintly perceptible: serenity? Curiosity? Amazing: she's flown in a clean trajectory straight from the blank infinities of sleep to something one could characterize as pleasant. Normal, like other people, waking on normal days. Expectant; anticipating good to come. Compared to her usual dawn aftertaste of despair, this sensation seems positively optimistic, untethered as an escaped balloon – a feeling almost like the first days of falling in love.

What has happened to her customary morning dread, the sharp stink of her panic? Where is her more orthodox heart with its quick metallic ticking, the grinding in her chest? Her mind searches for it, that familiar hemorrhage of fear, the known morning ritual of materializing terror – the terror of what she doesn't know as much as what she does – that has greeted her upon waking since July. She listens: as if it might be recoverable, lost for a moment here in the covers, lurking still in the chill air of the heatless room. It's gone, though, for this morning, receded like the tide for these quick seconds of semiconscious assessment, of her life coming into focus.

Then she remembers: she's in London. Yeats's house with its blue enamel plaque by the door. It's hers – her new home in the city. She's out of the rural purgatory of Devon, the red muck and bawling animals and isolation of her crumbling ancient farmhouse, home now in a poet's flat that seemed fated for her. All hers – she didn't have to share credit with anyone. But there he is, inevitably: Ted.

He'd met her at the train station the day she'd come house hunting last month, an inscrutable shadow shambling along behind through three dank, unacceptable maisonettes. Though it was later, after he'd escaped their latest failure into the tiled entrance of the Chalk Farm tube, his black back hunched in his coat and descending into dark as she watched him leave, another step, the ring of his boot on the stair, so quickly it was over—

It was later, on her own, when she'd seen the sign on her way to her London doctor's office, her infected thumb oozy and pink, rotting apple swollen, pulsing out its distress on her hand. Hurrying over the footbridge and down the Georgian arcade of Gloucester Avenue, her thumb in its bandages aloft and signalling her defeat, then around the corner and suddenly FLATS TO LET next to the blue sign. Address: 23 Fitzroy Road.

As if she'd conjured it: two years ago, she happened upon a freehold for sale on this same street before they'd ever dreamed of Court Green, of its acres of volunteer daffodils and cool twelfth-century walls, of their son born in a gush under its birded thatch, of their gardens, their fingers stained red with Devonshire loam. Two years ago in London, she raced home with Frieda in the pram to their tiny apartment off Chalcot Square – just a block away from where she lies now in her cold bed – bursting to tell Ted: what a benediction (if they could have only afforded it) to live on Yeats's street! Then three months ago in Ballylee, on the last shattering trip together, having climbed the spiral stair to the Irish poet's tower and thrown three pennies for luck, casting them eyes closed into the river sluicing the bridge below, she'd wished for something she then didn't know how to name – something, something she needed to fall into place, her life to right itself, her writing, her disintegrating marriage, something she needed to stop, Ted – she thought then it was Ireland for the winter that she needed. The far sea, its purifying salt and slow clouds, its ginger-scented turf fires in the grate, something equal to Ted's plan of flight to Spain; that's what she thought she'd been wishing for. But she was wrong. Their trip was a disaster. They left Ireland separately, Sylvia returning alone to Devon and the children. Ted wired her a few days later from London. For six years she had feared, even fantasized, shuddering at her garish imaginings, that someone would lure him away. Now someone had. He had come back just once to Court Green, to get his things; if she sued for divorce, he said he wouldn't stop her. He had left her. Her marriage was over.

There is no doubt in her mind: it was this house she'd wished for, unknowingly, from Yeats's tower. This house is going to be her salvation. God, she's made it. She braces for the chill and peels the blankets back. Her mauve wool bathrobe is retrieved from its position of abandonment on the coverlet, tugged over the shoulders of her eyelet-edged floral nightgown; her feet pivot to the hardwood floor. The cold hits her footsoles like a slap. Appropriate, this robe, its color: as if wrapping herself up in a bruise. Her heart feels light enough on this day that she can snatch a quick glimpse of objectivity, even endorse a little self-mocking criticism. In the corner beyond the bed, out of the children's reach, huddles one of the squat electric heaters she brought from Court Green. She tugs its cord out of the wall and scoots it, hugging her bathrobe to her, across the floor toward her desk.

She'd known this house was her omen as soon as she saw it; she's been counting on it (while the leasing agent sluggishly pondered her references) for a month. Jokingly, back at Court Green after finding the flat, she'd pulled out a volume of Yeats's plays from the bookshelves in the front parlor and told Sue the baby-minder she was looking for a sign. She needed benevolent spirits; she needed all the protection she could gather to herself. The page fell open, her finger marking a line in *The Unicorn from the Stars: Get wine and food to give you strength and courage, and I will get the house ready.*

In the fall orchard at Court Green, seventy-two trees hung with apples. She had borrowed a neighbor's long-handled picker and harvested all she could, a canvas sack slung across her breastbone, a three-legged ladder moving with her through the orchard, propped against the gnarled old trunks. Victoria cookers ripe in September, picked with Ted in joyless silence before the final Ireland rupture; then Pig's Noses and russeted Bramley's in October, all layered now in straw in the wine cellar at Court Green but for the bag she filled for London. The honey from her new bees, also, she extracted, leaving the bees enough to winter over, supplemented with plates of sugar syrup, pie tins slow with Tate & Lyle left beneath the bare-branched fruit trees. Potatoes and onions as well dug up, the potatoes scrubbed, the dry platinum hair of the onions braided in a day-long session before the movers came. Just prior to leaving, with Sue amusing the babies and toting the last loads of storybooks and toys out to the Morris Traveller, she carried her clippers and an old pillowcase across the front lawn and cut a treacherous armload of holly. It was downstairs now, arranged in her pewter vase in the unpainted parlor, its red berries plump and shiny, the white-tipped leaves still green and supple, sharp as razors.

The houses lining the mews this dawn behind Fitzroy Road are edged in pink, suspended in a pastel nimbus of foggy illumination as the sun creeps beyond their rooftops.

At her desk before the window, Sylvia sits in the sunrise quiet, her room, her papers, her flannel nightgown washed in thin blue light. She's risen today as she has every day since Ted left her in Ireland in September. While her two children sleep in their cribs, she has gone to her desk before sunrise, a habit begun as a way to give form to her suddenly nebulous days. Sleepless with the unknown, scenes from her marriage unreeling like a nightmare movie in her head, she needed a defense to stave off the creep of her misery.

It started as a helpful suggestion from her practical Devon midwife. With her husband gone and no help with the children, mornings before Frieda and Nicholas woke were Sylvia's only time to think or to write. Being alone had transformed so menacingly: with two babies in diapers, solitude had once seemed such a luxury. It had become, this fall, more of a sentence.

She wasn't sure, at first, that she could either think *or* write: her mind paced like an animal, desperate to flee, to connect, too frantic to do either. But something happened in those predawn mornings at her desk, some alchemy that distilled, concentrating her pain, dripping her fury into a purified essence, her own hot eau de vie. She had been struggling to write like this for years. Then Ted left, and the real muse moved in. Her poems had been flaming up, sparking, dangerous, for months. There was no sign of them stopping.

Blessed Sue the baby-minder – she'd arrived when Sylvia, too, was burning white hot, back at October's end, after a comedically unsuitable (comedic only in retrospect) string of temporary nannies – dour or disapproving or far too dear, one lasting all of an afternoon. The daughter of her Devon midwife's friend, a young nurse on break from her children's hospital job in London, Sue had been a godsend, a lifesaver. With Sue in the house watching the babies, Sylvia had not only been able to recover from the chronic viruses that had kept her feverish since summer – the endless flu, the sinus infections – but had also been able to work for unbroken hours during the day: twenty poems finished since Sue arrived, thirteen of them book poems. And with them the book: the manuscript of her second poetry collection. The poems as well as the London flat found, Nicholas weaned, Court Green packed up and closed, she and the children successfully moved to London: all this with Sue's help. And it was cheerful Sue who kept Sylvia as well as the children company, who cock-horsed Nicholas on her knees and admired Frieda's puzzle and erased the gloom with her chatter while Sylvia prepared dinner or tea each day. Who made it obvious that what Sylvia needed was not a cold, professional nanny but a mother's helper in the truest sense: maybe an au pair, a young, smart, energetic girl like Sue, someone to help with the children and the house, but someone, also, to help Sylvia keep her own loneliness at bay. In Yeats's flat, Sylvia has settled both children into the largest of the three bedrooms and put a desk in her own. This leaves a third bedroom for an au pair, to be hired as soon as possible, as soon as Sylvia can find a suitable girl.

That to do, and finish moving in: painting the walls and the floors. Unpacking the boxes in the kitchen: the copper wedding cookware, her mother's Bavarian dish set brought from Wellesley last summer. Sewing curtains and pillows on her second-hand Singer machine. Hanging the few prints and etchings she's brought, putting up book-shelves. Ordering a double bed, perhaps more furniture if the flat still looks bare after her new chairs and straw carpets arrive. Painting the three bureaus delivered yesterday – blue, she has decided, is her London color, inspired by months of watching dawn light: smoky dark blues, teals, navies, midnights. No more red: red was Court Green. The pink-washed walls trimmed in glossy white. The deep red carpet on the stairs, the Indian rugs in her study and the parlor and the bedrooms, the corduroy curtains she'd sewn. The few precious straw-berries from plants not killed by late frost. The hearts-and-flowers she'd enameled on the children's furniture, on the used beehive given to them in June, on her sewing machine. Court Green was the home they'd made with their own hands. Of course it was red; it was the inte-rior of her heart. It gave her a stab to think of it—

She wouldn't think of it now. Blue was for London. She'd already bought the paint.

She'd bought the paint, gone to the Gas Board and the leasing office, pleaded again with the post office for an earlier telephone hookup – it might be weeks without a phone in the flat – run errands and marketed in Camden Town, even put some hurried order to their piles of disheveled belongings. All this, again, accomplished with help: Sue had stayed one more day after their arrival in London. Without some sort of backup, caring for the chil-dren and finishing the move will absorb most of Sylvia's energy for weeks. She only prays that she and the babies stay well; as it is, she'll be too preoccupied to write until they are firmly settled into the flat. This, then, is her moment of satiation, the thrumming lull, the wing beat of a poet at rest. It was almost Christmas as well, a thought not nearly as grim as it had seemed a few weeks ago. There was shopping to do for the children, decora-tions – the holly was a start – to be made or found.

And she has a deep need, admittedly, to create this order. After the protracted months of not knowing how her fate would play itself, stunned by the melodrama her life had become, feeling herself flinch at every new, sordid revelation, she knows now where she stands: Her husband has become a liar and a cheat, a man she doesn't recognize. He has killed their marriage. He's carried it away, limp in his hands, and forked it over with dirt; she'll never find it again. She'll go back to her home in the spring. Who would know then, who could remember – daffodils waving their yellow heads by the thousands on the April hillside, lilac blowing over the nettled yard in May – what death happened there? The blood, by then, the gory evidence, would be gone, faded from sight. Now, in December, she has a wintering place, perhaps somewhat dormant as it is, but alive to all she has planned. She is a writer in a sleeping indigo city of writers, waiting for everyone else to wake up.

She's impressed, sitting at her desk, astounded even, at her own tranquility. Since July – since she first confronted Ted about his affair – she's been counting the days, the hours, for a moment like this: to feel herself rising above the ugly episodes of her recent life. It's her poems and this move that have done it, that are spoon-feeding her the self-confidence she needs. They are her nectar, her royal jelly; she'll emerge from this stronger than she was. She feels like a warrior queen, poised, victorious in her bathrobe.

No noise, yet, from the nursery. No grumbling squawk and cot rattling from baby Nick or birdlike treble chatter from her two-year-old girl. She'll take this moment of peace, then, if that's what it is, and put herself totally to rights. Before her, on and about the desk, are files of poems, all she's written during the fall as well as some of those that followed her first collection published two years ago. She picks up a string-tied packet that she dropped in haste yesterday onto a stack of unpacked boxes. Wrapped in brown paper is a spring-clasp binder with stiff black boards, purchased while she rushed about yesterday in the Morris wagon. Slipping the binder free and resting it against her lap, she lifts the top file from the stack before her on the desk, slides the sheets from between the file's manila leaves. She holds in her hand a manuscript, a stack of poems half an inch thick, composed on the reverse side of a variety of papers: crisp pink Smith College memorandum sheets; a handwritten draft of one of Ted's early plays, *The Calm;* and the opening chapters of her own first novel, which will be pseudonymously published, British edition only, just after the new year – *The Bell Jar.*

She's been thinking about this new collection of poems, their sequence, which to include, for nearly a month. Savoring the process, drawing it out, this pleasure of creating order, creating a truth, a logic and drive, out of their present seeming randomness. She knows certain things now: how many total – forty-one, just as in Ted's brilliant second collection, *Lupercal,* the one that made him famous; this numerical scorecard is less an ego indulgence than it is purely superstitious, salt tossed over her shoulder. She knows, too, something about the movement of the poems as a body, how they rise like a startled flock, flying as one, wheeling, spreading chaotically across the sky, finally alighting in the same tree. She knows the story she wants them to tell. It is her story. It is where she wills herself to go; it is an incantation. She's giving shape to her life, past and future, with these poems. Like the arrangement of cards in a Tarot deck as they are turned up, it is not just the poems but their relation to each other that matters. She knows where she wants to begin.

The first poem is 'Morning Song'; its first word is 'love.' She likes that, likes that it's a London poem. It seems symbolically right: she's wearing, this minute, the same flannel Victorian nightgown – threadbare now, a London draft blowing up the hem, standing the hair on her unshaved legs on end. As in the poem, her baby, now two of them, will wake soon, calling to her with their twinned morning songs. It started with love, the life she wants to order; she resists the coming of bitterness into her head, of Ted, of how frightened and bereft she has been, how brittle, on some subterranean level, she knows today's elation to be – she wants this moment, the sun blooming hesitantly through the window before her, her room filling with moody winter light, her manuscript complete in her hands, solely to herself, untainted.

It starts, then, with love: the mornings with her infant daughter in the cramped bedroom off Chalcot Square, Ted writing at first on the ridiculous rickety card table the Merwins had loaned, set up in the vestibule. It was his own little womb, she teased him. Too narrow for anyone to get by with Ted crouching enormously in his chair before his papers, facing the walls he had painted a deep vermilion. But that first London apartment was her birthplace also: she labored Frieda in their giant six-foot-square bed, an event – not the birth itself, but the existential act of giving birth to her child, a complete and separate being – she could see, then as now, as nothing but the beginning of her real existence. Becoming a mother: it was the galvanizing moment of her life. She would never do anything else to touch it, this ineffable transforming act. It drew her like a flame; it was a sound she couldn't help turning toward, literally also.

The poem itself she wrote much later, almost a year after, during that strange February of mounting anxiety: the second baby lost so swiftly, Ted's accumulating success and she secretary to his mail and calls, still not writing herself with predictable ease. The dismal prospect of an appendectomy and a week in hospital. In blue jeans and a rumpled shirt left over from Smith, the poet's wan wife, pushing a pram sans makeup. She thought, then, she was losing everything – her unblemished marriage, Ted, the words she could not seem to uncover – and she clung with a desperation she believed she had long ago exorcised. Not the desperation of a supplicant, but of a Fury. It was a month of red and white, a valentine mocking her, something she was part of and not part of, like her poem: the bloody clots, the walls in that claustrophobic apartment, the Irish hair, and the seductive voice on the phone, the lipstick – not hers – she was so sure of, and where was he? The red leather cover of Ted's *Oxford Shakespeare*. How dare he? She ripped it up: the tattered pages floated down, like snowflakes – but it wasn't snow. She'd been waiting every year for snow in England; she waited still. She wanted snow's erasure, its lustration.

And yet, something vanished like snow: Ted came to the hospital, parting the crowds of stubby nurses, cradling more paper in his enormous hands. Carrying offerings priceless as new life! – her wished-for yearly contract from the *New Yorker,* the newsprint cone of nodding tulips, thick steak sandwiches on crisp, unsullied butcher's wrap tied with twine. He'd come; it was all forgotten. She could see now, in the camera obscura of her mind, the scene played in mirror image: her own face as he approached her hospital bed, his hands full. Impossible, but she knew it as she knew the cries of her babies: her face peeled back to innocence, her eyes wet, the tears shimmering, incandescent, prismatic, rolling down her face. Ecstasy, her face. All joy, her life. They were reunited. Her marriage had not been damaged. She had never been so glad to see him.

Nick is roaring in his crib. The cot rattling begins. If Frieda isn't up already, she will be in moments. Just a cry, the squeak of a spring in a cot, and her children are reborn, vivid to her. She's Pavlovian; she always has been. Sylvia raises the spring clamp of the binder, slipping the start of her manuscript in: two slim pages. 'Morning Song' is first under a title page she has yet to settle; back to that later. For now, the process is begun. She closes the black cover and centers the binder on her desk. Retying the slackened belt on her robe, she unplugs the little heater – its hot red coil dies to ash – takes it in both hands, and walks barefoot out of her bedroom, the cord trailing on the hardwood, and down the hall to her children.

There is Nick in his pajamas: his fists curled over the coated teething bar of his cot, jerking it back and forth, squeaking the wheels and making the whole wooden cage buckle alarmingly. He stands more steadily in his crib than on the floor; at just under eleven months he's such a swift crawler Sylvia doesn't know if he quite has the incentive to walk. A grave look as he yells for his mother, and then he sees her coming across the threshold: his sleepy face blooms like a loose pink rose. Frieda, in her crib beside his, is amazingly still asleep, her sweaty fringe pasted to her forehead, her body stretched diagonally across the mattress, flannel-sleeved arms flung above her head. Suddenly, she looks so grown, her legs, her torso long and elegant, her babyhood evaporating. One of her hands has fallen outside of the cot rails. Before she goes to Nick, Sylvia gingerly weaves Frieda's small, flushed hand gently through the bars, back into the cot, and folds it over her chest; if she were to turn over, she could have broken her wrist. Sylvia's moved silently, not to wake her daughter, but no use: Nick continues to bellow, cheerfully now, and his sister is stirring. 'Hey there, Pooker,' Sylvia whispers to her little girl. Frieda stretches, eyes fluttering, moans. Nick's arms are out, welcoming his mother, and he is beaming.

He is also soaking wet, and so are his blankets and sheet. With Nicholas mouthing her sharp jawbone, his fat arms around her neck, Sylvia unbuttons his jammies and peels the bottoms off, down to the crackly acrylic feet, then pulls down his thick rubber pants. His diaper and soaker are both drenched, and he only stops bouncing, arms clenched at her chin, long enough to let her slip the wet nappies out between his knees. Urine sour, and perfumed with the powder of sleep: Sylvia breathes in her baby, his faint breath and soft mouth on her face.

Frieda is weeping, sitting up in her cot in a tangle of blankets, blinking, rosy with the heat of her own body. It's too cold to set Nick down on the rugless floor without so much as a diaper; Frieda will have to wait a moment longer. Sylvia pulls the catches on Nick's cot and the front panel drops. She hoists him bare bottomed onto her hip and with her other hand pulls the wet crib sheet off the mattress, kneading it into a ball.

'Frieda no,' Frieda sobs, her mouth a red O. 'Frieda up time,' she pleads, her baby teeth opaline in her mouth.

'Yes, sweetie, yes, I'm coming,' Sylvia calls over her

shoulder, fumbling with a stack of clean diapers atop the new bureau. One-handed, she manages to loosen two from the devilishly folded stack, picks up a pair of diaper pins and carries Nick to his sister's cot. 'Look, Frieda,' Sylvia exclaims, her voice bright with drama, 'it's Baby Nick come to visit! Good morning!' Frieda mumbles sleepily and watches as Sylvia lowers her brother onto the mattress, sweeping the animal quilts aside to make room. 'Here, Nicky. Let me put on your nappy and then you can play while I make breakfast.'

Already, as Nick rolls agreeably onto his back and Frieda, suddenly awake and good humored, pats his head and chirps encouragement, Sylvia rethinks breakfast. Downstairs in the kitchen, last night's supper dishes are undone on the drainer, the fatty rind of lamb chops curled on the greasy plates, larval and white. Sylvia's appetite has come back only in spurts; mostly, eating seems obscene, food absurd. Days have gone by when even preparing meals for the children hasn't sparked her body's memory. She had never been anything but slim, despite her trencherman's gusto; now she's lost twenty pounds. Her bones stick out like a refugee's. When she doesn't feel weak and desiccated, she feels lithe, pure and right-eous, surreptitiously proud of her boniness, how notice-ably it marks her suffering.

Though even starving hasn't stopped her milk. Nicholas weaned himself anyway, losing interest gradually as his curiosity about the world beyond her – Frieda's toys in particular – expanded. First the midday feedings went, then mornings; bedtime was the last abandoned rite. Though she feels an occasional pang of nostalgia – awake at night, alone in her dark room, or like this, his silky head, his happiness on seeing her – it was just as well that he had stopped. She had been so distracted during the last months of nursing that Nick's time at her breast had seemed endless. Even he seemed ambivalent: no longer driven by a passionate need, but caught with her in a limbo of faltering habit. He began to favor his cup; he fell asleep with a back rub instead of her. Now she sometimes sat in the tub and squeezed drops of her milk into the water, watched the tiny Hiroshima as it penetrated the surface, then the spreading grayish lacework, then it was gone. Her milk, just like that.

Yesterday had been so robust – in blue-skied welcoming London, help with the children for one last day, rushing through shops, even the nappy service man remembering her and calling her by name, Mrs Hughes, still her name – cooking dinner had felt celebratory, the chops sizzling deliciously on her new stove, the bright sprinkle of parsley over her own garden's boiled potatoes. And later, it wasn't just insomnia but excitement that kept her up late papering the cupboard shelves. She'd left the dishes at the sink. She'd forgotten to purchase washing-up liquid, would have to do that today. This morning, the distasteful battlefield she'd abandoned would haunt her: beads of blood jellied on the bone, edges of shredded pink, cooked smell of flesh. The single heater was doing a perfectly adequate job of taking the chill off the nursery. She'd dress the children first, then they'd all face breakfast and the day's momentous events.

Diaper pins clasped on Nick, rubber pants tugged on. 'My girl, what about you?' she asks Frieda, giggling now with her baby brother. 'Let's see about *your* pants.' At night, Frieda, too, wears plastic pants over a diaper, though during the day she has graduated to thick, cotton training pants. Lately she has been staying dry some nights; this has been one. 'What a big girl! You're all dry. Shall we go to the potty?' Frieda, who will be three in April, is nodding and grinning.

Her mother lifts her over the cot rail and sets her down on the floor, picks up Nicholas. Together they walk to the top-floor landing, then painstakingly descend the stairs to the bathroom, where Frieda's potty chair is pushed back against the tiled wall near the sink. On the potty's wooden back is a decal of three kittens wearing mittens. The trinity of kittens proved nearly as intriguing as the potty itself at first, with Frieda craning her neck for a better view as she sat. With a few successes, elaborately congratulated, under her belt, she's now devised her own potty ceremony. While Nick clings to the lip of the claw-foot tub and bounces, Sylvia sits on a small wooden child's chair, one hand steadying her son, the other unsnapping Frieda's blue pajamas and slipping her diaper pins back through the cotton cloth. Standing before her potty, pursing her lips, Frieda grips the hem of her pajama top in both fists and lifts it over her tummy. Chin down, belly thrust forward, she lets go of the top to slip the bottoms down over her hips. Top falls back down – Sylvia begins to correct her two year old's logic but thinks better of it, stays silent, observing – Frieda ignores the problem with the top. She hooks her thumbs under the elastic waist-band and tugs the bottoms down her thighs. When they reach her knees, her diaper flops out. This is evidently part of her plan. Frieda bends forward at the hips, pushes her pajama bottoms all the way to her ankles. She stands up, pajamas puddled at her feet, tummy out, rounded and velvet as a peach. Again, concentrating, her eyes heaven-ward, Frieda lifts her jammie top to her armpits, elbows akimbo. Thus totally, safely skinned, she drops her chin to secure the gathered top and starts to feel behind herself with one hand – Sylvia reaching out to spot her – and sits down.

Moments pass. Nick is tasting the edge of the tub.

Frieda sits like a pharaoh, back straight, shoulders slightly hunched, her hands cupped around the armrests of the potty chair.

'Legs together,' Frieda soberly recites.

'Such a clever girl, Pooker,' Sylvia says quietly, hesitant to disturb Frieda's focus but thinking a little encouragement might be well timed. 'Do you think you would like to sing?'

Frieda nods.

Breathily, Sylvia begins to sing 'Twinkle, Twinkle Little Star.' Nicholas bobs to the sound of her voice. A hissing sound begins: Frieda looks up, her mouth open in surprise.

In the warm nursery, Frieda stands nearly naked before the full-length mirror affixed to the inside of the open closet door. Sylvia, after praising, wiping, and stripping her daughter, has sorted through the bureau drawers for two sets of clothing and has now succeeded in nearly dressing Nicholas in a pair of fuzzy red coveralls. Again, she calls to Frieda:

'Miss Pooker, it's time to come to Mummy. It's time to put your clothes on.'

Frieda, topless in her padded underpants and wooly tights, turns to her mother but coyly looks away again, enjoying her own reflection. Nicholas, his turtleneck unsnapped, is wriggling away also, impatient to crawl across the room to where the toys are still tossed in a random heap around the celluloid rocking horse. The thin breeze generated by the heater's exhaust fan is causing two animal-head balloons, early Christmas treats sent by Sylvia's fretful mother in America, to skitter and bump along the wall. Nick's leather-bottomed booties rasp against the floor as he crawls.

'Come on, Frieda,' Sylvia tries again, sitting on her legs on the hardwood, a small jumper, turtleneck, and sweater in her lap, watching Frieda mug at the closet door. Now it's become a game: Frieda flirting with her mother's reflection, her mother beckoning to Frieda's. There is squealing. There is some kind of scuffling in the toys, exclamations of affectionate recognition. There is foot stamping; there is another even-tempered, firm request. Even this perversity of her daughter's fails to sand the edge from Sylvia's calm. She still feels patient, not exhausted or irritable; she could sit with the sweater in her lap for some time. The morning has buoyed her somehow, its small beauties – a child peeing in a potty, for that alone she could almost cry with gratitude! Her loose curtain of hair sweeping Frieda's soft, bare back, and Frieda's shiver from the tickle, like a pony. Her manuscript in her lap; the morning sun in her face. It was hard to decide what meant more.

She craves it now, this feeling; she can tell there's something waxing in her, like the moon. She can feel her own forces gathering – if slowly as the morning light. She loves it, she really does, her life: her weeping, stinking babies; their distractions and mushy kisses; these fresh, innocent walls. The sudden boundlessness of her choices. If she could only remember this. She could, really, almost weep herself.

'Frieda,' Sylvia tries once more, her voice suddenly thick with emotion, 'come to Mummy.' Frieda doesn't move; she's examining the inside of her mouth, turning her face from side to side in the mirror.

But Sylvia has an enticement. She's been saving this up, counting on its predictably hypnotic effect on her children. She'd like to think it's something to which she is no longer vulnerable.

She casts it out. 'Let's get dressed, Frieda,' she says. 'Daddy is coming. He's going to take Frieda and Nicholas to the zoo.'

It dangles like a charm.

2

The Couriers

November 4, 1962
Court Green

Twenty miles of hairline and lipstick, all the way from the Jaeger shop in Exeter. Sylvia's been staring at herself in the rearview mirror, gloating, her wedding ring ticking against the steering wheel, revolving loose on her skinny finger. On the passenger seat beside her is a new wardrobe, suit and skirts and sweaters and bangles, tissue-wrapped and crisply folded in candy-toned dress shop boxes. She's pulling into the unpaved lane and onto the back court cobbles, navigating the Morris between the treacherous whitewashed gateposts of the stable-cum-garage, easing the brake, cutting the engine. Now, before she tugs on the door handle and steps out, she looks again, adjusting the mirror to a better angle of her face. Even in the muted autumn light of the dark stable – afternoon sun beating in slanted prisms through the leaded window to her side, leaf dust illumined, floating at the corner of her eye – she's transformed. The hairdresser has worked a miracle. No more pale-faced married girl with a drab ponytail who cuts her own bangs at the bathroom sink. She's sleek as a cat, with a fringe framing her radiant face, her long braids circling her head in a crown. Her dark lips look dangerous, her hair glossy as a two-year-old's, the color of aged honey and as burnished as Frieda's.

If only she'd done this last week! Last week, she was the toast of London! Summoned to the BBC to record some new poems (did she have any new poems? Why yes, she just happened to have a few. A poem a day for the last month, sometimes two. Here, she'll read a dozen, and the three she finished writing *this morning*). Before lunch, handed an appointment from the British Council to head the American night at the summer's international poetry festival at the Royal Court Theatre. Finally, cheered by all of her old friends and colleagues at a literary party; a London critic had pronounced her the first woman poet he'd taken seriously since Emily Dickinson. And Ted? Ted, to her satisfaction, failed to materialize. His doggy spoor lingered in the corners, but he didn't show. Nothing, then, has burst her confidence; she's still drunk on the honey of praise, giddy with the promise of more. Who wouldn't want more?

So her cut left thumb is monstrous; not to worry. The whole hand's a wash. There's a gold band jangling at her knuckle, exposing the pallid cleft worn into her finger after nearly seven years, as cows wear a path around a hill – a circlet of skin white as a grub. She's never taken her ring off, and now she thinks she just might. It was a fake, anyway, a placeholder for the nice ring he was going to buy her when they had money enough – it was real gold, but cheap, and never intended to last. Five years, seven years tops. A cheap ring for a hasty wedding. That's how he's gotten loose, the fraud, on a technicality. Nothing, nothing is sacred. The Bloomsday, Bloomsbury bloom is off: it was just a rainy June Saturday in a worm-wood London parish.

Maybe, Sylvia is thinking with her sleek new head, she *will* take the ring off. For she is going back to London, and she is going to see Ted. She gathers her purse and her packages, keeping her injured thumb high and clear, and teeters over the narrow cobblestones toward Court Green's back hall. She listens at the thick oak door, her pocketbook swinging at her elbow: Sue has the children in the kitchen. They're singing Mother Goose rhymes. Sylvia steps back. She wants a few minutes more, before the children hear her, to settle in with her booty and decide what she'll wear on the train tomorrow. She turns toward the side of the house, boxes stacked on her fore-arms, and begins to walk quietly around to the front door, over the sloping lawn besieged with stinging nettles.

Thank God for birthday checks. Here's to her mother, and to her long-time benefactress, the Boston novelist Olive Higgins Prouty, always *Mrs.* Prouty; here's to the first real shopping spree since she left Smith seven years ago. She's got a smart camelhair suit, jacket and skirt, with a matching sweater. Two more skirts, both fash-ionably cropped to the knee, one cut slim of cerise wool, another in a tweed of deep blue and black. A black cash-mere sweater, good with either the skirts or the suit. A cardigan green as a duck's head. New pewter jewelry, earrings and a chunky bracelet. *Pussy-cat, pussy-cat, where have you been?* All soon to be put to good use. Sylvia has made a decision: she wants to move to London for the winter. She's so sure of this, so determined it's what she must do, she has braced for resistance and pressed the idea upon Ted – and to her astonishment, he approves. He's even offered to meet her at the station tomorrow, to have a look at her new work, even to help her look for a flat.

What, she'd like to know, picking her footing among the nettles, would motivate such magnanimity? He hasn't heard about last week's triumph; he doesn't know how she breezed into Broadcasting House and expertly delivered fifteen new poems, reciting each with the assurance of a gunshot. He doesn't mind the thought of having her in London because he doesn't think she's enough of a threat to worry about. He's got his regular programs broadcast on the BBC, his plays produced to accolades, his awards to squander on his manicured mistress and indolent holidays in Spain while his children outgrow their jackets. He's sunk right back into the chummy pool of their old literary circle since he's been in London, lurking there guiltily in the murk and the weeds. He's graduated recently from crashing on the sofas of various friends to house-sitting the vacant apartment of Dido Merwin's dead mother; Sylvia knows this, as Ted could no longer hide behind his homelessness as an excuse for leaving absolutely no way for her to reach him. That's where she called him to tell him about moving to London, and he's . . . *encouraging* her? He must think she'll sit meekly by in a distant flat in Kentish Town or Islington, entertaining the babies and rinsing nappies. Maybe she'll even type up his poems and sort his correspondence again, a dish towel flung over her shoulder. Ha! He'll see. She's the one stirring the cauldron now, bubbling thick with inspiration, her own scalding brew. Hers is the true muse. Hers is the poetry going straight to the bloodstream; they'll be jumpy as addicts for it now. His words are nothing but lies, lies and fish recipes.

No need to warn him; he'll soon see what force he's unleashed by his departure. Take off the ring; debark at Waterloo in a new camelhair suit – he'll get the message. She's no nagging domestic hag. She's a genius, a celebrated poet, a woman of thirty with style and self-assurance, on her way to London to house hunt. Utterly civilized. Look – her estranged husband at her side, lugging her case; children singing with the nanny back at home.

And there's a crunch at her rarely used front door: snails. They've colonized the door, wiping their snotty track all over the enamel, dozens of slimy mountaineers rappeling her entryway. Disgusting and spineless, leaving the door a glittery public trail of dried spunk. Just like Ted. She hates these everlasting snails, their pointlessness, their goo, their nasty probes. On either side of the step, under the twin boxwood bushes, are dented aluminum pans of old beer, Ted's Guinness. There are chipped saucers of flat ale all over the garden, a vain attempt to attract and drown the snails. They'd given up early on baiting; Frieda was out in the yard with her red tin spade every day. Drowning them seemed at least worth a try. Sylvia is scraping the one she's stepped on off her heel and onto the mat; there are, in fact, a few defunct snails effervesced in the beer-turned-vinegar, the pans crowded with floating twigs and fragments of leaf as well.

Sylvia shifts the weight of her packages to one side, juggling to free a hand and pluck snails off her door. This is what Ted has left for her: this harbinger of indifference, this smear over her threshold. A head on a stick: trespassers beware. As if she could be so easily deflected. It was *her* slimy disaster of a life now, and she was cleaning it up. He has no idea what she is capable of. She'll keep writing, and she'll kill these snails, too. She'll start a salon; she'll learn German. She'll take care of the grounds, the garden, the house, the moldering house; the children crying, awake in their beds. She'll carry their marriage, the life they'd made. She can carry it all on her shoulders. And she is going to carry it all, by God, back to London.

The snails are splashing her new shoes. Her fingers are sticky with goo. The snails don't seem to be dying, either – they're rolling in the pans, half submerged. Poking their heads out of their shells, sliding their filament eyes at her. She leaves the rest stuck on the door and lifts the latch. Inside, the water music of her children's voices and Sue's from upstairs now, the heat of the kitchen's Aga hovering at the ceiling in the hallway. She drops her boxes and bags on an armchair in the parlor and storms toward the kitchen.

Paper crackling, dumped in a chair – stomping down her pink-walled hall – there was a moment with just this texture, not long ago: Ted cut Frieda's hair. Last month, back for his clothes. The last time she saw him. He cut Frieda's hair in a bob. She walked in from the grocer's, baskets on each arm, and exploded – how dare he cut her child's hair, make *any* decision about the children he's abandoned without asking her? She'd sobbed then, her face hot and furious – Ted herding the babies out the door – cursing him on her knees on the kitchen floor, pinching up wisps of Frieda's shorn hair from under the high chair, fat tears plopping on the green lino. She'd been pathetic, a fool – as if anything he did could touch her. As if he held any power over her.

There's the white high chair and beyond, glowing radioactive at the center of her kitchen, the round oak dining table where they've eaten every meal since they moved to Court Green. Assia's table, poisoning her house with its toxic vibrations. No wonder she can't eat, her wedding ring rattling on the bone. She's been poisoned. Assia's planted her malediction at the heart of Sylvia's house, and it's been leaching noxiously for a year.

Assia's table in her house. It's a shock every time she thinks of it, as if seeing someone else's face stare back from the mirror. She and Ted had agreed to store a table at Court Green for the couple who took over their lease on the Chalcot Square apartment. A young poet and his wife, David and Assia Wevill. Assia, who has succeeded in seducing Ted. Who pretended friendship with Sylvia, all the while plotting to steal her husband. *Could you take our big table?* The black lashes fluttering, smutty with mascara. *It's too big for the flat, and I'll be happy to think of your family gathered around it.*

The ring. The snails. The table. Sylvia's been triply cursed, but it can't touch her; she's risen beyond petty subterfuge. The table, she decides, goes next. First, the snails. She opens the icebox and locates the last of Ted's jettisoned Guinness. She stabs at the bottle tops with an opener and wheels, a bottle in each fist, the cold of the glass a relief against her feverish left thumb.

'I'm here,' she sings, as she passes the stair. 'I'll be right up.' She marches out the front door, slamming it behind her. A snail or two dislodge, cracking and oozing on the granite step. She kicks them away. The weather has turned; the sun has disappeared, clouds bunching up gray overhead. Yellowed leaves are rolling and crashing in waves across the lawn. She can smell the green scent of the boxwood, medicinal, where she stands. Sylvia swings her arms out straight, one to each side of the step, and turns the bottles over, pouring the ale in a double waterfall onto the two pans at either side of the door. The Guinness chugs, frothing as it falls.

Tomorrow, she's going to see him. She tries the idea on, standing cruciform at her front door, preparing to kill the snails. She replays the words in her head, shifting them, the many ways they could mean. Which one is true? She's *going* to see him. She's going to *see* him. She's going to see *him*. She's going to see him.

She's going to see him, she thinks, simply that. There's no hidden message, no secret to her trip. She's done with him. She wants a new home that's her own; she wants a new start in the company of her peers. She wants to be known as Sylvia Plath, the writer, not Sylvia Plath, the wife of Ted Hughes. So what if he's there? What if he has other ideas? He'll soon meet with her frosty disdain. It's her own life she's interested in. She's got a new self, sleeked and costly and folded in tissue; she's got a self written in blood. She's ready.

The Guinness is finished, the pans foaming. She begins to pluck snails off the door, dropping them from her Olympian height into the pans of cold beer to drown. She pauses, holding a snail aloft, pinched between her right forefinger and thumb. She could crush its drab shell without trying; she can see the body writhing beneath the whorls. Its house feels no sturdier than vellum. Love, she thinks, it is finally *my* season. Lightly, she tosses the snail to the side, onto the lawn beyond the bushes. She has no need for poison. Let them live.

3

The Rabbit Catcher

She thinks she is ready.

He's at the door, eyeing her quizzically through the fogging glass, as if trying to place her. Sylvia has seen this expression before, at the train station last month. She'd been smug – the scene so perfect it was better than she'd fantasized. She stood under the four-faced clock in camelhair and lipstick, framed by the florid Victory Arch, queenly in her braided crown. Ted was late. A haggard, ragged black coat walking right past her. Truly hadn't known her at first and told her so. His craggy features muddied, unfamiliar, searching her face while trying to appear as if not.

Now she'd like him to stop – he's making her uneasy. She's grown deeply weary of surprises, even her own. She wants to keep this uncomplicated: just a transaction, the start of a simple economy. They both know why he's here. He'll come for the children every week; she'll hand them over, bathed and shod. Ted ducks his head, steps into the dark corridor and out of her way as she reaches behind him, pulling the door tight, sliding the lock in its groove.

'The children are in the flat, upstairs,' she tells him.

'They're dressed, but just starting their breakfast.'

Keep it simple. This part, at least, she's determined to control. No messy entanglements. She's the gatekeeper; at least for the foreseeable future, he'll stand at her doorstep for a neat exchange. Here, Sylvia thinks, is where they really begin to practice a new language, one of efficacy and avoidance, a replacement for their old, shattered familiarity. Perhaps she should have dressed – she's barefoot, still in her robe, her hair in a tangle down her back. She'd thought about it earlier, sitting on the nursery floor, her feet cold, watching Frieda conjure galoshes and oddments out of the laundry basket, Nicholas jabbering in the toy pile behind. But the morning had expanded so generously around her, spreading itself into the corners of the rooms. It felt clean, as after rain. She hadn't wanted to move. She hadn't wanted to disturb it at all. She'd just let it open, unhurried. She'll bathe and dress when Ted's taken the children for their outing. He's leaning now awkwardly backward to let her by – knocking the pram, which creaks on its springs – as she turns to lead him up the staircase.

The hallway crowds in, monumentally silent. Sylvia listens, knowing Ted is also listening, to the amplified beat of their feet on the stairs, the arrhythmic slap of her hand gripping the heavy Victorian banister. Her heart, stilled in her chest. This is the moment, in all her certainty about this move to London, that she couldn't imagine: how Ted becomes any random knock at the door – a nappy deliveryman, a meter reader, a temporary agency nanny. A man who takes her children to the zoo while she paints the parlor. He's come to her door; he has no key. He'll never have a key. Cell by cell, her marriage cools and stiffens.

'It looks bigger than I remembered,' Ted says behind her.

Sylvia turns around, faces him from a few stairs ahead, a rare occasion of towering above him. 'When were you here?' she blurts.

Ted looks up at her, confused. He points to the top of the stair. 'On Monday – there, I installed the baby gates. I carried the gee-up horse up the steps—'

Sylvia's face burns. Of course, he came on moving day. She'd barely noticed him in her excitement, the Yeats's plaque, her prize, pulsing its blue gleam all the way onto the footpath. The coveralled movers were stumbling about in the dark corridor, the electricity mysteriously not turned on, and then the front door blew shut, locking the keys inside the flat. There was a scramble through a window, and she'd lit candles so the movers could unload the van while she drove to the electric board. Ted had stopped by to check on Frieda and Nicholas; they'd set the zoo date, and Sylvia started the car. She had no idea he'd come inside, or that he'd helped. She'd assumed the movers put up the gates while she was gone. She feels so stupid. Already, the sands shift.

'I forgot,' she mumbles, drawing herself up. 'It was so hectic.'

'I peed in the potty,' announces Frieda, butter-faced at the landing.

So this is how it's going to be from now on. It's not terrible, Sylvia thinks. It's predictably awkward. It's bloodless. The scene in her kitchen mimics the unremarkable: her family gathered in the stark light of breakfast. Nick's high chair is pulled close, and he's painstakingly mouthing a thick slice of banana bread, smearing it into a featureless shellac on his tray. Ted sits beside the baby at the small square table, Frieda on his knee eating a piece of bacon and listening to a story in her father's deep, legato rumble.

Sylvia stands near the stove, her back to Ted and their children, whisking eggs with a fork in a bowl she holds at a tilt. Even little distances – her back to the table – feel vast; every remark and gesture is perilous. She'd like to simply turn around, address her children, ask Ted a question, but there's no easy way in. This is where estrangement becomes most manifest: it's not when one's husband has packed up and gone; it's when he's in the same room. Simple intimacy – there's no such thing. There is no small talk when one is heading for divorce, no robe sleeve meaninglessly brushing the back of a coat as a door is locked.

She ransacks her mind: Is there anything benign to say, any way for her to insert herself? She can hear her ownership of the day hissing as it deflates. Ted's presence is crowding her kitchen, backing her confidence to the walls. He's bigger than ever, hulking like a friendly giant over the children, who lift their flower faces up to him. He's bigger than she is.

She beats the eggs. Beats the eggs, involuntarily muted. She puts down the fork and checks the flame under apple slices browning in a pan. Her mouth hardly moves.

'Want tea?'

Ted looks up, turns his head. He pauses in his response, as if taking note of the weather in the room. 'Yes,' he answers, 'that would be lovely.'

What would be lovely, she'd like to know: the tea, or that she's offering? There it was again, her hostility. She could hardly keep it down. It popped out, like a foul burp.

'What?' he asks, looking around at her, incredulity in his voice.

She turns, the kettle in her hand. She shrugs. 'I didn't say anything,' she says.

'Oh,' he says.

She places a white china mug on the table before him. Nicholas is banging his empty, double-handled cup on his tray. Ted begins slowly to stand, as if not to startle Sylvia, lifting Frieda cautiously off his knee and onto a chair of her own.

'No – I'll get it,' Sylvia says, too swiftly. She puts down the kettle and turns toward the icebox for the milk.

Ted sits, settling Frieda as well. 'So will you come with us to the zoo?' he asks without looking up, cautiously floating his question, disembodied, into the room. Sylvia approaches Nick's high chair, gripping the cold neck of the milk bottle.

'No.' She is holding the baby cup. She is pouring the milk. 'I have too much to do,' she announces.

Ted leans his chin over Frieda's shoulder. 'Will *you* come with me to the zoo?' he whispers in her ear.

She does have too much to do, Sylvia assures herself. She's got plenty to do. There's disorder all around her. She isn't even dressed. She's got her manuscript waiting, letters she hasn't answered. She should put on her blue jeans and paint – she can unpack boxes later with the children around. She could walk to a phone box and make some calls. Finish her shopping. What a relief to have so much to accomplish. Days and days of tasks to keep her busy. Not a moment to spare. She needs her mind to lose itself, to efface the sense of endangerment she now feels. To bring her back to this morning, its unfolding. Waking clean as a baby. The faster she completes all she has to do, the faster her new life can begin. She can scramble these eggs, golden in their bowl. She notices the satisfying ache of her hand beating in circles, the ribbon of egg lifting and falling.

Two children are chattering brightly at the table. Sylvia pours the eggs into a hot pan.

Ted's hand is warming around his mug of tea. 'Fried apples,' he says, sipping. 'Are they ours?'

'Our very own,' she says with satisfaction, forgetting herself, the word *ours* in his rolling voice, a voice she hears in her sleep, dropping her into a groove so deep it takes her a moment to realize she's suddenly become a ghost from her past life. Then she stiffens. Something closes on her. She turns to face him.

'I didn't bring enough for you,' she stammers.

He watches her, not understanding.

'The apples. I only filled one bag – for the children. I mean, I didn't bring enough to send off with you. I left the rest at Court Green.'

Ted is watching her face contort. He doesn't look angry. Angry, in fact, is not how he looks at all. He looks, finally, as though he recognizes her.

'That's all right,' he says. 'I didn't expect you to. I didn't even think of it.'

Another moment passes. They listen to bubbles forming at the edges of the eggs, the sound strangely projecting, for each of them, from somewhere behind the other's face.

'You should have some now,' she ventures. 'You didn't have this year's Bramleys. Have some eggs with the children.'

The plates scrape against each other as she reaches into the box at her feet.

Sylvia wonders how some of these animals manage the cold. The elephants swaying protectively in their sandy lot, screening their narrow-hipped baby. The hippos, the motionless crocodiles. They're as foreign as possible here, with no natural defense against the bone-chill of an English winter. Today, it's very cold, but cloudless, and glassy bright: even in his sleep Nicholas is squinting against the sun, his little twisting face framed by a jumble of extra woolens at the back of the pram. Sylvia reaches in, tucks the blankets more tightly around him, and adjusts the pram's hood. She's got a scarf pulled over her head and tied at her chin, hair brushed now but loose to her waist, a pair of worsted pants and a sweater and coat tossed on at the last minute. Ahead of her on the narrow macadam path, Frieda is pointing and tugging Ted's hand, eager as a puppy. They're passing the giraffes' canal-side acre, pulled by force of nearly forgotten habit toward the lion house and the morning feeding of the big cats.

Leaned over the flat's banister in her nightgown, hair catching in her mouth, kisses blown to children whose faces and hands were newly wiped, nappies changed once more and potty tendered, their boots and mitts applied, jackets zipped. Ted asked her once again to be sure – she refused – before leading the children down the staircase, Nicholas at his hip, Frieda gripped by the wrist. She watched him wrestle the pram out of its cove under the stairs. He'd just told the children to sit on the hallway floor while he carried the pram out and down the steps – she could see him on the landing, the black wrought-iron railing catching on his coat pocket as he maneuvered clumsily, craning his neck to be sure the children were still sitting, safe – when she realized she couldn't bear to watch them go without her. She couldn't stand to be left

*behind, alone in the empty flat. Her children, sitting on
the doorstep, gazed curiously at their father struggling
with the pram beyond the doorsill, waiting to see what
he would do. Obediently still and jaunty-hatted, like an
audience of colorful, patient elves.*

*'Frieda, my helper girl, hold Baby Nick's hand—' Ted's
hand out, huge and flat and beckoning, his long legs strad-
dling the steps, protecting his family from any chance of
a fall.*

'Wait. Wait! I'm coming too—'

Their faces, all three, turned toward the stairs.

Why shouldn't she go to the zoo, Sylvia thinks, defiant.
The zoo is one of the reasons she loves this neighborhood, why she's so glad to be back. There's no reason to
deny herself. Ted asked twice, after all; he needn't have
asked her if he hadn't wanted her to come. And it was
Nicholas's first visit. She had a right to be here; it was
just as much her zoo as it was Ted's.

At Chalcot Square they'd been close enough to hear
the seals barking in their pools on mild summer nights.
Windows flung open, savoring their bed; the leaves on
the locust trees susurrating in the children's garden outside
their building. They had come to the Regent's Park zoo
nearly daily after Frieda's spring birth, dutiful new parents
but also notebook-toting gatherers of exotic fact: the exact
blue of a condor's legs. The oak leaf-patterned coat of a
Masai giraffe, its eyelashes long as baby fingers. The
thrilling roar of lions at feeding time: first a whoofing
from the belly as the cats listen for the metallic slide of
the keeper's door. Then the keepers appear, balancing
their wheelbarrows, and one lion starts. They all start: an
oceanic roar, a calling so deep and loud it enters the lungs
and inflates the body's internal sac, blowing it up like a

sausage case. How one's own chest expands, vibrating, exhilarated, how one is terrified on some deeply atavistic level by the lions' call. This is what they had always loved most, their unwavering point of gravitation: feeding time in the briny light of the lion house. Today, as on so many days in the past, they stand patiently in a crowd of parents with prams and mittened children, waiting for the doors of the filigreed old building to open precisely at noon, amused meanwhile by a nearby school of Emperor penguins who pop with a mystifying lack of effort onto their island out of falsely blue water, as if projected back-ward on film.

Nick is snoozing through his maiden voyage to the zoo, offering his parents a conversational gambit on their otherwise silent excursion through the exhibits. They wonder aloud, without direct address except to a concerned Frieda: Should Baby Nick be woken up? His nap is already running long; the lions, they decide, may do the job for them.

The doors are opening, and inside the building the lions have begun their huffing. One of the keepers, dressed in khaki green coveralls and heavy, steel-toed boots, has already appeared and is walking from cage to cage with a small canister of spice, a scent offered to arouse the animals' curiosity in an environment otherwise dull and uniform in its temptations. The keeper shakes a pile of cinnamon onto the sloping concrete; the dark-maned lion inside raises his head, panting obscenely.

Sylvia pushes Nick's pram toward the inner railing, beyond which the keepers will walk with their wheel-barrows of meat. Ted has lifted Frieda onto his shoulders and has moved in next to Sylvia. Along with the rest of the crowd, their voices are halted by the rising call of the lions. Sylvia can't yet see them, but from the full-throated roaring, echoing now off the brick walls, she knows that the entire team of keepers has emerged, pushing their barrows. The huge Victorian barn of a building is rank with sour humidity and the glandular musk of lion. She knows this routine; as the lions pace, the keepers stop at each cage, their wheelbarrows piled high with great roasts of crumbling, brick-red horse meat. Each lion gets a hunk or two, lifted from the heap with a pronged stick and slid through a rectangular grate near the floor. Most of the lions crouch down immediately on their haunches, chewing great gobs of sinewy horseflesh; one or two usually get worked up over it, snarling and batting at the keepers through the bars as they pass.

But today, there's something different happening. As the keepers break into view, Sylvia sees something furred and white in the pile on the barrows. It's unmistakable. Rabbits.

The first keeper marks his chart, then lifts a rabbit in both rubber-gloved hands, holding it aloft on his wrists like a sacred offering before tucking it stiff through the grate. The lion stands and walks, loose gaited, toward the rabbit. He sniffs, and slowly drops, his face low. Huge amber eyes gaze at the crowd over a white rabbit muff. The keeper turns toward the visitors at the railing; people are asking questions. The fed lions begin to grow quiet, the deafening cacophony dying piecemeal as each voice fades.

The second keeper is approaching, hands gripping the wooden handles of a wheelbarrow piled with rabbits. Nearly in front of Sylvia he drops the handles, marks his chart, and begins to pick up a rabbit, but pauses. He leans toward the visitors' railing, one gloved hand cupping his ear, the other resting lightly on the white fur. Ted's hands are holding Frieda's hands, and Sylvia senses that he's about to lift her over his head and down to the floor. She knows he wants to go. Sylvia wants to see what happens with the rabbit; it and all the others are piled with their heads facing away from her, their pink-fleshed ears contracted over their backs, their bodies curled into sickles, spines rigid.

'—some of them just play with it. But I've saved a big one for him. He loves his bunny. This one's nearly a stone.' The keeper before Sylvia turns his back to the zoo goers and picks up the rabbit under his hand. There is no blood, though clearly the guts have been scraped out. There is just a red hole.

'All right,' Ted says, his voice light, 'let's see the owls, shall we?' He smiles down at Frieda, who seems not to have grasped anything beyond the invigorating roaring of the lions, then up again, searchingly, at Sylvia. 'Shall we go?' he questions her.

Sylvia holds the handle of the pram. Amazingly, Nicholas is still asleep. She looks up again at Ted, then turns to the lion's cage, releasing her grip. The keeper has pivoted the rabbit in his hands to slide it head first through the grate. Its long, yellow-stained feet spring back in unison, devoid of any hint of life, like a piece of hardware, as they catch for a moment on the grate and then pass through.

Ted reaches for the pram with one hand. With the other he holds Frieda's. 'Sylvia,' he says quietly, 'let's go.' He starts to ease the pram away, out of the crowd.

The rabbit is sliding across the concrete, coming to a stop before the lion, who sits with his great head hung low on his shoulders. He eases his giant front paws down and out, to either side of his bunny; he lifts one paw and drapes it over the rabbit's back. He sniffs. There are abbreviated scars, naked patches, in the short plush fur on the bridge of the lion's wide nose, like tight tan velvet that has been scratched away, or a ripe cattail that has started to blow. The rabbit's white fur feathers beneath the lion's breath.

She's shrugged Ted off. She doesn't have to jump at his command any more. She's not even looking in his direction, but she knows instinctively that he's circling with the pram, looking back to see what she's doing, trying not to look like he's watching her.

And she's right. He's watching her, and he's driving the big-wheeled pram and Frieda in a long, slow, curving arc across the lion house, moving toward the door while glancing occasionally backward, the pram's broad chassis squeaking on its axles. Walking slowly, trying to seem like there's not a lot of obvious thought powering his motion. Ted's leaving as a lapwing leaves, flapping on the ground, feigning a broken wing at the edge of a meadow where its eggs are hidden.

Sylvia wonders if Ted fed the lions when he worked at the zoo. Before they were married, before they ever met. He wouldn't have thought twice, she thinks. He was a hunter, a country boy. The deaths of things were not strange to him. She wants to see the rabbit's eyes, but for some arbitrary hiccup of chance it has never turned in the right direction. She sees the lion's; it stares kohl-eyed and unmoved at her, at everyone. It licks its bunny in long, rasping strokes. With each lick the rabbit shunts by degrees across the slick cold floor, its dirty feet to the crowd.

4

Thalidomide

December 12, 1962
Night
London

A woman is crossing the moon.

The midnight sky has bled itself completely onto the darkened rooftops, erasing the houses and the black trees and everything else outside. Except for the lopsided moon: it pulses in its aperture, shrunken from its full luminous ripeness of three nights ago when Sylvia watched it from this same window in her new parlor. It's since been halved, funereally shadowed by the excruciating drag of the planets. Draped like a mirror after death, or like Sylvia's cheap new furniture, shrouded with old sheets as in an abandoned house. Though Sylvia's not giving up. She's been pacing the silent flat for focusless hours, jumping at the intermittent clank of the electric heater, watching the moon like a trapped fox. But she's pulling herself together, and she's got the paint can out, the brushes and the broom-handled roller. Newspapers on the floor, a tarp covering the just-delivered, wicker armchairs that will masquerade, for the time being, as a sofa. Newspapers spread on the glass-topped coffee table pushed out of the way, to the wall. She's set the raw pine bookcases on newspaper also; she'll paint them while she's working on the parlor walls and get this one room completed.

It's bad luck to look at the moon through glass, according to medieval superstition. Sylvia's done that before; she'll take no more chances. The parlor's quarter-paned windows rattle on their cords, hauled up with a screech against paint fumes. The cold rushes in, instantly dropping the temperature in the room. She looks to the homely electric grate on the parlor's far wall, the flat's only built-in source of heat. Some fanciful former tenant has framed it with an ornate carpentered mantelpiece to match the Georgian moldings; Sylvia's holly is stiff on its shelf. Trying to keep warm with the windows open wide is futile. She shuts the heater down.

She could have taken her sleeping pills and nodded off with Frieda and Nick hours ago. She thought about it, perched on her niggardly slice of bed with the shampooed children crowded into her lap – the only place they could all three gather with any comfort in this cold, in the stark-ness of the sparsely furnished flat. She wondered, while she turned the pages of Dr Seuss, why she shouldn't just amputate this misbegotten day and knock herself out? Night is the hardest, and this night, it had become unmis-takably clear, was going to be no different. But there was one mildly attractive alternative to the pills – something that would make her life incrementally better tomorrow, requiring nothing more of her than dumb, animal labor. She settled the children in their cots, switched off the upstairs lights, and carried the box of painting supplies into the parlor.

'All right then,' Ted said, having grunted with the pram, still filled with Nick, up the front steps and over the threshold, then kissed both children and assured them casually that he would come back very soon. More of the zoo, if they liked. He nodded briefly at Sylvia, then turned

toward the steps. Sylvia glared at him from behind the door, holding it partially open to let him pass. Nick was tugging her coat, cartoonish tears popping hugely from his eyes, gibbering desperately for help out of the pram. Frieda stood by, wordlessly observant. Ted was down the four steps, glancing left, then right, hesitating—

'What?' he asked, turning around, facing Sylvia at the door. 'What?'

She didn't speak. She assessed him coldly. His drooping coat hanging from his shoulders. His exasperated mouth; his distracted exhaustion. Her resentment, which had been this morning something loose, a floating thing, something that might just have broken up like so much cloud cover, had hardened over the hours walking beside Ted, grown diamondlike.

'What, Sylvia?' he repeated. 'What else do you expect me to do?'

Sylvia still didn't speak. Words were rushing past, flooding her head, too quickly to be stopped. His intolerable immunity – how could he simply turn his back, just walk away?

Her face was stony, impenetrable. She spit out the words under her breath. 'I know where you're going.'

Ted stared up at her where she was hiding behind the door. 'How could you possibly know where I'm going?' he asked. 'I don't know – I haven't the faintest notion where either one of us is going. I don't know where we're going.' He stood on the footpath in front of the house, his breath frosting white before his face in the darkening afternoon, watching Sylvia.

'Let me know when you'd like me to come back,' he said finally. 'To see the children,' he added, noticing her grimace and quick to clarify his meaning.

'*I'll let you know,*' *she said, cutting herself off with the sharp closing of the door. She stopped herself from watching to see the direction he would turn.*

If it weren't for the children—

She rummages through the paint box, knocking its contents against the scuffling cardboard. The rubber gloves she's sure she bought at the paint store aren't in the box, and she knows she hasn't any in the kitchen. She can't find a hammer or tape. Everything's gone. Whatever there was, it's been lost. She rolls up the sleeves of her old shirt and starts to pry the metal top off the heavy can of white paint with a kitchen knife. The metal plate wedges upward at a tilt, and she flips it by its edge onto the newspaper.

She peers into the cylindrical can as if down a well. Linseed oil has separated from the pigment, leaving a fatty yellow slick on the opaque surface. She dips the end of a coarse pine stick into the can and begins to stir in the oil. The paint gleams wetly, coating the sides of the flat stick and folding back upon itself as she stirs. Viscous, it sucks the stick. Air she's stirred into the paint rises through the thick liquid, tumbling up in bubbled lozenges, then bursts on the glossy surface like the gasses of a sulfur spring, the paint splattering in droplets and slowly melting in.

The thick of it. A drip, slow over the lip of the can. A bitter scent pinches in her nose, a sulfuric burn. Stranded – with this appalling loneliness. This greasy slick, this blank to fill. There are the bodies: whitened, oily and vaporous. Fornicating, grinding like demons. A tangle of legs and elbows, a butcher's bin of offal. Awful – this suck of vulgarity, these extra parts crowding the ones that are missing. A hip, a hip and a knee cocked, a sheet –

twisted and soaked, folding back into itself, drag heavy, caught between them. A gagging stink of perfume, of nail enamel, of paint that conceals how filthy it all really is – his cock slipping against her, his knee, their skin a slick nothing sticks to, certainly not the truth. The bone of it, the meat and the salt. Here it comes. Faster: Their faces shove up to the surface, up out of the paint – their eyes closed, lids bulging, mouths gaping, like death masks, like wax castings, melted yellow, oozing at the edges, fused. It's a mistake, a horror show.

The images flicker, grotesque, refracted on the vaulted surface of her stinging eyes. She rakes the box for a paint-brush and plunges it into the can. Each stiff bristle sinks individually, breaking the surface. A bed of nails. A torture. She lifts them, masked in white.

She slaps the paint up the wall, evens it under the stroke of the brush. It takes mere moments for her to realize she'll never get anywhere like this: the shabby unpainted room yawns away. She dips the brush again. Their fish mouths gulp at the surface. Assia rocks on her bulb, her rooty filaments clumped and dirty. He's spilling his milt into her, filling her little cup with it. It's all so dirty – the hairs will never come out of this paint. Sylvia could pluck at the sticky walls forever. She drops the eyelashing brush on the newspaper and searches the floor for the drip pan and the roller. She's gagging on the fumes. She wants to retch. She can't clear the particulate out of her throat. If it weren't for the children she wouldn't have to see him at all. No – not this way. It's unspeakable. It opens a hole gaping at the edge: Where would she be now without her children? And that idea's frightening twin, a tiny figure escaping across a crater: not seeing him.

Who was that? Blood spattered, clutching her stump, running barefoot in a flapping hospital gown? And the throbbing moon behind, pocked and scarred, indifferent as the dead. Her blood dripping, spraying in dark viscous drops. Drops that scar, that burn with a jellyfish sting, with an indelible acid, spraying over her arms.

The children – where are they?

Her rib cage, her body is shaking. She's shivering, trembling in the cold. It's not just the cold. It's this irresistible stench. How easily she rolls in it, this decay. She can't seem to help herself. It's ghastly, this attraction. At an impulse it squeezes out a steaming deformity. Some animals frightened into stampede – sheep, antelopes – will simply abort their fetuses, dropping them spontaneously in their bloody bags onto the dirt as they flee.

The children—

Her teeth are chattering, reflexive. She's trembling, running the long-handled roller up and down the walls. She can't make out the difference between the white paint and the white wall underneath. White on white on white. It's so cold; the mercury plummets with the night. At home in Devon, the apples she left on the trees, the highest ones she couldn't reach, are freezing. They were red; they were green. Their skin carried the perfume of spring. Up in the crowns of the trees. Unreachable. Daylight will thaw them, and they'll darken, rotting and monstrous. They will hang, heavy, revolving on their stems. Eventually they'll fall.

The children are safe, she tells herself. They're fed and washed and caressed; they're read to and folded into themselves in their beds. Their blankets are tucked all around them.

Thalidomide

She keeps painting. Her hair, her arms, and her uncontrollably shaking hands are freckled with it: drops she can't rub off. I did nothing wrong, she thinks. She paints. She'll do this all night if she has to.

5
The Applicant

August 12, 1961
3 Chalcot Square, London

The southwesterly wind blows in from the Atlantic over England's West Country, cooling and condensing as it gathers itself and rises in legendary mist up the raw granite plateaus and heathered hills of Dartmoor. The historic mining of Dartmoor has all but ceased: the extraction of alluvial tin and copper ore, the mining of arsenic and lead. Before the mines, there were abbeys, and before that, Romans and hill forts; before that, stone huts, stone circles, stone cists. Stones tell the story of Dartmoor; the acidic soil dissolves paper and pottery and bone.

In August, the last of Dartmoor's wild ponies are ready to foal on the upland heaths of the moor. In a few weeks, they'll be drifted into herds by farmers on bicycles. The colts and old ponies will be sent to market, to be sold as pets or slaughtered. The rest, those deemed sturdy enough to resist the extreme winter weather, will be turned out on the grassland commons for another year. They graze now among the still, wind-etched faces of tors in the flat light of a sunless Sunday afternoon, shaggy coated and immensely gravid, their soft whiskered muzzles tickled by lichen and milkwort, by purple moor grass, the ends of their long, blowing tails wicking up the green damp.

North and east as the crow flies beyond the moorlands, following the wet pastures along the river Taw, past a scant handful of half-timbered Elizabethan villages wedged into an aimless valley lush with oak and rowan and hazel trees bearded in moss, past hillsides studded with Scottish Blackface sheep and wall-eyed cows, over an arched stone bridge that spans the river, up near the crest of a curving cobbled lane in one of the bleaker of Devonshire's hamlets is an imposing, half-stone house situated almost in the shadow of a thirteenth-century church, the church, in turn, dominated by a monumental yew. Once a manor, then a vicarage, the run-down house is roofed with thatch in which generations of starlings have noisily reared their annual young under the eaves. Seven hundred years ago, the first thick walls of this house were settling in the red Devon loam; they're settling still, groaning with the effort to stay upright on their boggy West Country rise. They'll have to: The house's titled sellers have guaranteed it to stand for another twenty years. It needs paint and new plumbing. They've called in a woodworm service, too.

The house is empty. Behind the heavy door of carved and iron-braced oak is a shadowed back hall floored in worn cobbles; beyond, a bay-windowed kitchen with an Aga cooker, a scullery with a low stone sink and larder, a dim wine cellar under the stairs. What sun there is slants through the windows of a long, stone-sided hall at the front of the house, a room the new owners have imagined as a playroom complete with an upright piano and wall-to-wall shelves of children's books. There is a window seat and fireplace in the parlor; the plaster is crumbling beneath the wallpaper. Up the staircase, there are bedrooms and studies with views of the church and its yew and its toppling graveyard, views of the trio of giant wych elms shading the back quarter of the grounds, views of a tennis court overrun with vines and old roses. All the doors inside stand open.

Outside, a nine-foot wall of rough granite stones encircles the manor's three acres. On the lane side, a driveway draws itself closed in a pitch-cobbled courtyard flanked by a barn, a stable, and a falling-down servants' cottage. There are dahlias and snapdragons and spiking peach gladioli in the weedy flower beds; jasmine vines and dusty-leaved sweetpeas creeping over the vacant greenhouse. Nasturtiums and cornflowers have emerged under the twin laburnums, long past their saffron bloom; forget-me-nots grow rank beneath the boxwood bushes by the front door. The holly and lilac hedge framing the broad lawn belies the stinging nettles that have all but taken over the grass. Encroaching on the tennis court is a wild bramble of purpling blackberries, tight knots at the end of erect stems, dark tiny fists.

Under the sixty-foot elms is an ancient moated mound, all that remains of an Iron Age hill fortress. In spring, its sides and ramparts are blanketed with daffodils and narcissi, a sea of waving green and white and two-toned yellow that spreads through the sloping, grassy orchard.

In the front garden, the fruit from the few cherry trees is weeks out of season. But in the orchard four kinds of apples, eaters and cookers, are ripening. The poorly pruned branches of the apple trees are fully leafed out, the verdurous leaves waving faintly, turning palms up in the breeze; they shield the mostly undersized, embryonic fruit. The apples are hard, waxy finished, and woody, some still thumb-sized and puckered, with the exception of the Devonshire Quarrendens, the rarest and earliest apples in the orchard.

No one is certain if the Devonshire Quarrenden was first grown locally, or if it came across the English Channel from France. Its name may have derived from Carentan, a city in Normandy; for most of its three centuries the Quarrenden has been a garden apple, commonly called the 'Quarantine.' No one disputes that it's an attractive variety: a flat crimson apple with downy sepals and a long, thin stalk, small in the hand, aromatic, with the distinct flavor of berries and honeyed wine. Its only flaw is that it won't keep, and once the apples mature, they drop. It is nearly the middle of August, and the Quarantines are ripe.

The sky is pinking behind the yew, and soon the church will be readied for evensong. The medieval iron chandeliers will be lit, giving a glow from within to the three stained-glass windows, and the Anglican bell ringers will stand by at their ropes, weathered pitch cobbles worn to a gloss beneath their feet. Until then, the only sound will be Quarantines plopping into unmowed grass, bruising, their thick scent, sweet and berried, guttering suddenly like candles from the preciptious drop.

Continuing in the same north and east direction across England, eight hours by car, four hours by express train from Okehampton Station, to the neighborhood known as Primrose Hill in London, in a five-story building across from a handkerchief children's park patrolled each morning by watchful nannies and young mothers with tottering charges, up a dingy staircase and in through a low door, the new owners of the Devon manor house can be found: Ted Hughes, the newly acclaimed Cambridge-educated poet from Yorkshire, son of a tobacconist, and his American wife, Sylvia Plath Hughes, a writer also, a scholarship girl raised by her widowed mother. The Hughes's daughter is sixteen months old. They've spent all their savings, plus loans from both their families, to buy the house called Court Green.

Through the cramped vestibule hung with coats, past a card table folded against the wall and books and sheafs of paper stacked there too, beyond the floral wallpapered bedroom with its green corduroy curtains and the tiny bath floored with marbly black linoleum, into the cheery-papered galley kitchen lined with copper pots and translucent china and down a step into a narrow parlor facing the street, a room so compact that one reflexively draws one's shoulders in upon entering, Court Green's new householders appear to be entertaining. In fact, they've just hosted a tour.

The Hughes are giving up the three-year lease on their Chalcot Square flat. They moved in a year and a half ago, which leaves another year and a half, until February 1963. For their ad in the *Times* they listed the rent as six guineas a week plus gas and electric, and a fee to cover the reconditioned stove and the new American-style icebox Sylvia purchased just before Frieda's birth. Of the eight interested parties, two couples have arrived for the Sunday tea-time showing.

Seven pairs of knees are now clinking like crowded glassware in the parlor. Three are crammed onto the sofa, backs to the broadside of Ted's poem 'Pike' and a framed antiquarian etching of the Magnae Deorum Matris – great mother of the gods, crowned in a garland of wheat, shaking her sistrum with the moon between her knees.

Ted leans against the opposite wall of bookcases, Baby Frieda wedged under his elbow like a football he's about to maneuver through a line of defenders. She looks, though, more like something out of a garden, her auburn hair curling weightlessly, like silky spider threads, about her face. She's got fourteen small opal kernels of teeth, duly admired, and bells on her new white shoes. Her legs dangle and ring, like wind chimes.

Sylvia, meanwhile, is a hummingbird. Heartily recovered from a miscarriage earlier in the year, from an appendectomy just after, she's more than four months pregnant with another child, carrying tight and high on her slim frame, light on her feet. She's hovering, dipping, gathering tiny chalices of sweet wine in the kitchen, porcelain teacups on trays, flitting back, drawn by a flowery scent, by honey in her living room. The owner of the seventh pair of knees in the parlor, lacking a spot on the sofa or against the wall, has scraped Sylvia's desk chair around from where it was tucked under a small table, the table tucked in turn under the window, and she's perched on the chair at the far end of the room. To one side before her is the Hughes family; to the other, on the sofa, is her poet husband and a couple equally keen to take over the Hughes's apartment. Evenly divided, three facing three. The flat, of course, is the focus of this gathering. And yet the applicant in the chair, from her position at the head of the room, seems almost to be the real point. She seems even more the point because Sylvia can't pull herself completely away.

Maybe it's the way this applicant, Assia Gutmann Wevill, looks: like a chic Grimm's heroine, a fairy tale enchantress. She's gray-eyed, and her hair falls in a long, gleaming, obsidian sweep. She's perfumed and lipsticked and polished and dressed in a bright coat stylishly flaring at her knees, a hothouse flower of a coat. Maybe she's Snow White. Maybe she's Rose Red. Maybe she's Gretel, come to the wrong house, and her trail of crumbs is gone, eaten by a bird.

Maybe it's what she's said, or how she's said it. Frankly, that hasn't been much – a basic conversational wit and humor, an appreciative aesthetic sensitivity, a quick litany of where the Wevills have been and where they'd like to go. Like Sylvia, she's a foreigner in England, though her pedigree is far more appealingly exotic: German-Russian from Berlin, then Italy, Tel Aviv, Vancouver, and most recently Mandalay. She writes advertising copy; she knows the words that sell. She remarks on Sylvia's taste, the most interesting Chalk Farm second-hand shops, and the tan that lingers from the Hugheses' recent holiday to the Normandy coast.

But now the conversation has dwindled to almost nothing. Teacups click on the saucers. It's clear that both couples want the flat. The room has stilled, quieted; all but the noticeable thrum of Sylvia's curiosity. The man who is not Assia Wevill's husband is inspecting the books on either side of Ted: annoyingly snoopy is how Sylvia will later, for a while, think of him. The moment grows heavy. Six adults gaze into their cups, reading their tea leaves, waiting for someone to break the spell.

Abruptly the annoying man speaks up. He pulls out his checkbook, chattering. Everyone looks on politely, sipping their tea or sherry, as if trapped by a boorish conversation at someone else's dinner party.

So sorry, she's saying over the telephone, they simply didn't realize how hard it would be to disengage themselves from their first London home. It's Sunday night, and Sylvia and Ted have cooked up a plan. Sylvia's on the phone with the annoying man, and she's told him they're ripping up his check. They've decided to stay, she lies. The baby born here, and the neighborhood . . . et cetera. Hope you'll understand.

'All right,' she says, dropping the phone onto its cradle with a flourish. 'One down. Now where's the other number?' Ted flips a grease-smudged scrap into Sylvia's long-fingered hand. Frieda's been put to bed, her cot set up in its space between the sofa and the bookcase. They've pulled out the sherry again, congratulating themselves: this feels like the right thing to do. In truth, they are moving eagerly on, their life telescoping out from this claustrophobic walk-up; what does it matter to them who takes their exiguous flat? But surprisingly, it does.

'Hullo?' Sylvia says, elbows on the kitchen table, her free hand fingering her braided bun. 'Assia, this is Sylvia Hughes—'

Her voice carries through the apartment, moving over it lightly, like a fine mist. It settles over the painted floors and the glossy molding that traces the rooms. '—you'll have to visit us there. It's Ted's dreamscape. Our own Avalon, complete with apple trees and the bones of pagans. Ted's older brother spent a year somewhere in Devon as a gamekeeper, long ago. Before the war. He spent all his time hunting pheasants. Ted says it was the happiest year of his life.'

Her voice lingers, coating the bedroom wallpaper, sifting down over the folds of the jackets and wraps in the red-painted vestibule. It glazes the surfaces of the furniture: the top of the compact enameled table where they sit, the spines of the books, the bureau in the hallway by the bathroom. It covers the Olivetti typewriter and the neat stack of typed pages on the small table before the window in the parlor, the pink pages of a manuscript that will be completed, to Sylvia's great relief, in a week's time, her first novel, 274 pages of a novel she's titled *The Bell Jar*. Like their cramped life on Chalcot Square, the story of the bell jar is an episode she's getting out of her system.

Like mist, Sylvia's voice will evaporate from this apartment, and that's just fine with her. Yet she relishes the idea of bequeathing the flat – stifling or cozy, depending on one's mood – to another pair of fledgling writers. The Wevills seem like their sort of people, Assia particularly. They don't deny it: Sylvia and Ted both believe in signs. One last act to indemnify the good auspices of their move; after the applicants departed, they fished the crumpled list of callers, names and numbers, out of the wastepaper bin under the sink. Then Sylvia picked up the telephone. The hand-off feels, in its small way, fortunate.

6

Barren Woman

May 19, 1962
Court Green

The orchard floor, three weeks ago thick with a thousand daffodils and fragrant white-starred narcissi, is littered now with apple blossoms. They fall like confetti – random, frivolous, a moment of glitter. Throughout the stone-walled treescape, the blossoms hang in suspense, dropping weightless petals onto blades of tall grass, onto the hard-tamped ruddy soil. They yield at the least breath of wind, shed like cells or bits of pale tissue.

Sylvia's headed for the warmest corner of the back grounds at Court Green, where the Hugheses have dug and planted their vegetable beds. She's pushing her four-month-old son's pram with a bucket banging at her wrist and the end of a watering hose slung over her shoulder, dressed in mud-laced brogues and dungarees, her shirt-tail trailing beneath her buttoned sweater. She can smell the mineral tang of the turned topsoil as she approaches. The trees defloresce in the distance.

This is her first spring in her first garden, and she feels like a self-made Persephone, driven, not born, into ripeness. She's baffled by her garden's easy fecundity – the relentless creep of the weeds and the mint, the spontaneous green emergences – as well as the equal ease of its everyday losses, the casual squanderings of nature. She can't quite imagine what it would be like to be so free. Since childhood her life has been that of a disciplined conscript, the battles waged mostly in her head. The risks of freedom have always discomfited her, no less than her ardent heart – the heedless vulnerability, the shrieking rush of every thing at once. The threat that she might fail. And yet she has been fighting all these years for her own flowering, brooding over the life she was impatient to get started. Cultivating her words like fragile cuttings, nursing them to root in their windowsill jam jars. Fruitfulness: she yearned for it; she willed it from herself. But she needed it calibrated, poised, meted out with judicious caution, as you would offer crumbs to a wild bird. A decade ago, the surge of her desires nearly killed her. Now, almost thirty, she's stunned as if from a blow by the thought that she has everything she ever wanted.

She wants to hoard it all, every pink-gummed infant grin, every leaf, every moment watching the clouds knead outside her study. She carries disbelievingly the burden of abundance, the glut of her own good luck: the luminous intensity of days with tiny children, the eroding old manor and its creaky beneficence, the churning vegetable theater outside. And Ted, as breathless as she is with the tag-team passings of babies and householding. Throughout their marriage Ted has talked Sylvia down from the ledge of her anxieties; his body and his voice have been her unfailing succor. His skin fits her better than her own. These days, she's equally soothed by the solid daily presence of his tools, his fishing gear, his library books on husbandry. Each night she falls into bed, her back and muscles and nipples sore, her fingertips rusty with dirt.

She listens for the breathing of her family, the breathing of her aged house. Her heart is like the heart of an elephant: enormous, swollen, her emotions huge. She feels caught in the crush of her own gratitude, clutching all she has.

It is the third weekend in May, and only a few tight apple buds remain closed on the branches, their leaves miniature and flocked, their petals veiled, snug and secretive. Most of the blossoms have opened, receding from a deep lipstick pink to a blush as the petals began to unfurl. The fully flowered blooms bear only a memory of color, faded now completely to a tender whiteness.

The sky has whitened also, become shredded with cloud cover from the east, the afternoon sun shouldering through in moments of brilliant, magnified light. A tree, or a group of trees, will brighten in a moving spotlight of sunshine, branches illuminated with almost painful clarity, ancient apple bark revealed to be curled back in brittle insect-drilled strips, edged with dying moss.

A strong breeze ripples the grasses, and suddenly a whole row of apple trees releases its shower of petals, a slant of sparkling white like a snowstorm, a drift of sun-caught flakes atomizing the orchard with their faint poignant scent.

Sylvia regards the apple trees and the wind that has unloosed the blossoms in a burst of sunlight. Then she turns her back to the orchard, a single brown braid swinging slightly as she carefully positions the pram alongside a border of ox-eye daisies and a tangled old rosebush fat with blowsy, cameo flowers, taking advantage of the intermittent sun for the baby's nap but shielding his face with the pram's bonnet.

A woman has followed Sylvia from the direction of the

house, the latest in a string of guests from London, company with whom to gape at Court Green's unfolding splendors. But it's not just a game of lady-of-the-manor that prompts Sylvia's invitations: It's a way for her to temper the disconcerting vividness of her days. The cooling objectivity of visitors is a relief; she takes refuge behind the scrim of their distractions.

The young couple who took the flat, the Wevills, are this weekend's houseguests, just arrived on the train a few hours before. Assia's slipped off her heels and walks barefoot and tanned across the lawn in paisley-patterned capri pants and a shimmery tangerine silk halter, carrying a basket and kitchen shears, a Cashmere cardigan pulled over her elegant shoulders, gold wire bracelets jangling. Assia's long, loose, fine-textured hair is the rare spot of pure black in Sylvia's garden; it absorbs what light there is.

Sylvia glances up from Nick's pram, heeding the blowing orchard, sunlight catching in prismatic aureoles at the tips of her eyelashes as she focuses. 'Look,' she calls to Assia. Sylvia nods toward the apple trees, whose century-old limbs creak lightly and imperceptibly sway. 'There go all of our apples.' The blossoms continue to blow down, drifting in a steady westward fall across the hillside orchard, noticeably blanketing the ground.

'It's lovely nevertheless,' Assia replies, her voice thickly glottal and very German. 'Like a scene out of Tolstoy.'

'Yes, you're right,' Sylvia replies, watching the profligate trees. 'But I think of all my pies, and the apple cakes—' Her own voice is shaded with genuine regret.

'I can't cook,' Assia says. 'I'd gladly give up a few apples for this. And it smells like paradise, doesn't it,' she adds, safeguarding her welcome, looking around. 'One would never need perfume.' Beyond the daisies and heady roses edging the vegetable bed, extending to the lane past the trio of wych elms in full leaf, the entire nine-foot wall surrounding the grounds is obscured by blooming lilac in white and shades of lavender, the heavy conical sprays aromatic, nodding on their branches. Wild and thorny and lush, more roses are bursting in trembling sprays by the tennis court and alongside the stable, and honeysuckle and jasmine vines continue their promiscuous ascent over the roof of the greenhouse, their scent drifting into the kitchen late in the day. In the flower beds, the tulips seem girlish, bending their heads together, shaking and arranging their petals. The Asiatic poppies have just broken the soil and thrust their stems upward, dangling their heavy, furred pods.

'I do feel a bit like I'm Eden's caretaker, or its chaperone,' Sylvia replies, ducking into the role of confident hostess. She hands her own gardening gloves to Assia before kneeling at the edge of the turned beds, where already the flowering creepers of pole beans are climbing their trellis, Argus-eyed, and the green stalks of baby onions have grown crowded and weedy. 'I hardly exaggerated when I told you this was all Ted has dreamed of since he was a little boy. After I thin these onion sets and water, we can pick some lettuce from that shady patch behind the strawberries and have it with the thinnings in a green salad tonight.'

'Is Ted always so helpful with the children?' Assia asks, positioning herself on one hip in the grass beside Sylvia. 'I was impressed that he took your daughter along with David to Dartmoor, rather than leaving her here with us.'

'Oh, Frieda loves tromping around on the moors,' Sylvia answers. 'She's good company. Though I'm sure

Ted will have to make a point of spotting ponies and not just playing Adam. If it weren't for Frieda's nap, he could easily disappear until dark, just poking along the banks of the Taw.' Sylvia is systematically pulling weeds and thinning the onions from left to right in the bed before her, tossing the weeds into the grass behind and the creamy-tipped shoots into the basket Assia carried from the kitchen. 'We follow a shared schedule with the children each day,' she continues. 'I have the mornings in my study while Ted potters about out here with the babies, and after lunch we switch.'

Assia has pulled on the goatskin gloves over her polished fingers and, following Sylvia's lead, pulls a weed or two from the edge of the bed. 'What are you writing now?' she asks.

'I've finished a novel, but only for the money,' Sylvia shrugs. 'I'm thinking of starting another, and I write poems of course, here and there, when they come. But I'm really just settling back into my routine after the baby.' She pauses, feeling minutely, uncomfortably exposed. 'Ted couldn't very well take Nicky along, not yet,' she adds. 'He nurses every three hours. He'd starve.' She lifts an onion thinning, the length of a scallion, and draws it toward her knee, knocking grains of soil from the shallow white roots clumped at the end of the knuckle-sized bulb. 'Can you smell it?' she asks Assia, holding the delicately pungent onion under her own nose. 'It's glorious! I can't wait to cry real onion tears.' Sylvia drops the shoot into the basket and continues thinning the plants.

Assia cocks her head vaguely in the direction of the pram where Nicholas sleeps. 'Do you think you'll have more children?' she asks.

'As many as we can, until we run out of room or I collapse,' Sylvia answers with a self-deprecatory laugh. She lifts her eyes away from her muddied hands and looks at Assia. 'Seriously, I've never felt so right about anything as having babies. I feel I was somehow born with my children. I think they've made everything else possible.' Assia meets Sylvia's gaze, her thickly black-lashed eyes round, the irises light, wolflike and gray. 'Won't you and David have children soon, now that you've settled at Chalcot Square?' Sylvia blurts, startled by the strange intensity of Assia's eyes.

'I've had more than my share of chances for children,' Assia replies, absently pulling a weed and placing it in the basket. She turns again to Sylvia. 'You know, David's my third husband.' Sylvia looks up from the onions, her interest piqued. 'I've had six, or maybe it's seven, abortions.'

Sylvia scoots on her knees toward her right, her trowel in one hand, pulling the basket along the edge of the bed and motioning Assia to follow. 'Seven?' Sylvia asks, both fascinated and horrified. She squelches her horror; she wants to hear the details. 'I knew one girl in school who had an abortion – she's an actress now. What did they do? How did you do it?'

Assia rolls her eyes skyward, tipping her chin up and rocking back on her wrists in the grass. 'Let's see. There've been so many.' She turns again toward Sylvia. 'I imagine I've done just about everything. I've been curetted of course. That's very expensive, but as safe as one can expect. You check into a nursing hospital and pay an outrageous amount, a hundred pounds or more. Once I took a shot of something with ergot in it.'

'Isn't ergot poison?' Sylvia asks, her own eyes widening.

'Yes,' Assia says coolly. Her gray irises are almost color-less in the light. 'Of course. That's the point.'

'What do they do in the hospital?'

'They give you sedatives, things to relax you. Then they scoop it out and you're done.'

On her hands and knees, Sylvia leans forward, putting her weight on one flattened palm and dropping her eyes toward the onions, the end of her braid dusting the surface of the soil. 'I miscarried our second baby last year,' Sylvia says. 'But it was so early, my doctor told me it was perfectly normal. I was only a few weeks along. It happens all the time. I got pregnant with Nicholas right away.'

'I tried the gin bath, also,' Assia continues. 'My father is a doctor. So I know that there's really no medical basis for it, it's hardly more than an old wives' tale, but I tried it anyway. While you sit in a very hot epsom salt bath, you drink a quart of gin.'

'Did it work?' Sylvia asks, turning her head and flicking her braid back over her shoulder.

'It did,' Assia answers ruefully, 'but it made me so sick, I think I would have had the baby orally if it hadn't worked otherwise.'

Sylvia clears the row before her of weeds, then leans back slowly, haunches on her feet, hands on her knees. 'Really, I'm amazed,' she says, beginning to stand. 'Did you so dread having children that you didn't think you might try it just once?'

Assia hesitates. 'Maybe it's partly that,' she answers carefully. 'But I think it had more to do with the reasons I married.' Again, she pauses. 'And the war.'

'You told me you escaped Germany,' Sylvia coaxes, picking up the bucket and hose and moving around to the other side of the onion bed.

'Yes,' Assia answers, leaning to her side for the basket.
'I was very small then, only a schoolgirl. We left Berlin
right before the Nürnberg laws were enacted. We had to
– my mother was a German, but my father was a Russian
Jew. They would have been arrested.'

'Did I tell you my father was German?' Sylvia asks:
'He emigrated as a teenager and became a professor of
German language and entomology – an expert on bumblebees. He wrote a book. But he died when I was eight.
My mother says he'd never seen a doctor in his life, and
it turned out he had diabetes mellitus. He had an embolism
after his leg was amputated for gangrene. He died a miserable death rather than show weakness.'

Assia's lips curl in a small, private grimace. 'I saw men
wet themselves and swallow their tongues in fear in front
of the Nazis,' she says quietly.

Their faces are suddenly washed with light, and Sylvia
looks up. Above them the clouds have dissolved almost
completely. She turns to Assia. 'Wait just one moment,'
she says, holding up a finger and jumping to her feet. She
runs over to Nicky's pram and peers in, fusses with a
blanket inside. She looks up at the sky again, squinting,
and walks back to where Assia sits in the grass. 'I should
really wake him up now so I don't have another night
like last's, but I just can't resist. I so rarely get any girl
talk. Okay,' Sylvia says, taking a breath, 'go ahead.'

'I don't know . . .' Assia says, her voice trailing. 'My
father got us out. Then he got us out again, in Italy. By
then we had fake passports, which we used to get to Tel
Aviv. But it had been too much for my mother, seeing
the arrests and our neighbors disappearing, the fake
names. Pigs' blood poured on our doorstep. My father
got us out, but she blamed him. And he was too passive,

or maybe indulgent, to argue with her. That's how I ended up married for the first time. She talked me into marrying a man in Palestine. He was a British officer – he was *her* escape fantasy.'

Sylvia's eyes are enormous, her pupils round and dark, and she drops her trowel into the red dirt. 'You mean she lived through you,' she says to Assia, who is nodding her head.

'Now you see,' Assia adds.

'Assia, my mother is just like that,' Sylvia says. 'She's been living through me for as long as I remember. She can't leave me alone, and I can't get far enough away. She really was a saint, scrimping and sacrificing so I could have everything, but she expects me to turn my life over to her in return. When Ted and I were on a camping trip across America – I was pregnant with Frieda, but I don't think I knew it then – we saw catfish eating their live young at the edge of a lake, as they were being born. I thought, "Oh! Just like home. Thank God we're moving back to England." And yet she's my mother. My father's dead; she's what I've got.'

'I was only eighteen,' Assia says.

'I'm almost thirty and *still* I can't get away. My mother's coming this summer in fact – for a month. I'm sure I'll be climbing the walls, but I'm desperate for the baby-minding—'

'I had to find another man,' Assia says.

'That was your second husband?'

'Yes, one of my college professors. Just like my father, he spirited me away to another country, England this time. But then I met David.'

'And that's when you followed David to Mandalay?' Sylvia asks, crawling on her knees toward the last row of onions. 'So why not now? Don't you want children eventually?'

'What do you think,' Assia says, leaning from one elbow to the other, 'do you think we're always attracted to men like our fathers?'

'Ted is nothing like my father,' Sylvia scoffs, flexing a hand dismissively. 'Ted is a force of nature. He may be strong like my father and brilliant, but he doesn't question his virility, and neither do I.'

'Hmm,' Assia mulls, turning the onion thinnings in their basket, 'perhaps that's the answer to your question, and mine also.' She pauses in her response, her fingers working. 'David is very dear. He's ten years younger than me. You could say that we've been growing up together.'

Sylvia lifts the last of the tassellated thinnings in her dirty hand and shakes them, readying to toss them toward the basket, but she sees that Assia has arranged the onions carefully, all facing the same direction, the pale roots matted together like thread. 'That's so funny,' Sylvia says, looking into Assia's face and smiling as she places the shoots into Assia's gloved hand. 'That's just the sort of thing I do.'

Assia also is smiling, scrutinizing Sylvia with her porous, unnerving gaze. Her black hair is gleaming in the sunshine, and the crown of her head looks hot to the touch. Her smile is odd; it reminds Sylvia of swimming up out of sleep in the hospital after her appendectomy, right after she lost the baby. The nurses always had that same kind of smile: plying their thermometers, leering meaningfully into her half-conscious face, eager for signs of weakness or infection. So submerged and swiftly passing that it almost doesn't register, a thought occurs to Sylvia as she meets Assia's intent, ravening eyes: *Nothing good will come of this.*

Sylvia looks quickly away, busily slapping her hands against the thighs of her dungarees as she stands. 'I've still a few chores out here in the vegetable beds, watering and such,' she calls out in an oddly loud voice, startling herself. 'If you'd like, you could take the onions into the kitchen and wait for me there.'

'Oh no, that's quite all right,' Assia replies, standing and carefully brushing the seat of her capris with her glove. 'I'm enjoying our time out here, getting to know each other. And this is all new to me. I've never been much for gardens. If you don't mind, I'll just tag along until you're finished.'

'Certainly,' Sylvia answers, without looking in Assia's direction. She bends down, picking up the end of the garden hose, which lies uncoiled on the lawn like a long, lifeless snake or a green umbilicus, all the way across the yard from the spigot at the side of the house.

'Can I help?' Assia asks, reaching for the bucket where Sylvia last deposited it in the grass.

Sylvia glances over. 'Oh no,' she answers. 'That's actually not for water. Look inside – it's full of ashes. We collect them from the fireplace and sprinkle them over the garden for fertilizer. It's very good for onions, but it's messy. I don't think you're dressed for it. Although,' she adds, 'you could turn on the water for me.'

When Assia loosens the spigot, the hose leaps in Sylvia's hand, water shooting in a clear, forceful arc, falling back as the water pressure equalizes. Assia begins to wander back toward the vegetable beds, pausing to inspect Nicholas in his pram, then turns instead toward the greenhouse, where the most tender of Sylvia's seeds are still propagating. Assia peers through the window glass, her still-gloved hand at her forehead, shading her eyes.

Sylvia waters her garden, a thumb over the metal hose coupling for control, her free arm snapping and pulling the hose around the edge of the beds as she steps backward. Assia's still poking around; Sylvia pretends not to have been watching her wander the yard when Assia calls out from across the lawn.

'Sylvia, I would love to see your book – *The Colossus,* isn't it? Would it be all right if I take a look? Maybe some of your good fortune will rub off on me. Of course,' she adds, 'I'm not serious about it, as you are. I just play with poetry. Decorative arts are more my métier. Needlepoint. I can put it in my handbag and forget about it—'

'Be my guest,' Sylvia answers, a bit dryly. 'You'll find it in the parlor, on the little walnut secretary. The American edition, with the blue cover – it just arrived by mail.'

As she watches Assia descend the flagstone step and enter her house, Sylvia continues to tug at the hose to keep it from crushing her seedlings. Just for a second as she works the hose Sylvia notices how the grass springs back, supple and resilient, in the spots where her feet or the hose had flattened it moments before, as if she'd never touched it at all.

Low voices and bacon frying. The sounds and aromas of Sunday morning float up the stairs and reach Sylvia, who is lying on her side in bed, nursing Nicholas and trying to convince herself that she might still sleep. For the fourth night in a row Nicky has cried through the night; if the Wevills hadn't come she might have moved him for a few hours into the carry cot in Frieda's room, but for graciousness' sake she kept him in the bed and didn't sleep herself, again. It might be a growth spurt; it might be teeth, though Sylvia has run her index finger along the baby's gums and hasn't felt so much as a swelling. Whatever it is, she feels the familiar sense of ruin; she's enervated and raw, all of her senses on edge, yet beholden to meet the day and the guests. Ted has obviously already gone down. It was time.

Voices, pricking in her head. Sylvia smooths the back of her hand across the cheek of her baby, sated now and calm, then gently slides the tip of her pinkie into the corner of his mouth to break his latch on her breast. His chin flutters, eyes slowly opening; a dribble of milk runs out of his mouth as she rolls him, milk drowsy, back on the mattress before turning on her hip and setting her feet to the floor. She opens the bedroom door a crack and the voices blare sickeningly, but she can't tell to whom they belong. Down the hall, the guest room door is closed.

Quickly she buttons her nightgown, slips her arms into the sleeves of her mauve bathrobe, and leans over the bed to lift Nicholas up to her shoulder. She begins to softly pat and rub his back as he raises his head, unsteadily at first, to look around. She'll wait on the nappy change; he would need another in a few minutes, anyway.

The voices continue to amplify, becoming more distinct as she descends the carpeted steps, nosing Nicky's fluffy head. Ted must be at the cooker. Assia's deep, gritty voice is the one she couldn't make out from upstairs, layered with Frieda's high, singsong trill. That's all, just the three of them. Sylvia turns the corner into the sunny back kitchen and sees Ted, as expected, in a pair of rumpled khaki Bermudas and an untucked pullover before the gleaming black face of the Aga, against a back-drop of shiny copper pots. Assia, shoeless but dressed in blue jeans and a plain blouse, is seated at the big oak table – her own table, in fact, a detail she teased through the dinner conversation several times last night. Sylvia's spattered copy of *The Joy of Cooking* is open on a chair, homeric, and a stack of her prized, well-thumbed *Ladies' Home Journals* slump at Assia's elbow, but Assia faces out, toward another chair on which Frieda, in a diaper and her pajama top, is assembling the elements of her miniature china tea set piece by piece. Sylvia squats under the kitchen's thick wooden lintel, cradling Nick's head with one hand and the stone door frame with the other for balance, to meet Frieda's squeal and kiss with her own.

'Good morning,' Sylvia croaks to the room, wincing at the echo of her own voice clanging in her skull.

Ted has stepped away from the bacon and frying potatoes to lean sideways toward Sylvia, greeting her with a brush of his lips. 'Shall I put on your water for coffee?' he asks.

'Please. And make tea for the two of you. Did you pull out the rest of that ginger cake to warm?'

Ted nods and adjusts the kettle before stepping across the hall into the larder.

She turns to Assia at the table. 'I trust you slept better than I did. Where's David?'

'My sleep was glorious!' Assia crows, stretching her arms. 'How could it not be, in this paradise riotous with spring? I woke to the sun lighting up the branches of your elm tree, and then the birds started under our window. David's still in bed, but I couldn't resist the morning light. Maybe I'm not the city girl I always assumed I was.'

'Ah, but after the riot of spring comes the ruin of winter,' says Ted with mock gravity, returning with half of a cake carefully wrapped in waxed paper.

The ruin of winter. Sylvia feels the scrape of those words inside her, efficient and deadly. It's not the abundance in her life that makes her uneasy; it's the idea of loss that exists alongside, like some terrible hibernating animal nested within her walls.

'What did you think of Burma, then?' Ted asks Assia, placing the cake inside the warming oven.

'That's different,' Assia answers, swiveling in her chair to face Ted at the stove. 'In that part of the world, all of nature feels like exotica, even in its purity. People don't seem to belong in that context. But here,' she says, addressing the view from the bay window, the oak- and laurel-covered hills undulating away into the early haze, the heather dotted with sheep and stone, 'I get a sense of the old England. Surely the gardens are cultivated. Someone planted your apple orchard a hundred years ago. But there's a dark wildness here also. Something uncontrollable, but with a human history as well. There's an archetypal current to the place.'

'That's it,' Ted nods, 'that's just what attracted me.'

Sylvia listens, expressionless, and doesn't sit, rocking side to side on her hips, burping Nicholas. She watches Assia, who is curled now, catlike, over the spindle-backed chair, her bare arms twined across the chair back, another cashmere cardigan draped across her shoulders like a limp, expensive trophy. It dawns on Sylvia that Assia is wearing the same outfit Sylvia wore yesterday, though Assia reeks of Chanel, not dirt or urine-soaked nappies. Even her hair today is gathered into a loose braid, which flicks and glints over her shoulder as she preens. Sylvia steps farther into her kitchen and jerks out a drawer, collecting silverware and folded linen napkins, then reaches up for a pitcher from the cupboard. A swag of bay leaves hangs from the lintel; Sylvia picks one and hands it to Ted. He nods, preoccupied, listening to Assia, then looks down at the leaf, uncomprehending.

'For the potatoes. For flavor,' Sylvia says. 'I know what you mean about the sun coming through the elm,' she adds, addressing Assia crisply at the table. Assia has gone through Sylvia's books and magazines; now she's exploring the children. She's affected yet another provocative pose, assisting Frieda with her precarious towers of toy teacups and saucers, aping a maternal interest. 'We watched the sunrise from the guest room on the morning Nicholas arrived, and before that the full moon. He was born in the very bed where you slept, Assia.' Sylvia pauses for dramatic effect, patting the baby's back. 'It's warmer there than in our bedroom, and because of Frieda's birth at home we prepared ourselves for the rather messy procedure.'

'Indeed, he arrived in a torrent of his own making,' adds Ted, turning potatoes at the stove.

There is a low, rumbling eruption from Nicholas. Everyone turns in surprise. Frieda laughs with gleeful relish.

'Editorializing?' asks Assia, with raised eyebrows and a smile, stacking the tiny saucers.

'Precisely,' says Ted, 'though this sort of torrent occurs with more regularity than his initial one.'

The seat of Nicholas's nightgown begins to radiate liquid warmth, followed by real damp blooming at the crook of Sylvia's elbow. She reaches for a tea towel. She feels glum and irritable, her rattled weariness becoming something darker. Then she notices Frieda. Her eyes bright and eager, Frieda's little pink hands are clasped at her chin, awaiting the next surprise. Sylvia goggles her eyes, making a silly face. Frieda convulses with laughter, stomping her feet on the floor.

'Speaking of the mysteries of nature,' Assia adds, now holding her manicured hand lightly over the stack of teacups to keep it from tumbling, 'all of this natural glory embedded itself in my dream life. I was just telling Ted when you came downstairs, Sylvia.'

'It sounds very much like a pike – the coloring and mottled spots, and the spiky snout,' says Ted, leaning against the edge of the stove, a kitchen mitt in his hand. 'Did it have striping on the fins and tail?'

'Yes, I don't know – I don't know anything about fish,' Assia says, 'but it seemed so vivid and exact—'

'I was obsessed by pike as a boy; they truly had me in their thrall. I couldn't get enough. I fished for them every day,' says Ted, turning to lift the steaming kettle off the stove. 'I dreamt about them also. I wrote a poem about them once.' He fills the teapot, replacing the lid and leaving the tea to steep.

'It was the poem that hung on our wall at Chalcot Square,' Sylvia adds, rocking Nicholas, who is beginning to wriggle for a nappy change. Sylvia tries to soothe him, unable to tear herself from the exchange between her husband and this woman who, she increasingly senses, is fingering her life like so much yardage. 'It's in the parlor now; you probably saw it last night, Assia. Or read it before. It was published in *Lupercal* two years ago. You couldn't miss it – it's called "Pike".'

'I don't know,' Assia answers, holding one of Frieda's teacups and absentmindedly stroking the smooth porcelain surface. 'I don't know anything about animals. But this was a long, muscular fish, green and gold, with a golden eye.'

'Certainly a pike,' Ted adds, nodding at Assia.

'But what happened?' Sylvia asks hotly, just submerging her annoyance.

'Nothing really happened,' Assia answers, shrugging. 'I dreamt of the fish – the pike – I saw it in great detail. Finally I saw that in its huge eye, this glittering, gold eye, was a baby. Curled up, pulsing and alive. And that was all.' Assia looks up, from Sylvia to Ted, still cradling the tiny cup.

Sylvia stares in disbelief. She tastes the pounding of her sleepless, tannic heart, squeezing in her chest.

Ted stands at the stove, his arms crossed before him. He meets Assia's gaze and looks away. He turns away. He turns to the stove and picks up the teapot in his mitted hand. 'Would anyone care for some tea?' he asks, his voice booming, turning again to recover the room.

'Served at my very own table,' Assia answers cheerfully. 'Now there's a welcome twist.'

Ted approaches the table and sees that Assia has no cup. He glances over his shoulder, the teapot in his hand, and begins to elicit help from his wife, who stands behind him, holding their infant son. 'Sylvia—?' he asks.

'No, don't bother—' Assia says, lifting one of Frieda's toy cups playfully and looking to the little girl for approval. Frieda grins and picks up a cup for herself.

'This will be just perfect.' Assia nods. She holds the cup out to Ted, delicately pinching the curved handle between her thumb and forefinger. Ted leans down first to Frieda, pretending to pour her a great steaming arc of tea. Then he turns to Assia and fills her little cup.

7

Lady Lazarus

June–Early July, 1962
Court Green

It is the black husk of another life that blows through her: the cold planetary blank of the crawl space, lightless beneath her mother's cellar; the flaking of dead stars into her eye as she bashes her head against the edge of the concrete foundation. It is the Morris climbing the lane and pulling into the courtyard after midnight, headlights sweeping the darkened windows of the bedroom and extinguishing as her husband turns into the stable. It is the crush of the tires on the cobblestones she hears from their bed.

It is the fifteenth of June. Sylvia climbs the stairs in her dirty canvas work pants, wet through the knees from a morning of scrubbing floors, carrying Nicholas on her hip and a tin of baking soda with a spoon balanced in a cracked teacup in her other hand. Minutes ago she was wearing a beekeeper's veil, the whole contraption, all new. The cloud of cheesecloth spread out before her over the picture-frame brim of the straw hat beneath, giving her a dreamer's view of the low mist of wood smoke curling about the ankles of the apple trees. As never before, she saw her world through a veil – she'd eschewed even a hat at her simple wedding. Their sixth anniversary is tomorrow.

It is the new queen who is the bride today. The bee man is still in the orchard searching for her, pumping his bellows in a hazy landscape of fern and meadow grass and purple-tufted thistles. The bees grow sleepy as he checks the brood combs with his smoker, puffing the nurses and the workers to the edges of the frames, looking for the sleek, auburn body of the young queen. When he finds her he'll mark her with a drop of nail polish, a little red drop on her back. She'll take her bride flight, chased by the drones; then she'll never leave the hive again. Like a bridesmaid in attendance, Sylvia painted the hand-me-down beehive herself, a green gabled house positioned under the semaphoring trees.

Upstairs, Ted sits on a chair in their bedroom, his hair dusted yellow with pollen, his forearms and collar sticky with propolis, his fingertips green-stained from mowing the lawn. He was up first thing, bringing the baby to Sylvia in the bed before she even awoke, then off to the Taw at dawn light with his tackle in his old army rucksack. He's been outside all morning as she's been in, scouring the house until the bee man arrived. The bee man brought the swarm humming furiously inside a vibrating box.

Ted is holding ice cubes wrapped in a tea towel to his purpling lips. His forehead is lurid, lumpy and hot, his eyes swollen almost totally shut. When he shifts his weight in the chair, dead bees fall out of his loose cotton shirt and skitter crisply on their velvet over the gray floor-boards. They stung him six times, swarming his head. They chased him as he ran, the bee man pumping his smoker uselessly, trying to mask the banana scent of fear.

'We smell of smoke,' Sylvia says quietly, as she sits

down on the edge of the bed beside Ted's chair, propping Nicholas into a sitting position among the pillows. Nicholas sucks his fat hands and a large wooden bead.

The yeasty aroma of burnt twine and peanut shells drifts from their clothes and their hair. Sylvia scans her husband's mottled, darkening face. He looks wretched, a miserable Cyclopean monster. The curtains exhale behind them at the open windows.

'I thought you said they didn't like white,' Ted mumbles, his mouth swollen, his voice pulpy and slow.

'That's what the rector told me. He said they're attracted to black. But you didn't put on the hat. Did you think you could keep them away with that napkin?'

'Not a napkin. My handkerchief,' he answers gloomily.

'Even so.'

They listen as Nicholas smacks his toy. Sylvia opens the tin of baking soda with the edge of the spoon and knocks a few clumps of powder into the cup. She leans forward toward the bedside table, pours a bit of water from the drinking glass there into the cup.

'Where's Frieda?' Ted asks.

'Feeding her babies downstairs,' Sylvia answers, stirring the baking soda and water into a paste. They can just hear Frieda from the playroom, the rise and fall of her toddler prattle mimicking with disquieting accuracy the fawning neighborly emptiness and bitter private remonstrances of adult conversation.

'What did the bee man say?' Ted asks.

'Not to run,' Sylvia answers.

'It's too late for that now, isn't it,' he responds wearily, his words thick.

'I'm sorry,' she says, giving him a weak smile. 'I was just trying to cheer you up.'

'What did he say for the stings?' Ted asks, unamused by Sylvia's risk at humor.

She holds up the cup. 'Baking soda and water paste.'

Ted sighs, pressing the ice pack lower, to his chin and jaw. 'All right then. Shall I keep the ice on?'

'Yes, for a moment more.' She continues to stir the paste, the solids of which continuously separate from the liquid and settle in a silty clog at the bottom of the cup. 'Did the dentist give you any painkillers?' Sylvia asks as she stirs.

'What?' Ted replies, his voice muffled and distracted.

'For your bad teeth. Did he give you anything yesterday in London, a prescription?'

Ted looks at her. She can't gauge his expression; his face and his eyes are too swollen. His countenance is unreadable.

'No,' he finally answers.

Sylvia gapes at him, scoffing. 'Unbelievable, the dentistry in this country. It's barbaric. I thought the whole reason you went into London and not just Exeter was to see a better dentist. And still they didn't give you anything?' She shakes her head, indignant for him. 'How do your teeth feel?'

Ted's chin drops; he looks at the floor. 'My face is worse.'

They are quiet for a moment, listening to Nicholas, Frieda in the background, the scraping of the spoon in the cup.

'Did they fill your teeth, at least?' Sylvia asks, her tone more gentle.

Ted's breathing is slow and measured. He sighs and pauses. 'Yes.'

'Gold, I hope,' Sylvia mumbles.

Ted shrugs vaguely.

They give you sedatives, things to relax you. Then they scoop it out and you're done.

Sylvia looks up at her husband, his weirdly colored, oddly distant face. 'Does it hurt?' she asks quietly.

'Yes,' he answers, not moving his mouth.

'I'll get you some aspirin in a moment,' she says tenderly. 'I'll finish the mowing, too. Can you take the ice away now?' she asks.

Ted withdraws the ice pack from his mouth, resting his hands in his lap. He sits utterly still as she surveys the welts on his head, on his ears, his neck, his lips.

'You look fine,' the nurse said nervously. 'Just a little swollen.'

But they wouldn't give her a mirror. She could feel the right side of her face under the bandages. She was sure she was blind in that eye. It felt like a meteor had crashed there.

'You're going to look a fright for my mother,' she says, her voice low.

'When's that, now,' he mutters unhappily.

'Thursday,' she answers. 'And Rose says Percy is worse next door. She's sent for their daughters. I listened to her braying into the phone all yesterday while I hung the laundry. July is going to be a long month.' She taps the spoon against the edge of the cup and drops it the last few inches to the floor; it hits the softwood with a flat, contracted ping. Holding the cup in one hand, Sylvia dips two fingers into the slushy paste and gently begins to smooth it over the hard, knotted bee stings.

Her fingers on his skin. His softness, the radiating heat of his burning face. It feels oddly different to her, new in a way. New as the stranger who came back to her hotel in London six years ago, as she was leaving Cambridge for spring break. The ex-Cam poet with the broody cowlick, with the voice she could hear in the soles of her feet. The one with Shakespeare in his pocket who met her at the train station with his friend. His friend, his groomsman, who soon disappeared. All the next week in Paris, magnolias blossoming along the river, she could think of nothing but him. His fingers on her throat, her ribs. Magnolias blossoming, flushed and heavy scented, parting like lips as she walked through the gravel of the Tuileries.

The cool milky paste is dripping down his neck. Into his thick dark eyebrows, down his shirt collar. Neither of them says a word. She holds her hand to this new face. Ted doesn't even look up. He doesn't move. She catches the drips with her hand. She wipes them away with her finger.

Sylvia rakes the lawn her husband mowed, the blades cut down like overrun soldiers, broadcast with random finality over the yard. Her shadow looms over the clipped grasses. She covers their shocked faces with a bag.

Old Percy across the lane, blue-faced, wheezing, is dead. Three months ago he had stooped through her April daffodils in his billowing jacket, waving, his eyes soupy in his collapsing face. He had called to her through the window glass. She couldn't understand what he was trying to say: the wind was eating his voice, as something else had eaten the rest of him. What was he doing in her garden? It wasn't a public park. She couldn't hear and turned away.

All that is left of his flesh pools into the satiny cushions of the coffin, his nose flinty and steep, his eyes like currants baked into a fallen cake. His wife has had him set up for viewing in the parlor in front of his telly, that dead, too. The villagers troop by to gawk at the corpse, holding their hats as they shove close to the box. So lifelike, they yawp to the widow. They gabble with sock-puppet sincerity; they trade recipes. Rose has colored her hair. Sylvia slides her eyes over Percy's dead face: the powder that chinks his wrinkles, the book wedged under his chin to keep his mouth shut. So lifelike, she nods, as she backs out the door.

Already the mattress has been slumped down the staircase and tumbled outside to air; it lists in defeat against the cottage wall. A freshly laundered sheet flaps at the window like an escapee. Parakeets hang from a hook in the doorway, whistling and butting their bells, bobbing their senseless cucumber heads.

Sylvia cleans. She paints and weeds and mends. She scrubs, echoing through her house, her yard, in wet-kneed pants, alert to signs of corruption, wary of anything frayed or soured or askew. She drags the ash cans, freighted with grass clippings, out to the lane.

She glues the shredded edges of the wallpaper in the parlor. She washes every window in the house, sunk with age in their wormy casements. She hangs garlic in a braid along the mahogany sideboard in the kitchen, a dented horseshoe in the back hall. She throws netting over the ripening cherries, cushions the melon vines with hay. She whitewashes her children's furniture, trims it with small painted hearts. She sends for more of the pink memo paper from Smith, her covert fetish, its pages stiff like the face of a shield.

Workers have cemented the playroom floor, sealed off the cold stones from inside. Still she knows they are there: the stones that never change. Under her house, muttering below the linoleum. She puts down a rug; she hears nothing. She hems the checkerboard curtains and pulls them shut.

Hearts on the sewing machine, hearts on the beehive. Little painted hearts, sometimes flowers and leaves or a bird. On the trestle table in the playroom. On the piano. On Frieda's little rocker, on the doll bed made by Ted. Pink hearts a tripwire over the doorways. Hearts on the mirror in the hallway. Hearts and a garland on the baby's cradle.

Sylvia stands on a chair outside the guest room. She holds her fine sable brush; she paints a glossy red heart on the threshold. Downstairs, the nail-studded door opens in the back hall. She listens, her heart ticking like a bomb. Has it come? Is it over? Soft voices foam into the house: it's only Ted, Frieda, Nick. The heavy oak door groans on its hinges and clicks into the lock. Her fat, black anxiety rolls back, for a moment, like a stone. She paints a leaf, flowers, steps down off the chair and checks her work. It looks just perfect; it looks just as it should.

'I can hardly bear to watch.' Aurelia Plath is hamster flat against the warm red vinyl seat of her daughter's car, clutching her pocketbook in her lap. With her other hand she grips the door handle, darting a worried glance in Sylvia's direction.

'Mother, please stop it,' Sylvia says tensely, her neck craned over the seat as she drifts the car slowly backward. 'I've done this for years; I know what I'm doing.'

Sylvia's easing the clutch and reversing out of their parking spot on Cathedral Close, the lane that runs alongside Exeter's thirteenth-century cathedral. The opposing traffic approaches around the curve that rounds the cathedral green, the cars hidden until the last moment by the jaywalking crowds of sweaty summer tourists and by flickering patches of leaf shadow thrown from the mature hawthorns and plane trees shielding the cathedral from the street.

'You're right, it's my fault,' Aurelia apologizes. 'It's just so hard to get used to English driving on the wrong side.'

'It's only wrong to you,' Sylvia mumbles under her breath. 'Could you please roll your window down? It's stifling in here.' She pulls into the street and steers herself into the steady wave of traffic. Aurelia cranks down the window glass but pretends not to have noticed her daughter's rudeness. She gazes out the window, concentrating on the neglible view through the full trees.

Sylvia drives the short arc of Cathedral Close, past the lathe-and-plaster facade of Mol's Coffee House and the Georgian Royal Clarence Hotel. She pulls to the stop sign at the High Street intersection and prepares to turn left, her signaling arm out the window, into what would be oncoming traffic anywhere but England. The insistent blinker clicks like a surfacing memory.

A long parade of cars is inching narcoleptically down the High Street, keeping Sylvia waiting at the intersection. She watches the traffic continue to pass, willing it to stop. Three more weeks; she needs to get a grip on herself. This is all her mother wants to see: the picturesque thatch. The baby skin. The pink-checked curtains. The hollyhocks. She's here for a tour of her daughter's heart, the nice part; she wants to see everything nice. There's no need to give her anything more. She can protect herself; it's only three more weeks.

'I'm sorry the day isn't turning out as planned,' she apologizes stiffly, keeping her eyes on the passing cars.

'It's just fine, darling, there's no need to apologize,' Aurelia responds, relaxing at the milder tone in Sylvia's voice. 'I don't know that you could see that cathedral in one afternoon anyway, and we've had a full day as it is. I'll have a chance to study my Michelin before we go back. We still have lots of time this summer.'

'Right,' Sylvia replies with scant enthusiasm. The cars clear ahead of her. She steps lightly on the gas and pulls onto High Street, heading west toward the river.

'I'm just glad we found that charming toy shop – was that on Gandy Street, with the oil lamps on the walls of the buildings? I do hope Frieda will like the paper dolls. Don't you? They're not as pretty as the ones you used to paint—'

'I'm sure she'll be very excited, Mother. But we should reinforce them with tape before you give them to her. Frieda's a little young for paper anything. She's still at the stage where ripping things up is endlessly fascinating.'

'Well, I hope not – they were expensive,' Aurelia says, a trace of hurt in her voice.

Ignore it, Sylvia thinks, both hands on the wheel.

'I would have thought they would carry more baby things in a toy store,' Aurelia says, veering the topic in a safer direction. 'I did want to find something for Nick also.'

'He's a baby, Mother,' Sylvia says. 'He doesn't need anything.'

'I don't know about that,' Aurelia protests. 'When you

could hardly walk you formed your blocks into the shape of the Taj Mahal—'

Sylvia sighs. Here it comes.

'—just like the image on our bathroom rug. Babies are brighter than you think.'

'Mother, I *know*,' Sylvia says, growing exasperated. 'I *know* about babies. But you gave both of the children piles of presents a week ago. They don't need anything more. They're too young to know the difference.'

'I wanted to bring a few other treats, just little things,' Aurelia continues with a wistful pang, groping for a benign connection. 'But I didn't have any more room. The suitcase was getting too full of chocolate chips and molasses and fluoride toothpaste. I can't imagine why they don't sell such common items in England. So peculiar . . .' She glances at Sylvia for a nod, any signal, of friendly commiseration. Sylvia keeps her eyes on the road. Aurelia moves on. 'But my true preoccupation was that box of dishes. I never took my eyes off it from the time I left Wellesley until you picked me up from the train station. I was afraid one of the stewardesses on the plane or one of the porters would kick it, though I labeled it "fragile" on every side.'

'Mother,' Sylvia replies, trying to let her genuine gratitude for her mother's gifts soften the annoyance she feels at yet again having to express her gratitude, 'I really do appreciate all that you brought for us. I love the dishes especially. You know I always wanted them.'

'You always liked that forest green border,' Aurelia notes with satisfaction. 'It's hand painted, you know. I think the color caught your artist's eye.'

'I think you're right.'

'And they're quite valuable now, also. They're nearly

antique. I doubt you could buy a set like that at all, even if you'd kept your job at Smith.'

'I'm sure they're irreplaceable, Mother.' Just ignore it, she tells herself.

'I would have given anything for a job like that,' her mother sighs.

Sylvia doesn't respond, gripping the wheel.

'And I was looking at your garden. There's a nice sunny spot to plant the corn right by your trellis of broad beans,' Aurelia says.

'Mother, it's July. It's too late to plant corn.'

'Oh,' Aurelia says, her voice pinched with disappointment. 'Well then, you can save the seeds and get an earlier start next year.'

'Right,' Sylvia replies automatically, watching the road. Always – something she could do better. Some way that she's let her mother down. They are driving alongside the Roman walls of old Exeter and out toward the banks of the river, which they will follow north and west for much of the trip home, along the same route across Devon that Vespasian's legionnaires had followed, hundreds, no thousands, of years on this road. She feels its pull under her, fundamental, innate. An ancient path; they'd been following it all her life. Whatever she did, whatever pearl she dropped at her mother's feet, it would never be enough.

'Well, it will be so soothing to get back to Court Green after the morning bustle of Exeter,' Aurelia blathers, bridging the stiff little gap in the conversation. 'Though I'm sure you really don't have to worry about Ted or the children,' she offers reassuringly. 'I'm sure they're just fine without you.'

'What do you mean?' Sylvia asks, braking at the next

stoplight. 'I never leave them. I never leave Nick.' Her voice goes suddenly tremulous; she flashes a tiny fearful look at her mother.

'Sylvia, I didn't mean anything,' her mother replies blandly. 'I just meant that Ted has been gone so much this week—'

'What do you mean by that?' Sylvia asks, defensive, gathering herself up on the seat. 'Don't criticize Ted. He's got to go to the dentist for his teeth. He has things he must do whether you're here or not. I'm not going anywhere.'

'Sylvia, of course I'm not criticizing Ted,' Aurelia answers, puzzled, quick to explain herself. 'I only meant that I'm sure he doesn't mind keeping the children alone for a day. I just meant that I don't think you need to worry about them.'

'I worry about them all the time, Mother,' Sylvia says, her voice welling despite herself. 'All I do is worry about them.' She is gripping the steering wheel, staring ahead now at the lozenge of Exeter trapped in the windshield, one foot on the brake, the other poised over the gas.

'Darling, of course you do, I'm sorry,' Aurelia says, scrabbling for balance. 'I don't mean you don't worry about them *at all*. I just meant that you could take a day for yourself, and they would be fine. Ted said it would be fine.' Uneasy, she watches the side of Sylvia's face, which has receded into impenetrable shadow. Sylvia stares at the traffic signal, which urges her mindlessly to caution.

They'd been gone all morning. She maneuvered her mother first through the shops along the flower-potted sidewalks of the Princesshay markets, then to an early cream tea on the quay. Aurelia, who had been appalled when she and Ted quit their teaching jobs to move back to England and live, they hoped, solely by their writing, insisted on picking up the check, blinking with anxiety, her thin bony fingers feeling around the inside of her little coin purse. St Peter's Cathedral, thank God, was free. It reposed dramatically in fawn-colored stone beyond its copse of protective trees, humbler buildings crowding in on all sides of the grounds. They crossed the sun-beaten green to the Gothic western entrance, as tall as Court Green's trio of elms. The carved saints were stacked up to the windows, standing on each other's shoulders with their faces ground away by the centuries, shimmering grittily in the heat.

Inside, the cathedral was brilliant with uncharacteristically hot July sun, a kaleidescope of golden light ratcheting through the stained-glass windows on either end of the vault, as if honey were pouring, liquid, through the glass. The immense stone room was blinding in the concentrated light, a world of amber-toned compartments magnified and mathematical under the ribs of the flying buttresses. The whole glowing interior seemed to be respirating in the heat. A sweet waxy musk of incense seeped out from deep in the pores of the stone. It was like being inside a hive: the capped windows in their gilded hexagonal fittings, the marble-skinned martyrs writhing like pupas up the walls.

'Watch.' *Her father stood in sepia light by the fence of their house in Winthrop, across the bay from Boston. The coarse-textured sand inched right up into the yard, blowing in little eddies between the salt-bleached pickets, drifting over the shells that bordered the grass. It was 1937; she was four years old, almost five. He would be dead in three years, and they'd move away from the ocean. The door of her childhood would close.*

Her father waited, perfectly still before a snaggle of battered geraniums, tall in his nubby brown suit, his hands held out and stiff. He was uncompromising; he could wait forever. Suddenly he clapped his hands together in a trap, then folded down onto one knee. Flicking his head to one side, beckoning her over. He held his cupped hands to her ear. From inside came a stifled, frantic vibrato. 'A bee,' he said, smiling down at her like a god. 'It won't sting me. I know which ones to catch.' The bee buzzed and buzzed in its cramped black cave. Slowly her father opened his blunt fingers. The bee shot out, sputtering like a backfiring motor; it droned again and was gone.

She watched it fly, amazed.

Her father watched it too, grinning. Then he tugged one of her sun-blonde plaits and stood, his broad hand cantilevered on his knee.

The cathedral was humming with holy, golden judgment. It sizzled at the back of her eyes. She held their bags from Jaeger and the toy shop, the library renewals for Ted that she'd forgotten to drop off in the car before they entered the church. Her mother was gawking at the long Gothic ceiling in the nave. All that light pouring in. Sylvia was ill; it was making her ill. The barefoot saints muttering at the door, the honeyed light bucketing down on all their heads. All that sorrow, all the wringing of hands. What made all that gold so bright was the blackness yawning behind it.

She stepped quickly out of the pew where she was resting the bags. 'Mother, let's go.' She took hold of her mother's elbow, began pulling her down the side aisle and out of the cathedral. 'I have to go home. I have to go *now*.' Confused, her mother fumbled for the toy bag and the library books, trying to help. She jerked her mother's arm, gripping it hard. 'Forget it. Let's just go.'

Sylvia stares now at the traffic signal. 'They are fine. But I'm not fine.' *Stop*, it says. *Stop*.

Her mother is watching Sylvia with mounting fear, holding her face steady, trying not to betray her own flailing emotions. *Is it back? Is it over?*

'I have everything,' Sylvia says, her voice breaking into little chunks. The light turns green, and she eases the clutch, turning right onto the road that lies along the river, waving her arm cursorily out the window to signal. 'I never thought I would have all this. My beautiful children,' she says. 'My husband. I have everything. My house and my writing. I never thought I would have it.'

'But of course you were going to have it, my darling,' Aurelia argues, reassured by what she misreads as a simple overflow of emotion. 'Of course you were.'

'No—' Sylvia says. 'I wasn't going to have it. I didn't think I would ever have it. I was afraid I was going to have *nothing*.' She pauses, bracing herself for the words her mother has never been willing to hear. 'That's why I broke down. That's why I tried to kill myself.'

There is a moment of thick, airless silence.

'But that's over now, Sylvia,' Aurelia finally replies, her words measured and motherly, calmly declarative. 'That was so long ago. You put so much pressure on yourself. You didn't really want to die.'

'What?' Sylvia says, incredulous. 'What?' she says, stabbing furious glances in her mother's direction while watching the road. 'Of course I wanted to kill myself! I wanted nothing else *but* to kill myself.'

Aurelia's face drains of all color.

'You know I did, Mother. You know I did,' Sylvia says, her voice both pleading and insistent. 'That's why you locked up the knives. That's why you locked up my sleeping pills.'

'No, Sylvia,' says Aurelia, scrambling, 'you didn't really. You didn't really want to die. That's how you gashed your head, that's why you've got this scar—' She reaches toward Sylvia's temple to brush away her bangs with a finger. But Sylvia's arm flies reflexively off the steering wheel to block her mother's touch. Aurelia recoils, stunned; her face begins to melt off its bones. 'Sylvia, no,' she insists, her eyes brimming, 'you were trying to get up. You were trying to help yourself. You were vomiting up the pills. You were crying. That's how we found you.'

'I was dead for three days!' Sylvia cries out. She swings the wheel and pulls over, the tires spitting stones on the narrow grassy shoulder of the road as she brakes at the edge of the river. 'How can you deny it? I was dead for three days under your house! The only thing I did wrong was to take *too many* sleeping pills!' She glares at her mother, who is trying not to blench. Aurelia's eyes are glossy with tears; she is too frightened to cry.

'I was trying to help you,' Aurelia trembles. 'We were all trying to help you. You were so hard on yourself.'

'Help me!' Sylvia says, shrill, disdainful. Her voice has grown rich, echoing; she feels it moving over a dark plane, blank and windswept. 'You *killed* me. You're the one who gave them permission to electrocute me. You told that quack doctor to give me the shocks.'

'No,' Aurelia says, quietly beginning to sob into her chest. 'No. I was trying to help you. Everything I've ever done has been for you.'

'Help me?' Sylvia repeats, bitter, her voice caustic with mocking sarcasm. 'You won't even admit what happened. If you won't admit the truth, how can that help me?'

Aurelia is slumping against the door, holding her purse over her chest, quietly crying. Sylvia's hands are still on the steering wheel, watching her mother's collapse. She is breathing fast, her heart pumping. She's aghast, amazed by the ominous force of the words as they come out. 'I should be dead, Mother. I'm living a resurrected life. Everything I have is a miracle. My whole life is a miracle—'

Aurelia is sobbing harder, nodding her head, tears dripping off the underside of her nose as she nods, clicking open her purse and looking clumsily for a handkerchief.

'"*Let's just pretend it never happened,*"' Sylvia says. 'That's what you said to me when I got out of the hospital. But I'm telling you now, it's all a miracle. You have to understand it. This is why it's so precious to me – *so precious to me*.' It scares her even now to say it. She says it. 'I should be dead.'

Her mother is crying helplessly, wedged between the car seat and the door, a cowering animal. She is nodding her head and wiping her nose with her handkerchief. She doesn't look up; her mouth hangs open in a gash. It awes Sylvia to see it, this stunning, unspeakable power.

She turns her head, searches the dashboard to locate the car's starter. Her hands are still gripping the steering wheel. She turns the key in the starter and steps on the gas; there is a sudden metallic grind from the engine, and she jumps. It's still running. She never turned it off. She flicks on her signal and glances into her rearview mirror, preparing to reenter the line of traffic.

She listens to her mother's quiet, steady keening beside her as she pulls onto the single-lane road. The green Devon landscape revolves past the windshield and away.

She enters the house blinded, as by a bright explosion.

Her pupils flare, adjust, and the rooms of her house emerge, washed in the submarine light of summer afternoon. Her life takes tangible shape again, returned to her in high relief: the curtains she's sewn wavering at the windows. Her pewter candlesticks, her braided rug; her Chesterfield sofa and its worn blue velvet undulating like a reef at the edge of the parlor. The playroom abandoned for naptime, the debris of toys and storybooks scattered over the floor. Her mother follows behind, brittle, her face wrung like a rag, carrying more packages. The ringing of the telephone begins to surface. The house is otherwise still.

'Ted?' Sylvia calls, peeling off her purse and bags. She hears his chair's faint scrape across the floor of his attic study. Another ring stiffens in the air. 'I'll get it,' she says to no one, anxious to pull her life close, crossing the parlor and turning into the hall, where the phone table is centered against the wall between the staircase and the kitchen. Ted's feet are clattering down the attic steps.

'I've got it,' she calls, as she reaches the phone table, rounding her voice: calm, efficient. As her hand extends toward the black receiver, she sees Ted turn the corner at the top of the carpeted stairs and hesitate in the blue shadows. She raises her chin to him and sends him a tight, hopeful little smile – a tiny intimate motion between people long married, almost a reflex, almost benign. She picks up the telephone, cutting off its shrill pulse. She brings the receiver to her ear. 'Hullo?'

A second of dead air, then another, hisses at the other end of the line.

'Hullo?' Sylvia says again, her hand already tensing to

hang up, her swiftly shaped composure going liquid at its center.

Ted is walking quickly from the second-floor landing down the remaining flight of stairs.

The line crackles with the oceanic suck of a hand covering the mouthpiece. The hand slides back, and the caller speaks into a tinny void. 'Hello,' says a deep, gravelly voice devoid of affect. 'I'm calling for Ted Hughes.'

The muscles and joints and pearly taut sinews of Sylvia's body go slack with immediate relief – it's nothing, it's only for Ted – and then something in the caller's muffled, genderless voice sets off a rush of blood from deep in the cage of her being. It has a Germanic edge.

'Who is calling, please?' she asks, her vocal cords tightening.

There is no answer; just the vibration of air in the line.

'Who is this?' Sylvia asks, her voice suddenly gummy with fear. Ted stops halfway down the stairs, listening, his head bowed like a mourner's.

The caller hesitates. 'I'd like to speak to Ted Hughes,' it asks with sudden, false briskness.

Sylvia grips the phone and holds it tight to her ear. The bones of her hand whiten under the skin. She twists to face Ted, her face an appeal of helpless terror. He does not meet her terrified eyes; he cannot look at her. He listens, his head bowed, his shoulders sagging, as if he holds the ancient weight of the rafters on his back.

'Who – is – this?' Sylvia demands, drawing herself up, her desperation mounting, throwing off panic and dread like sparks.

The caller says nothing.

She knows this voice: It is the voice of her nightmares. Not the voice itself, but the ceaseless void it comes from.

Sylvia's voice rises up in a wave, crashing into the receiver of the phone, flooding the mouthpiece, the full force of her fear transforming, becoming an unchallengeable furious anguish. She has been betrayed. 'I know who this is, Assia,' she says. 'I know it's you.' She jerks the phone away from her face, as if it stung her, and stabs it at arm's length into the air at Ted. 'It's for you,' she says to him, looking away, her face contorting.

For a second, for hours, no one moves.

Ted descends the remaining stairs slowly, as if walking through a wall of water. He takes the phone.

Sylvia's mother is trying not to tremble by the front door, hitching herself as close to the parlor furniture as she can, trying to disappear. It doesn't matter; Sylvia has ceased to notice her. She's been absorbed, become part of an already operating machinery. Sylvia is pacing away from the phone table, into the kitchen streaked by thick bars of dusty sunlight, her back to the stairs where Ted has carried the phone up the steps to the second-floor landing and is whispering hoarsely and clearing his throat. Sylvia's bare arms are crossed over her chest; she is gripping her arms with her hands, squeezing with her long, fine fingers.

Within seconds, Ted has finished speaking. He begins to again descend the stairs, the receiver still in his hand, the base of the phone at his side, his fingers curled under the cradle. As he takes a step, another down the stairs, Sylvia turns and swings her hands down and out to her sides, regnant. Everything, suddenly, goes dry. The sea light slides back, evaporated. In the potent, magnetic air everything looks bleached and static – the walls, their faces, everything but the pitch-black, glossy phone.

Sylvia's upper arms glow white with the imprints of her own hands. She rushes forward, the blood blooming under her skin, her face febrile, lit by a ghastly inner radiance, to meet Ted at the phone table.

The receiver is still in his hand. As he sets the phone down on the table and readies to fit the receiver onto the cradle, Sylvia snatches the telephone's cord out of the air and pulls, grimacing, yanking the telephone itself off the table, yanking again, the table falling, the drawer crashing out and the pens and pencils and scraps of paper tumbling and sliding to the floor, the cord ripping out of the wall socket and snapping into the air, its wires bursting like a coppery flower out of the end of the striped fabric cording. Sylvia pulls the phone out of the wall and feels a surge of electric current, a charge, the million filaments of the wires exploding, burning all along the line from London, all along her nerves, electrocuting her, burning the shadow of the moment into place, shocking her again with their lightning stroke, straight to her electrified heart. He had betrayed her.

As Sylvia pulls the telephone out of the wall, the cells in her brain are charging, the synapses going off like cannons, like fireworks, setting off little tails of smoke, the scent of scorch electric in the air, and silence behind, everything over. Sylvia pulls the telephone out of the wall: dead air. The voice on the other end cut off, severed, extinct. Dead air. And that's not all that's dead. In the moment the cord sails up and snaps and shoots its sparks in the potent hall, Sylvia knows how futile all of her protections have been, all she did to sandbag her slipping hold. What's dead is the life she saved from herself. The moment has cut her loose, stripped her of everything that tied her to her perfect, ordered, resurrected life. In the eye blink of a god, in a heartbeat, all that she clung to rises up with her like smoke, like ash, into the charged, dead air: The cakes of soap. Her wedding ring. His gold filling.

8

Tulips

Early August 1962
Court Green

Her baby is propped on her lap, as directed. With her photogenic house behind her, she faces the orchard and the flourishing garden, the banks of rampant flowers that the camera won't see. The overcast sky, an impenetrable slab of heavy, shadowless light, presses itself to the landscape like an ether-soaked cloth. The poppies and the dahlia blossoms struggle, tossing their breeze-blown heads. She holds Nick steady under the arms, her fingers splayed over his footed coveralls as he frowns and stares and flails his fists. Frieda sits beside her on the grass, pensive in her ironed dress and Mary Janes, hands busy with a toy, a wooly dog with felt eyelashes tucked loosely under her elbow, a doll buggy off to one side.

Ted fumbles with her mother's camera, waiting. Her mother passes through the composition like a nurse, collecting the tumbled doggy for Frieda, arranging, rolling the buggy out of sight. Kneeling beside her daughter for the final tableau, prim in her traveling suit. Nick flexes his toes and squints.

Sylvia submits. She's hollow-eyed, pale, subdued. She gives off a low-voltage hum; she knows they can hear it.

If they were to cut her open, she would glow, phosphorescent, like the cobalt-boned eels she and Ted caught on their honeymoon in Spain. She hated Spain. The whole country was a graveyard. Ted draws the camera to his face and holds it steady, stepping back into the soft soil beneath the rustling pole beans. Stumbling in his own dirt. He doesn't care – he's as closed to her as the sky. His paradise is but a phone call away. Or was. It's winter now, all right. It's so cold it burns. Her sweater is buttoned almost to the neck. She stares down the slit of his single, guilty eye. Yes, she'll give him a picture: her shredded little soul, overexposed. The bloody tatters of their marriage dangling from her wrists like the layers sliced back on a cadaver. She scrapes her face together into a smile.

The shutter clicks. It's time to rush her mother to the station. The flowers go on dreaming, kicking in their sleep like dogs.

9
A Secret

December 13, 1962
London

Adrift in a warm, salted sea. Utah, the Great Salt Lake. Floating on her back, held in the cupped palm of July, 1959. A rim of sagebrush hills, antelope blond, gathers the lake. The sky a gouache of arid, infinite blue pulled taut and matte-finished overhead; the night's future stars a certainty behind, waiting, like spilled salt, to be tossed into the air. Already a hologram of moon, bony and blue-veined as her feet. Ted floating somewhere beside her, lake water washing between them as if it is itself an irrevocable bond. Her baby, rocking in its secret. The late sun a hand to her forehead, the smoky green water lapping her neck and the fine soft hair at her temples. The mysterious ache of new pregnancy. She closes her eyes. Happiness strokes its fingers across her face. It isn't merely happiness; it isn't anything so crude. She feels contained.

Her eyes are closed. She hears the faint tidal rocking in the caverns of her ears. The warm immersion, the holiness of it. She can taste it: the salt in her mouth. The wet trickle curling over her ears and down her neck. Into her pillow. The moment stills, her face washed by something unbearably pure. The salt stinging in her eyes. All at once, the vision contracts at the edges, pulling into itself. The colors, the textures intensify, grow richer, stranger, dizzy with brightness, pulling forward at great speed and bursting in a moment of light that shrinks to a pinprick and snuffs out, leaving nothing but the wet, aching darkness behind.

She's crying. She's been crying in her sleep, through her dreams, the tears running down the back of her throat, into her ears, wetting her hair, sorrow washing out of her in her sleep.

She lies on her back, motionless, her eyes closed, the tears brimming through her eyelashes and spilling in a seamless trickle over her cheekbones and down the curving flange of her ear. She doesn't resist. She doesn't even try to think. She lets it come, lying soundlessly on her bed, the back of her head saturating the pillow. She surrenders to it, the tears coming and coming, like birth.

From far off in a vague distance her children's voices begin to materialize out of the disintegrating night. It's not night, it's morning – the windows pale but lucent, the sun lightly rummaging through the paint-stinking clothes she dumped last night on a chair. Her children, across the hall: they are calling for her from the other bedroom.

Even the eyelet on her nightgown is soaked. It clings to her throat. What would be left of her – just a skin, empty, the rest gone. A cicatrix. She takes a deep breath; it clatters in her ribs. She takes another, wipes her hands across her face. She braces herself to rise.

Up the gravel-crusted footpaths of Primrose Hill she rises, pushing Nicholas in the pram. Past the traffic crossing and wrought-iron palisade at the undulant edge of Regent's Park Road, the last decaying sycamore leaves cartwheeling, hand-sized and yellow, over the flagstone footpath, slick black taxis and their soundless occupants flickering by like penny theater scenes at the edge of her sight. Across the green lawns spreading on all sides, she walks in the last granular light of afternoon. Frieda's mittened hand curls around the curving chrome chassis of the pram. Sylvia leads her, a docile calf, toward the playground at the foot of the hill. But the summit exerts its own pull, its cloud-marbled arc of changeable, potent sky drawing Sylvia's muted attention.

It is quiet at the top of Primrose Hill. Only a few distant walkers tugging their coats about them and hurrying toward the shops and beyond, to Hampstead; no one at the crest. The hawthorns splayed alongside the ascending footpaths are black-jointed and lacy against the colorless light, bare but for their red berry tassels. At the playground a couple of older children are puttering unsupervised in the high-sided sandbox, their open jackets flapping. Sylvia lifts Nicholas, blinking himself awake, into the wooden saddle of the infant swing.

Frieda has run to the edge of the sandbox to watch the older boys filling their dump trucks. She waits, her hands knotted behind her. The elastic frog on one of her rubber boots has come unclasped. The boys' hands and faces are raw with cold, red and chapped from the damp sand. Sylvia pulls her head scarf tighter, glancing around for their mothers. This would be the day *not* to run into any of her old neighborhood crowd. She's swaddled her grisly, tearstained face like an unpresentable baby: another appalling surprise. She takes cover, harrowed and benumbed, behind the deflecting solidity of Nick, who is content to merely dangle in his swing, snowsuited, in his pointy tufted hat, contemplative and sleepy, his feet lightly swaying. He knits his infant eyebrows and studies the sandy slab of concrete below him that records with faint shadows the infinitesimal orbit he's making.

The ornate Victorian street lamps suddenly blink on at the edges of the footpaths, their thick glass globes haloed with tawny light. It is nearly four o'clock, nearly dark. The passing of hours has escaped her. All day she has been caught in the gaping lags between the simplest questions and her ability to respond. Time and again Frieda's curious, patient face has suddenly materialized out of her thoughts – real, before her, standing in bare feet on the kitchen linoleum, or now, in undone boots – a request for a cookie or a puzzle or a cup of water echoing, empty of meaning, in her head. The clouds roil at the crest of Primrose Hill, concealing the receding western light. It's there, but hidden, glowing now and then at the edges in slow, observable time.

The sound of car horns ribbons up on the empty air from Prince Albert Road behind her. As the remaining light drains from Primrose Hill, unseen bulldozers scrape a space for the zoo's new aviary on the far side of Regent's Canal, cut their belching engines, are silent. Her fingertips, she distantly observes, must have worked the frog over the hard rubber toggle on Frieda's boot. Frieda is swinging; the back of her red woolen coat comes and goes. With every push on her daughter's weightless back, the grit beneath Sylvia's shoe chafes, grinding, eating away the concrete underfoot, the leather of her sole.

The Earth is turning. Westward, toward her and the hill she faces, like a mill wheel scooping up days, holding them up to the sun for a moment at their zenith, then turning them out at her, drenching her with unwelcome recollection. As she stands on Primrose Hill, her back to the still and lightless flat on Fitzroy Road, the life she left behind begins to roll forward. All of London, now, falls away before her, sinking and glinting at the skyline; she can feel the inexorable marble turning of the Earth beneath her feet.

The Gothic, beaded towers of Parliament and West-minster Abbey, the serpentine Thames, the sinuous green downs of Salisbury Plain roll toward her, monumental and blank and ineffectual. The melancholy dolmens and toppled bluestone of Stonehenge, Bath's lustrous golden facades relinquish the light as they sink from view. Past Exeter Cathedral's helpless, faceless saints hugging their time-pocked columns come the elderberried hedgerows and patchwork hillsides of Devon, the fields of barley and the ragged cattle and her apple trees. Among them her beehive, sheltered on its painted stand. Her garden, dying back under the giant elm. And then her house appears, her cobbled court and rotty thatch; the nine glazed panes of her French kitchen window rise and revolve away. The dank, moss-covered church rears up over the picket of lichened gravestones she could see from her study. The yew, as always, has caught the setting sun in its black-green needles. The butcher, the post office, the bridge over the river, the slate-roofed village flash forward, and suddenly she's on a grassy hillside flanked by stone walls and hedgerows sprouting late dog roses, by the giant tufted fingers of a Victorian-era monkey puzzle tree at the gate, by stunted English oaks growing close to the ground. Not again: she's standing at a swing set with a view of the purple mass of Dartmoor looming out of the patchwork heather, beyond the borders of the village play-ground. It is September, three months past, and she sees herself alone, speechless, pushing a child in a swing at sunset.

It was September: a vicious and despairing time. Ted was gone, just *gone*— Her mind raced ceaselessly, picking over dead conversations. Draping wet laundry across the steaming, cast-iron doors of the Aga, choking on the fraudulent cheer of her nursery teas, she rehearsed for future scenes – showdowns, pleadings – and analyzed merciless replays of recent ugly vignettes, already glittering malevolently in her memory. She agonized: what she should say, what she shouldn't have said. What was the truth? She had desperately wanted to know. She couldn't find it for the slipping of her mind. For all the stillness and silence she lived inside at Court Green, the hours and days she would go without hearing another adult voice, without speaking, she couldn't escape the roaring in her ears. There were always the voices whispering their terrible, urgent advice.

This is all she'd known then, killing time – a phrase whose accuracy made her wince – with her children at the village playground, the inescapable facts: Ted was having an affair. He was sleeping with Assia, sleeping on floors in London to see her. Sylvia didn't, beyond that, know where he was or what he would do. She had wanted to know it all – the truth, all of it – she knew there must be more. But in the glare of these particulars alone her mind was a bedlam of horrified torment and disbelief. Months later, standing in the cold London twilight, her face still flushes with shame: he knows everything about her. She has no secrets – he's always known more than she has known herself. Where would it go now, all that was her, now that he didn't want it?

Her children are still swinging. Still, Sylvia stands by absently, one cold hand clenched deep in her pocket, letting their movements, the shapes of their bodies against the fence, the incremental slump of Frieda's socks wash by her. In September she'd written to her mother about the majestic view of Dartmoor from the playground, as if that made her life less forlorn, less cramped and scared. What was it he had said to her? His words had fallen like blows, and now she couldn't remember. It was too exhausting to concentrate on the hard things, the elemental truths of the self. She couldn't then, and she can't now – she notices again how her self slips away, uncatchable except by the most strenuous effort. It was slippery, the self, like a baby in a bath.

That's all she needs. All, more likely, that she can manage: a bath. Hot as hell. As hot as she can stand, tropical, so hot she breaks a sweat. So hot and long her fingers pucker. Scalding hot, a brandy's sting – she'd have a brandy too, a cat's eye in the tub: the burning and the numbing, a fossil stiff in amber.

The little deaths of all these leaves: the stunted oaks, the London planes, rolling by in tatters on the grass; she dreads this recycling of days. The shadows of her children are flying out over Dartmoor, over the rooftops of London, out over the world as she watches. The older boys have vanished, teased back into the dark by their invisible mothers. All along Fitzroy Road the other mothers will be just preparing their suppers as she heads back with her children to their dark flat. Eyes downcast, her scarf pulled close, she'll pass the glowing, knee-high windows of the garden flats and see all those other mothers headless at their cooking. They'll be chopping their vegetables, making their stews, ringing their puddings with cream on the other side of the steamy basement glass.

10

The Jailor

December 14, 1962
London

Framed within the glossy red grid of a Jubilee telephone kiosk is a two-year-old girl wearing a
carmine coat as red as the booth in which she
stands. Her smaller brother is balanced on a chrome-
edged shelf meant to hold parcels, and her mother is dropping coin after coin into the call box. From her
circumscribed spot on the kiosk's damp, cast-iron floor,
the little girl looks out onto the hill where she played last
evening, now blanketed in a layer of blue fog hovering
thickly over the grassy slopes and sports fields like a sterile
sheet of cotton batting. The morning rain continues to
fall, a cold, steady mizzle dribbling irregular trails down
the glass-paned kiosk windows with their streaky views
of Primrose Hill. The pennies chink in the coin box; her
brother is starting to cry. Outside on the corner, his pram
is soaking wet. Her mother pulled the bonnet up, but the
gabardine cover would not snap closed over the pillowcases of dirty laundry she had piled into the bassinet. She
hunches into the telephone, away from the public indictment of her soggy buggy parked on the corner of Regent's
Park Road for all to see.

Sylvia's umbrella, snagged on the hook so thoughtfully

provided by the General Post Office, is dripping steadily into the top of her overshoe. Nicholas is struggling, whining and grasping at her wet coat; she holds him firmly on his high awkward seat in the crook of one arm and flips the worn pages of her address book with the other hand. No one, no one is answering. Not the mothers who used to meet in the gardens in front of her old flat, the ones who could seamlessly carry on a conversation while digging out of a baby's mouth sand from the box where the neighborhood cats buried their hard little turds. Not the wives of the poets with whom she exchanged recipes or sly asides, not the poets themselves. Not the Telephone House, where her application for service was filed over a month ago. If she could set up just one tea, one visit.

The pennies fall and return. No answer comes. The ringer drills its pointless holes into empty space.

The neighborhood has gone steely and lusterless in the rain, which has gradually seeped under Sylvia's clear plastic cap and into her thick hair as she stands at the phone, and now trickles in cold rivulets over her stiffening scalp. Even this simple plan – the launderette, setting a date for a visit with friends, maybe a baby-minder engaged for a few hours – is a death by a thousand cuts. She's scuttled with the loaded pram, dragging Frieda from the shelter of tree to dripping tree down the footpath at the edge of the park, looking for the nearest public phone; her skull crinkles, fragile and papery as the abandoned husk of an insect after the seven-hour stupor of her sleeping pills. It's just her luck to find the phone here: mere steps from Dido Merwin's disapproving front door on St. George's Terrace. She's passed this corner what must be hundreds of times in the past, to and from dinners at the Merwins' a block and a half from Chalcot Square.

But she never noticed the box at the foot of Dido's street; she'd never needed it before. And now she's got no choice but to use it, crouching in the shadow of a woman who's never liked her, her soiled linens in the street.

The doorways to the shops on Regent's Park Road are garlanded with meaningful swags of greenery, blatant seductions for holiday shoppers. Colored lights blink garishly in the windows of the flats above. A girl in The Queens Head, the pub across the street, is wiping a tabletop with a filthy rag and staring at her through the window. Sylvia turns her back, searching her book for someone else she might call. Dido is out of the question; now that Ted was gone, there was no reason to keep up the pretense of friendship, a pretense Dido most decidedly abandoned when she offered, unasked, to house Ted. The windows of the phone box have begun to cloud, fogging up with the heat of three damp bodies. Her mother in Wellesley (fast asleep, thank God, no temptation there), the solicitor: both just as risky as the only other choice she's got left, and nearly as expensive. She turns to the front of the address book, just out of curiosity – not because she's going to use it – looking for the loose scrap of paper on which she wrote the number of Dido's mother's flat, where Ted is staying. The back of an envelope, blue airmail, the thick uneven line of her Sheaffer pen – she knows exactly what the paper looks like, the deckled edge where she tore it from the aerogram, but it's not there. It's not in the back of the book either, not tucked between the pages. She can almost see the number in her mind, she's looked at it so many times, willing the solitary girlish aperçus and Arabic loops of her intent penmanship to reveal something other than the practical: some divination, a sign. She checks again, more slowly, fanning the onionskin pages under her fingertip, Nicky crying at her side and attempting to crawl down on his own.

It's disappeared, slipped from the book. And there's no one left to call *but* Ted.

Cautiously, hugging Nicholas whimpering at her neck, Sylvia leans to the right, edging beyond the glass-encased RATES & INSTRUCTIONS poster, which shields her partly from view, to glance cautiously up Dido's short, sloping lane and its block-long row of grand houses separated from Primrose Hill by its own hairpin strip of garden. None of the curtains is moving. Still, Sylvia can feel the prim Palladian reproach of St. George's Terrace. Lord Byron's scandalized widow died here a hundred years ago, humiliated; she read it in a biography last month. She's sure Dido told her that Robert Frost had chucked her under the chin here as a baby. Or maybe that *wasn't* here; maybe Dido had snagged this manse from one of her several discarded husbands. The nerve of her judgments! No wonder Dido is sheltering Ted; she and Assia have so much common ground.

By what unearned privilege has Dido come by this house with its view of the hill? Sylvia had always found Dido's tales of bored superiority, crammed with obscure allusions and multilingual self-flattery, hard to take, let alone to keep straight. Dido's nonchalant sense of privilege bred an overbearing generosity that only succeeded in making Sylvia feel meager and resentful. She's trying now to cantilever the phone directory up onto the writing shelf, to look up Dido's mother – if she could just remember her last name. Had she ever known Dido's maiden name? It's probably of little consequence: who could know how many times Dido's mother herself had been married. She slaps the directory shut.

She's got no choice. Again she picks up her address book, this time running her forefinger over the tabs to 'M.' She reads and quickly memorizes the number, turns the book over to keep her place, and reaches into her coat pocket for four pence. Her finger traces a modulating crescent over and over on the dial, the chrome disc ticking back each time into place. A pause, and then the double burr.

'Hello,' answers Dido's throaty, smoker's voice.

Quick, a deep breath – poised and cool: 'Dido, it's Sylvia.'

'Sylvia,' Dido drawls out, exhaling through her nose. Sylvia can just picture her: standing in her marble-surfaced kitchen, tapping her ever-present cigarette pack. One bony hand on her hip, the boyish slouch and wide red hair band, a halo of smoke ringing her flawless black bob. 'How nice of you to call. Where are you these days?'

'I'm in Devon.'

'Oh,' Dido says, breathing evenly into the phone. 'I thought you were back in London.'

'No—' Sylvia answers. The muscles in her neck contract.

'Did you get your telephone replaced, then?' Dido asks.

The calculated malice! 'No,' Sylvia responds, 'I'm calling from a public kiosk.'

'That's astounding,' Dido says, 'as there's a baby pram looking just like yours, the one we bought for you, in front of the telephone boxes on the corner here on Regent's Park Road. Filled with bags of money, it would seem, from the look of it.'

Except for the muffled gasps of Nick's weeping into her coat collar, there is only foreboding silence from Sylvia's end of the telephone line.

'In fact,' Dido continues, 'there's a charming little girl in the box I can see from my window who appears to be the very image of my lovely goddaughter, and she's licking the glass. What's all that crying about?'

Swinging Nicholas onto her hip, Sylvia tucks her chin into the earpiece of the phone, holding it steady, and reaches down to take Frieda's hand, easing her away from the kiosk glazings. She quickly wipes her fingertips first across Frieda's warm wet tongue, then onto the seat of her own wool coat. Her hand comes back wetter.

'Would you like to bring the children in out of the rain?' Dido asks. 'I've still never seen the baby.'

'No thank you,' Sylvia says. It's no use. She pauses, just long enough to kick dirt over her composure. 'Dido, I've only called because I need Ted's number.'

Dido takes a long drag on her cigarette. 'Well, Sylvia, I'm not at all sure I should hazard giving it to you. He's staying at my mother's flat, you know, and I fear you may start badgering her housemaid as you did my catminder this fall when Ted was staying here.'

'That's ridiculous,' Sylvia scoffs. She – the downright lies! She hardly called at all – the cat-minder hung up on her *twice,* and she could hear Ted's voice in the background—

'If only it were so,' Dido replies. 'And I can't risk having her quit now, as I've only got until the end of the year to finish an inventory and get the rest of my mother's furnishings off to the auction house.'

'So Ted will be moving again,' Sylvia interjects, careful to keep her voice hollow with indifference.

'I would guess so, unless he'd like to stay on in an utterly barren set of rooms,' Dido answers dispassionately. 'Which might not sound unsatisfactory to him, come to think of it, after this fall.'

Nicholas is bawling into Sylvia's sweater, rubbing his head into the lapels of her coat. She can hardly hear over his hiccuping sobs. 'Whatever do you mean by that?' she asks raggedly, struggling with her voice, running her palm over the back of Frieda's hair where she's buried herself against her mother's skirt.

Again Dido inhales deeply, her voice tight and adenoidal as she begins to speak. 'I only mean that after the endless harangues and accusations you've been hurling at him the last few months, perhaps if you'd give him some peace he'd have a chance to think this through.'

'It's already thought through,' Sylvia replies, holding her body as rigid as the phone. 'I'm getting a divorce.'

'Well, if that's the case,' Dido answers blandly, 'you've nothing left to badger him over. Let your solicitor do it.'

'I'm calling him for the children, Dido,' Sylvia confides, convincing even herself, her attention diverted by the shock of Dido's easy reference to a solicitor. Has Ted said something? What has he said? Everyone must know: they're nothing but formalities to each other now. She feels suddenly chilled, the puddle in her overshoes leaching its way up her heavy knit tights. The morning marketers parade by, swinging their lumpy mesh bags and peering moonfaced through the distorting glass of the kiosk as they pass.

'. . . on my way over there now,' Sylvia hears Dido responding, her voice not exactly friendly, but slackened, like her jaw line before her face-lift, 'just waiting for a mover to arrive to pick up a few trunks and old relics I've decided to ship off to the auction house as well. Winter cleaning, you might say. I'll be staying at my mother's as well until I leave for New York. We've leased this house through the spring. I'll let Ted know.'

Success, such as it is. Sylvia tastes a sudden rusty flavor of doubt at the back of her throat. 'Please tell him not to come until Monday,' she responds. 'I'm busy with guests this weekend,' she adds, collecting herself.

'Of course,' Dido answers, inhaling. 'If that's all, then—'

'Yes. Oh – Dido—' Sylvia says with overdone breathlessness, a sloppy attempt to mask her secondary agenda, another favor, as spontaneous thought. She cringes at herself: why does she even bother? Dido will sniff her out like a dog. 'Millie –' she continues, '– your old cleaner. Does she still work for you?'

'Then you *do* have bags of money in your pram—' Dido says, exhaling smoke through her nose.

'Don't be ludicrous,' Sylvia answers irritably. 'I'm working my fingers to the bone and I've got little to show for it, certainly not from Ted. But if I can get a mother's helper, I *will* have bags of money. I absolutely must find a nanny right away. I hoped Millie might do some baby-minding for me as she did when Frieda was small.'

'Like everyone, Millie loves Frieda, and I'm sure she'll love little Nicholas,' Dido says evenly. 'No need for the hysterics. I'll have her ring you.'

'My telephone hasn't been connected,' Sylvia says, her face growing hot.

'Oh,' Dido says, the sound of her cigarette box tapping again on the countertop. 'You do have bad luck with phones. Then give me your address. I'll tell her to stop around.'

'I'm at number twenty-three Fitzroy Road,' Sylvia responds formally, 'Yeats's house.'

'Yeats's house?' Dido repeats in disbelief. 'You've come back to this district? More than that – you've moved right back into the neighborhood.'

'Of course I came back,' Sylvia answers. 'This is my home – my other home. My doctor is here—'

'*My* doctor, you recall, to whom I recommended you as a patient—' Dido corrects.

'He delivered Frieda,' Sylvia responds, peremptory. 'My favorite shops, my grocer, my parks, all that I love is here.'

There is a pause, broken only by the sound of Dido inhaling. 'More than you know,' she says. 'Perhaps too close for comfort.'

'There's nothing I don't know,' Sylvia snaps. Something, maybe her certitude, clatters in her chest.

Dido smokes, holding the phone in silence. 'All right, Sylvia,' she finally answers, her voice receding and skeptical. '"Whatever flames upon the night / Man's own resinous heart has fed."'

'Don't quote Yeats to me,' Sylvia says, imperious. 'That's why I came. I know what I'm doing.' As she hangs up the phone, Sylvia turns around, holding Nicholas, pink-faced and blotchy, his little body heaving with residual sobs, her own blood thumping. A phone slam: a pathetic, gutless gesture. Her damp skin prickles with disquiet. The rain continues to fall, the sky congested and close. This can't go on: her future arrested, held in suspense by the weather, the barren, the absentees, public humiliations she can't escape. She's got to get her own phone, a lifeline. It's Friday, nearing noon. Lunch hour, then afternoon naps for the children. She could lose the whole day, stuck at home in the dying light, like yesterday. Then the weekend, two more days incommunicado, a prisoner. The laundry will wait.

'All right,' Sylvia mutters to herself, scanning the street. The canvas awnings over the shops are dark and saturated, the scalloped overhangs sheeting with rain. Before her, across Regent's Park Road, a short lane of narrow houses cuts through to Chalcot Road and beyond, past her new flat, to the post office at the corner of Princess Road – spanning the length of the entire four-block-long district, a much faster route than the park road's broad curve along the perimeter of Primrose Hill. She knows what she's doing. 'All right,' she says aloud, gathering her address book and coin purse and sliding her pocketbook over her wrist, leaning her free elbow against the door of the booth. 'We're making a run for the post office. Quick like bunnies,' she says to the children, hurrying to the pram and pushing back the bonnet, revealing a miraculously dry spot for Nicholas to sit behind the pillowcases of drenched laundry. She swivels her head protectively up and down Regent's Park Road, over her shoulder toward the intersection of Primrose Hill Road and the faster traffic behind them, before gripping Frieda's hand and darting with the pram across the street.

The useless umbrella, requiring one more hand than she has available, is furled and tucked beside Nicholas in the pram; her head in its plastic cap is tucked toward her chin against the rain as she hurries with Frieda down her shortcut's footpath, the old familiar stones beneath her feet a mosaic of slate and the browned lace skeletons of leaves. It's a route she knows by heart but has avoided for days now as she's taken the long way around, the safe way, by the park. By the park she loves, yes, its single rolling crescendo of hill stippled with centurion trees, but the long way, the way of circumvention, the way she was walking, warily, hurrying then as well, to her doctor's office when she'd seen Yeats's house for lease. It was *not* just a path of avoidance, out of her way, the farthest route from the tube station, the shops, the phone box: a month ago it was also a manifest sign, a legitimate omen. It was the route she took to find her new life, circling at the edges of her old one.

Shoulders clenched below her coat collar, Frieda's hand beneath hers on the handle, Sylvia pivots the pram at the half-block angle in the lane and pivots again a few houses down, turning onto Chalcot Road. She looks straight ahead: she's just a block from her own new corner, then another block, broken by a mews or two, from the post office. She can do this route, too. She knows what she's doing, the pastel houses lined up like children's toys around the garden square – no reason not to – the familiar swing and the mothers' benches at her left shoulder now, no one on the street – it's raining, it's a work day – her old flat on the right, its Doric-columned entrance like a sentry box. She dares not look up toward the third-floor windows, the little flat overlooking Chalcot Square where Frieda was born, just a block away from where she lives now.

'Let's hurry, Frieda,' she calls to her daughter, breaking into a trot, passing as fast as she can through this no-man's-land, the nineteen houses between her old flat, where her husband's lover lives, and her new home, her new life in Yeats's house on Fitzroy Road, barely out of sight on the other side of the next street.

The flimsy corner door swings in and bangs, jangling the chimes hung above it, as Sylvia shoves the pram through the doorway, maneuvering over the jamb and into the Princess Road post office. She stops just inside the door to untie her rain cap and stamp her boots on the mat; Frieda stamps, too. On a table set to the side, within free reach of customers, lay baskets for various classes of letters, brochures and forms, and several scales, one with individual lead weights and a bowl in the shape of a silver urinal. At the far end of the room, a long hardwood counter with chipped mouldings spans the full length of the storefront, from the misty picture window facing the street to the cashier's grate at the other end. A three-foot-high wire mesh topped with brassy finials encloses the counter, protecting shelves stocked with twine, envelopes, gum erasers, pots of ink, and glue. A tall, middle-aged clerk with greasy hair sits in a criminal hunch behind the bars, his thick assiduous fingers stacking matchsticks into an elaborate model deployed on a sheet of newspaper. He doesn't look up at the sound of the opening door.

'Excuse me, sir,' Sylvia says, approaching the clerk while pulling off her gloves by the fingertips. 'I would like to speak with the telephone manager.' Smiling, friendly but firm.

The clerk looks up, blinking, holding the burnt tips of two matches in midair. 'There's no telephone manager here, madam. You'll need to ring the head postmaster at the district office.' He looks down again, carefully dipping the matchsticks into a glue pot and affixing them to his model.

'No, you see,' Sylvia continues, leaning into the mesh railing, her gloves dangling from one fist, 'I *have* been ringing the district postmaster. I need my telephone to be installed, and my request for service has been on file for a month. I've got the letter of confirmation, and it says my service was to be hooked up "as quickly as possible." All of my forms have been filed through this post office.'

'Well then, madam,' says the clerk, putting down his matches and resting his huge meaty hands on his thighs, seeming pleased with the assurance of satisfactory performance from all sides, 'it appears your paperwork is all in order, then, and you merely need wait for the engineers to ring you for an appointment. I've no doubt you've made it onto the waiting list, as the letter you received confirms.'

'Waiting list?' Sylvia asks suspiciously. 'The letter said nothing about a waiting list. It simply said my order was to be processed as quickly as possible.' The bells over the door chime unevenly behind her.

'And that, indeed, madam,' the postal clerk responds, rising from his stool in arthritic segments, like a metal chaise unfolding or a stork lifting jerkily into the air, 'means that you've been put on the list, and now you are waiting.' He spreads his wide, flat-nailed fingertips on the counter and smiles paternally.

Sylvia stares at him. 'But this is preposterous. I don't see why I must continue to wait; I need a telephone now, and I'm willing and able to pay. I have small children,' she says, waving an arm in the direction of the pram, where Nicholas has fallen heavily asleep against the laundry, his face tear stained, his mouth a slack pink O. Frieda stands beside him, gripping the pram, sucking the wet end of her mitten, her eyes wide, startled by the sudden blare of her mother's voice turned in her direction. Sylvia gives the clerk an uncompromising look, tapping her nails on the counter. 'I simply insist,' she says meaningfully, 'that my telephone be hooked up.'

The postal clerk's smile sets, becoming just perceptibly hard. He runs one hand over his thinning, slicked hair. 'I daresay you'd have your line if you were back home in America, madam,' he replies, pausing for emphasis, 'but this is a country nearly bankrupt by the war. It may seem far off to you, but it is not to Englishmen. Our telephone service is state run, and there's only a certain amount of money set aside for telephones each year. It's the end of the year. We've run out of money. You can thank the Germans for your lack of a telephone.'

Sylvia's cheeks burn. She feels the heat of other bodies in the room, the soft feathery sound of breathing behind her. She lowers her voice, leaning farther toward the clerk. 'Please, sir,' she pleads, her tone solicitous and meek, 'there must be some way I can get a phone. Could I pay the quarterly tariff now? What if I pay for the full year of service?'

The clerk is shaking his head as Sylvia speaks. He continues to shake it, a look of mournful discouragement on his face as he tells her, 'I'm afraid that won't help. You see, young lady, there are certainly other customers ahead of you on the waiting list. It wouldn't be right to serve you first. It just isn't done.'

'But I have small children—' she says plaintively. 'I'm alone.' She whispers to the clerk, her lips nearly touching the wire bars. 'My husband is dead.'

'I'm very sorry, madam,' the clerk says, still shaking his head. He pauses, his chin just wagging. He sighs, lifting his eyes to Sylvia. 'Have you considered shared service? The waiting list is generally shorter.'

'That's a party line?' she asks cautiously.

The clerk nods. 'You might get service by January.'

'January?' Sylvia exclaims, deflated. 'How long will it be otherwise?'

'For your own service?' says the clerk. 'February. No later than March.'

Sylvia groans, leaning her forehead against the mesh. 'But I can't wait that long,' she moans, feeling her face sliding out from under her control, her eyes filling and salty. 'I can't wait,' she says, looking up at the clerk again. 'I have to have a phone. I'm trapped. I'm alone,' she says, gritting her teeth, trying to stem the impulse to cry. 'What if I need to call for help? There's got to be something you can do.'

'Surely you can get help from a neighbor,' the clerk responds, his voice blandly hopeful.

'How can the engineers ring me for an appointment?' Sylvia asks angrily. 'I've got no phone.' She straightens her back, takes a deep breath, begins to turn on her heel and finds that all she sees is filmy with tears.

'Madam, I assure you there's nothing I can do,' the clerk says to her as she is turning from the counter. 'You'll get your phone. If it's any comfort to you,' he says, smiling wanly, 'I can tell you that this process is entirely out of our control.'

At the door, at the end of the vague, glassy line of postal customers she sees as through the back of a water-fall, a man holding a dark spongy newspaper he'd tented over his head steps aside. Sylvia pulls Nicky's hat down over his ears, his sleeping face hot and flushed under her icy hands. The bells jingle as they leave, stepping out into the rain on the corner, turning back and retracing their steps in the steady drumming rain.

Under her feet, the wet flagstones of the footpath: buckling with tree roots, stained with the tarry gravel of workmen, catching her heel, laid randomly slab to slab as they are in Yorkshire cemeteries. She looks up, livid, panicky: Chalcot Road opens before her, or closes. From the point where she stands far into the wavery, watery distance, at the road's end, identical houses line each side of the street, the creamy, three-story classical facades of the houses exactly the same, the columns and Georgian cornices and sooty terra-cotta chimney pots alike, the black wrought-iron railings following each other end to end in domino order, repeating down the street and receding to a vanishing point three blocks away. Fitzroy Road has disappeared, off to the side, unseeable, offstage. In the silvery wash of the distance, she sees herself reflected in tear drop, all the way down the street as in a hall of mirrors, her selves growing smaller and smaller, her tiny faces turned in surprise, or turned in something, an expression she doesn't want to see, the last little face centered precisely over Chalcot Square, hovering, a captive of her past.

II

Cut

Wednesday, October 24, 1962
Court Green

Pot at a boil, kitchen steam, onion dice, blade—
This is silent astonishment, Sylvia pale at her
butcher block, the knife dropped as if burning, clattering, the tip of her thumb sliced off. The baby still beats
his tray, the two-days' nanny takes her handheld tour of
the toy box.

Blanching, her face and her thumb, and sensation held
in suspense: no pain, no fear, no shock. Twilight itches
the windows. Church bells go off like a clock.

And then the blood comes. Oozing red, seeping up to
the surface, dark and bright and thick, welling at the
sheared top of her thumb without spilling, a shiny crimson
dome engorged and rising, and then the flood.

And then the flood. Twenty-eight days – a phase of the
moon, the agony drag. The spurt, the pad, the jangling
belt. The dangling flap to hide in her skirt. She was bloody,
cursed and dirty, answered the door on moon-day to her
pretty young nurse, a fat pad snagged to elastic between
her legs. Hardly dressed for a week. Cramping gut,
cramping womb, her head hot, and her lungs a rattling
muck. Oh, her lungs, they hurt.

They hurt, the twenty-eight days since his cruel desertion,

a month of mothering her fatherless son. One last chance: in Ireland, but he cut it off. He cut her dead.

Blood is running down her wrist. She pulls back the sleeve of her blouse. 'Sue?' she calls to the young nurse, her new nanny, in the playroom. 'Sue?' she calls, her voice distant and thin.

And what's come since? The sleepless dark, and flu, and poetry: all she's eaten, all she's slept. Twenty-one poems in twenty-eight days. She's burned through them, burned with fever, day after day, hit the mother lode, the richest vein. My God, think – it's the real red thing.

Sue, glimpsed through the doorway, is smiling, laughing, her head at an endearing tilt, on her hip on the red rug with Frieda. A felted duck, a squeaky cat in her lap, a pile of grubby dollies at her knees. Nicholas bounces in a walker, crowing, banging his block. Sue's head turns frame by frame: in the kitchen Sylvia's slim, elegant arm is held up like a jewelry model's, blood cascading off her elbow, flush upon flush.

The relief of blood – the ache, the break of tension. Something came loose, slipped free—

Sue stands, saying something mild to Frieda, who turns back to the toy box to dig. Sue stops in the kitchen, presses Sylvia's right forefinger to the nearly severed flap of skin at the top of her cut thumb, asks where to find bandages and iodine. Blood is pooling in the chopped onions.

The bee poems. 'The Jailor.' 'A Secret.' It didn't surprise Sylvia that it was so often likened to childbirth. She'd thought the same, even as a teenager, smugly appropriating a metaphor she hadn't earned. Even after the babies were born, she thought she knew. She didn't know at all, until now. It was both – sex and birth. Sex – not the shared experience, but the private one. The pleading desperation, the sweaty fury, the greed, the full heat of surrender. But it was birth most of all. 'Lesbos.' 'A Birthday Present.' 'Stopped Dead.' With Frieda, she'd had nothing for the pain, on her knees on the bedroom floor: its barreling, breathless violence unmitigated. Even with Nick, the midwife's portable tank of gas had run out. Then she was pushing. This, too, was how she felt the poems: the brutality, wave after wave of it. And then, oh God, she felt the head. Were all the doors open? Were the windows? The plates of the skull folding, slipping tectonically like a world, to get through her bones. The thrill – it was irreducible, the only true thing. It was glorious.

Blood is pooling in the onions. Sue has the gauze, the root-beer glass tincture of iodine.

The blackberry blood of childbirth, richer than earth. Birth and poetry: the signs of her true womanhood smearing her thighs, dark drops on the plank floor of the guest room as she rises. Her body the body of a woman delivered, glowing in moonlight at her desk, the moon rising out of the yew beyond her study.

Sylvia takes a step back, steps in the dark drops of ruby blood on the kitchen linoleum. The decapitated cap of her thumb pulses under her fingertip, a little animal, with every beat of her heart. Sue holds the iodine, ready to douse Sylvia's thumb.

'It's going to hurt,' Sue warns.

Sylvia lifts her forefinger, sticky with blood. Holds out her thumb. At the first red splash of iodine, she winces. The sting, it's real—

(Sue holds the bottle steady.)

Do it again.

12

Elm

April 19, 1962
Court Green

Old ragged elms, old thorns innumerable. My poor house, she thinks ruefully, watching coal smoke chug and curl from one of the two brick chimneys at the crest of her thatched roof. The elm tree beyond it waves and clacks as if for rescue in the high, gusting wind that has been blowing all night, the tiny, heart-shaped leaves so fresh on the branches they're almost undetectable from this distance. Only twigs, black sticks, the tree bursting skyward into the chimney smoke, all of its frayed nerves on edge. Sylvia stands in the hard rain's hush, under a contracted, cold noon sky. Now and then the wind blows stinging pricks of icy rain up into her face as she holds her umbrella and watches from the soggy green churchyard overlooking her soggier front lawn, where the workmen who are sealing her floors have piled their sacks of gravel and bitumen and cement.

It's another tempest, another spongy April day of piti-less English weather, another day without spring. Restless, she holds her umbrella and slowly paces the boundary between the church grounds and Court Green, peering down the sloping bank of the cob retaining wall faced with unquarried rubble, stepping back and forth between the tilting pickets of collapsed gravestones reerected at her property line and the uneven rows behind, all of them grown mossy and mineral stained, their faces etched by spreading patches of vividly colored lichen: orange, red, mustard gold. The steady, deafening hiss of the incessant storm is punctuated now and then by the forlorn bleats of animals, cows and sheep, left out to graze or stand numbly in the rain.

'Why did you stay?' she was asked last week; the interviewer came down from London to record her for a radio program on Americans who live in England. Why indeed? It certainly wasn't for the weather or the closeness of the sea, though maybe she once thought it would be. All she could think of was the miserable Yorkshire seaside resort Ted had taken her to the year they were married, the charmless boardwalk clotted with chip papers and squabbling gulls, the muddy flat slurp of the ocean. The people on preposterous holiday in their raincoats, huddled in blackened inns. The tape recorder clicked chidingly on the parlor tabletop; she stopped herself short of saying something truly insulting. Her in-laws would in all likelihood listen to the BBC broadcast, and so, she had newly realized, would her neighbors.

No, she told him she stayed for the butchers: the English butchers who cut things up while you watch. Theirs was a dismemberment she could follow as she'd follow a narrative: knowing then where everything went, where everything goes, not the blank ignorant horror of wondering where all that blood came from. Not the cunning hermetic miracle of America. After years of British life it still struck her as so blatant, seeing whole pigs hooked by their trotters and turning at the ceiling, she feeling sick looking up at them, fascinated, sawdust clogging her shoes, the pigs revolving, lurid, blinking off and on like a red light district.

She told him she stayed in England because it wasn't America. She made a joke of it, but she'd meant it: she was shrugging off American rules. She wanted her own rules, out in the open. And Ted's, of course – they could live as they pleased, as writers. Ted had hated teaching as much as she did; it was a long, slow death with an audience. Here, she could have her mornings in her study, she could birth her babies at home, she could walk in the scudding rain while Ted made lunch; she could do as she liked. It was all up to her. England wasn't like America. She felt no scrutinizing eye upon her. But now, to her agitation, they've been noticed.

Ted has been invited to tea by the bank manager's wife, whose sixteen-year-old daughter is being primed for university. The town is fawning over him. They've all seen his photograph in the dog-eared doctor's office *Vogue*; they've heard him weekly on the BBC. Now, curious and flattered, they've come lowing through the sodden garden, stumbling past the sentinel holly and the intrepid daffodils, batting their eyelashes and shoving their daughters forward, the silly cows. No more casseroles, no crocheted baby hats for Nick. No gifts of January oranges for her confinement or sugared cakes for Frieda. They were coming for Ted Hughes.

And he was going. He would go that afternoon and impress them even more, bend over the girlish verse with a kind observation, the loan of a book or a record. While she stays home with the workmen forking their barrows of concrete onto the playroom floor, tracking tar and mud over the bare floorboards in the hall, leaving her no peace, cooped up in the rainy gloom of the drafty house.

Endlessly filling the gurgling Bendix, typing Ted's drafts, taking Ted's dictation. She stands at the edge of the churchyard regarding her front garden's forbiddingly high gate, which leads toward the street and the church and past to the village, the roadbed rutted and eroded by God knows how many generations of market-driven hooves before it was finally paved.

Flanking the cobbled walk that marks the path from the street to the north church door, the parallel rows of pollarded lime trees are not yet leafy enough to hide their knotty, cankered prunings. They're stunted and grotesque. But the churchyard yew is full as always, its needles green-black, its branches impenetrable and upright. It completely hides from Sylvia's sight the lych-gate behind it where the rector meets coffins on their pony carts at curbside, the footpath thick with mourners, littered with bruised petals. Her house is a shambles, she thinks, unpresentable, and Ted's family is coming for Easter. It's Maundy Thursday now, appropriately, a day for enforced charity. Tomorrow or Saturday they'll come – Ted's lazy mother to be waited upon, his spectral, shell-shocked father, even Uncle Fat Pants. She bristles at the injustice of it; she can't possibly get any work done if she's pulled into pieces like this, supervising the workmen and the children, entertaining the relatives, fending off the neighbors, coaxing the garden to life in this unrelenting winter, her poems left idling, grinding and pointlessly grinding to no conclusion, engines that won't turn over. She's up at two and at six, stupid with lack of sleep. And meanwhile Ted will be off, whetting the fantasies of schoolgirls, ignoring her—

Sensing him out of the farthest, intuitive range of her sight, she turns her head to see him looking for her through the parlor's bay window, between the bookcases, his pale face passing in shadow behind the glass, like a fish swimming just below the surface. Like a fish crossing the shadow of a watcher on the bank, he vanishes, sinking back into the dark of the house.

He ignored her when she told him to keep Frieda away from that crow, she remembers, hastily stepping back from the visible edge of the churchyard, turning and squelching through the green mire toward the church. She trudges through a mist, her breath and the damp heat of her body steaming a trail behind her. Squatting in the nascent, crumbled-earth garden, holding Frieda still and quiet between his knees, Ted coaxed the crow over; Sylvia watched him, puffing in two layers of jackets over the tennis court, mowing the new lawn in the tensing weather yesterday, the skin of her knuckles cracking in the cold. A morning between rains, and three acres of grass to her knees. She should have stayed at her desk! Her latest batch of pink paper from Smith had just arrived, wheedled from a former colleague with an office next door to the English Department's supply closet. But the monotonous weather had become unbearable to her, the black downpours relentless since November, the frigid east wind blowing straight through the heatless house; she couldn't help herself. To spite her, the momentarily clear sky was loading itself with leaden clouds – predictably – the wind whipping up like a spell. Ted was coaxing the crow, a fledgling baby, sleek feathered, glistening blue-black, hopping on horny twig legs over the red dirt, hesitant. Ted hunched, whispering, encouraging Frieda. 'Don't do it; it might bite,' Sylvia called across the yard, low and again, not so loud as to scare the crow away, a perverse desire to see herself proven right. The crow hopped forward, puzzling, the tips of its wings tucked back over its blunt tail, formal in its cutaway. Frieda's small, creamy hand was held out flat, leftover toast on her palm, Ted supporting her elbow and nodding. The crow stabbed its sickled beak, snapping, and Frieda shrieked.

Sylvia passes the yew tree, its black branches held vertically in surrender, raindrops shearing off as the tree sways in the wind. *Her father had held her steady, her eye at the door of the hive. She breathed in the sweet honeyed musk of beeswax. He brooked no mistakes, no opposition; he was an authority. He handed down judgment in red pencil by lamplight each evening, rigid in his leather chair, correcting papers, threatening distress at the lectern next day in his sharp, Germanic baritone.* Was this a man, then? Inviting chance, or refusing insurrection? *He studied bees because he was poor and had a sweet tooth, he announced. It was no whim. His every action showed strategic ambition.* Refusing a bird for the pure serendipity, the curiosity, of a bird? There was only a small, neat drop of blood. Frieda was happy with the novelty of the bandage. Her initial whimpering and panic at the sight of her own blood had transfigured into a grave, third-person recitation about the crow, as if it had happened only remotely to her.

All these daughters – impetuous, primping, boy crazy, angling for attention. Showing up on her doorstep clutching their dreadful school anthologies, peeking around her down the hallway, breathless and babbling, for a glimpse of Ted. These children with no discipline, no core. The interviewer last week had come with two horrid little girls. Despite her instructions, despite her firm warnings, they rampaged through her house during her cheap moment of glory, snatching Frieda's toys and waking the baby. Sylvia listened to the little girls' squealing and slamming of doors as the interviewer's tape wound and unwound on the reel. Chagrined as she was, she also had the uneasy feeling that it was a just punish-ment for indulging her ego. The BBC hadn't called her for herself, she suspected; despite her *New Yorker* contract, despite the grants, her poems were still only trickling into magazines. *The Colossus* had hardly been reviewed. The producer most likely thought of her because she was Ted's wife. There would be children screaming in the background.

She can see nothing through the mullioned windows of the locked church. There are no lights on inside. The diamond-patterned panes are rain-filmed and murky, virtually opaque. Shouldn't the church be open? What if someone needs to pray? she wonders. She thinks of knocking the iron sanctuary ring to see if the rector is really inside, spying on her silently through the louvered window in the belfry. Where are her guts, she thinks with scorn. She's got no self-control; she's merely looking for excuses to keep from going back to her study to face her unfinished poems. The laundry, mowing the lawn, a crow nip, walking in the rain, a spontaneous urgency to bake – any and all will do. Percy's crisis next door had satisfied that need most of yesterday. She was doctoring Frieda's finger in the kitchen, Ted beating a retreat up the stairs, when she heard Rose's shouting, then the banging on the door. Rose's hair was crazy and loose. Her buttons undone, she clenched her slip. Percy was having a stroke.

Sylvia hesitated. Ted had turned immediately around and run after Rose toward the cottage. Frieda was methodically gathering and eating the bits of cheese and raisins Sylvia had scattered over a plate to distract her.

Nicky was still asleep. She had a sudden vision of Percy in his windbreaker at the foot of the Roman mound as she'd seen him a few days before, coughing thickly into his handkerchief, the elm crusty-barked and stiff next to him, drooping its clusters of callow chartreuse leaves, blood-spotted at their centers, rustling like sistrums. There was a battalion of several thousand slender, green-stalked narcissi at Percy's feet, their white heads pinging and bouncing in the fine sea-spray drizzle. She imagined him abruptly as an angel, ascending to the churning heavens from the mound, his feet and face and jacket blue, the starry narcissi bowing and waving good-bye, blinking their tiny gold eyes.

But it wasn't going to be like that, and Sylvia knew it. The pull was irresistible. She ran coatless out the door, banging through the back gate. Ted was already on the phone to the doctor in the dim cottage. Sylvia stood behind Rose at the doorway and gaped. Percy was jittering in front of his television as if electrocuted. It was terrifying, priceless material: it was like observing her first electric shock therapy from a casual distance. Had the point been to shake her back into life? That's not what it had felt like. It felt like an execution. As she watched, Percy had already begun his retreat. He had become an awaited death, diminished, not a person. The trail had forked.

Last night she still stood listening at her back door, wiping out pans and eavesdropping on the unseeable comings and goings at the Keys'. The somber, purposeful knocking, the click of the doorjamb, whispers, footsteps slow and even down the lane. The rector? The doctor? Looming over her the moon, a day from full, was snagged in the elm despite the wind's effort to blow it free. Sylvia stood in its glare and watched it hang, tugging at the branches.

It is a struggle, this mood of dis-ease, this gnawing of dissatisfactions, as helplessly compulsive as the last primitive, rabbit-brain weeks of pregnancy. 'Full of yourself—' her mother used to say. 'Aren't you full of your-self—' Admiringly, when she was small. It meant something else later on. She feels belabored, her thoughts disorganized – not empty, like the inexpressible nothing she felt before her breakdown, and after. Nothing like that. Far from that. She has new poems, drafts and drafts of one in particular piling up on her desk, unfurling like a bolt of cloth, sliding in every direction. Why not her? When will it be her? The villagers frown over their swedes at the greengrocer's, casting glances at her and brightening, making up excuses to start a conversation. 'Oh, Mrs Hughes—' She wonders if it was even Ted who suggested her for the BBC broadcast. Again! She hates the thing inside of herself that knows the bottom and nothing else. It's her own faulty character, this disorder of her heart.

She needs to get back. Nicholas must be stirring by now; her breasts prickle, hard and tight with milk. Sylvia turns the corner of the church, toward the south porch, and her elm and her home come back into view. Flinty headstones teeter in every direction; the cobblestones are brightly mortared with moss. Rainwater gullies over the uneven pathway. She hears the oceanic boom of the tree crashing around past Court Green's roofline, like a wave curling up over the house. Someday someone would find the elm still there, its roots deep in the foot of the Iron Age hill. Archaeologists would come looking for it. They would punt out in their skiffs down the undersea A30 and beach on the shores of the mound, its moat filled and flooded to encompass all of what had been Court Green. Her three submerged acres would lie at the bottom of the pool, the cob walls, the reed-and-wheat straw thatching all crumbled to fish waste. And there beneath the rippling surface, amid the frilled white reflections of the narcissi and the jagged elm leaves floating on the water, they would see her disintegrated life – her Dutch tea set in shards, her sewing machine florid with rust. All at the slimy, red-earthed bottom, all decomposing, all but the elm. The smoke-blackened, hand-sawn Elizabethan elm rafters from Ted's attic; the thick, six-foot elm plank that was her writing desk; the three-trunked elm itself: inscrutable, impervious, perfectly preserved, like the bog men found with hair still growing, undigested seeds in their intestines thousands of years after they sank from view. It was good for coffins and wagon wheels. The elm, immutable, would outlast them all.

The rain beads the dark dome of Sylvia's umbrella, gathering at the dentate edge and dropping to the ground in crystalline, elliptical chains before her face as she raises her eyes. The granite bell tower, the most ancient feature of the church, looms at her shoulder, its Norman walls spattered with celadon flecks of lichen, like a painter's drop cloth. Under the oak-shingled spire, eight bells wait for Sunday; a ninth sanctus bell rings the hours all week long. Twenty feet up the south side of the tower, a sundial melts into the wall, hardly noticeable, camouflaged by its abiding stone face and weathered wooden frame the exact gray as the granite of the tower. Its lines of declination fan outward in rays, predicting the movement of the sun; its iron gnomon, purposeless today, bleeds a ruddy stain onto the tower wall. Engraved across the top of the dial plate is a motto: LIFE IS LIKE A SHADOW. Sylvia reads it, considering its dense music, its fugue. 'Life is like a shadow': she speaks it aloud, plucking it out, considering. 'Love is like a shadow,' she says. The words fill her mouth.

13

The Night Dances

December 14–15, 1962
London

She should have known: the endless tears. The long, long naps, today and yesterday. Then tonight's comfortless supper. 'Please—' she fantasized pleading as the three of them crouched miserably together at the little table in the kitchen. Trying vainly to capture his red-faced, wailing attention, begging: 'Please—' She watched him wearily, held his dripping spoon for him; she waited with it, suspended, as he shrieked. An inconsolable tyrant, catastrophic in his terrycloth bib, his soft crew cut of neutral-toned baby hair standing upright in indignant outrage. Frieda, bearded with stew, merely looked on, a mildly interested gawker.

Afterward, the sobbing, effortless collapse, a matter of minutes. She should have known. She could have guessed. Part of her did know – once both babies were in their cots, she simply didn't take the sleeping pill. A glass of brandy imported up the stairs and her papers hurriedly fanned out on the bed: the typed final drafts of the new poems, the ones still bound for the manuscript, spread over the coverlet to be sorted. A working table of contents, mostly blank, and the ledger of those she'd already sent to magazines or sold open on her desk before the window;

a set of carbons to submit, and her latest maroon journal for updating. Too much for one night, even with a second wind. But she willed it, books and brandy and papers arrayed around her, warding off interruption. She picked off the easy targets first: matching poems to the magazines most likely to buy them. She banged out letters at the same time, nothing before her but her own pale, hectic ghost on the black glass, raindrops trailing silver down the panes. The worn, rewound end of the typewriter ribbon grew fainter with each keystroke. The words faded, barely brushing the surface of the bond. She hit the keys harder, her stiff fingers icy. She crammed every last cheery reassurance and breezy, tactical quip onto the pages, manually aligning the sheets when they got too close to the paper's edge to advance on the rubber platen, filling in words by hand around the aerogram spaces left for her mother's address or Mrs. Prouty's. She warmed to the shell game of poem sequence playing in her head. She was no failure – look: the *New Yorker* has taken 'Amnesiac,' the *Observer* would publish 'Ariel' and 'Event,' *Punch* wants an essay. The stack of letters and submissions grew as the tide line in her brandy glass receded: fat envelopes addressed to her family, *London Magazine,* the *New Statesman,* the *Atlantic,* the Third Programme, all efficiently stamped and ready to be posted tomorrow. *I'm here,* they all announced; *here's proof.* And finally, with mathematical predictability – a cry, but odd.

She could have guessed. She feels it in her nerves before he even stirs. Still that primordial instinct remains intact, the one that so many times before had gotten her up and shambling from the bed, the bodice of her nightgown dampening within from the fine milky spray aroused by the mere rustle of a wakening baby.

Cautiously, holding her breath, hoping for reprieve, she opens the children's door from the bright, chill hallway. Nicholas is sitting up in his cot in the dark. Frieda remains resolutely asleep, her long-lashed eyelids clamped together despite Nicky's wail and the faint, angled blue glow of moon and street lamp cutting across the floor. Nick's bedding is wet, but with something having the texture of runny, tepid oatmeal. He vomits again as she lifts him out of the crib.

She rocks him, little oven, sponged now and calmed, very slowly, side to side from her hips, the light low and contained, billowing from the candles left over since moving day. Nick is heavy, limp with fever, sobering as black coffee; he sinks his full weight into her shoulder, into the cradle of her crooked elbow, slowing his mother to the pace he needs. Sylvia lets his weight anchor her. She breathes him in, the unfamiliar odor of sickness on his skin threaded by the sharp fresh scent of soap. The candlelight flares and shrinks with her slow rocking, with the heater's draft. The candlelight flares and shrinks, throwing its inconstant spotlight in turn on her typewriter, arrested; the welter of smelly crib sheets and pajamas, damp towels piled into the laundry basket; the bed still papered with poems, a random mosaic of pink and white tesserae, blind to each other as kittens.

Is she here, or there? She's stopped, subjective, in this shadow play. He found her out. He hauled her back to wordlessness, back into the body they both still inhabit. She holds him over her heart, pressing against her breast and collarbone, feeling the tension in his small body fade at the mere touch of hers. It feels like relief to her also, the wonder of unresistant physical contact. Her own body is a desiccated thing, a bone house, deprived of the elements necessary for its survival. Skin on her skin. Warmth. Sustenance. Could you die from this? she wonders. Could you die if no one ever touches you? She feels corrupt, finding such covert, selfish satisfaction in her baby's feverish body, the compact comfort, the hot, yeasty loaf. His fat, foreshortened feet dangle at her lowest rib, kicking her lightly; his inexplicably filthy ear blazes against her neck. That heat – it's life flaming through. At their births, it was her children's starting heat and heft she was stunned by, their solid human otherness: Frieda's narrow infant shoulders creamy with vernix, like a channel swimmer's. Their slow unfolding, over days and weeks, after all that time curled inside her, wrinkled and red as poppies. Their newborn faces, roving in sleep – smiling, frowning, grimacing, eyelids fluttering, trying all the different frequencies of emotion for the first time. Their faces now, so often unreadable, leaving her to guess. 'Dat!' Frieda will shout, excited, exasperated, pointing to something she hasn't yet learned to name. 'Dat!' Nick mimics, 'dat, dat!' Merely pleased by the form of a sound he can master.

But before language, before words, all they know is corporeal, measured by their bodies and by hers. She should have read it in his torrid little face – at dinner, the post office, before. Nicholas doesn't sleep but drifts, tensing and digging his jaw into her neck when she falters, stepping even slightly out of the soothing, metronomic dance she's set in motion, her body their pendulum. She rocks her baby side to side, side to side. Her fingertips memorize the rough spot at the back of his head where his hair has rubbed off. He needs her now. She leaves the poems where they are.

Feverish, a child takes on an eerie, radiant beauty, its skin even more lush, dry with the consuming inner fire of a cinder, velveted as the lips of a foal. With a warm damp cloth sprinkled with rosewater, she swabs Frieda's forehead, smoothing the fine minky hair at her temples, running the tip of the cloth over the graceful contours of her daughter's small face. *Rosenwasser for Christmas cookies, for handkerchiefs, for a child's fever.* Nicholas is restively asleep beside his sister, his hold on his mother a slackening knot that eased just enough as Sylvia heard Frieda call for her, and gag—

She takes the cuff of the top sheet between her fingertips and eases it down, revealing Frieda's bare chest, thin and blue as milk and bowed, well made, like the bottom of a boat. Sylvia sweeps the damp cloth lightly over Frieda's skin to cool her. The little girl is burning, alarmingly so, though Sylvia has not been able to look for the thermometer or the rubbing alcohol, still packed in one of the boxes downstairs in the parlor. She is afraid to leave her children for that long, afraid that Nick will fall out of the bed, afraid that Frieda will have to vomit again before she can bound up the stairs to help, and their only place of comfort, the only place she can care for them both at once, will be irretrievably soiled. She has no more clean sheets; all she brought from Court Green have been used up over the week in the babies' room. Now they molder inside her wet pillow slips in the pram at the bottom of the stairwell.

Under the soft gilding light of the candles, Frieda opens her eyes and gazes into her mother's face. Bending over her child, moving the cloth gently over her skin, Sylvia sees herself reflected in Frieda's guileless blue eyes, glassy with fever, as her own shadow grows up the wall, a mountainous giant of head and shoulders, taller and wider than the windows. Frieda looks so little once more, no toddler now but merely a baby, her body a neat, vulnerable package, lost among the bedclothes as she so often seemed as a newborn, her skull like the skull of a bird's. Delicate and brittle as the skull of a bird. Guilt clutches Sylvia's heart as she waits for Frieda to ask again for Ted. But Frieda doesn't, not tonight, not in the still, broad hours of this endless night. Her whole world is here, reflected in her eyes – all she knows of safety and love. Her whole world has shrunk to the aureole of a candle, to the feel of her mother's hand against her burning cheek. Again, as before they left her breast, Sylvia is the empire, complete. This Frieda is not the child who is learning to tell secrets all by herself – cupping her hand at a willing ear, blowing into it an incomprehensible roar that modulates to a whispered non sequitur delivered with pride: 'psst – a bee,' 'psst – a cloud,' though that child will be back tomorrow, or the next day. This Frieda is the child who once sat on her mother's lap, a wristwatch held to her ear for the very first time: her tender little face first blank, then flowering into a laugh, hearing the tick.

It is this responsibility, this power she wields, that Sylvia can hardly bear: she is, in every practical sense, all they have. She is the boundless shadow looming over them. They rest fitfully inside it now, her giant darkening the crown molding, blown up the wall behind the headboard. They are so tiny – their sweaty hair plastered to their scalps, their quick, illuminated breathing. Her heart wells with a sorrowful, guilty love, a tart hurt she can taste, this grief for all she lacks. There is no one to hear them, no one to come to their aid; there is no sleep, no father, no phone, no rescue.

Morning flares blue, then copper, then white, like the flame of a candle. Light arcs unmitigated across space, through the bald windows and over the blank walls of Sylvia's bedroom, shadow to shadow, as the day languidly expands and passes. The children are sick, are weepy, are listless, are fussy, are bored. Sylvia misses her piano. She sings to them, hums her tone-deaf lullabies, finger plays the German singsongs of her childhood. The mesmeric, plaintive Lorelei coax naps from their rock on the Rhine. '"*Help me! Help me! Help me!*" *he cried* . . .' jump Sylvia's two fingers, slim rabbit ears chased by a huntsman over the blanket. She guesses at what might comfort and amuse: cool applesauce. Soupspoonfuls of rosehip syrup, tangy and sweet. Mugs of diluted blackcurrant juice that she's warmed on the stove, another of her grandmother's remedies, good for the tummy. Dry toast cut into animal shapes with cookie cutters. Storybooks no one has the patience for.

When did she become so porous? The pink occident light of declining afternoon filters the cloistered world of the bedroom where she nurses her sick babies, flushing her closet door, her pillow shams, the pearly candle nubs, the children's sleeping faces with a pacific, rosy luster. She cannot remember when, exactly, since yesterday, her body and her needs so completely shaped themselves to her children's, when motherhood overflowed its banks and carried her, willingly, deep into its current. When did she change into a nightgown, pleating it into a thick tube between her hands, like stockings, and dropping it over her head in one efficient move? When did she gather the puzzles, the diapers, the bottles, the cups and plates? When did she collect the heap of new poems, loose sheets hastily plucked off the bedclothes and weighted beneath a candlestick on the bedside table, and shove them into the drawer of her desk, dismissing the idea that she might try to work while the children rested – impossible – in unison? When did she squeeze into bed with them, capturing one under each arm, nosing their sour little heads like bouquets, like the perfumes of a rare flower? Like the seductions of a night lily, like the potent pink dust of the stargazer. Sleep swells as she breathes in the breath of her hot babies. It rocks her at the surface of awareness, rocks her until she slips under, too.

She revolves on an island, floats and rocks in a cold gray December jelly churning a mash of salty ice into chunks at its surface. The stars rearrange and fade, throwing the shadows of passing planets on the wall. The stars fall, hurtling through a black heaven, white-hot flakes of pain bursting inside her eyes, blistering her head, making her sick. I remember this, she dreams. I remember this, her stomach heaving.

14

The Detective

December 16, 1962
London

She's ruined, gray and mottled as something gone very bad, her head and gut full of the foulest, most unthinkable garbage. No, her head is full of pulsating, metallic rot; her gut is utterly emptied, gagged to the last fleck, down to her scraped-out bare toes. She has been sick all night, clutching the porcelain rim of the toilet, virally poisoned, retching, weaving fever dreams, her unhinged mind rambling over weird, ghastly scenes. Snails crawling over the bathroom walls wearing the faces of Ted and that woman, their sluggish moist tracks glistening on the tiles. Their sidelong eye-slide of lies, their miniaturized fear of tumbling into the foamy acrid soup in the commode. Or she and Frieda and Nicholas a rick of bones, heaped together on the dusty bedclothes, discovered months from now by the two leasing agents in their matching dark suits and bowlers, their twin faces verdigris'd as the faces of undertakers. She sprawled, convulsing, on the relievedly cold floor in the loo, Nicholas and Frieda unaware and dead to the world upstairs, exhausted themselves from their own influenza ordeals, collapsed on her bed, the mattress of which she managed to drag – how? by what superhuman effort? – onto the floor of the nursery in the morning. And lay there all day, sipping water from a cup, shivering and sweating, the babies tossing and muttering beside her, taking turns in their cots. She lay immobilized, flinching at the sound of the children's penetrating, mosquitoey voices.

Night, again, has ground itself around. She has made it all the way downstairs, shaky, sallow, barefoot, in her nightgown, each step an excruciating jolt to her frangible head, with her wastepaper bin from the kitchen and a note for the nappy service man. In a sudden, brief spasm of clarity, Sylvia's remembered that the rubbish truck comes Monday morning and so will the nappy man. She hasn't the strength for two round trips down the staircase to the entrance hall, one with the trash and one with the heavy, awkward diaper pail, though the flat reeks of rotting rubbish and all the week's diapers are used up, the children bare bottomed. It is beyond all human comprehension that she might even *attempt* to rinse the stinking nappies. But she has switched off the stairway light to spare her eyes, her blinding headache a blacksmith's anvil banging and sparking her brainpan, and she has tacked her note to the house's front door, asking the nappy man to ring and wait while she brings the soileds down in the morning. In the phosphorescent glow of the moon beaming a shard of bluish light through the front door transom, Sylvia tamps her trash into the mysteriously full bin behind her pram, under the dark stairwell.

'What are you doing with my rubbish bin?'

Sylvia startles at the sudden bark of a man's voice behind her, and the bright light just as suddenly shining at her back, as if she were the subject of a criminal pursuit. She turns around, squinting. A middle-aged man with tiny, wire-rimmed bifocals is frowning and narrowing his eyes at her disapprovingly, standing with an ordnance map in the open doorway of the house's ground-floor flat. Behind him are unpacked cartons, stacks of paintings with their stretchers showing leaned against men's-clubby furniture. A radio natters in another room.

'I ask you again, madam, what are you doing with my rubbish bin?' he demands.

'I – I – I'm sorry, I thought it was put here by the agents,' Sylvia stammers, clanking the lid carefully – painfully – back down on the can.

'You are mistaken, madam. The leasing agents have provided no such convenience. I was told, and I presume you were also told, that the tenants are to purchase their own rubbish bins.'

'I'm sorry,' Sylvia apologizes, her head pounding. 'I've just moved in this week. I didn't realize.'

The man surveys her unhappily. 'You must be Mrs. Hughes. I was told a Mr. and Mrs. Hughes had been given the larger flat because—' he pauses, continuing to inspect her, 'because of their "greater need," as the agents termed it.'

Sylvia stands uncomfortably, clammy skinned and unwell.

'I was told you have two children,' the man continues.

'I do,' Sylvia answers, breathing shallowly, 'two small babies, two years and almost one. They're upstairs. We've all come down with the flu.'

'Yes, I thought I heard babies crying.' The man nods almost imperceptibly, considering this deduction, crossing his arms before his saggy brown suit. 'So your husband is upstairs?' he asks.

For a moment, Sylvia eyes the man just as steadily. 'No, he's not,' she answers, offering nothing more, too beleaguered to work up any explanations at all.

The man watches her. 'I also required the larger flat,' he says, meting out his words slowly. 'In fact, I have it confirmed in no uncertain terms that I saw the first-floor flat and expressed my interest in it before you did. Nevertheless, the agents approved your application rather than mine, and my two growing sons will have to sleep on bunk beds.'

'I don't know what to say,' Sylvia responds weakly, wincing with effort. 'Perhaps it was a matter of credentials. My mother was my reference. She's a professor in America. She has very impressive credentials.'

Disdainfully, sniffing audibly and looking down at her over the tops of his bifocals, the man scoffs. 'I am also a professor, as well as an international scholar of art. I have *also* lived in America, where I was appointed the art critic for the *Buffalo Evening News*. My credentials are impeccable. No,' he continues, his voice dropping, mumbling to himself and gazing vacantly at his ordnance map, 'no . . . it was clearly something else.'

'I'm sorry, but I'm very ill; I really must get back upstairs,' Sylvia whispers, feeling the blood drain from her face as an ominous percolation starts deep in her intestines. She takes a step forward toward the foot of the staircase.

'May I ask where you moved from?' the man asks with sudden urgency, still standing fully in his doorway, leaving only a matter of impassable inches between himself and the oversized pram.

'Devonshire. Just north of Dartmoor.'

He nods knowingly. 'My wife has left me for a man from Cornwall.' He glowers with hostility at the map in his hands. '"As you value your life or your reason keep away from the moor." So said Holmes. He also said a concentrated atmosphere elicits a concentration of thought, but I disagree.'

Sylvia nods hollowly, single-minded to get back up the stairs. She takes another step toward her neighbor, whose intractable position remains the insurmountable obstacle.

'How much rent are you paying?' he blurts.

Taken aback, her bowels churning, Sylvia stammers again, 'I'm not exactly sure – I don't remember – I made out a check for the full year in advance—'

'Aha,' he says, smiling, looking grim and pleased. His eyes glitter tinnily behind the lenses of his glasses. 'No wonder they considered your need to be greater than mine.'

Sylvia stares at him blankly. She would have done anything to get Yeats's house. She cabled her mother straightaway; she cleared the savings account. No one could have possibly needed this house more than she did.

Her neighbor does not move aside, fixing her instead with his unpleasant smile, relishing this exhumation of diabolical skulduggery, when his face begins to knead into a grimace. 'What is that infernal smell?' he asks, sniffing the close hallway air.

Sylvia, her congested head impenetrable, cannot smell a thing, though she fears the culprit can only be her basket of vomitous trash, or her rotting wet laundry still packed into the pram, or herself. She folds her arms over her chest, furtively ashamed, hugging her flannel nightgown to her skin in the cold.

Her neighbor scowls at the cumbersome pram before him. 'Why don't you move this perambulator into your own flat?' he complains bitterly. 'As you can see, it's blocking the corridor. This isn't your private storage, you know, this is public space. The lease reads that we are to keep this area clear.'

'But I can't move it upstairs – it's too big and heavy,' Sylvia responds, incredulous, hopelessness whinging her voice.

'Then you should get a smaller one.'

'—I have to have it – I need it—' she appeals, 'how else can I manage my errands and my shopping with the children?'

'Have your husband help you,' the man pronounces.

'But my husband isn't *here*,' Sylvia says, her head thudding at what seems an impossible argument, doubly impossible to resolve in her enervated state. She pauses, gathering the remnants of her strength. 'Excuse me, Mister—?'

'*Professor* Thomas.'

'Professor Thomas, perhaps you could do me a small kindness. I'm expecting my nappy service and my husband tomorrow – he's been away on business. He doesn't have keys. When they ring, could you let them in? My husband will move the pram. I'm so sick, you see—'

'I simply can't,' he crisply replies. 'If I haven't already left for work, I can't imagine that I could hear *your* bell. I've been nearly deaf since I was a youth.'

'But – you heard my babies crying—'

'Mrs. Hughes,' Professor Thomas sniffs, 'if you are so sick, why aren't you properly dressed? Where is your dressing gown?'

'I just came down with the trash—' Sylvia explains, reddening like a chastised child, her head reeling, '—I thought the ground-floor flat was vacant—'

'Aha,' Professor Thomas cuts her off, brandishing his ordnance map as if to silence her, 'but as you can plainly see,' sweeping his arm across the threshold to his open parlor, 'I've been squashed into a flat too small – to satisfy your "greater need" – and as I have two impressionable sons who visit, I can't risk any scandal.' He assesses Sylvia, eyes her clutching her nightgown. 'Evidently you have many resources on which to call for favors. I, however, cannot allow any false conclusions to be drawn. Good night.' With an air of victorious finality, he steps back into the doorway of his brilliantly lit flat to let her pass.

Sylvia hurries past him, as much as she is able, hunched over, holding her wastebasket and her gathered nightgown, queasy, her face blanched and glazing with perspiration. She rounds the staircase's turned newel post and seizes the banister, stepping gingerly up each riser, feeling his cold eyes on her back as she retreats up the stairs into the darkness.

15

Ariel

October 27, 1962
Court Green

The frozen breath of horses, smoking in the cold violet dark of a nearly deserted stable. A spray of fading stars, an argentine flake of moon melt in rectangles of glassy black on the icy cobbles of the open yard. It is nearly sunrise, the morning after a hard frost, low autumn fog packing the riverbeds and the cleaves of heath-covered hills and blanketing the sunken fields. Sylvia carries her saddle and tack over her forearms, lays the burnished leather saddle and stable rubber on the rack to the side of a turquoise stall door. Inside, assembling out of the blackness, the ears of a chestnut mare, gray muzzled, her blaze flecked with mud, pivot separately, then swivel in Sylvia's direction. At the far end of the row of stalls, another door is already open, a pitchfork leaning against the wall, a single bare bulb on a dangling cord glaring from the rafters of the pitched barn roof. There is a clanking of metal: grain canisters, water buckets. Horses nicker like gassy uncles, swish their long, coarse tails, crunch oats and sugar-beet pulp and hay suspended from nets in the corners of their stalls. Sylvia slides the iron bolt on the lower half of the Dutch door and nudges it open with the toe of her boot, holding cross ties and a head collar in her hands, her tender left thumb heavily bandaged and stiff. Her regular horse stands in the indistinct light of the stall: a steady and mild-tempered cob, a cross of Dartmoor pony and farm horse, ruddy-coated and aging, wearing a green rug, her winter coat long and her thick, short legs shaggy, unclipped for added insulation against the cold. A good teaching horse for a beginner. *Always work the horse's near side, the left.* Sylvia steps into the stall, approaching the horse from the left, and stands at the animal's shoulder, stroking the plate-like disk of her cheek, her crooked white blaze, looking into her enormous, placid brown eye. This is old Ariel, the horse on which Sylvia takes her weekly riding lessons, this day's Night Mare, not mythically perched in a yew tree, nested in the scattered jawbones of poets, but instead dozing in oat straw and crumbly fresh manure. A sharp ammonia stink rises from the floor of the stall, a green vegetal fragrance, granular and toasty, not unpleasant. She pats the horse's jaw a last time, then fits the loose framework of the head collar up over Ariel's face.

Footsteps sound down the covered stableway. It is the teenage daughter of the riding instructor holding a stack of loose flakes of oat hay in her arms, wearing tall, black rubber boots with a red seam running around the sole. 'Going for a hack this early?' she asks Sylvia in a stage whisper, deferring to the early quiet, hugging the load of feed to her quilted jacket.

'Just for a walk in the pasture, past the river,' Sylvia whispers briskly, occupied with her tasks, moving with confidence around the horse, focused and efficient, clipping the second of the cross ties to a ring at the right side of the stall, stooping under the rope at the mare's shoulder and unhooking the rug at her chest. *Safety first. Remove rugs back to front*. The horse shudders daintily, her coat and thick skin rippling, as her rug comes off.

'Good thing I haven't brought her feed yet, then,' the girl replies. 'When you're back and she's cool, could you give her crushed oats and half a flake of hay? I'll scrub her water bucket.'

Sylvia nods. She's folded the rug and put it away on a high shelf at the front of the stall, then stepped toward the door, where she left the brushes and currycomb. As the girl walks away, Sylvia takes up the brushes, loosening the caked, dried mud from the horse's coat with a gentle, circular massage. She brushes neck and belly and loins as the horse patiently submits, turning her impassive head to watch.

Everyday life is out of sight, three miles away up the road. The whole world is still. There is no threat of intrusion. The children are asleep at home with Sue; no one will miss her. She'll be back before breakfast. No one even knows she is gone – her mother's anxious, sententious letters can't find her here; Ted's insults can't find her. She's inviolable, indestructible in a stone-walled Dartmoor stable. Sylvia draws the brush over the teeth of the currycomb, knocking loose the dirt and the shedding, auburn hair. She runs her hand reassuringly over the mare's left flank as she crosses her broad hindquarters to brush the horse's off side. No more of Ted's pedantic directives: *Study* King Lear *for an hour. Think for an hour. Write for an hour*. Who was sentimental, the charge he'd condemned her with? She, stripping away all artifice and falsity, ripping history and familiar comforts to shreds, risking everything, or he, carrying the same life everywhere? His lumbering West Yorkshire mouthings, his rods and reels and fanatical fish visions.

His chipped Beethoven records, over and over and over on that antiquated gramophone. When he left, he took all of who he'd been for most of his life; he hauled it off in a few boxes. All, or nearly, that he'd brought to their marriage. Good riddance. No one, ever again, will tell her what to do or who she is. Sylvia ducks under the cross ties once more to exchange the brushes for Ariel's bridle. A rooster crows, disembodied in the limitless distance of bruisy dark. The high northern uplands of Dartmoor, a paddock's length away on the other side of the Taw, are a firewall holding back the hot crimson flare of morning. Cawsand Beacon, over two thousand feet above the sea, broods above the shadowed village of Belstone. Its densely wooded foot and hillside common spread along the riverbed, not much more than a swift stream here, close to its marshy source, though the Taw widens and matures as it travels the forty miles through farmland toward Barnstaple Bay on the northwest coast of Devon. On a clear day, from the top of the hill, you can follow the river's path all the way to the Atlantic, to Appledore and the sandy western beaches.

It is her birthday. She is thirty years old. She's been waiting, watching this movie unreel in her head since she started her lessons two months ago. She's going to ride to the top of the highest hill in Southwest England, arriving with the sun on the anniversary of her birth. The morning of her rebirth: the start of another life, like a cat. The mare stands nearly free, head collar unbuckled and refastened around her throat as Sylvia lifts the bridle reins over her keen ears and neck and eases the jointed snaffle bit into her tractable mouth. She smooths the felted cavesson, buckles the cheek pieces, the throat lash; attaches the curb chain. She collects the blue-and-white-checked rubber- and wool-stuffed saddle from the rack, carrying it back to Ariel over her arm, the hornless pommel at her elbow, and lifts it up over the horse's withers and shoulder blades. *Slide the saddle back, with the coat, not against.* The children deserve security, her mother writes. You should come home. You should get a job teaching. You should be brave and ladylike and passive, be like your mother, make a martyr of yourself. Make sacrifices; control your emotions. Hold it in. Hold it in till you bleed. *Your father took over the dining room to write his book on bees; every night for a year I diagrammed the arrangement of his papers before I moved them off the table for supper. Marriage is a compromise.* It was infuriating. The children deserve plenty – but what do *I* deserve, Sylvia contests. Why is the woman always expected to give up on life? She's a writer, not a teacher. She *can*; she *does*. *She* is the arrow, not him, nor him, nor him, these men who would have her be charming and quiet, reciting the names of insects in Latin, stirring something at a stove. Her mother is ashamed – her daughter's marriage an unholy mess of adultery and mayhem, and now she's turning up her nose at golden opportunities to slink meekly away, to be clutched to the suffocating bosom of her loving, sacrificing family – just as she was ashamed of Sylvia's breakdown. She'd be even more ashamed if she knew it was Aurelia whom Sylvia had really wanted to kill: her nagging, selfless mother and the whole tribunal of faultfinders sitting in judgment of her, for whom she performed like a circus act. The lady on bareback, circling and circling for the kibitzers, the critics with their fat red pens, and getting nowhere.

Ashamed and afraid, that's what her mother's letters convey. Wringing her hands over the Atlantic. Afraid of life, of anything that isn't neat and proper, of Sylvia's ferocity most of all. *Bombus impatiens. Bombus perplexus. Bombus fervidus.* Sylvia buckles the girth, pulling it snug around the mare's generous belly. *One notch at a time – don't pinch.* Gently she slides her fingers under the wide band, smoothing the leather and skin. Sylvia has nothing to fear; she's come through a *kesselschlacht,* a burning cauldron of hell, her own Stalingrad, and she's pure passionate righteousness on the other side. No apologies. She's finished proofreading the pages of *The Bell Jar.* The book has already gone to the printer; there's no turning back. She wrote 'Daddy' the day after Ted left, 'Medusa' last week during her fever. She's purged of sufferings. The sacrifices are over.

'All right, you sprite,' Sylvia addresses the elderly horse, her tone low and soothing, as she hangs the loose head collar over the wall of the stall and takes the reins in her right hand, leading the saddled mare out through the doorway and into the silvered yard. The night sky is withdrawing by degrees, the broad dome of Cawsand Hill a languorous, ultramarine sweep hovering over the corrugated tin roofline of the stable. Ariel's shoes click on the cobblestones. Sylvia swings the stock gate open and leads the horse out onto the bridle path that runs, bordered by impenetrable hedgerows, between the paddocks down to the river. A grizzled granite fence encloses the stable: the fence, the stone side of the barn, the bare limbs and rough trunks of the trees, the pitch of the roof closest to the moors all blanketed by avidly green moss. At the fence post, where Sylvia turns her horse around and ties her to the gate for mounting, a flaking hand-painted sign warns ALL RIDES AT OWN RISK!! Beside it, hung along the length of the fence on barbed wire, are the mossy skulls and curling horns of bygone Dartmoor sheep, their perfect, human teeth gleaming in the emerging pale blue light.

Sylvia checks her saddle, slips the stirrup irons down their leathers. Holding the reins in her left hand, she grips a shank of brown mane low on the horse's neck and fits her left foot into the near stirrup iron, bracing her right hand on the saddle and taking a couple of hops before launching up and onto the horse's back, amazed, as always, when she's done it. *Heels down, toes up, weight on stirrups. Reins in the near hand only.* Settling into the saddle with the reins clear of her bad thumb, Sylvia gives Ariel's sides a tap with her lower legs. The horse doesn't move. Sylvia tries again, pivoting her heels and her knees exactly as she's been taught, thighs tight to the saddle, giving the horse a squeeze with her calves. Ariel takes a step and begins to walk heavily down the muddy, leaf-strewn track.

The slow clumping of Ariel's hooves on the damp grit reminds Sylvia of something: a hand clapped again and again over a telephone receiver. Head bobbing in sync with her dilatory gait, her mouth reluctantly sensitive to her rider's hands, ears twitching independently to noise-less noises, the horse's neck is the split frame for all that Sylvia sees. On either side the hedgerows slump, propped up by the stooping rowans and hazels planted behind them, as if exhausted by the effort of holding back the relentless winds of the moors. Despite the prickly deter-rents of whitethorn and blackthorn and wild rose, some village sheep have scaled a hedgerow and stand stupidly at its summit. Their topaz, coin-slot eyes glint in their dull black faces. They stare after Sylvia vacantly, like mental patients, bleating their senselessness, clouds curling from their nostrils. Frosted hawthorn berries, protected by their blackened crowns of thorns, by the dying brambles of spent blackberry vines, hang over the trail: the prisms of a rare chandelier. Black eyed, red hawed, rime beaded – the fruit of the May tree. The fruit of May, the unlucky month for marriages: The month when her luck ran out. You could smell it in the flowers, the sickly sweet stench of death. Yeats was right, she thinks: *Horseman, pass by!* She was going to London on Monday, her baptism as a writer on her own. It had nothing to do with Ted; this would be her singular debut. She was to be interviewed at the BBC for a series called *The Poet Speaks,* followed by a recording of new poems. Perfect for her: what had she gained by Ted's leaving but her voice? What did she do now but listen to the beat of her own words, feel them and hear them as they formed – audacious, supple, ruthless, dazzling – in her mouth? This was no dead meter, no finger count learned by rote from old men. Her poems were lifting off the page. They hung in the air like a risen soul.

The trees, leafless and not, crowd into a canopy over her head as she approaches Belstone Cleave, the gently canting banks of the river – an inky cave of varietal greens, a misted grotto of snapping branches the color of old pennies, all of it sugared with hoarfrost. Ariel's shoulders rock rhythmically, mimicking a boat in gentle swells. In the silence the river roars, though it's hardly more than inches deep, tumbling over slimy stones and partially submerged tree roots. The rocks, the tangled limbs of the trees, the plank footbridge, still every surface is furred with rank moss, scattered with leaf: ochre, yellow, taupe, tigered orange. As they cross the river, the mare stretches her neck to snatch at the tender grasses growing along the banks, and halts. *Never let a horse eat with a bit in its mouth. Stay in control. Look where you're going, not at the horse.* Sylvia checks the horse's head, opening the reins to get her attention, looking up – not at Ariel, but at the steep incline before her. Beyond the thick foliage at the water's édge where she cajoles her errant horse, the landscape opens: a coppice of birch and oak trees braces itself against the side of the towering, heath-covered moor, which rises above a grassy, sloping common scattered with grazing sheep and wild ponies not much smaller than the horse she rides. Where the eastern side of Cawsand Hill meets the tree line, the world is on fire, sunrise chasing the fog back. The coppery crowns of the trees, the clitter-strewn ascent, even the sheep are lit up, red blazing with a shimmery golden heat at the horizon, tonguing the whitening sky, gilding the tatty, twig-matted backs of the oblivious infantile sheep.

Day is breaking, and she can't wait. Impatient, pulling the reins tighter, Sylvia thumps the horse's sides, clucking her tongue, urging Ariel into a trot toward the hill. A horse can trot forever, her instructor has said. At the sight of the distant ponies, the mare forgets the tempting grasses and raises her head, lurching forward with her ears alert. *Keep your hands down. Sit up straight. Don't make chicken-feeding noises.* Sylvia bounces jerkily up and down, jogging almost out of the saddle with the uneven beat of the horse's gait and the awkwardness of her bandaged thumb. She's forgotten her crop. She grabs the reins with her right hand as well, her fists pumping – *No!* – with the horse's head, her body tensed and curled over the horse's neck.

'Whoa—' she calls to Ariel, tugging the reins, trying to press her weight into the bouncing stirrups with the balls of her feet. Raw earth and tawny matted grasses pass beneath her, a close-cropped frozen knit pounding by, the damp, matted hair of babies, crushed quartz, mica, tourmaline ground to mud, the morning sky creating itself in streaks of garnet and azure. She braces, tensing for the slip of her heels out of the irons, a repeat of the runaway gallop hugging the neck of the first horse she ever rode, careening down the streets of Cambridge just after she'd arrived in England, the honking and dodging cars, pedestrians diving into shop fronts, she clinging for dear life, anything to keep from under those hammering hooves. *Remember: Fear runs down the reins.* 'Whoa—' she calls, checking the reins once, again, feeling for the horse's mouth, straightening her spine, and Ariel slows enough to bounce Sylvia backward into the saddle, where the driving force of one of the horse's hind legs bumps her up and out just enough to miss the jolt of the opposite leg. *Rising trot: Head up, hips forward, knees bent, weight in heels, beginners take the mane.* As she rises Sylvia grabs a handful of mane halfway up the horse's neck. Suddenly, as her seat touches down behind the pommel and the mare's muscular haunch sends her up again, her body catches the rhythm of the horse's gait. Her pelvis tilts, and again she meets the saddle on the downbeat. She's got it; she's posting, rising with the motion of the stride, perfectly balanced with the thrust of the horse's body.

The gilded sheep trimming the fescue and tormentil don't even raise their heads. Morning continues to bloom, the growing light warming the uplands, pools of sun spilling into the dark contours of the iced hills, spreading like stain. The mare moves with ease alongside clumps of bracken; dry, crumbling, pumpkin-colored hart's-tongue fern; crisp bell heather still flowering mauve in patches; sharp, silvered gorse. Ariel gives a melancholy whinny as they pass an assembly of ponies, who silently lift their whiskered faces and watch her trot by. Ivy Tor smolders at its edges like a burning sheet of paper. Sylvia rises, pauses, rises, light on the horse's back, feeling the long muscles of her thighs, the roll of the mare's shoulders, the tempo of bodies in concert, the hard under the soft: bone, leather, flesh, bone. She has been living almost entirely in her head, her body fading, even shrinking with inattention. Her body has been a shape on a page. But now she feels it – real, womanly, her small breasts lifting under her sweater, her ribs high and open, her shoulders sculpted, cantilevered; her hair catching like a flag across her face. She's tough, and strong; anguish has burned her down, a hard, brilliant gem smoking in the ashes. She rides past a hut circle enclosed by the remains of a low wall grown over with turf, older than history. Past cairns, piles of stone and mounded sod, centuries-empty graves of the long dead. Tors behind her, ahead, an earthscape of rock eaten by wind and years. She is threading up the hill, circling clockwise up the sheep track, leaving the river and the village behind, riding toward the sun, toward the Bronze Age stone row called the Beacon, the outdoor temple the locals know as 'The Graveyard,' a triple row of upright granite boulders leading five hundred feet to a double burial site, two stone cists sunk into the crown of the hill. *Never ride on the moors alone.* She was doing it, she was almost there, giddy with independence, the green wind flavor of it, this first real ride alone, defiant – so early, so high, no one would even see her. Her riding instructor would never know she took the horse beyond the common. She was Lawrencian, the woman who rode away. She'd slipped through.

It tastes like desire – to listen to herself, to trust her

own instincts. Whenever she'd done it before, she'd been right. *The ones you love will leave you*: it was the rhythm beating in her veins, in her ears, all her life; it was her terror, but it was true. She knew it like a shaman knows, like a visionary priestess, a mystic. *A wobbling table from Dido's attic, the vermilion wall he pushed it against, the stratified coats on the rack, typescripts and carbons and Shakespeare – his proselyte's Bible. The red leather binding had ripped cleanly in half, brittle as an old sheet. She waited for the door of the flat to open, furious, bits of white paper fluttering down. The walls gushed like blood. He pasted the handwritten pages of* The Calm *back together, his only copy, his first play. He sat there and glued each flake into place.* But she'd sensed something, and she was right. If not then, some day: she would always be left. She knew. That intuition, that deep vision of her self – it was her gift, as words were her gift. It was her fate, her *wyrd*: what is to come. Her weirdness, something to be proud of. Ariel: spirit of poetry, lioness of god, sacrificial altar, birth of the immaculate soul – it was all coming together, *now* and *now* and *now*, hoofbeats pounding. Her god is dead, again. The muse hangs over her life like a moon. She will ride this fate right through to a fiery ecstasy, to a resurrection on a hill, a self that was naked and real.

As she rounds the ascending curve of Cawsand Hill, the lowest stones of the triple row come into view, above the acres of rime-whitened bracken, now melting, and the swampy outline of treacherous, emerald peat bog tufted with cotton grass. Sylvia takes a deep breath and stills her hips: she simply stands, her weight in her stirrups, pelvis steady, shoulders back, her breath no longer misting under the sherbet-colored sky, the sun's forehead burning as it finally rises over the distant oak-scattered range she rides toward. The wind plays her face. She fills her lungs with it, this cellular hit of liberty, the heady elation of steering her own life. She is stripping off expectations, the dead rules, the hands of all who would hold her back. With almost no encouragement but the shift of Sylvia's weight in the saddle and on the reins, the mare slows her pace as she approaches the stone rows. Sylvia holds her balance: the sun bursts free of the skyline, blazing, enormous, the whole sky a fever of red, lighting her hair, spinning it into golden filaments that fly about her face as she drops lightly back into the saddle and eases Ariel to a walk, turning her up the hillside, westward, to follow the stones.

She keeps the reins taut but long, and lets Ariel pick her footing up the rows, the sun burning at their backs, warm through Sylvia's barn jacket. The boulders pass on either side of her, sharp-edged, erect, firmly set into the shallow, gritty loam, not at a constant distance but aligned by some design known only to the beings who placed them. Telling her what to do, how to live – she will unpeel the shadow Ted has cast over her life. Always pontificating, plotting her every move by Tarot or the shifting of the planets, but piddling his own life away, sneaking out mornings to stare at a bobbing fish float. Sneaking out to the crowded bed of an adulteress, thinking he could mask the stench of her with lies and craven silences. Looking for a way out, looking for escape. He would never have the guts to do what she's doing.

'"Oh thou mein Herr",' Sylvia intones, pleased with her transgressions against the sacred, with her effortless stupid joke, '". . . what strange fish / Hath made his meal on thee!"' She's at the crest, the cists straight ahead in

the dripping grasses, pocked and ruffled by lichen, encircled by a ragged crenelation of haphazard stones, all that
remain after centuries of sightseers have carted off the
rest for keepsakes. She guides Ariel around the perpen-
dicular blocking stones that end the rows, taller and wider
than the others, bright with the new sun beating their flat
surfaces, and clears the perimeter of the curb circle, at
the center of which the empty cists collapse upon themselves. The hollows into which the stone slabs were
lowered have eroded with time, filling with bilberry and
ferns, their sides disjoining, the stones folding like a deck
of cards. Who had been buried here between these
perspiring stones, their ashes now blown to the four
winds, scattered over the desolate moor tops, the bleak
sweep of empty heath and damp grasslands rolling luminous for miles all around, flying high above a blue misted
valley that pours toward the northern horizon like an
ocean? Her house is somewhere down there, secret as
these heaped stones, sheltered by treetops, embedded into
the vaulted hills beveling a foggy riverbed, the richly
textured pasturelands glittering, sunlit, with barley and
wheat and corn. She, too, could fly to it, right over the
side of this hill, like the songbirds now waking, the linnets
flitting erratically in the ling. She could fly to it like Ariel,
who prances foot to foot and tosses her head, impatient
with Sylvia's restraint, piqued by the radiant, boundary-
less expanse at the moor's summit. This morning, another
daybreak composed itself behind the wych elm. Bands of
yellow light spread across the back courtyard from the
kitchen window, flooding the frosted lawn suddenly
broadcast, out of nowhere, with cornflowers and late red
poppies. Poppies, the blessing after the battle. Flanders,
Waterloo, the *Iliad:* ordinary fields gone scarlet, blood to

flower, haunted by the memory of death. She could see them from her study window, the only other room alight in her somnolent house. Home. She loves it with a fierceness even now, miles beyond it, miles above. Sentimental? No – she's a fighter, a warrior queen. A woman demanding her place among men. If they could see her now, holding her horse back, threatening to bolt down this grass-bright hill! She's a fighter; she will flee nothing. She has entered the deed to Court Green in her name at the bank. Her poems come to her like truths, every word taut and hard. Ariel dances beneath her, eager to go, light on her forelegs, impetuous. This new life is hers to make. The old one was nothing but a role, a mask to cast off. 'Oh love,' she mutters, high on her impatient horse, strands of hair lashing her forehead, her eyes, 'you don't know how tough I am.'

She holds the reins tight, ankles pressing into the girth, the mare's neck arched, jaw flexed, hindquarters tensed, her body compressed like a spring. Fog churns and dissolves on the moors; the world foams below. A wisp of distant gray marks the route of a westbound train; a pinpoint necklace of headlights traces the roadbed of the A30. Her heart is poised, the blood beating loud in her ears, pounding against the insistent whipping breath of the wind; the shock of dew, its spray, glazing her warm skin. *Ripeness,* she thinks, *is all.* Ariel rears. Sylvia lets her go, striking off in a bounding canter, a gallop, all four feet in the air at once, momentum snatching her, propelling her forward. The rush, the drive, the muscular inevitability of it, the throb of the horse's motion under her too late to stop, her body lit, sparking at every nerve, flying – her body, this heedless pounding speed. She believes in what she feels. She belongs to no one.

She is no daughter, no mother, no wife. She is herself, held by nothing under the pure blue dome of sky, attended by granite and sheep and curious ponies, trilling warblers drunk on sloes in the bushes. It is her birthday. She is thirty years old. She is sitting at her desk, her toes buried in the red wool plush of an Oriental rug, a cup of hot black coffee smoking at her wrist. *Free*. Daylight rises like a curtain beyond the curtains of her study. Her children sigh in their sleep, stir under their blankets, in the room beyond the wall. A purple dawn, a toppled graveyard, a vision she bows her head before. Blue cornflowers, red poppies mouth her name, cascade across the stage at her feet.

16

Death & Co.

It's ringing.

It's ringing.

It's ringing.

It's ringing and it wakes her up.

She opens her eyes. It's still ringing. The shrill tandem bleat of a telephone. She opens her eyes: shadows, black and blacker, the edges of furniture, dark heap of Nicholas in one of the cots. Frieda is curled up against her, steamy, back to back on the mattress on the nursery floor. The phone continues its urgent ring.

Light floods the upstairs hallway, loitering along the edge of the cracked door. She rolls onto her knees and the palms of her hands, up off the awkward mattress with its desultory bedding spilling loose over the hardwood planks, up toward the sound.

But she has no phone, she thinks, floating high above her dream self, cautiously widening the door, the angular glare from the bathroom flaring up the staircase, down the hall, spilling over her bare feet, over her nightgown, the braided cord of the ringing telephone stretching across the hallway and disappearing into the vacuous darkness of her bedroom. She leans over, curling her fingers around the receiver, and as the ringing abruptly quits and she lifts the earpiece toward her body, she notices scuffling, gasps, and sharp skittering taps over the bathroom tiles at the bottom of the stairs. Black feathers, white tipped, a wing extended three, four feet across and flapping aggressively, glimpsed beyond the banister rail. A blunt reptilian claw skids partially into view. Lunging, a wing flaps and contracts. A hiss. Then a spurt of blood, gobbets of veiny red dripping down the tiles, sprayed over the leonine leg and enameled curve of the cast-iron bathtub, all she can see. A nude, wrinkled head pops up with a liquid smack, dripping, incarnadine, glossy with blood, and looks at her with its soulless, 180-degree eye. A garnet eye, a beak hooked like an oyster knife. She turns away, drawing the cold receiver to her ear.

Mrs. Plath? asks the caller.

I'm not Mrs. Plath, she says.

Mrs. Plath, I'm afraid that your husband is . . . gone.

What do you mean? she asks, terrified, her heart searing, concurrent with awed fascination at the immediate adrenaline pump of her fear.

He's gone. He's dead. An embolism. His heart – it burst. A blood clot, a flaw.

A flaw? She can't believe it. No. It can't be true.

To his heart. It went straight to his heart. It was too much.

Too much? There's the sudden sledgehammer of guilt. She would do anything—

Too much.

She's stunned. She can't believe it. *But what will I tell my children?*

You mean the girl, the boy?

Yes. Her body is going liquid, it's flooding away . . .

Only tell the girl. It won't matter to the boy.

This stops her. She's back, maternally vigilant. *What do you mean, because Nick is so young?*

Who's Nick?

The boy. Such a comfort, pragmatism! – the chance to wrap oneself in the cloak of practical circumstance, sure and efficient. She's always loved this part, the bureaucratic grid. Filling out forms, say: the simple, clear questions; dutifully outlining dates, addresses. The neat unequivocal order of facts.

That's not his name.

What do you mean? she asks, confused.

The boy – the one you favored over the girl when your husband got sick.

Now she's really baffled, unless this is all euphemistically reductive. A stereotypic judgment of her skill as a mother? She had a newborn and an active toddler – what more could she have done? She was tired, she was exhausted, and it was always, always cold. Sick? *But my husband didn't get sick.*

Yes, he did. He got sick, then they amputated his leg, then he died, then you sold the beach house in Winthrop and moved in with your parents.

No I didn't. That was my mother, Mrs. Plath.

Who is this? the caller demands.

This is Sylvia Plath Hughes.

This isn't Mrs. Plath?

No.

Oh. Wrong number.

The line goes emphatically dead, blood bursting like a tomato out of the receiver, wetting her ear. She holds the phone away, horrified, as worms begin to rice out of the mouthpiece, flabby and flaccid, flapping in unison: pink fringe. The worms ooze longer and longer. She drops the phone. It clatters on the floorboards like a kitchen knife. The handset begins to vibrate and she reaches for the receiver, slick with blood, wipes her hands on her nightgown as she brings the ringing telephone again to her ear.

All-righty, says a pert bloke.

Who is this? she asks, her vocal cords tightening.

Cheerily, in an Irish brogue, the caller begins to recite:

> *Now that we're almost settled in our house*
> *I'll name the friends that cannot sup with us*
> *Beside a fire of turf in th' ancient tower . . .*

This is the engineer, madam, calling to hook up your extension.

But how did you get this number? I don't even have a phone.

Who is this? the caller demands, drawing himself up.

It's Mrs. Hughes, she answers, her voice suddenly gummy with fear.

Oh. Wrong number.

She leans down and picks up the phone by the scruff of its neck, replacing the receiver on the cradle, observing herself immune, as if accustomed, to the feather flap and ripping, the rending of flesh from the bathroom, where the tiles are smeary with meat. The phone rings again as the receiver connects, and she's not surprised.

Hello, Mrs. Hughes? the matronly voice asks. *I'm ringing from the nanny placement agency. We can place a highly qualified nanny with you straightaway.*

There she is: it's Rose Key – dressed like a schoolgirl, her fat, capitulating knees showing, saddle shoes and anklets, clutching her cardigan over a nylon slip, with garish hair. Another appalling surprise—

No? says the agency lady. *Then perhaps you'd like to wait. We have a German au pair who will be ready to be placed very soon, as soon as she's made some of her own domestic arrangements. Very exotic and unscrupulous, but fascinating. Would you like to speak with her?*

She's not sure. Her tension spikes in objective wonderment: What will she do? Seconds pass, vacant. *Um, all right,* she responds unconvincingly.

Hullo? says the German au pair. Her voice is low, thick and gutteral. *I love children,* she says, crossing her tanned, slender bare arms, the phone cord snaking around them. *I've waited a long time for the right children.*

Sylvia slams the receiver down, flinging her hand away as if shocked. The phone immediately rings. It rings and rings. And she can't help herself. The spooks in her childhood closet? The pathos of 'The Little Match Girl'? The delicious terror that she might trip and fall onto the tracks of the Boston subway? She never could resist the temptation to run her tongue over those tender fears. She picks the receiver up.

This is the overseas operator, says the bored Marylebone voice on the line. She pauses to exhale, the end of her cigarette brightening as she takes another puff. I have a call coming through from America.

I don't want the call—, Sylvia says briskly, pulling the receiver away from her ear.

It's Mummy, Sylvia, says a spidery, faraway voice.

Sylvia holds the phone inches from her head, wrestling with indecision.

Sivvy, it's Mummy. It's very expensive to call at this hour—, she says, turning the age-old blade of guilt.

Finally Sylvia abuts the receiver to her ear.

Sylvia, I'm so worried, Aurelia says.

YOU'RE worried? YOU'RE worried? Sylvia thinks. You're not even having this dream.

I've got the house all ready, Aurelia says assuredly, as if she might vanquish resistance by sheer breathless trajectory. *The children can have your brother's room. And you can share your old room with me, just as before – we can be roommates, just as when Grammy and Grampy came to live with us.*

Why can't I have the guest room now that Grammy's dead and Grampy is in the nursing home? Sylvia asks, nibbling but suspicious, like an old fish.

Why – Aurelia stalls – *why, I thought you'd want it just the way it was before. We can pretend it's all just the same. You know, pillow talk, just the two of us.*

NO— Sylvia says, suddenly struggling free. *No – I'm not coming back there. I'm never coming back.*

But Sivvy, Aurelia pleads, *you could get a high-paying teaching job anywhere in Boston and still live at home. You could save so much money for the children. You could even go back to Smith if you wanted. I've called*—

You WHAT? Sylvia bellows into the phone. *Who did you call?*

I just called Mrs. Prouty, Sylvia, Aurelia says, scrambling. *Just Mrs. Prouty.*

I'm not coming back! Sylvia shrieks at her mother.

Sylvia, Aurelia says, her voice hardening. *Don't speak to me in that tone. Don't you forget that Mrs. Prouty's generosity put you through Smith*—

You would have made an exceptional teacher, Sylvia! Mrs. Prouty's stentorious voice breaks in. *A rara avis, Sylvia. With your education, all to waste* . . . she adds pityingly.

We put our faith in you, Sylvia, her mother remonstrates, the hurt in her voice ratcheting strategically.

ME?! she says, incredulous. *Faith in ME? No, that's wrong – that's backwards—* Her nerves effervesce in defeat. She's being overrun.

Sylvia, Aurelia whispers meaningfully, *Mrs. Prouty paid for all of your hospital expenses. She paid for your new psychiatrist at McLean. Don't you owe—*

She hangs up: her mind drafty, emotionless, disengaged; she simply hangs up, because she's done for. She knows it's there, lurking right around the corner, just out of sight. Just waiting, opportunistic, like a dormant virus. The phone rings.

Hello, she says angrily. She should be angry; it wasn't supposed to be this way ever again.

Hello, is this the home of Ted Hughes? asks a heavily accented female voice.

Who is this? Sylvia asks, her desperation mounting, throwing off dread like sparks.

I'm a producer from the BBC Third Programme, calling for Douglas Cleverdon, says the woman.

Sylvia begins to deconstruct the accent: It's the Irish producer, not Assia. It's the redhead wearing lipstick from two years ago, when they lived on Chalcot Square. It was only a voice, but Sylvia could just tell: a fun-loving redhead with lipstick.

I'm calling about Mr. Hughes's play, The Calm. *We're very interested and we'd like to meet with him about it,* says the Irish producer.

It was always there, always, at the back of her mind.

No, I won't go there again, Sylvia answers.

But aren't you already there? says the woman.

What? Sylvia asks, scalded by panic.

You're already there, says a voice. *You only need to push.*

What? she says again, falling through space.

You're ready, says the voice. *Just push.*

Wait— Sylvia says, confused. *Is this a party line?*

Push! says the voice.

Sylvia looks down. The phone cord is a twisted umbilicus, blue and weird, dangling from under the hem of her nightgown. Fat clotted drops of black blood plop to the floor between her bare feet.

She's a very good pusher. Both of her midwives had told her so. But she can't push like this – not with a phone in her hand, with the scuttling over carrion in the bathroom. She hangs up the receiver and sets the phone down on the floor. She braces her hands on her knees, squatting with her feet spread for balance, and pushes. She can feel the murky ringing in her uterus, the electrified shrill, but she doesn't quite have her bearings. She takes a step back, out of the hallway, placing her hands on either side of the nursery door frame. Gripping as tightly as she can, she bears down. The phone is ringing and ringing.

She's groaning. She's roaring. She's afraid she's going to pop all the blood vessels in her eyeballs.

She's pushing, and she's getting tired. She's been violently sick for a whole day now; she doesn't have much energy in reserve. It's hard work, pushing and pushing, getting it out. She stops to take a breather, picks up the ringing phone.

Ted? she says, too cautious to hope. But there's no one on the line. There is only a dial tone suspending itself in the phone's black ether. And she realizes that the ringing hasn't stopped – it's a car horn, not a phone. She sets the receiver on the floor and walks hesitantly toward the windows, stepping past the children, little Nicholas in his crib huddled, rump high, against the refrigerated air. Frieda collapsed in her frilled flannel nightgown as if dropped from a great height, her two Carrara feet exposed, delicate relics at the blanket's fluted edge. Under the sickly green glow of the streetlight, her mother's car, the old gray Chevrolet, is all packed up – to drive across America? No, it's the hoar-frosted Morris, shiny black and brand new, ready for the channel ferry and their trip across France just before they found Court Green. Then she must really be pregnant; she's always been pregnant on road trips. So it *must* be Ted down there, behind the wheel, waiting to take her away – the beach at Berck-Plage, the amputees sunning at the veterans' hospital on the sand, learning to turn the pages of their newspapers with prosthetic hooks. To Spain, to Ireland, somewhere, away from here.

Wait— she calls out the closed window, though he won't be able to hear her. Her breath blows up and frosts the glass, erasing her reflection, making her impossible to see from inside. The Morris idles at the curb, intentional as a London cab, as a hearse. She turns, running back through the room to the hallway, and snatches up the phone to call for help.

Hello, this is the international operator, says a dusky female voice with a German accent. *You have a call coming through.*

In a sudden access of foreboding, she knows it's not Ted waiting for her outside. *Father, I know it's you,* she says into the telephone, afraid. *Operator,* she says, *I won't accept the call.* Hobbled by the inertia of the unconscious, she moves excruciatingly to hang up, frozen like a child in her defiance.

What have you got on under that nightgown? thunders a German baritone. *Put on some proper clothing. You can't go to the door like that, practically naked!*

It would kill your father, Aurelia breaks in, *to know what you did with all those boys. I know. I dreamt it, and he died. Don't you remember? I told you while we were lying there one morning, in our twin beds—*

No! Sylvia pleads. *It wasn't me! He wouldn't go to the doctor, he was sure it was cancer and he refused to go – it wasn't me. I was a good girl. I tried so hard to be good.*

But you prattle something too wildly, Aurelia scolds. *That diaphragm episode with your McLean psychiatrist, and that French boy at Yale . . . Your father's precepts therein you do forget.*

Sylvia drops the phone, melting into sobs. She crouches on the floor, hugging her knees, broken down. It's there, waiting, the flicker at the end of a dark black tunnel, available, if she wants it. Does she want it? No. She can't be sure. When she was twenty, she mourned for her unlived life: all she would never experience. It seemed so sad, but ultimately a necessary sacrifice. Now the shock is that her children, so priceless, are only so magnetic. After a pivotal point, it's not about her future or theirs, but about the present and the past polluted into nightmare, from which she could be entirely, obliviously relieved.

The phone rings.

Sylvia's hand reaches through syrupy time, through the slow yawning gape of dream, for the phone. The chimerical reel immediately snaps free, spinning on its axle, when her hand connects with the black Bakelite receiver. She hears flapping, crisp and rhythmic.

Who is this? asks the operator. She recognizes her own voice: haughty, womanly, resonant. Unflinching and confident, rolling with insinuations.

This is Sylvia Plath, she says.

Behind the back-lit stage scrim that her bedroom wall has become, Professor Thomas crouches, holding a cup to his ear, eavesdropping, an ordance map in his lap that he masturbates behind as he listens. The paper flaps rhythmically with the jerking of his hand.

That's right, her voice says to herself. *Can you remember that?*

Of course, Sylvia answers meekly, without confidence. *It's my name.*

Grimacing, his mouth a sagging rictus, Professor Thomas's face falls away in oozing chunks below his bushy white eyebrows. Old meat falling off the bones. His eyeglasses glint in the light.

It should end here, Sylvia dreams; it should end right here, before the next question. She knows it before the words are formed.

This is the best thing that's ever happened to you, isn't it? her self asks her self. *This is just what you needed to break free. You've never felt more alive—*

Professor Thomas is holding out his cup. He offers it to her, spotlit behind the sheer scrim, bobbing in his hand. *Here,* he grunts, gritting his teeth, his eyes rolling back under thick, blue lids, *are you going to be sick?*

17

Magi

December 17, 1962
London

Not so rash, not so foolish as to smile or offer
a weightless, friendly greeting sure to be read,
then, as malignant or callous, though he has, as
he understands it, been summoned – yes? – implying,
at the very least, détente, a truce, for the moment in
which he will be performing whatever service Sylvia
seeks rendered. The downstairs neighbor, a Professor
Thomas, has let him in, had listened resentfully for the
rude electric buzz of the doorbell, muttered a sequel to
his earlier protests, and stands in the hallway watching,
sourly, skeptically, as Ted trudges heavily up the stairs,
ducks his head at the abbreviated half landing, lets
himself through the fastened baby gate, and lightly but
unambiguously knocks at the door to his wife's flat.
His face he keeps blank, just blank.

The door flings instantly open.

Sylvia stands on the other side, her blue-tendoned fist
bloodless around the doorknob, erratically dressed in
layers of clothing under her robe, holding Nicholas, a
clammy little phantom clinging to her ribs like a monkey's
child. Her face lucent, her skin seeming waxen, almost
iridescent – she is still feverish – and her eyes glittering,

Sylvia also seems vaguely ethereal. But the black enmity of her glower is anything but conceptual. With a whimper Frieda stumbles, headlong, dazed, wearing only the unsnapped top of her pajamas, across the floor to Ted, who is caught in medias res of his nervous humming of 'Sir Patrick Spens' and gathers her up.

The threshold of Sylvia's flat, no abstract, separates them. Avoiding eye contact but listening, listening, they wait. At the door to his flat on the ground floor below, Professor Thomas listens for them listening. Sylvia's high pique hovers, ventilating the stairwell. Ted hums, caressing his daughter's cool legs and bare bottom and back, comforting her, Frieda's matted head burrowing under his jaw, her arms slung over his shoulders.

'"Syngynge he was, or floytynge, all the day . . ."' Sylvia accuses under her breath, her face pinched with intolerance and grayed exhaustion.

Ted says nothing. They stand on the landing in opposition, one on either side of the door, each holding a diminished child, listening for Thomas to stop listening. Finally he retreats, shuffling, sufficiently deaf indeed, and thus disappointed, into his flat.

As soon as they hear the click of the door downstairs, Sylvia's unforgiving eyes lock on Ted's. 'We could have died this weekend—' she hisses, even the acute angle of her long, sharp arm around Nicholas seeming aggressive and intractable.

'Let me bring her inside, Sylvia—' Ted whispers.

'That's right,' Sylvia responds, stepping aside, her voice shrill and snide, 'you know what to do for them. You're so devoted. You're so wise.' When Ted has entered the flat carrying Frieda, Sylvia scrupulously closes the door, snapping the bolt with the side of her hand, then turns to face him, the untied belt of her robe dangling at her hips, her feet bare and thin.

'I came as soon as I was told to,' Ted says quietly to the foyer floor. 'Dido told me you were busy with guests—'

'I was *busy*,' Sylvia whispers, pitiless, rocking Nicholas mechanically, 'keeping these children alive, dousing their burning bodies while nearly out of my head myself—' She notices Ted lift his gaze, the almost imperceptible flake of movement as he looks around, cautiously, in the manner of a hunted creature plotting the split-second opportunity of escape. 'What is it?' she asks him, seizing upon his bifurcated attention. 'Figuring the sums in your head? I can tell you exactly; I know every pound by heart. The two chairs, the coffee table, the straw mats; the book-cases I bought more cheaply because I assembled them myself. All my years of scrimping and going without and putting your career first, and now when it should be paying off, all that work, *this* is what *I've* got. I see the receipts from Selfridge's in my sleep, a roll call of the discount casualties, the dead and the merely wounded—' She registers his face modulating, flinching, responsive, and she drills on. 'What about you? How much have you spent on your abortionist? Where is the money from my grants, which was to pay for a nanny so that I could write, but which you squandered on yourself?'

She stalks him into the parlor, where he has ventured in search of a blanket, air, a covering for Frieda, some-thing to shield their daughter from the velocity of her mother's wrath. He finds some soft woolen thing on a wicker chair and picks it up, draping it, with one hand, over the child. 'We both agreed we would live on those grants, Sylvia,' he counters with the deliberate delicacy of a doctor delivering bad news, pinching the blanket up awkwardly, trying to get it up over Frieda's shoulders. 'Don't revise our history now,' he says, his flat tone cautionary but dispirited, fully cognizant of the pointlessness of any attempt to argue. He is avoiding her face, trying to keep from a full engagement with her overpowering valence. 'We agreed to live on the grant money so that we could both write.'

'But I didn't get to write, did I,' she retorts, feeling the withering sting of tears even as she drives them back, drives her irrefutable point home. 'As soon as I was back in my study, you were rolling in the scent of Chanel. Filthy with it,' she continues, her face collapsing beneath the bitter taste of scorn. She is listening to herself, full of self-pity and hypnotic disgust. She cannot stop. 'Your face in it. Like a pig. *That's* your "View of a Pig."' She hugs Nicholas, who is dull eyed, contracted into himself from the visceral shock of the last three days. 'And I with a nursing baby.' Again, the vision of herself abandoned brings the pinch of near tears. 'Revision . . .' she sneers. 'Everything I've accomplished, I've done *despite* you.'

'I didn't plan this, Sylvia,' Ted says, wretched, his fingers knitted into a buttress supporting Frieda's weight under her blanket, her small pale face turned away, hiding.

'What do you think we are, figments of your imagination?' Sylvia adds. 'Something you can excise? You think these children—' She pauses, suddenly cowed by the profundity of her children's realness, here, hearing everything, doubtless sensing the ineluctable pall of her hopelessness seeping out of her pores *All the weeping and the gnashing of teeth and the children of the Kingdom cast out into darkness—*

They stand together in the loveless parlor, swaying out

of sync with the quiescent children, who are young enough yet to retreat from an alarming glut of stimuli back to the cushioning amnion of sleep. The wall heater creaks and ticks. Sylvia's holly, cut a week before, corrupts in its vase, the berries shriveled and dropping, the scalloped edges of the brittle leaves browned and dangerous, like rusted wire.

'Were you ill, Pooker,' Ted whispers to Frieda with strained concern. 'Did you have a bellyache?' Frieda tightens her clasp around his neck. 'What about Nicky?' he asks Sylvia.

'They've both been vomiting since Friday night,' Sylvia reports with the weary matter-of-factness of the battle worn.

'Tell me what you want me to do,' he offers.

'I've gotten nothing done,' Sylvia blurts reproachfully. 'No shopping, no work. I've run out of everything – nappies, food, towels, clean clothes. Christmas is a week away, and I've done nothing for these children. I won't have your desertion ruin their lives as well as mine—'

'You needn't do anything,' Ted answers without hesitation. 'If you're sick, I could drive you and the children to my family for Christmas—'

'*IF* I'm sick?!' Sylvia rears.

'If you are *still* sick. If you *like*,' he corrects himself.

'Are you mad?' she fumes. 'You think I would submit to that humiliation, asking for your family's charity when they know what you've done to me?'

'Sylvia,' Ted interrupts, 'my mother—'

'They're your family now, not mine. They've offered me nothing.'

'It's not true,' Ted says, shaking his head. 'My mother—'

'Your mother *what?*' Sylvia challenges. 'Your cowardly,

gossipy mother ran for cover when your sister crucified me the last time we spent Christmas in Yorkshire, a mistake I swore I'd never make again. Stuck in that slovenly house for a week? Now you think I'll go back for another dose of mortification? Isn't the scandal *here* enough? "Fare Thee Well," and you telling anyone who will listen it's all the fault of my irrecoverable childhood, not your own doing? You think I'm so lacking in self-respect I'd be packed off to relatives, hunch over my petit point – my "decorative arts," as your girl puts it – while you resume your debaucheries elsewhere? I'll be no Anna-bella, no Lady Caroline Lamb to your slaughter.'

'What?' Ted blunders, utterly mystified.

Sylvia fixes him with a caustic, death-blade look. 'You've already set this up to get me out of your way, haven't you, Lord Byron? "Mad, bad, and dangerous to know." *I* know. I'm sure you think delivering me into your family's custody will keep me from writing as well.'

Ted is shaking his head in disbelief. 'Sylvia,' he mutters, 'that's insane.'

'That's always your trump card, isn't it, Ted?' she savages him, stung by his use of the word. 'When *you* can't bear what *you've* done, you blame *me*. You tarnish me with all I entrusted to you.'

This is the impasse, the speechless stalemate. The children are limp in their arms, incontrovertibly rejecting the chance to witness the full collapse of their parents' short-lived, fragile accord. Whatever civility they had warily hammered out in the last month, the flat hunting, the tentative settlements and divisions and schedules, is crumbled like chalk. All of it nothing but theory in a free fall of alienation, no common language between them, just the squalid silence of their estrangement. Just the terrible convulsive breathing of the fallen nestling trying to die. *She couldn't wait for that baby bird to die: gasping in its shoe box for a week, keeping them both awake at night and sick at heart with its brave mournful cheeping. Ted taped the cardboard box to the bath hose and hooked it to the gas stove, finally, in the kitchen of their apartment at Smith. She was relieved, and ashamed of her relief – the bird's innocent misery an oppression she was desperate to escape.*

'What can I do?' Ted ventures, breaking the perilous silence.

Sylvia watches him, his cowlick falling over his eyes, watching her, his chin resting on Frieda's back. 'Do something concrete. Bathe these children. Sterilize Nick's bottle. Listen for the nappy man. Stay with them while I run to the shops and the launderette.'

'I can go for you,' Ted offers.

'No—' she snaps. 'I want to get out of here.'

'All right,' he says, backing instantly down. 'All right.'

Upstairs, after she's put Nick down to finish his nap in his cot, found a pair of nearly clean socks and her Wellingtons, sat on the bed to steady herself, her superheated brain cells popping like soda, a sidereal spree glimmering before her sore, abraded eyes, she knots more laundry into a dirty bath towel and listens to the awkward clinking of Ted feeling his way around her unfamiliar kitchen. She's not going to stay here, no – fastening the buttons on her overcoat, coming down the stairs, hanging on to the handrail. No. Like a lamb to the slaughter. She's got to get out.

'How do I . . . Sylvia?' Ted calls from the kitchen.

'What is it?' she asks impatiently from the hall by the front door. Frieda is still draped over his shoulder, unbudging. Ted is examining the alien baby bottle caddy at the sink.

'How do I do that?' he asks sheepishly.

'Boil it. Figure it out,' she answers, her fingers gripping the doorknob. She's got to go.

18

Lesbos

Late September–October 11, 1962
Court Green

Tiny grasshoppers leap randomly out of her path, airborne flakes of jade. She walks through the high, blonded grass and dying fern of the orchard, carrying a tin of golden syrup to feed her bees. *There's no use putting more energy into Ted,* the midwife had counseled her a few days ago; Sylvia sat sobbing on a ladylike upholstered sofa in a room with a view of the moors, black-footed Pekingese puppies toddling like chubby infants at her feet. She clutched Ted's cable from London in her hand – it was waiting for her when she returned home from Ireland alone, holding her breath, crossing from Dublin wondering if he would meet her at the station. Her knuckles stung; she'd scraped them on the sliding compartment doors of the train from Holyhead, trying to move all of their heavy luggage into the racks by herself. *Who knows when he'll have a change of heart. Think about yourself now,* the midwife said, bringing tea on a tray, *you and the children. You go to your study in the mornings; it'll be good for you to have a routine. I'll come by in the afternoons to visit, help you with the chores.*

She did come by in the afternoons, bringing her apple

ladder, her honey extractor, two kittens as a surprise for Frieda; burlap sacks to store the onions and to cover the combs they harvested. *Now you'll have to feed your bees,* she told Sylvia as they cranked the handle of the centrifugal cylinder in which they'd loaded the uncapped, dripping combs. Dusty late September sunlight fanned in through the open doors of the barn, a deception of the cool afternoon. Glass mason jars that Sylvia had boiled were lined up on the cobbles, ready to be filled. The job was messy, but the women kept their jackets on under their aprons. *There's not much pollen left to forage, and without enough honey the colony won't last the winter,* the midwife explained, her kind, pragmatic face set determinedly as she spun the galvanized crank. *They close up shop, so to speak, but they still need to eat. Tate & Lyle, corn syrup, even granulated sugar is fine.*

Tate & Lyle, that's what Sylvia has brought; she pries the metal lid off with a butter knife. As the syrup oozes slowly from its tin onto the pie pan she sets in tamped-down grass near the entrance to the hive, she watches the bees; the guard bees come to inspect her, pinging around her shoulders as if on elastics, beyond the cheesecloth draping of her veiled hat, and buzzing back to the hive to report. A few aging scouts and foragers returning from late reconnaissance in the fields, their wings all but shredded from the summer's flights. But the most dramatic activity is the commotion at the hive door, where bees are pouring out, not in. There, workers are pushing the larger drones out the gabled entrance. Hovering, humming, cowering in clusters, the fat-bottomed drones try to crawl back up the wooden frame past the waiting line of workers, who pinch the male bees and push them away, literally dragging pupal drones clear of the hive and dropping them into the grass. As she watches, Sylvia realizes what the workers are doing. The midwife has told her about this. Winter is coming; there will be no room for bees who have no purpose, who eat up all the honey, whose only job is to mate with the queen in spring. The workers, the sisters, are doing what has to be done. They are evicting the useless drones. They are getting rid of the men.

He's back, but he's leaving. It is almost over. Rubbing her forefinger over the satiny waxed surface of her elm-plank desk, her coffee cold, waiting for him to finish packing, waiting to drive him to the train station with his junk. Metallic light falling from behind the steaming roofline, sifting over the yard, baking the damp thatch; early autumn rusting at its edges. Property line bracken dried up and curling like claws. Skinny fingers feeling his pockets for change. *Will he marry her?* A crash in the guest room. Clumsy – stumbling over his tackle. Beethoven's same tattoo scratches across the gramophone he's set on the floor, needling the old grievances. He's humming along.

Humming along, breaking up the god-awful hush. He blew in like the fog a week ago, covering everything, erasing all the landmarks, honesty and routine and love – but she was armed to the teeth, priming her artillery, caught in the cellar with her flashlight, failing batteries casting a jaundiced spotlight on her secreted valuables, the fruit of six years' hard labor. Her apples, her onions, her potatoes, her six maiden jars of honey. Six years of sweat and faith, and this was what she had to show for it.

All week the clouds have poured endlessly by, lie upon

farrago upon prevarication. She's had to drag the truth out of him, bit by bit. *When, exactly? How? Where?* And still she's faced the facts, obvious no matter what he says: that the life that had made her so stupidly happy was a fraud, an illusion. That the hallway mirror, with its loving border of hand-painted hearts, frames the face of a man who is dead to her.

Livid and harsh, utterly apart: that's the face she's shown, listening to him empty the closets, box up his papers, Frieda trailing him down the hall squeezing a cat, thumping his rubber waders down the attic stairs, sheared like Joan of Arc thanks to him. Like living in a house of wax: that deceptively transparent, that destructible, that glazed. He hums, so pleased with himself. She's divorcing him; she told him straight off. He can't even look her in the eye, the bastard – afraid of the medusa head he'll see, the levitating snakes and the sudden, deadly stiffening.

But she has to be surgical, to the bone. She has to be practical. Divorce is the only possible solution, the absolutely magnetic choice – if it is a choice, of which she is doubtful. He has left her no other choice. *The bird flies itself to the hunter*— Dostoyevsky. Ted's dragging this out has been killing her – the deceit, the evasions, the sickening suspense, all of it leaving the stink of rot somewhere beneath the surface, something foul tamped into the walls. She wants a divorce. She has to want it.

She listens to the disconsolate creaking of her house, its resigned settling. She can hear everything; she can practically see it. It is the pellucidity of truth she sees through, its awesome clarity. The rustle of the appliqués on the baby's animal quilt beyond this wall. The dead mouse putrefying under the floorboards in the larder. Ted cocking his big head in the guestroom, contemplating his defection, stomping down the stairs. Like life in a house of wax, in a mausoleum, that stifling. She has sequestered herself in her study morning after morning, avoiding him, hating him, keeping her mouth shut, refusing to walk the plank. Bent over a sheet of paper, grim and stubborn, skinny and brittle, her body wasted and careworn. After today, he'll be gone. *Will he marry her?*

A declaration, not a question – that's the act that shields her from the dismemberment happening outside her study. She keeps stacks of reusable paper under her desk: old manuscripts, drafts, Ted's and her own, words she can reclaim to protect herself, to urge herself forward. Thrift and omenizing at the same time – a practice as old as her marriage. She's been using the reverse of *The Bell Jar* typescript to draft her poems since she got home from Yeats's tower. She scans each page before she turns it over; sometimes the very words she reads help her get started. What she's written these last two weeks, then, the poem each morning before breakfast, has been laced with the question she asked herself at the end of her novel. How did she know, she had Esther Greenwood wonder, that madness would not reassert itself? How could she be sure she would make it? Now that Ted is back, packing up at her insistence, Sylvia wants stronger medicine for her poems. She wants to assert the act of will that endows her own survival. Not Tarot; not prayer. Like her bees, all those maids, those frugal ordinary women, huddled in a ball at the dead dark center of their hive, a sisterhood rationing its store of honey to last the winter, she's going to make it through this poor and benighted time. When she was ready to type the final version of 'Wintering,' the last of the sequence of bee poems she was writing when he showed up and interrupted her, she put away the chapters of *The Bell Jar,* that potboiler.

She reached, instead, for pages from Ted's play *The Calm*, the first one – his answer to Shakespeare's *Tempest*. Sylvia wants calm, no more tempest: stasis in this time of darkness. She wants a woman's story, not a man's. She wants her fingerprints all over his page: *her* page, *her* words, *her* survival. His manuscript was right there, under her desk, to reinscribe. *The bird flies itself to the hunter.*

He says he's worried about her. He's told the doctor, the midwife, probably the neighbors about her breakdown. Worried about her – my God, what a laugh. They nod at her, stiff masks of skepticism on their faces no matter what comes out of her mouth. She says, *the window broken by the wind, a loose limb;* she says, *the fever didn't break for three days.* She stands in the produce market with her baskets, harrowed, listening; she says, *I hear gunshots.* She thinks, *he told me he was going hunting, but he never came back.* And they nod, scanning her face, the butcher, the grocer, the postman: disbelieving everything.

There he is, big and black, packing the car with his life – his moldy books, a knapsack that reeks of fish. And she sits inside, packed too: hate up to here. Just waiting for him to go. Then she'll be off to the coast of Cornwall, with the kids and the kittens and the sleeping pills, off to visit some people who'll have her – zen orphan depressives ensconced in a faux-charming guest cottage, an invitation complete with cute décor and milk allergies and neurotic gossip. All fake. And moon jellyfish by the thousands washed up on the touristy shore; they'd rather kill themselves than be stuck in Cornwall either. Dreadful, but she's got nowhere else to go, and she's got to have somewhere to go. She's got nothing; at least it's something. She'll go. She'll spread on the sand with the suicidal jellies in their peek-a-boo nighties, see-through ovaries displayed like sliced pimentos, raw and overexposed as she is – melting crystal blebs in which if she hurries she might see her way to a future.

Ted's strapped his suitcases to the roof rack. Both doors of the Morris stand akimbo, the backseat flat for his fishing poles. Hugging his Yorkshire voodoo by the gate, he leans into the trunk. The corduroy nap has worn thin at the elbows of his shabby jacket. His bony wrists, his elbows, his back, that seam across his shoulders that's pulling, behind the panes of the car's rear window – a rift she can see, even from this irreconcilable distance.

In his telegram, the one waiting for her by the back door when she returned from Connemara, he said that the trip had been sentimentality, a gloss. It was pure viciousness. She knows what he really meant: her faith in him, all she believed in, was nothing but vapor. Carbon monoxide. He's standing, turning around, blinking into the sun, and she abruptly sits back in her desk chair – away from the window, out of sight. She won't let him catch her looking. He's become the part of herself she no longer recognizes – not like an amnesiac, but like a country at civil war. Now she'll make him understand that she's real; there's nothing sentimental about her. Now she's drawn the line. She's kicked him out; she's ended it. *Will he marry her?* He's told the doctor she's reckless, but he's wrong. She's not reckless; that's not it at all. She's afraid to wait.

19
The Other

December 18, 1962
London

She's escaped – lighthearted, light-headed, the snowflakes whirl: silvered pinwheels strung high between the lampposts, pasteboard angels and flocked stars glittering down the kaleidoscope of Regent Street, their illuminations, blue-red and sparkling white, leaving tracers streaming the avenue punctuated by the taillights of passing cars, all of it a magic lantern show reflected on the cold, benumbed faces of the marveling shoppers. She erupted from the Underground at Piccadilly Circus – Eros, child of Chaos, directing six-way traffic on one bronze foot – and headed first toward stylish Jermyn Street, to Paxton and Whitfield, to Fortnum & Mason; then north beyond Nash's graceful curving quadrant to Hamley's toy shop, to Liberty, to Dickins & Jones; to an early movie, her next stop, the first she'll have seen in nearly two years. Back at the flat she's got clean clothes, groceries, mail; while Ted fumbled over the children yesterday morning, she invested the necessary time at the phone kiosk trawling her address book, turning up an invitation for Christmas dinner, a last-minute baby-minder, neighbors for a toddlers' tea. With Dido's Millie installed at home with the children for the afternoon,

195

Sylvia moves strategically through the holiday throngs, horizontal with bags and packages, pausing to let someone pass who's carrying even more than she, in homely ecstasies over this sudden gulp of liberation, brimming with gratitude for the innocent flimsiness of commercial good cheer. The swags of greenery, the bell ringers, the theatrical window displays, the heat in her cheeks, her swanky new get-up back from the cleaners: She's heady with London, this glorious venerable bustle, this Dickensian urban hum, and she gapes like a child in the midst of it. Waves of black-suited businessmen in bowlers, sprigs of holly tucked into their lapels, carry little glossy satchels in their bare-knuckled fingers and string bags of oranges imported from Spain. Chic young wives in fur hats pose for the doorman as he swings wide the heavy, brass-trimmed portal under Liberty's Tudor awning. Fierce, harried mothers like herself – gathering loot, scouring toy shelves, insisting that the aproned clerk climb his stepladder to reach for the last wooden train or the one baby doll whose packaging isn't crinkled. She's found a striped rubber ball and that last wooden train for Nick, fine flowery cottons and crocheted trimming for doll clothes, Swiss chocolates and sticky candies, blown-glass baubles and red satin ribbon to hang gingerbread hearts on the tree she'll decorate in secret on Christmas Eve, after the children are asleep. She's even eyed the velvet toreador pants at Dickins & Jones for herself, making a mental note to come back for the January sales and splurge with the last of her birthday stash.

Faith, hope, and charity – the traffic lights blaze crimson at Oxford Street and the crowd halts, black backs and black hats, more shops and more angels and more snowflakes flanking either side, hovering impatiently, neon flashing in a syncopated rhythm, the brightly lit windows festooned and lavish with desirables. Ahead, backing onto Cavendish Square, is the august London Polytechnic, where the Lumière brothers showed the first moving pictures in its vaulted, Palladian theatre and where Sylvia is headed now in the deepening tourmaline twilight of winter's approaching solstice. Farther on, just out of sight, Eric Gill's sculpted Prospero restrains Ariel from flying out over the entrance of Broadcasting House; inside, somewhere, on Douglas Cleverdon's desk, is a packet of Sylvia's new poems, the transcript of the twenty-minute recording from October that the producer thinks is wonderful – the note she got from him today says so. But someone else still has to approve; it's still not for sure. Please, she thinks. Just this once, for Christmas – *the greatest of these is charity. . . . For now we see through a glass darkly; but then face to face; now I know in part; but then shall I know even as also I am known.* Her new poems on the Third Programme could galvanize her move to London; this could be the break she's hungry for.

The light goes green, and the crowd swells across Oxford Street. It's worth celebrating this much even so, she thinks, checking her watch, checking her reflection in the nearest shop window, feeling smart, feeling rich, dimly registering the squeal of brakes, car horns, carols surging from open doorways; walking in tempo with the bustling crowd. No time for tea, but she'll make it just fine to the movie, all of her purchases in tow. *Through a Glass Darkly* – the latest by Bergman, her favorite, about a girl going mad, the subject that just doesn't wear out. Even better, it won an Academy Award for best foreign film of the year, boding well for *The Bell Jar* with its pub date only a month away. She could even consider this professional research, she thinks, rearranging her bags, jockeying for her pocketbook.

The black tide of shoppers pours forth, divides, and there, just ahead: Assia, like a tiger lily walking the December streets, gaudy, exotic, exuding her sexual scent. It drifts down the sidewalk toward Sylvia, curling like smoke around the heads of the other oblivious pedestrians. Even from the back, Sylvia would know her anywhere – that mannequin carriage, that head sleek as a taxidermist's bird. She is hurrying somewhere, she is late, working her way steadily through the crowd, adorned with kidskin and jewelry, polished black boots, her small, tailored handbag ornamenting the elbow of a coral pink coat; hair so unnaturally dark it's almost purple. The black crowd is suddenly stagnant against Assia's boldness, the machinery of her silks shearing forward. This isn't the glass house of Chalcot Square; it's not even the congregatory terraces of Regent's Park Road. It's the center of teeming London, and still, for Sylvia, Assia's draw is magnetic. Her pull is irresistible, like the moon's: Sylvia follows, helplessly bound to an unknown fate that this other woman, victorious, commands. Sylvia follows, lugging her unwieldly packages: hooked, like knitting, like a side of meat. Up the block, through a sea of unsuspecting faces, winding like a funeral procession of two toward the door of a bookshop, where Assia grips the tarnished doorknob in her gloved hand and enters, briskly turning only to shut the door tightly behind her, rattling the glass pane in its glazing, thunking the holly wreath and bells hung from a wire slung through the transom. Sylvia stops and stares.

Books, new and used, are brandished shoulder high in the plate-glass window, displayed on shelves draped with evergreen boughs and artless tinsel garlands. All the current rivals lurk there – Sexton's *All My Pretty Ones,* Katherine Anne Porter's *Ship of Fools,* Akhmatova's *Poem Without a Hero,* Shirley Jackson, Janet Frame, Lessing's *Golden Notebook.* Assia's perfect, so true to life, standing inside at the counter, her lips moving soundlessly behind the pane: wide gray eyes questioning the shopkeeper, smiling cosmetically at just the right moment. That fine nose like something chipped off a Greek statue by a tourist; the marble luminous skin, cool as a morgue. Sylvia is rooted to the spot, gawking, wordless, the little match girl standing outside, scratching her pitiful flares. What could she possibly say? She has so much to say! And all of it merciless; all of it useless. The damage is already done. Assia turns her elegant back, disappearing after the shopkeeper down the aisles of books stacked to the rafters, inserting herself deeper into the heart of all Sylvia cherishes, into her new life, this last untainted bastion, into Sylvia's intimate mystery of words. And Sylvia can only watch, silenced behind the cold glass, without a voice, her thoughts derailed, her nerves shot, utterly divided from anything she might do to change this, to rehabilitate her innocent hopes, all the afternoon's shallow pleasures turning to ash like the apples of Sodom. Her own fevered reflection – her sallow transparency in the unflattering glare of shop light, the grief ringing her eyes, the baggy wool she can see now hanging off her bones – revealing her true and sudden poverty, which is written all over her face.

20

Stopped Dead

December 18, 1962
London

Hung out over a dead drop, her bundles forsaken across armrests and velvet in the balcony's first row, the curving balustrade with its polished brass rail and glossy molding all that keep her from plummeting over the edge into the pitch-black below, a netherworld alive with the random rustle of unseen watchers. Watching and waiting, tense in their seats, masticating popcorn – a plague of insects eating the place alive. Behind her, overhead, a cone of light cuts the plenary darkness, filtering forward from its slit in the wall. The two loaded reels of the cinema's projector spin, their flickering hiss muffling the obscenity of rasping mandibles, of crunching sweets, the tic of wings and voracity.

Her life unspools in black and white: a stark landscape drained of blood. On an island in a cold northern sea, a woman is waiting for God, moonlight washing over her nightgown in the cobalt hours before dawn. The music wells, a single aching thread of Bach on which she dangles, suspended between one world and another. *Defiant, Arachne waited for the goddess: It was her own incomparable skill that gave art to her spinning and weaving, not a gift of the immortals. Athena could meet her chal-*

lenge if she chose. Waiting among the whisperers, the planes of their faces brilliant with light. Watching and waiting among packages wrapped up tight, poised in the shadows on the upholstered seat, her long legs crossed beneath her, her slender arms folded into her winter coat.

The film threads through the teeth of the projector, framing a longing for God, for a pure and selfless love, for a meaning behind this mortal torment. A father and a husband argue in a boat, dead in the water – whose love is more flawed? The husband impotent against his wife's anguish, or the father watching?

Side by side, Arachne and the patroness of weavers threaded their looms, stringing their warps between the heddles, wrapping weft thread on the bobbins of their shuttles, buttoning their mantles beneath their breasts to free their arms as they worked. They wove swiftly, sweat rising on their brows, ribs resting on their looms' breast beams, beaters keeping pace, their concentration complete. Athena's tapestry was impeccable, designed to humble the haughty girl: above the city of Athens, the gods dazzled on their Olympian thrones, winged Nike victorious at their center, the whole encircled by graceful, leafing branches of Athena's symbol, the olive. But into each of the four corners of the fabric she wove a cautionary tale – the story of a mortal whose pride had offended the gods, and the fate each had suffered as a result.

The warning came too late for Arachne. Finished with her work, she stepped back from her loom so the goddess could see. Into her tapestry Arachne had woven the fear of Europa recoiling from the waves over which Zeus, in the form of a bull, was stealing her away. There was Leda, powerless beneath the beating wings of the swan, and

Asteria violated by an eagle. To Alcmēna, Zeus appeared disguised as her husband, and Antiope thought it was a satyr and not the Almighty who seduced her. Arachne pictured Danae overcome by the golden shower that produced Perseus, and Aegina assaulted in flames. Arachne depicted not just the deceptions of Athena's father, but those of the other gods as well: Poseidon, too, in the shape of a bull to deflower Arne, and as the swiftly moving river that filled Aloeus's wife with twins, and as the ram that mounted Bisaltis. Apollo, Dionysus, and Cronos were pictured in the myriad forms into which they had metamorphosed for the purpose of deceit. Arachne embellished her ungodly collage with a maidenly border of dainty, entangled flowers and leaves.

There was not an ungainly stitch in Arachne's rendering of the depredations inflicted by the rapacious gods; she stood contemptuous by her subversive embroideries, watching Athena's face knead with indignation and envy for the girl's unmistakable craft. Finally the goddess could stand the affront no longer. Athena took up her shuttle and beat Arachne between the eyes before ripping her impudent tapestry from the loom.

From her husband's bed, from her father's, a woman discovers how she has been betrayed. And still she longs for the light, and the parting of the whispering crowd, and the face of God emerging through the dark door. For her.

Athena's insult was more than Arachne could bear. Outraged, she knotted a heavy skein of her own wool into a noose and hung herself from the castle beam of her loom. But death was not sufficient punishment in Athena's eyes; it was unresolving retribution she was after. She lifted the girl, easing the rope, and sprinkled a potion from Hecate over Arachne's head. The herbs of the great mother of the gods, Magnae Deorum Matris, contracted Arachne's head and body into tiny orbs, her legs and arms into filaments. She hung, a spider, from her own thread.

Sometimes one is so defenseless, says the young woman to her husband on the night she will wait for the door to open. It opens, and her face is incandescent with longing. As her family listens for the approach of the ambulance, she tells them she has seen her god: it was a spider, a rapist, with a cold, stony face.

And Sylvia is hanging, hanging by a thread. Like Arachne stripped to her waist, dangling, her forehead and shoulders gleaming with sweat, the purple bruise rising at her temple, and gray-eyed Athena breathing hard beside her, gripping her by the hair – sometimes one is so defenseless – tipping her vial of wolfsbane and yew into the dying girl's braided crown, whispering into her ear, *Seek all the fame you will among mortal men, but yield place to the goddess.*

21

Poppies in October

December 18, 1962
London

Fog roils over the great carved porticoes and patinated mansards of the buildings, gushing out of Little Portland Street and Cavendish Place, lapping and curling in an opaque misted sheet down the broad sidewalk, banking the limestone architecture, swallowing traffic, insulating the headlamps and the street lamps in an aural haze. Fog has obliterated her London, rolling on forever, closing in. Only the obdurate spire of All Souls Church, needle sharp, perforates the opiate density.

Black silhouettes of approaching pedestrians erupt like bathers from a colorless ocean. Hunch-shouldered bowlers with their collars turned up. Red-mouthed women hugging their coats, averting their eyes. Averting her own, stumbling down the marble staircase out of the theater, over the lobby mosaic trampled unnoticed by how many thousands over time, soul after soul, which she must have crossed as well when she arrived and purchased her ticket. A horseman stripped bare, struggling with a serpent – THE LORD IS OUR STRENGTH the tiled message mocked her just inside the bronze doors, before she stepped out into a world where everything has disappeared. Cast out into darkness. Where did it all go?

Smears of red in the vaporous darkness: only paint on a diminishing bus. Christmas wrapping. The muted mouths of women. Where is the gift of conspiracy that had saved her, life giving her what she needed, numinous and real – poppies bowing their heavy heads at her feet. When did she step beyond grace?

Disembodied faces veer to either side, glance haltingly, dully before they look away. The weeping, the keening, the mouths crying open. She lurches forward into mist and night, wrenching her bags and packages through the passing decorous crowd. Had they only been flowers, not what she had made of them? She had felt their truth in her cells, pumping through her veins. Where did it all go – the poppies she cut for her desk, her birthday: she'd held them in her hands. She'd lifted a lit match to their stems. Sealed them, burned them black. To make them last, to keep them from bleeding to death.

22

The Courage of Shutting-Up

December 19, 1962
London

Molten umber, mahogany, earth: two rooms, blazing, in which a man is reflected as he reads. Two rings of cairngorm flecked with topaz. A man floating in brown, sepia toned – brown coat, face, hands, light. First in an office in Broadcasting House, bookcases crammed, play scripts and typescripts piled on the desk, in boxes, hastily cleared from a chair where the producer motions for Ted to sit, conversing and thumbing meanwhile through last week's opened mail, searching for an oversized envelope neatly slit along the pasted flap, mumbling self-deprecatorily and finally easing a thick packet from a slumping pile. *Oh yes, here it is, you've seen all these, no?* Douglas Cleverdon must have asked, or something like that, in a scene projected without sound, without dialogue, a projection, in fact, not of the retina but of the mind, a fish-eye exchange Sylvia can only imagine, Cleverdon glancing over his shoulder, then, yes, and cocking his eyebrows at Ted seated in the proffered chair in his aged corduroy jacket. Yes, they concurred, brilliant work, like nothing she'd done before. *Just as you've been telling me, Ted,* the producer would have added, giving him all the credit, as if she were a puppet, a doll, a thing of his creation. *I think we really must get a programme out of this. This one,* he might have said, selecting a sheet from the sheaf of her poems, *I'm utterly knocked out.* And Cleverdon began to read, aloud, the first few lines of 'Daddy.' Listening, basking, Ted's smug smile, the Cambridge leer, his nod of complacent approval dissolving as the words formed in the stale air of the office. Loaded, immediate, indefatigable, words demanding to be heard. *Actually no,* Ted would have interrupted, feigning benign curiosity, *no, I don't think I've read that one yet. May I—?* And the producer, in midthought and phrase, stammering, *Oh yes, really? Yes yes, quite right, perhaps she's sent me things so new even you haven't read them yet. It sounds from her note as though she's been writing at a gallop. Here, have a look – what of this one, 'A Secret,'* or the one published in last Sunday's Observer, *did you see it? 'Event' I think it was, yes, here,* paper crackling as he passed the pages and back-folded newsprint into Ted's outstretched hand. Ted in Douglas Cleverdon's office at the BBC, her poems in his lap, high in the Art Deco building of Portland stone from which no desertion was possible, no craven leap through the window onto the Langham's porte-cochere, say, or shimmy down the double marble colonnades of All Souls next door or blood-pumping disappearance into the crowds strolling Regent Street below. There was no escape for him now. He read her new poems, all Cleverdon had, turning the neatly typed pages swiftly – those he knew about – and others more slowly, absorbing the accounts of his bastardies. His secrets, he was rapidly discovering, were out.

Now, in her parlor: where he's come straight from the BBC on the tube, rapping on her door unexpectedly, surprising her in her painting clothes, asking about the poems he's just read for the first time, his face shifting and grim. How much more is there; who else has read them; may he see them all?

She's said nothing in response to his questions. Nothing, like Cordelia. Instead, she left him confounded in the parlor, turning away and mounting the stairs. Her heart thudding, a cannon. Espial of her wretched tidy bed through the balusters, the room's desolate order. Bureau drawers on newspaper in the future au pair's bedroom lined up for paint in the center of the floor, the first coat drying, a task to keep her busy, to keep her mind occupied, any measure of resistance against the limitless free fall of dispossession. The babies were playing in the nursery; Frieda scolding and piling all the toys up high. Sylvia's heart a cannon, dangerous and pounding. In Cleverdon's office? Those were just the beginning, a smattering. He might try to stop her now. In the nursery, Frieda snatched a toy out of Nicholas's slow, fat arms. 'No!' Frieda chided. Undaunted, Nicky picked up something else from the floor, a picture book, and gave a gummy little cough. 'No!' said Frieda, grabbing the book away.

He was downstairs, waiting. Quietly drawing the children's door mostly closed, Sylvia entered her bedroom and approached her desk. This was it. She had nothing else left. Her heart near to bursting in her chest, she gathered it all: every file, everything she'd written since May, teeth sown from the slaughter of a serpent. Every poem she let him read this fall, everything she's chosen for inclusion in her new collection, everything else, all of it, and she brought it downstairs and handed it to him. Resolute, without a word, masking her hopelessness. He sits now by the windows in her parlor, reading, and he does not speak.

In her eye, the window behind him a rhomboidal block of miniaturized light, a convex transparency of wicker chair and fingers on a page and bookcase behind and kickshaws – Arabic glasses in sapphire blues and purples arranged on the makeshift mantel – reflected all in brown and brown and brown, a hemisphere of dark and glittering brown. Ted sits with the files open in his lap, going over each poem, line by line, each event refracted through her singular intemperate eye.

While he reads, she watches: she has done the same for nearly seven years. One leg crossed, horizontal, broad shoulders slouching over book or page, his features gone boyish and slack, utterly receptive to the written word. A notebook and pen balanced on the arm of his chair. The occasional sigh and settling, the regular sough of fingertip down the edge of paper, the scratch of his pen when he comes across something worth recording. On his back – floating down the duck-littered Cam, relishing a sofa of worn grandeur in the library at Yaddo, in the damp grass of Hampstead Heath, in bed, legs crossed at the ankles, a pillow or a rolled-up sweater propping his book on his chest as Beethoven sonatas play over and over on a phonograph, or birds call, or rain beats down. A sleeping newborn replacing the pillow on his chest. In September, in Ireland: Sylvia threadbare with the tension between them but hoping, for a few days anyway, that words could bridge the gap. The two of them stooping like giants over the poem Yeats carved into the wall of the winding stair at Thoor Ballylee, crows erupting out of the roofless apartment above, Ted's finger tracing the rough letters engraved into Norman stone:

And may these characters remain
When all is ruin once again.

Words: his absorption, his sheer amaze in the pliancy
of language. At its best – Shakespeare, Eliot, but also
boys' adventure comics, or a children's book on foxes,
on otters – she could almost see the revolutions of his
mind, the words proceeding off the page in a gilded
stream, as in some quattrocento annunciation, toward his
beatific face. She has watched time and again, for nearly
seven years, for his reaction to *her* words, the indescrib-
able contraction of the fine muscles in his hands, around
his eyes, the acute suggestions forming, his opinions that
she had trusted above all others, his approval her sustenance, his encouragement her guide, the leonine poise she
knew so innately when he was about to rise from his seat
and call her name.

No longer. She observes him coldly, his body hanging
heavily on its frame as he reads in the chair by the window.
The poems before him now are evidentiary, the tally of
his crimes. She is girded for doubleness, anger and justi-
fications, the same old friable rationalizing. Her heart a
mortar in her chest, she is daring him to stop the unstop-
pable, to plead with her to call Cleverdon or the *Observer*
or the *New Yorker*, to concoct an excuse to shut her up.

'The Rabbit Catcher.' 'A Birthday Present.' He turns
the pages, slipping them to the floor as he finishes, each
sheet skidding farther out than the last. Around him the
unheard cries and crunch of bone, the convulsive snap of
electrodes, the sickly stench of burning hair. 'Words heard,
by accident, over the phone.' 'Stings.' Around him the
intolerable ringing, ringing, ringing of the telephone; the
rustle of linen, the tears, the soiled bed of their marriage.

He reads, taking her in. Not merely her words, her blistering vision of how he has failed her, but the thunderclap of her artistic bravado. Her unflinching authority – that of a surgeon taking up a scalpel against her own disease.

She sees him across the room, the muscles pulsing under his skin. He holds a page in his hand, leaning forward, elbows steadied on his knees, reading. She watches him from the threshold, from the distance of imaginative assembly: not merely spurned wife but poet, the crafter of their temporal life into language, performer of the act that was her preservation, if not theirs. The worst blows to their marriage were no more real, no more solid, than her poems; she used them, tempered them, their objectifying alchemy – for her – cooled and hardened.

But not for Ted. Ted is quiet, he does not speak. He turns the pages, astonished and brutalized; he reads. 'Fever 103.' 'Burning the Letters.' The pages fall. Her words hurtle on, meteoric, the fiery husk of planets transforming cold to heat; death to naked, throbbing, furious life. His hands are full of her, page after page: the agony and the rage, the flames licking, the layers peeling back, the fresh new thing emerging in its glistening skin, awesome and terrible to behold.

Sylvia watches. She watches Ted's forefinger slide down the back of a page, a finger down her spine. Lifting, turning, the page floating to the floor. Like a snowflake, a free and inimitable thing, riding the air. Ted, too, watches its flight. Humility, distress complicate his face, clouding his brow and the cast of his eyes, a response of involved confusion – respect, horror, tortured admiration for the undeniable marvel of what she's accomplished, a genius he can't possibly deny. And as he reads, on and on, she sees it. She reads it in his eyes: she has pierced him. She's gotten to him, the one she wanted most, through to some vital place, Homer's soldier, mortally wounded, his head bowing like a poppy under the weight of his helmet, heavy as a poppy on its stem.

Around him whips the deadly hush of winter, the wind in its silent rising. Around the two of them, the sweep of wind flattening the dead grasses of the moors and the dales, the blown hills, the unmoved swale of cemeteries, of houses returning inexorably to the earth. Their two thousand days – the roar of springs, of summers, of autumns. Now, winter's silence. He hears nothing, but he feels it. They both feel it: the chill.

Sylvia stands at the threshold to the room, shocked witness to the gravity of her success. She sees it with her own eyes. Ted bows his head; he reads on. She takes it in, her pupils imperceptibly wide, her expression from the distance of the doorway as inscrutable as it was when she refused answer to his questions and turned her back to climb the stairs. But she sees. She's gotten what she wanted. They will see it on the page as she sees it in his eyes, the mark of her triumph, this, her Cadmean victory.

23
Nick and the Candlestick

December 20, 1962
London

She bites the thread from a topstitched hem. Wrapped in layers, her fingers numb, she sews curtains and doll clothes at her desk in the frigid midnight flat. The electric iron seethes, steaming the windows blue. An ice age of black corridors, creaking floorboards, primitive fear. Paring knives glint menace from the bottom of the sink in the kitchen downstairs. Copper oozes green, dripping acid. Dripping grottoes, echoing caverns, subterranean penetralia lie undisturbed for centuries. The gills of her manuscript ripple in the wall heater's faint eddy.

She too has mastered it, the meaningless dark, etching her own magic gallery on shadowy walls. Wrapped in reindeer hide, forehead streaked with soot, under shuddering light the artist performs acts expedient, sacred, essential as meat. Charcoal, manganese, ocher, iron oxide: rubbed with tallow into stone, blown into patterns through reeds. Handprints that will sustain their unique whorls and scars for the next forty thousand years. Real wolves, real lions stir at the flare of firelight.

Sylvia's left hand feeds cloth to her Singer; her right turns the crank on the wheel. At her sewing machine, she lifts the presser foot and cranks the needle high, releasing the velveteen for the parlor curtains. Bits of pattern tissue curl like fortune-telling fish beneath her toes. She plucks pins from the seams, tugs basting thread free. The iron tears and sizzles.

Sylvia presses her finished curtains and lays them aside with the set for the au pair's room, the one for the kitchen window. The parlor's wall heater ticks and echoes and ticks. The faucets drip. Apple peelings curl in a pile on the drainboard in the kitchen. Hours evaporate, leaving their crystalline pyres. She changes the bobbin, rethreads the machine, single-mindedness her protection. She takes up the pattern pieces of a tiny nightgown and bloomers in white lawn embroidered with ladybugs. *I have my writing, my children, my home.* Here elastic gathers a waist. Here is a perfect French seam. Here is eyelet hand stitched to a neckline and hem. Here is the heat and spice of an apple cake baking, its scent rising on the flat's chill air, subduing the sharp assault of the vinegar in which her tarnished copper steeps. Mastodons, panthers, sulphur-colored bulls, a lyre of pointed horns decorate the flickering passageways. Red ocher horses gallop – black maned, black hooved, muscles tensed, nostrils flaring. Sylvia gathers skirts, bastes crocheted lace for little dresses of Liberty cotton: soft roses, Victorian florals. She cuts the pattern for a miniature red coat of felted wool with black glass buttons dimpled like ripe blackberries.

She leans over her machine, turning the crank clockwise, the muscles aching in her right arm. The pads of her fingers grow tender, threatening to blister. The needle surges, white thread arcing and tightening in an even, decorative stitch along the finished seams. *A thin crimson skin against the underlying snow of pale flesh, the peel*

coming off in a gyre that curled to her elbow before it
dropped. She chopped the apples in half; their five-petalled
cores mimicked the shape of their blossoms. A seedbed,
a star: the orchard flowers in the memory of the apple.

She pins the collar on at intervals, turning the infinitesimal seam allowance under, pressing with the sharp tip
of the hot iron. She has nearly a yard of the red wool left
over, enough for a play suit for Nick. She sews on the
coat collar, easing the material, pulling pins as she goes.
She leans over the little coat as she removes it from the
machine, trimming the threads, her fingers mirrored in
the reflecting nickel of the face plate. She turns the collar
to the right side and with her pinking shears grades the
seam allowances to make them lie flat, raising her little
torch against the vaulting dark, not fearless but hungry
and cold, deep in the vast impassive dark, utterly hollow,
under everything.

24

Berck-Plage

July 12, 1961
Lacan de Loubressac, France

Not the Causse de Gramat, all earth skin and bones, its arid plateaus of bleached limestone, its stony oak ravines plunged into their own shadows. Not the high thin pastureland etched by Roman road and raccoon-eyed sheep. Not the *limargues*, the abrupt grassy sinks formed by rain's acid leach through porous stone; not the shepherds' huts built into drystone fences, their arched doorways opening onto uplands scented with horsemint and wild thyme and pungent ivy. Not the river valleys overhung by ruined castles, the green, rich alluvial soil, rows of slender Lombardy poplars screening the fields of strawberry and tobacco, the plentiful salmon, lamprey, eel, pike. Not the dense chestnut forests, not the groves of truffle oaks, the wild pigs rooting among damp leaves and lichen in the shade. Not the Padirac Chasm, the underground river flowing clear with emerald water, dammed weirdly by minerals, where the residents of the *causse* descended by torchlight to hide during the Hundred Years' War. Not the stalagmites, the stalactites, the eerie crystalline grottoes, the caves dripping with calcium glitter, prehistory's concreted ooze. Not the arcaded galleries of Lascaux, the pale cliffs and dark catacombs of the Vézère Valley, the Magdalenian wonders in ocher and reindeer bone about which Ted and Bill Merwin have been conversing and corresponding since their introduction in Boston in 1957, the year of Ted's first book and Sylvia's dismal slog through two semesters on the faculty at Smith. Not, in Sylvia's case, lifting a finger, as she had forewarned her accommodating hosts before crossing the channel into France in the Hughes's brand-new car, their first trip away since Frieda's birth. Not, it turned out, merely no housework, but no walks, no exploration, no socializing, no digressions from her incommutable holiday agenda, to which she expected Ted, as well, to adhere.

Instead, a week's appeasement. Sylvia sketching, napping, eating, working on her tan. Taking long showers until the water from the cistern ran cold. Lolling on the stone *bolet*, the broad outdoor porch of the Merwins' restored farmhouse, with her portable typewriter and her correspondence and the nearly finished manuscript of her novel. Writing letters amid the potted geraniums and the diving sparrows, beyond the raftered bedroom where she's rearranged the furniture. Sitting in potent silence through an impromptu visit by the Merwins' elderly neighbor. Glaring at the rusty delivery van that pulls up unannounced through the courtyard gate and cuts its engine in front of the open front door, rising from her chaise and glaring over the porch rail as the driver climbs out of the cab with the weekly bread from the local baker. Lunching from trays supplied by Dido, who smokes and cooks in the vaulted kitchen downstairs, rinsing lettuce and beans in the shallow stone basin, concocting solitary chores and ingratiating feasts to mollify the ferocious rigidity of her invited guest.

Foie gras d'oie, bitter young greens dressed with walnut

oil and salt, *petites fritures* of bony trout, potato galettes with *cèpes* hunted from under the pines behind the house, *tourins* of onions and garden tomatoes and young garlic, *petit pois* stewed with a few of their own velvety pods, *tarte aux pêches*, wines from the terraced vineyards of Bergerac. Snifters of Monbazillac and armagnac by the limestone fireplace while the bats sweep blacker than the black night out of the eaves. Desperately polite retreats upstairs at the earliest hour decent, candles blown out, whispers dismayed or righteous in the dark bedrooms, stars showering down upon the shadows of the trees. Ted's presence required always: standing by while Sylvia sketches, carrying the typewriter case outside, seated at the table, by the fire, on the terrace next to Sylvia. Ted tempting the fates to follow Bill into the grassy orchard of gnarled plums, goldfinches launching themselves out of the blackberry cane, the rough walls buried in eglantine, lined by mossy walnut trees and bird cherries, the two men hacking stumps and boulders from the scanty soil, clearing ivy and burning brush with the valley opening wide down the hillside, the thin skin of the river winding and glinting far below, Ted within earshot, always, of Sylvia's fortified encampment on the terrace.

One day, a delicately negotiated drive into the Dordogne Valley, four uneasy adults folded into the Hughes's compact Morris to tour a small, vibrant cave nearby. Down the shelved galleries the animals ran by in silence, red horses, mastodons, sulphur-colored bulls, chased across the centuries by arrows, muscles tensed, nostrils flaring. Queasy from the humidity, the clammy walls, the faint winey updraft, Sylvia, three months pregnant, sulked by the concession stand, addressing a postcard to her mother back in London.

This is what the Hugheses take back from their visit to Lacan. The pacificatory meals, the stalled conversations. Sylvia's tan. Presents for Frieda, who has this week bestowed on her harried but delighted grandmother her first genuine toddle across a room. Notes for a couple of poems. A basket furnished with a picnic of robust proportions, even by the standards of Sylvia's current appetite.

Ted is packing the car. Sylvia stands behind him on the grass inside the slumping garden gate, passing things over, offering urgent instructions. Dido emerges through the stone-silled doorway out of the cool, late morning shadows of the house, carrying a sweater Sylvia left behind and the picnic she's packed in wicker.

'Next time we come we'll leave both of the children with my mother, and we'll all go off to explore,' Sylvia announces. 'I know Ted would like that.'

Nodding, forbearing comment, Dido thrusts the picnic basket forward. 'Meanwhile,' she says, 'you may as well have a leisurely drive back. Here are some provisions for the journey.'

Sylvia takes the basket in both arms with customary protest. 'You've really spoiled me,' she says, eagerly peeking under the napkin knotted across its contents.

'Just keep the linens and the basket,' Dido adds in reply to Sylvia's rising noises of concern. 'Don't worry about it.'

'I know – I'll have my mother take them back with her to St. George's Terrace,' Sylvia responds. 'She'll be staying there again once we get back. I don't think I could suffer all four of us under one roof for more than a day.'

Dido manages a stony smile of commiseration, glancing toward the bottom of the orchard, feeling her pocket for cigarettes.

'She's just loved having your house as a home base, Dido,' Sylvia adds briskly, reddening at her failure to acknowledge the favor before, well trained, despite evidence to the contrary, in the surface conventions of civility. 'It's been so convenient for us. In her last letter she asked me to thank you again.'

'No need,' Dido mumbles and waves one hand, cupping the fingers of the other around the tip of her cigarette as Ted stoops over her, clicking the flame of her proffered lighter.

The shrilling of cicadas drifts from the tall grass in the walled garden. Dido inhales, building a justifiable pause into the brittle niceties. She and Sylvia both swing their attentions toward Ted, who has circled purposefully around the wood-trimmed side of the çar, climbed into the driver's seat, and started the engine.

'Where's Bill?' Sylvia asks, glancing around.

'Oh—' Dido answers noncommittally, exhaling and gazing toward the sloping garden. 'I think he went to the orchard to put some tools away.' She calls his name in the direction of the trees, where the plums and walnuts sink away down the hill toward a thicket of scrubby oaks. For another moment they wait, hesitating in their good-byes.

'That's all right,' says Ted, hastily ending the awkward suspense, rounding the passenger side of the idling car to open the door for Sylvia. 'Just tell him to ring when he comes through London on his way to New York.' He holds the door while Sylvia settles into the seat with the basket. He walks back around the car, embracing Dido on the way, and while she calls bon voyage, her arms crossed, the ash of her cigarette dangling as she lifts a hand to wave, he releases the emergency brake and engages the clutch.

'Good-bye!' Sylvia calls, beaming with exaggerated gratitude and wagging her arm out the window as the Morris pulls away down the unpaved lane, crushing stone beneath its tires. 'Good-bye!' she calls to Dido, who smokes at the gate, nearly eclipsed by the rising cloud of dust.

Because she has turned around, pulling her bare sunburned arm back into the car, adjusting the windshield visor against the strong sun, adjusting her cotton dress with the willow basket in her shrinking lap, Sylvia misses the expression of unqualified, aghast relief that slackens the tight features of her hostess, now joined by Bill, as they wave the car off down the road, back the way it came, west and north across Central France on the *Route Mauve*, past the lavender fields of the Quercy, the wheat fields of Orléans rolling green to Chartres, the cathedral bristling against the skyline toward the sandy shore of Normandy, to the sherbet-colored bungalows and beach-combing invalids of Berck-Plage, and the channel ferry home.

Sylvia unties the linen napkin that Dido has sacrificed to secure the makings of the picnic she's prepared. As Ted navigates cautiously down the hill's decline, steering in low gear past the potholes, tires sliding here and there on the broken stone, Sylvia picks through their bounty with her slim, balletic fingers.

'Look, Ted, it's a feast—' Sylvia gloats, not bothering to see if Ted is, in fact, looking, which he is not, just listening, quiet, his eyes on the road. 'Fresh peaches, a crock of pâté from the Spanish duchess who came for dinner, the one with the château near here – duck rillettes, a loaf of that good bread, a little Cabeçou cheese wrapped in its leaf, roasted lamb from last night, green walnuts, olives, a bunch of radishes, *marrons glacés,* a cherry clafoutis sprinkled with crystal sugar, and plum eau de vie.' She holds up the slender glass bottle of clear liquid, its cork coated with wax, catching the moted light slanting through the windshield. 'This should keep me till Limoges.'

'Maybe you'll want to rest while it's still cool,' Ted says.

'I feel like a million dollars,' Sylvia says, greedily surveying the cornucopia of dainties. 'Dido likes to kill you with kindness, and I'm happy to oblige. This week has been just what I needed.' Ted makes no comment as he drives past the hedges of sloe and the knotty walnut trees flanking the lane, the high shelf of the unexplored *causse* at their backs. The shuttered windows and red-tiled roofs of the village come into view ahead; a sheep bell clanks in the ripening air. Sylvia reaches into the basket for a twisted paper filled with wrinkled black olives. 'I think we really ought to consider giving up your Maugham Prize, Ponter. I would hate to lose the money, but I don't want to go traipsing all over Italy. It's too much trouble.'

'But that's why we bought the car,' Ted says, his voice weary though it is only eleven o'clock. Already the sun is high, the summer light unmasking every leaf and stone. He lowers his visor against the glare.

'It would be so much better for us in the long run to buy a place like Lacan,' Sylvia says. 'I don't want to travel with two babies. I'll never get anything done; I'll be chasing after one or the other of them all the time. What we really need is a house. Something big and old that we can fix up, a place we can remake to suit ourselves. I want a study just like that sunroom off Bill and Dido's terrace.'

Ted is watching the road, silent, his eyes on a flock of sheep flowing down the incline ahead and around them, toward the streambed and the oak shade down the hill. He slows the car to a crawl. The sheep skitter and bound in confusion, climbing each other's matted backs to get out of the way, their nostrils flaring. At the sight of the car in the road, the shepherd leans on his wooden staff and bends over to pick up a rock, which he throws toward the sheep on the downhill side of the lane, showing his dog the direction he wants the flock to move.

'I have to hand it to Dido,' Sylvia continues idly. She bites the bitter skin from an olive, tasting its salt. 'She's so lifelike.'

The shepherd hunkers his way down the slope in his black felt hat, gathering more rocks and hurling them down the embankment past the car. Ted lets the Morris idle, waiting for the last of the sheep to pass. They scatter down the stony hillside, fat and wooly on their match-stick legs, and disappear, revealing a gap in the tree-lined vista where the implacable sprawling ramparts of the Bretenoux castle appear, perched on their distant cliff over the filmy river valley, the sky pouring blue into the hole. The silly clonking of the bellwether echoes down the steeply sloping road long after the flock has moved on.

25
Gulliver

December 21, 1962
London

Behind her, against a midsummer backdrop of mature shade trees and genteel East Coast suburbia, Ted parsed the unfamiliar American currency for the taxi driver who had dumped their suitcases and trunk and crates of books onto the curb in front of her mother's house, a fare of $3.35 from Boston's South Station to Wellesley in 1957, three dollar bills and some silver change, which Ted held out hesitantly in his open palm for the driver to pick from, as if feeding a squirrel or a wild bird. Sylvia couldn't wait; she practically skipped up the concrete path past the unpruned junipers flanking the front door, the lank petunias growing toward the light, and let herself in. 'We're here!' she yelped up the stairs, excited, the prodigal daughter returneth with a Cambridge degree and a job offer from her alma mater and a poet husband, brand new − new to America, anyway − the screen door banging on its hinge, Ted struggling up the walk with the crates, and Sylvia turned around to see her mother bent over the dining room table on which she had been arranging and rearranging all of the wedding gifts and cards of congratulations from family and neighbors, Sylvia's favorite professors at Smith, old classmates from

Haven House and Lawrence, when they learned of her marriage in London the previous June. Clocks, linens, crystal, pewter, copper pots banked to the edges of her grandmother's Austrian tablecloth, sparkling, gleaming, buffed to high luster after a year of proud maternal display and much handling. Confiture, double boiler, fish poacher, demitasse. 'We've arrived!' she squeaked as her mother straightened, going red in the face, still wearing a stained housecoat over her welcoming dress, a rag in her hand.

The bicarbonate bubbles and foams. Sylvia stands at the kitchen sink, fluorescent with wakefulness, her bony hips against the metal edge of the linoleum counter. It is some time, hours, after midnight. Her sleeves are rolled to her elbows; a dishcloth is tucked into the waistband of her apron. Fresh apple cake sweats on the drain board, warm to the touch. She sprinkles another spoonful of bicarbonate over her tarnished wedding copper, neutralizing the acid of the vinegar bath in which they've been soaking all night. The surface foams like the rush of incoming tide and subsides. Sylvia unscrews the cap on the copper polish and dips a remnant of soft flannel into the tub of polish, thick and white as cold cream.

The foam subsides and her hand plunges into the hot water. She rubs the flannel in circles over the curved surface of a copper bowl. Polishing pewter is not so satisfying: the yellow patina fades but not dramatically, leaving a milky shadow that must be buffed away. Copper, though, readily bares its new soul: the dark tarnish turns first green, then black, transferring onto the flannel, wiping away. With her cupped hand, Sylvia rinses the bowl clean. The warm water sheets off. The copper glows,

pink and unblemished as the cheek of a baby. Like rubbing
a fist against a dirty mirror – suddenly one's face appears.

*The foam subsides; racing waves rake the churning,
spiraled intricacies beneath the water's surface. Gulls
mourn overhead, riding the relentless breath of the shimmering sea. High shadowless clouds belie the violent sun,
icy white and still against so celestine a sky they register
the shock of temperature backward, like the sudden gush
of cold water from a tap that one expected to be scalding.
And yet the sand is hot, blistering to the soles of her bare
feet; hot from the grassy dunes and the salt flats skimmed
by horseflies, from the pastel bungalows and the shell-
pocked concrete bunkers where the postcard vendors and
ice cream stands take shelter, hot right down to the dark
wet shadow of the tide line where she walks, gathering
seashells for little Frieda, ankled in the cooling Atlantic
on the Côte d'Opale, the beach at Berck-sur-Mer, across
the Strait of Dover from England and home and her one-
year-old girl.*

*In its foaming retreat, the seawater tumbles a luster
onto the dulled surfaces below. Chinese hats, crimp-edged
keyhole limpets. Bubbles clear as glass, popping at the
pinhole tidal retreats of whelks and periwinkles. Tiny
hinged clam shells, coral hued, open like butterflies:
Papillons, they are called, on which she and Ted supped
last night by the dozens, steamed with butter and wine
until the shells lost their fingernail gleam. Sylvia collects
a handful and places them in Dido's wicker lunch basket
with a chambered conch, echoing and secret as a fetus,
and looks up, shielding her eyes against the harsh
aluminum light.*

*Ted sleeps on his back at the corded edge of the dunes,
away from the shouting and the kites, the holiday fami-*

*lies, the war veterans from the convalescent hospitals
scouring the horizon pointlessly. Sylvia, though, despite
herself, has gotten as close as she could to the heart-
pounding edge of damage and ruin: swinging her basket,
strolling intentionally along the village arcade in the direction of the hospitals overlooking the beach, sliding her
gaze toward the bony men with their empty sleeves, their
orthopedic boots, their ghastly burns and wheelchairs
parked on the gray slab of concrete at the edge of the
barnacled breakwater. A man with a crutch and a pinned-
up trouser leg struggles before her as she circles back on
the beach, his head down, looking for shells that he can't
pick up or just watching his footing, she doesn't know
which. He hobbles in Ted's direction, toward the new
lighthouse built to replace the one blown up by the Nazis,
toward the fishermen in their faded blue shirts stacking
baskets of herring in the distance, their flat-bottomed
berckoise boats run aground onto the sand between tides.*

*Swiftian in his repose, Ted sleeps through the halting
journey of the one-legged man who passes by, the tip of
his crutch strangled with seaweed. Immovable, Ted sleeps
through the distant calling of the fishermen, the parade
of barely clad* jeunes filles *in their vivid bikinis, oblivious
to the coital stirrings in the reeds and the sallow thorn
around him. Even on his back he appears a man-moun-
tain, an immutable backdrop to the industry of sandy-
bottomed children dragging tails of ruffled kelp fronds.*

*Tomorrow they will be home to Frieda. Sylvia hopes
her mother will remember to put the baby down for a
nap early so she'll be awake when they arrive. She can't
wait to be home. She veers up the beach toward Ted,
over the dry expanse of whiffling sand; in just the two
weeks since they passed this way on their drive south to*

the Merwins', her pelvis and ankles and knees have loosened, awash in the solutions of maternity. Unsteady, she switches the hand in which she carries her basket of shells, noticing the fullness of her belly.

'Ted,' she calls as she approaches, her voice ribboning off in the dampered air, cast out impersuasively with the calling of gulls.

'Ted,' she calls as she gets closer, the blowing sand duning against his legs, in the folds of his unbuttoned shirt; the depth of his retreat into sleep nearly knitting him into the marram grass and ranunculus on which he rests his head. 'Ted . . . Ted,' she calls to no effect.

She stands at the sink, her hands in the water, wedding copper glimmering beneath the surface.

She stands before him, shadowless in the high light, her apprehension rising, floating bloated and vulgar like the drowned, suddenly and vividly aware of the final moments of Ted's dream, his inadmissible escape. Another moment free of her, just another moment more, *asleep among the reeds and the grasses that bind the dunes, the sand that grain by grain blows away.*

26

Getting There

April 22, 1962
Easter Sunday
Court Green

Finally, on Easter, the clouds rolled back and out, at last, ascended spring.

Spring light. Perfect light. Light silvered and tender, stirring the black, drenched, amnesiac earth. Young lush of spring, dew beading at the tip of every blade, in the ruffled trumpet of every quivering, golden-eyed star on the hillside. Velvet of petals, of calyx, of sepals. Jeweled light. April light clear and shadowless, the sun writhing like a god past winter.

Ted's family is hardly waved out of the cobblestone court and down the gravel lane and out into the street for their long journey back to Heptonstall, soporific with Sylvia's midday dinner of cloved ham and scalloped pota-toes and pineapple upside-down cake, when she and Ted charge back through their house and outside to stammer over their acres of glorious daffodils, their gardens shud-dering to life, the splendor of the flawless afternoon, their sheer fantastic luck. The distant ringing of cowbells, voices, birdsong floats by on the clarity of the thin, green weather as the Hugheses gloat over their land, their white-washed manor, bowing to the whorls and fairy rings of their volunteer flowers, cutting armload bouquets of daffodils and narcissi to sell at the Monday morning market.

In her haste for the sun-soaked garden, Sylvia has not bothered to change out of her girdle and best cotton blouse; she's unsnapped her stockings and rolled them off to save them, pulled on her Wellies barefoot, thrown her mackintosh – not quite believing in the sudden shirtsleeve warmth – on top of everything. The damp grasses brush the hem of her gray flannel skirt as she bends over the daffodils with her sewing shears, snipping a half dozen at a time, holding them sheathed in their pliant green blades. The very *relief* of spring, oh God, at last! As her bucket fills, she meanders alongside the garden's front path, parallel to the orchard slope where Ted is harvesting, the daffodils so thick there they close like the sea after his cutting, leaving no trace of the loss.

Even Ted has admitted he dreams of losing Court Green. Not dreams – nightmares. Already it has become something much greater than a house or a home: a hibernaculum, for each of them, of some kind of ecstatic regeneration. The neighbors, the rector, the postman, all periodic audiences to the Hugheses' ongoing battle to reclaim the lawn from the nettles, to harrow the overgrown tennis court, to sow invisible vegetable seeds in the frosted, slushy earth, to patch and repaint and somehow stave the rotting of their half-stone house as the rain drummed, month after dreary month, on the thatch – all of them have assured Sylvia and Ted how lovely Court Green would be come spring despite them, a bower of cherry blossom and old roses and a dozen kinds of daffodils, swifts in the eaves and pheasants sunning on the ancient mound among the apple trees. Still, they haven't been prepared for the occult pleasure of it all, wave after wave of dazzling wonders, the feast it is, their true soul house, presented in all its glory today, finally, against the clear blue heavens. It is, simply, paradise. Even the rain become lovely, streaking the windows in mercury drops when Ted's family arrived – the sanguine, straw-mulched garden vegetating, fresh with promise, beyond the clean glass; the green tulips coy with their unreleased silks. And the floor men finished by Easter, just this side of miraculous! Sylvia and Ted proudly conducted the tour for the relatives, pointing out the heirloom treasures they've picked up for pennies at auction; where the plumber bored a three-foot-long hole through the eight-hundred-year-old stone to hook up the Bendix washer; saw the sun, at last, beating onto the gleaming, newly painted floorboards upstairs.

That the Devon spring should make its long-awaited appearance on Easter only adds to its perfection. Court Green's beauty is not just spiritual but carnal to Sylvia, body and blood. She has never borne the cold and the dark well, never been at her best during the grubby oppressions of winter. Like Demeter's daughter, April is when Sylvia comes back to life. April, indeed, was the month she let Ted wash over her like a baptism six years ago; April the month of both her parents' births. Even Frieda had the good sense to arrive five days late, on April Fool's. Sylvia's springtime resurrection this thirtieth year is coming in the sanctity of her study, in the ease she is finding there again, Nick only thirteen weeks old. Just as after Frieda's birth, a spurt of good poems right away. These April poems with all their complications and darkness: except for Thursday's 'Elm' not perfect yet, but she liked them, their startling texture, the notable absence of the panic to please and the technical stiffness that had so predictably intruded upon her before she and Ted made the decision to leave America. Here, all around her, in its dreamland resplendence, is the terminus of their journey.

The house seems the distance of a veritable daffodil industry behind her. Even so, she hears Nicholas's bleating complaint from the upstairs nursery as he struggles to wake from his nap. From the foot of the orchard, Ted hears the baby, too, and stands to listen over the sudden interference of Rose Key's voice blaring from the lane cottage, intended to hijack Percy's attention over the volume of his television set.

'Let me *do* it, Perce, that's not . . . put it down, you'll hurt—'

Ted is already heading downhill toward the house, swinging his full buckets. He waves his garden snips with one hand, motioning Sylvia back to her place among the flowers on the path. 'I'll bring him to you,' he assures her as he crosses between the boxwood bushes on either side of the front door.

'Thank you,' she calls automatically, inattentive as she stoops again to the flowers, fluidly commingling two distinct actions: genuine appreciation and absorption in the task at hand.

'All right, all right – just wait for me,' Sylvia hears Rose say in a tone of anxious exasperation. Silently eavesdropping, Sylvia gathers up her bucket and scissors and stealthily steps closer to the lilac hedge rife with fat green buds bruising mauve at their tips. A moment later the smarmy ballroom music emanating from Percy's television abruptly halts, replaced by an announcer gravely intoning the predicament of a wayward family of swans. Sylvia listens, picking flowers along the border of the hedge that separates her front garden from Court Green's lane and the Keys' stone cottage, adding stems of grape hyacinth, snowdrops, primroses of varying hues to a bunch she will take to her study. The doctor said one more stroke would have killed Percy on Wednesday. Now it sounds like Rose, despite herself, is destined to drive him to his grave. Lowering her bucket, now full, Sylvia crouches against the lilac, listening, hidden by the abundant foliage opposite the Keys' front door. Rose continues to chatter at Percy who, unequipped with dentures since the strokes, sounds not much different from Baby Nick, gurgly and assonant. Rose's voice ebbs and flows as she frets and scolds from room to room.

'Hello?' Rose calls suddenly from her open doorway. Sylvia ducks low to the ground, holding her scissors still. She hears Rose handwringing out on her step, accompanied by the TV's insinuations.

Now Frieda erupts from Court Green's open door, a merry bunch of daffodils in her fist. Spying her mother right away, she runs, squealing, arms wide, over the path and toward Sylvia, whose desire to conceal herself has instantly vanished. Ted follows behind carrying the sleepy baby, Sylvia's big Brownie camera around his neck.

'That's the trick to get her off her pony,' he says, grinning, motioning at the bouquet.

Her family is coming to her in the pink and supple light, her breathtaking, enchanted family, the sun's rays breaking out over them. Ted towers over their little daughter in his dear rumpled trousers, flawless, beaming like a god, all but immortal in the shadowless light.

'Stay where you are,' Ted says, leaning down to Sylvia, once she's caught and released little Frieda, to hand her Nicholas. Together they admire and exclaim with their children, Ted helping Sylvia out of her mac. Isn't our garden the most magical garden anywhere? Aren't our flowers the most beautiful?

'Just stay there, don't move,' Ted says, his palm out flat like a London bobby's as he backs away, holding the camera and Sylvia's coat. Sylvia settles herself in the cool grass, sinking into the field of flowers, dropping her scissors, tucking her skirt under her bare legs with one hand and feeling for nettles. Frieda squats in her Easter dress, toddler style, grasping her daffodil prize beside her euphoric mother.

'Were you riding the gee-up horse, Pookus?' Sylvia asks. She was so unbearably lucky! Her incredible, weird luck. To have all this – spring and summer and years to come. The world at their feet. Ted is focusing the camera on her and the children among the daffodils. He sees them seated in the grass, the white and yellow heads of the flowers trembling before them, the sharp green sheaths bending and parting, the black-limbed elm rising behind against the robin's egg sky. Frieda clutching her fistful of gold blooms. And Sylvia in ecstasies, laughing, a baby in her arms, her luminous face turned on her little girl, seeming more content, more part of herself, than he thinks he's ever seen her, beginning to be the writer she has always struggled to be, the clouds, quite literally, thankfully, lifted.

'Did you load that color film, Ponter?' Sylvia asks, giggling with Frieda, cuddling drowsy Nicholas. Frieda continues the dramatic, garbled story of her ride on the gee-up horse, and her bear's ride, and her dolly's. 'I'd love to send some of these snaps to my mother,' Sylvia says, tucking the edge of her Wellingtons well under her skirt.

'She won't believe it,' Ted exclaims, his eye to the camera's viewfinder. 'It's too glorious. Tell Mummy what you've got, Pooker Pie,' he coaches Frieda.

'Daff-a-dee!' Frieda chortles.

He was so good to her! She could hardly imagine what she's done to deserve it.

'Sylvia?' Rose calls over the lilac hedge.

Sylvia ignores the intruding summons, getting silly instead with Frieda, getting Nick's wide-eyed, newborn attention.

'One more—' Ted says, the shutter clicking.

'Sylvia, yoo hoo,' Rose calls again.

Frieda turns, smiling, toward the sound of Rose's voice.

'Pooker, look at Daddy in the flowers—' Sylvia encourages. 'Rose, just a minute,' she says, annoyed.

'Just one more, Frieda,' Ted calls, keeping the camera in focus as Frieda beams at the hedge, looking for the peek-a-boo face through the leaves.

So shatters the fragile meniscus of spring. Sylvia takes a deep breath through her nose, balances on the finger-tips of one hand as she rises out of the grass with Nicholas, paradise lost. Rose blathers on as if anyone is listening.

'. . . bouquet for Easter?'

Nosing the baby's head after a feeding three evenings before, Thursday night scudding in past a cold and drippy twilight. The winds that blew through the house, right under the feckless doorways as she'd finished 'Elm' over lunch alone in her study, had finally eased off, which she realized because she could hear voices in the front garden over the deafening silence. Ted had been at tea with the bank manager's family for hours. He'd missed Frieda's egg and bedtime. She listened, sniffing the baby's sweet bouquet.

'So if it's not a real secretary, how do you know if, um . . . ?' asked in girlish sotto voce.

On the garden path, under a few rash stars and bare

trees, stood Ted and the bank manager's sixteen year old, toeing the cobblestones and flushing, their faces lit like stunned deer in the sudden light of the open front door, caught in this backwater's envisaged fertility rite.

'How do you know what, Nicola?' Sylvia interrupted, brandishing her baby. Thick-legged Nicola, her arms full of Ted's record albums, back against the budding branches of the laburnum. Cuffed anklets and a polka-dot head scarf, a baby blue mac à la Brigitte Bardot by way of England's dairyland. 'How does he know that the secretary sleeps clenching her "buttocks tight," is that it?'

'Sylvia,' Ted pleaded.

She glared at Ted. 'You're very late. The workmen were here until supper. I needed help with our children.'

Nicola's face was ghostly. She hugged the albums to her chest.

'You can let your mother know she needn't send you to escort Mr Hughes home, Nicola,' Sylvia said icily.

'Nicola was hoping to borrow some LPs during her Easter break, Sylvia. I offered,' Ted appealed, his voice cautious and measured.

'That's fine,' Sylvia answered carefully, staring them both down. 'Take them all. Keep them as long as you like. We're expecting company, and we really can't be bothered again. Mr Hughes has a great deal of writing to do. We both have a great deal to do.'

Hesitantly, Nicola began to offer the albums she'd brought to return.

'Just keep them. Keep those, too,' Sylvia said, shielding the back of the baby's head from the drafty doorway with his blanket.

'But these are the Beethoven records that Daddy

borrowed,' Nicola protested, holding them out. 'Mr Hughes—'

'It's fine,' Sylvia snapped. 'Just take them back with you. I'm going to save Mr Hughes from himself. Believe me, he'll thank me later for the sacrifice.'

'It's fine, Nicola,' Ted said quietly. 'Why don't I help you with the records. Sylvia needs to get Baby Nick out of this damp.'

'I'm going to my study,' Sylvia corrected him. 'I've got work to do.'

27

Medusa

December 21, 1962
London

She is head down when the doorbell rings, on her hands and knees, painting the floor for the unmaterialized au pair. On her hands and knees she draws her brush across the scuffed and roughworn planks, crawling backward toward the door. Insomnia has left her in a state of dynamic paralysis, moving perpetually, her thoughts unfathomable. She is on her hands and knees and gray as this first coat, prostrate with the ineluctable weight of Ted's silent, anguished approbation, a gravity that pins her ever lower, deepening, as the hours ache by. Her manuscript is still in the parlor, untouched, sacramental, where he left it. She dips her brush into the can and spreads the heavy linoleum paint, masking the flaws that time will eventually, inevitably, uncover, despite this unyielding effort. At the intrusion of the doorbell she raises her head reflexively; the children regard her from the hallway with their moist fists of apple cake, their covered cups of milk.

With effort Sylvia pries herself up from the floor, scooping Nick onto her hip as she enters the hall and cracks the door to the flat. She pauses, silent, for signs of the professor in the lower flat. At another reproving hiss from the unanswered bell, Sylvia descends the stairs.

A gold-braided maroon uniform has capsized on the steps outside, engulfing a sullen teenager who pushes a yellow envelope at Sylvia and a fat receipt book. 'Western Union,' the uniform says perfunctorily. With Nick held aside from the chilling draft of the open doorway, the telegram squeezed in her hand, Sylvia signs the receipt, which the delivery boy then submerges in the enormous pocket of his jacket before he lists away. Standing barefoot in the hall, too numb to hope or dread, she tears open the sealed flap of the envelope and unfolds the wafer of paper it contains. The words swim at first, unpunctuated. It's a cable from her mother in black block letters: URGENT CALL COLLECT AT ONCE EMERGENCY LOVE MUMMY.

Riding the tide of wild panic, Sylvia has rushed to the phone box across the street from the post office on Princess Road, an arguable step or two closer than the kiosk at St. George's Terrace, relievedly free of the gauntlet of Chalcot Square. Both Frieda and Nick are in the perambulator, stuffed into coats and hats over their pajamas. Sylvia is calling her mother, breathlessly waiting as the operator wades through endless static for a connection to the American exchange. The morning is cold but crisply clear; Sylvia leaves the glass-paneled door of the phone box open to the pram outside. The scent of fresh bread from the bakery at the corner makes Sylvia's stomach roil. It is her mother's unnerving talent to divine Sylvia's most vulnerable moments, a gift for appearing, omniscient and generously pious, at the lowest possible tide.

Another bell rings and the pupils at Primrose Hill Primary School are excused for recess, their racket erupting gleeful and steady as they stream onto the playground on the other side of the brick wall where Sylvia stands, holding the pulsing receiver. Turning her back, she concentrates her hearing on the transatlantic buzzing of the phone. She waits, fearfully, for an answer. It is the middle of the night in Wellesley. If it were Aurelia's ulcer, someone else – Sylvia's brother, her aunt – would have sent the telegram. Maybe it was Grampy, or Mrs. Prouty – dead, moneyless, sick? The line jangles, jangles; finally there is the click of response. She listens to the operator ask for Professor Aurelia Plath to accept the charges of a collect call from Sylvia Hughes, followed by her mother's self-conscious, 'I accept.'

'Mother?' Sylvia whispers into the receiver, heart clutching. She hasn't sought her mother's voice since Aurelia left Court Green in August.

'My darling! It's you!' Her mother's tremolo vibrates over the line. 'Where are you?'

'I'm in London, Mother. I'm in the street. I haven't got my phone hooked up yet.'

'Have you moved, Sivvy?' Aurelia asks, and after a pause punctuated by the schoolyard shrieking, 'Are Frieda and Nicholas all right?'

'Yes, yes—' Sylvia answers, plugging her free ear against the pandemonium in the schoolyard. 'That's just an elementary school behind us. The children are here, they're fine.' She can hardly hear herself. Frieda and Nick are craning their necks to see beyond the pilastered gate, fascinated by the uproar of screaming, racing, tumbling older children. Sylvia nudges the pram slightly closer to the gate, giving them a better view, and pulls the door to the phone box shut, instantly reducing the noise level to a muffled, high-pitched incoherence. 'Mother, just tell me, what's wrong?'

The line crackles with interference. There is a delay in Aurelia's response. 'But you *have* moved to London,' she repeats.

'Yes, didn't you get my letter?' Sylvia asks.

'No, I haven't heard anything in weeks,' Aurelia answers, emphatic.

'I wrote to you, Mother,' Sylvia says, counting the days backward in her head, distracted by the habit of duty, righting the keel of her daughterly fealty. 'You've just not received it yet. I just wrote this weekend, telling you all about it.'

'So you're all right, sweetheart?' Aurelia asks, stalling.

'Yes!' Sylvia says, impatient. 'Tell me what's wrong with *you!* Is everyone all right? Your cable said it was urgent. What's happened?'

'Oh, darling,' Aurelia answers, hesitant, her subterfuge bobbing to the surface, 'I was just getting worried. I thought you would call me right away when you got to London.'

'Mother, I don't have a phone,' Sylvia answers, vexation countermanded by relief. The schoolchildren's shouts rise and fall at random, raucous and piercing. 'It's almost impossible to call within this district, let alone to the States. But I wrote to you right away, all the details. You'll see. You should have my letter any day.' Six hundred times! Six hundred times she's written to her mother since she left for Smith at seventeen, flooding the envelopes with reassurance, gratitude, filial praise, innumerable dazzling inventories of accomplishments for Aurelia's delectation, the convenient distance of letters keeping their intrusive bond remote, but advantageously – for both of them – intact.

'Well, I was frightened,' Aurelia hedges. 'There was

such a whirlpool of events and decisions to be made, and I hadn't heard . . .'

'Mummy, thank you for being so worried,' Sylvia soothes, momentarily unguarded, attracted into the open by the tantalizing lure of maternal sympathy. 'But really, we'll be fine. The flat is lovely; the children are happy. I'm relieved to be back in London.'

'And living in the home of Yeats – how proud you must be!' Aurelia gushes. 'I'm sure it will give you years of inspiration, remembering all the wonderful poems and plays that he wrote there.'

'Oh, he didn't actually write anything here, Mother,' Sylvia says, chagrined by her sudden scramble for approval as she listens to Aurelia's expectant breath on the line. 'He lived here as a child. But it was the first thing he mentioned in his autobiography – his first real memory was of my house, looking out the window—'

'I can picture you and your brother the same way, looking out Daddy's study windows in the Winthrop house, watching the ocean,' Aurelia says, sucking Sylvia back like the sea to her early childhood: the high, briny horizon, the gulls' cries and sleepy massage of afternoon sun shafting through glass. Winter days with her maternal grandmother in Point Shirley, on the other side of the sandspit from the Plath home: the kitchen steamy and warm, scented with chowder and gingerbread; the Atlantic heaving against the breakwater, snow at the tideline icy and salted. 'But when Daddy died . . .' Aurelia continues, her voice fading off, the background roar of the connection rushing to swallow her unspoken feelings. 'It was much more practical for us to leave. I sold the house as well as Grampy and Grammy's, and we combined our households. I had you children, and that's all that mattered.'

No matter how bitter the flavor of the distance Sylvia has protected herself with, her mother's voice and breath can lure her back into their shared need, dragging Sylvia in to digest every aspect of her individuality. Tentacles of emotion wind through the phone line, drawing them tight.

'Oh, but I love Primrose Hill. It's not like that at all for me,' Sylvia responds, kicking free.

'So your arrival at Yeats's flat is a great success?' her mother asks, the starch of age-old, sub-rosal skepticism firming her solicitude.

Unnerved, Sylvia scrambles to recover from the sudden constriction that is her response. Her mother's eye, invited or not, is once again upon her. Aurelia's beatific pride in being front row center for Sylvia's every memorable event – first word, first poem, first publication at sixteen, marital collapse at twenty-nine – is the culmination of her long-suffering motherly ambition, even the merciful remedy, it would seem, to the graphic shame of the summer at Court Green. 'I feel just what you feel, Sivvy' – the tears in runnels down her quivering face in July – 'he's broken my heart, too.' The unendurable blubbering, the consoling martyrdom. The suffocating scrutiny, each of them distorted and distorting by the focus of a too-close lens magnifying their mutual debt. Out of Aurelia's sight, connected only by ink or by cables anchored to the ocean bottom, Sylvia has labored to shore up the otherness between them and escape. She knows she could never again endure the naked exposure of last summer.

'Oh yes, Mummy, it was the perfect thing to do,' Sylvia says, true to the script, almost gay, straining to resurrect her old plucky self, dead since July, for her mother's benefit. 'It's just what I needed. I've been welcomed back with open arms. I'm so busy I can hardly stop for tea, a real deluge of activity since we arrived. Already I've been commissioned by the BBC, and gone to the cinema, and shopped for Christmas on Regent Street. And I've just sold two more of my new poems to the *Atlantic*.'

'Wonderful, Sylvia!' Aurelia crows. 'Did you make sure to give your editors your new address for the checks? And have you seen Ted, then?' she slips in.

Sylvia cups the phone, buying time as the 74 bus approaches. 'Wait, Mother, here comes the bus.' Even with the door shut the booth roars with diesel noise as the bus whines by on its way toward Kensington, giving her a moment to assemble her story. 'Oh yes, he's been by,' she says nonchalantly. 'We took the children to the zoo together, and he'll be coming to visit them once a week or so. He's agreed to a monthly allotment and regular visits will remind him.'

'Get the money you deserve for being a devoted wife, Sylvia,' Aurelia counsels. 'Get your divorce finalized before he . . . embarrasses you.'

'Oh, it's fine. I hardly think about it at all,' Sylvia says convincingly.

'Darling, I'm so glad!' Aurelia praises. 'I thought it might be awkward to be in London with Ted, but I know you're a brave girl. Don't let him ruin your wholesome future.'

'Oh no,' Sylvia answers. 'It really doesn't matter to me one way or another. I have so much to think about just getting the three of us settled and establishing myself here. I've been painting and sewing like a demon. It's been quite an adventure.'

'Well, that's part of why I was so eager for you to call, Sylvia,' Aurelia says sweetly. 'Now that you've got yourself and the children to London and the flat is secured, I thought you might like an extra special Christmas present – why don't you fly home for Christmas, my treat?'

Sylvia stiffens.

'I've got three weeks of vacation coming from the university, and Mrs. Prouty said she'd help with the tickets,' Aurelia entices. 'You know how I would love to watch the children open their presents on Christmas morning! And you could simply relax and enjoy yourself, now that the hard part is over—'

Sylvia is lithic with desperation, her footing a crumbling slope washing out through the black cable of the phone, back into her mother's riptide of emergency love.

'You wouldn't need to do a thing, darling. I would do it all. You need only come home and be taken care of,' Aurelia adds brightly.

'Mother, I can't,' Sylvia says, resisting, sweat breaking out on her brow. To believe in a mother's tenderness! How she yearns, simply, to *believe*—

And yet the days of her over-observed girlhood, housed like specimens in the bell jar of predetermined expectations, expand in the warming air of the phone box, drawing off all the oxygen. The smallest details grow sharp and particulate, acrid in their preserving vacuum. 'It's your vacation, just as you said,' Sylvia croaks. 'You need that holiday for your health – you don't need to spend three weeks cooking and cleaning and washing dirty diapers.'

'But, darling, it's Christmas,' Aurelia cajoles. 'We miss you and we're worried about you. I need my daughter happy and productive and rested more than I need three weeks of idle sightseeing or visiting friends. You and the children would be *my* present! And *you* should take the break *you* need after all Ted's put you through, and to help you prepare for the days to come.'

It is not hard for Sylvia to come up with reasons not to go. Her breakdown ten years ago was the clearest indictment of her compulsive dependence: to chase the bait of her mother's acceptance, to earn love, to be *good*. She cannot go back to her mother's womb: crawling in, crawling back defeated, no better than when she was twenty. But it is harder to isolate her reasons, now, to stay. Her body and mind push outward, down the street, past the warning chorus of screaming, running children, toward the terraces of shops milling with customers on the other side. The bakery with its iced cakes and plump fragrant loaves, the sweet shop, the hairdresser. The dairy that handcarts bottles to her doorstep at dawn. The whistling butcher in his stained apron mopping the footpath in front of his shop. The newsagent's, the post office, the draper's, iridescent silks pouring over their bolts in the plate-glass window. Real bread, flesh, real milk. She takes a whiff of self-preservation. The deep breath freezes her lungs.

'But, Mother, the whole purpose of my move to London is to work,' she begins. 'My future and the children's depend on my success here. I told you, I've already gotten a commission from the BBC – they've asked me to write about my childhood landscape.' *Here, Mother. Here's your gift, the return on investment that left you bankrupt of self, ready to cash in on mine.* She takes a breath and continues the recital of her current triumphs, thin as it feels in the December air. 'A producer in Norway has asked to translate "Three Women" for the radio there, and he never would have heard the program if it weren't for the BBC. There's simply nothing to compare in America. And I've been submitting to more magazines – I'm selling lots of reviews and articles, too, and now these poems, and this little novel coming out. I need to find an au pair so that I can get back to writing right away. I've got to finish assembling my new poetry manuscript as well and send it out to publishers.'

'That's all wonderful, darling, but precisely the argument for your coming home,' Aurelia counters, tenacious. 'Save the money on the au pair for another month. I'll take care of the children while you work. You can write right here – what better place to evoke your childhood? I could drive you out to Winthrop for your research; you could interview me. You can put me to work – I'll edit your manuscript for you. I did it for Daddy, remember. You know I'm an excellent editor.'

Sylvia doesn't answer, feeling for a way out of her mother's enveloping altruism.

'*I* can be your mother's helper, Sylvia,' Aurelia adds selflessly. 'Just as Grammy and Grampy were for me when you were small, after Daddy died. And if you wanted to go back to teaching full time, I could take early retirement and raise the children. That would certainly be easier for you than piecing a living together poem by poem.'

Sylvia is nearly faint with the confusion of their egos, their repeating histories, hardly able to breathe, afraid of what she might say – unshaped, uncensored, undefended by the veil of dramatic personae, the reliable justification, however shallow they both fear it to be, of art. She feels so entwined, so smothered, Sylvia is not sure who is whom, tight in her mother's cobra squeeze. Now Aurelia is grasping for the children, too, the words that she has sacrificed so much for – the usurpation Sylvia has fought and defied since she was twenty. She knows this: *She does not want to be her mother.*

'This is so generous of you, Mother, but I just can't. I need to stay here and struggle through.'

'But why, Sylvia,' her mother persists, trying to push past Sylvia's resistance, 'when you have a family who would do anything for you? I worry about you there alone, especially on Christmas. Why should you struggle through when you could live here, all of your family and old friends around you, good schools, and opportunities for the children—'

'Mother,' Sylvia says, her resolve condensing in the winter cold, 'I'm not ever moving back to America.' Is it her imagination, or has the street suddenly gone silent, the schoolchildren and their tide of shouts washed back into Victorian brick?

'There's no need for you to struggle when we're here to help you. You can't have much of a Christmas for the children if you're working so hard,' Aurelia argues, her dream of rescue bobbing away. 'And I was so looking forward to the joy of having my grandchildren in our home for the first time.' The true mother of her daughter, Aurelia has enough pride not to ask for an invitation to visit that she knows is not forthcoming.

'They'll have a lovely Christmas, just like all the lovely Christmases you created,' Sylvia chants, free to be magnanimous at arm's length. 'All the old traditions. I'm going to decorate the tree with cookie cutouts, glazed hearts, just like you always did, on Christmas Eve. We're going to make springerle and German punch and gingerbread. I've already been baking.' *Your stooges, Mother, gingerbread hung on the tree – glancing around the parlor with their wary raisin eyes, watching for witches, for Perseus.* 'You should see the surprises I have planned,' she says, pouring sugar over everything, the gratifying sparkle of familial legend. 'I'll write you all about it. The flat is really looking inviting and cozy. I've been sewing curtains – yellow broadcloth for the kitchen, blue velveteen for the au pair's room, and the parlor—'

'You can wash velveteen by hand, you know, if it's cotton—' Aurelia advises, scrabbling to keep psychological pace with her daughter.

'—painting the floors. I've got a blue theme for the decor, really elegant but simple,' Sylvia continues.

'I hope the Christmas package arrives' – Aurelia frets – 'not just presents but decorations, too, some of the glass garlands I thought you'd like, packed very, very carefully, so open them with caution. To make things more festive for the children – and I sent each of them exactly the same number of wrapped gifts. I know Nick is too little to tell the difference, but Frieda is getting so clever she just might, so I didn't want to take a chance—' she adds.

'It's come already, Mother,' Sylvia reassures her.

'Oh no, it couldn't have,' Aurelia says. 'You must mean the *other* one, with the balloons and the toothpaste—'

'Yes, that's right—'

'No, that's not it. The real Christmas package I mailed later,' Aurelia says.

'It's beginning to get cold out here, Mother. I should really get the children inside—' Sylvia says, feeling a bruise of guilt at her mother's familiar, scrupulous care.

'Sivvy, before you go –' Aurelia says, feeling blindly for a hold, 'the niece of a colleague of mine at the university is coming to England next month. She's a young married girl, an aspiring writer. I haven't read anything of hers yet, but her uncle said he would give me an article she published in her local newspaper. He says she would love to meet you and get your professional advice. Would you mind if I give her your new address?'

'In January, Mother?' Sylvia responds, carefully shifting

Aurelia's request to her own advantage. 'You know, I'll be absolutely swamped then – with the BBC and my silly novel coming out and all that. But I could make time, I suppose – for a friend of yours. Why don't you tell her to write and suggest a date for tea at the flat?'

'That sounds perfect, Sivvy,' her mother replies, gratitude fountaining in her timorous voice. 'I don't know what will become of the Christmas package,' she continues with enduring anxiety. 'I mailed it to North Tawton as I hadn't heard from you. I wanted it to arrive in time, but you never called me to tell me where you were.'

'I've already filed the forwarding orders, Mother,' Sylvia reassures. 'But it's getting so cold now, I really must get us three inside.'

'Oh, Sylvia, we'll miss you so on Christmas—' her mother laments.

'I'll miss you too, Mother, but I'll write you every detail,' Sylvia fawns.

'Don't forget, I'm here, darling—' Aurelia says.

'How could I ever forget you, Mummy?' Sylvia answers. She hangs up, her mother sucked back into the line like a genie into a bottle. She hangs up, holding the receiver down, down as it struggles and finally stills.

She pushes open the panelled door of the phone box, nearly gulping for breath. The incoming rush of cold and silence hits her with renewed clarity. Not even life insurance when her father died – her mother suddenly having to work full time, sometimes two jobs at once, living with her aging parents, pooling their savings, the bleeding and all the surgeries – sharing a bedroom until Sylvia left for her Fulbright at Cambridge. *Her hair, what her mother proudly called 'German blonde,' in plaits down her back, arms crossed as she watched Aurelia sign the slip of paper in her meticulous secretarial hand. It was the day after her father's death; it was settled. She'd come home from school crying, with a contract written in pencil. Her mother had signed it, promising she'd never marry again.* Nothing to show for her life but her children. No life but the furious girl breathing beside her in the dark, the words they passed back and forth – the alphabet learned at Aurelia's feet, poems for each other they hid under napkins at dinnertime. All those letters. And this unworthy daughter, Sylvia thinks – her volcanic resentment, guilt, anger, shame hardening on the surface of her thoughts – begrudges it all. Sylvia steps out of the phone box, closing the door behind her.

At the scrape of the door Frieda and Nicholas pivot toward their mother, brilliant cheeked in the cold, cheerful, excited, their noses running. Sylvia doesn't bother to look in her pocketbook; she knows she doesn't have a handkerchief. Her knuckles white on the handle of the pram, petrified, she stands like a stone on the footpath as the people pass by.

28

Purdah

It is solstice, the longest night, the veil of the year worn thin. It is the night of the universal goddess in her solitary labor: the birth of eternal return, time revolving forward and back. In her hands the curtains rustle; she hangs silks purchased this morning on Princess Road, color stirring pavonine in the lamplight of her bedroom.

Concatenating shifts of gold. Curtained, veiled, screened from the moonless street, she embraces the fate – stirring, rustling, revealing its inconstant hues beneath her fingers as she draws seclusion across the insulating glass – that she has, for lack of courage, or for courage, chosen. There are lampshades in matching saffron at her bedside, at her desk. Fresh wallpaper striped in a honeybee's plush, floors and baseboards banded black. A queen's cell, amber lit. Gold and black: honeybee, daffodil, laburnum.

Pregnant with Frieda at Yaddo in the fall of 1959, plotting their retreat to England a month later, she had dreamt of a room in London, its bed set prophetically among acres of daffodils. The scent of soil carnal and dark in her sleep, the yellows so rich she could feel them through her eyelids.

It meant nothing at the time, a dream; no pattern, no context. Pure enigma. Now the queen cups of the daffodil; now the cede of Taliesin's honey isle. The patterns unloose, breaking into facets: eyelash, breath, lip, eye.

Her second Fulbright year, just returned from their honeymoon summer in Spain. Their marriage green still, at her own anxious insistence concealed from the spinsterly proctors at Cambridge and the possibility of censure. Ted jobless, aimless in Yorkshire, in London; waiting for the mail, bored with his poems and clumsy gropings at a play, writing letters two and three times a day that only made his balls ache with longing for her, and telling her so. Living like an eyelash only, a fragment of herself, unable to think – what, in turn, she wrote to her mother, justifying her marriage against the mandate to achieve. She needed him to be her best self; together, they were one complete person, one mind. Torn from his side, Eve from Adam's rib, the distance left her bereft, in wrenching agony. An eyelash only.

Six-sided the cells of the hive, six thousand the facets of the eye. Ocelli, the simple eye: modulations of light and dark. Ommatidia, the compound eye: many jeweled lenses hexagonal as honeycomb, each sensitive to color, to movement, to the position of the sun in the sky. Six thousand images become a pattern of reality, a composite of any moment in time or space.

Was it an argument over cufflinks, that year she went back to teach at Smith? Sulking in the twilit park after her self-righteous departure; the slammed doors, the nonstarting car. Boys with flashlights were hunting for night crawlers in the tree shadows. Then Ted stormed by, looking for her, not seeing. She followed him tree to tree, hiding and waggling pine branches until he noticed.

*Rushing to keep their reservations, feeling foolish, feeling
greedy, oysters on their peacock shells for dinner. Later,
the passing cars of Northampton lit his face over hers in
the dark, beaming fine, slivered rays through the drawn
blinds.*

Six years of marriage, six jars in the bat-black cellar.

*In Court Green's wine cellar, guarding her jars of
honey. The fallout of her words settling irradiated on the
dusty jam tops, on the forgotten bottles – ruby, garnet,
jade. Its batteries nearly dead, the faltering flashlight
under her armpit projected a cone of yellowed light
toward the dank ceiling, half framing him as he turned
away, a featureless black shadow, the negative of the
man, to pack his things.*

Weaned on royal jelly, on honey, still the queen's life
a self-determined purdah, lived within the sheath of the
hive, invisible to all but her sisters. Six days a virgin –
then the world known only by the sun washing through
the milky wax of translucent cells, honey-drenched, the
hexagonal walls illumined gold. Her world a gold thing,
the art of her body priceless, and only that. Groomed,
fed, fingering her silks, attended all her life. No wind, no
dew, no bee's-purple calyx. *Magnae Deorum Matris.*

*The startled drone pinged away, stalling first in confu-
sion, sputtering over the resigned geraniums, the crisp
hydrangeas, and she watched it fly, amazed. Her father
watched it too, grinning after it, his authority confirmed.
In the direction of its flight, high meringue clouds levi-
tated over the postcard Atlantic; from the other side, the
screen door to the kitchen – the clack of sink-damp
crockery. The* Bienenkönig, *the bee king, tugged one of
her sun-pale plaits and stood up, his broad hand on his
knee in counterweight. 'Your mother needs to do some-*

thing about these flowers,' he said, brushing sandy bits of grass from his trouser leg.

Ocelli and ommatidia, the clarities shifting.

Ted agonized, seated in the parlor with her manuscript. His shattered assent, and she holding her breath, the dagger in her hands.

But they cannot see red, the bees: the leonine velvets of the queen, dark red; they cannot see poppies or apples. Blind to the cover of his *Oxford Shakespeare*, blind to the heart of their house. Red is black, or simply blank. No red, but shifts of light and shadow invisible to a woman or a man. And swift – six thousand times swift, frame by frame. To the bee with its fast-forward eyes, the movie of human life is nothing but a series of stills: the incremental sway of the cloaks and hats, the blood splashing vermilion up the walls, the bits of paper fluttering down. Daffodils, the swinging golden chains of the laburnum – to bees, flowers blink off and on like stars, like real stars ticking south as the dawn of the waxing year approaches, the sky heaving to purple behind the curtains.

Mr. Crockett, her high school English teacher, pulled up a second tatty armchair to the card table where she sat in the patients' lounge, her back to the view of McLean's seasonally groomed grounds, the wooded landscape patchy with a shell of dirty snow and pine needles. After he sat down across from her, Mr. Crockett, the only visitor she requested during her six-month stay, turned out the bag of Scrabble letters that he had brought with him every week since she tried to kill herself in August. It was now almost Thanksgiving. Concerned about her slow improvement, Sylvia's new psychiatrist had begun to wonder if further treatment might have to include another round of electric shock therapy. 'All right, Sylvia,' Mr. Crockett said mildly, without pressure or expectation, turning the letters over, pushing them with one index finger into a random grid. The game had progressed over time from agonized attempts at a reintroduction to the individual letters of the alphabet, to identifying uncomplicated words – dog, in, and – or playing with anagrams, teasing out simple riddles. Bloated from months of failed insulin treatments, morbidly depressed, Sylvia could only manage an erratic engagement with language, alternately furious or demoralized by its cloaked indecipherability. 'All right,' Mr. Crockett continued, 'I wonder if you can see words in this group.' She leaned her elbows on the table and looked dully at the four letters before her, fingers tangled in the hair at her scalp, which she recognized, without affect, as greasy and unwashed. One hand dropped to the table, lowered slowly like a flag; she fingered the letters but did not move them. 'How about T-O-P-S,' Mr. Crockett spelled, his voice in her head coming as if from a distant echo chamber. 'How about P-O-T-S,' he spelled, 'how about S-T-O-P.'

Six months at McLean. And then revival in pieces, in little bits, the words like stars surfacing, beading the expanse that had gone hopelessly, mindlessly blank.

Back from his first, lengthy meeting at the BBC, the promise of a contract for The Calm *practically in his pocket, Ted wore an expression of blank confusion, unable to process the scene: his little desk in the vestibule cleared, and books and paper everywhere, everywhere – loose, in pieces, in little bits, floating over his shoes as he stepped through the front door. And Sylvia simply standing at the end of the red hall. It was a puzzle, anagrammatic, with some kind of unthinkable meaning. It was red and white and black.*

Each page, each poem an image, a facet in the pattern of her reality, a mirror – Lady Lazarus, Ariel, the beekeeper's daughter, Sylvia.

'It says POTS, Mummy,' Sylvia said, holding her mother's hand at the intersection, across from the entrance to Harvard's Arnold Arboretum. 'It says POTS!' Aurelia was watching for traffic to pass, her baby son, three months old, only loosely wrapped in his carriage due to the muggy Boston summer. She glanced over at her small daughter, following Sylvia's finger pointed excitedly up at a STOP *sign. Sylvia was reading. She was two and a half.*

Shifting, revealing the nuanced shimmer, the gleam of meaning from another angle as the whole, like a world, revolves. A knuckle's strained pallor, or a shoulder polished by the sun.

Arms folded in judgment at the end of the hall, she ransacked his face for signs of lipstick, red smears on his collar. He looked confused. Her imagination flew into hyperspeed, light years past the sudden senselessness of what she'd done, searching for justification, excuse, anything but recognition of the pattern hidden among all those scraps of paper, their black words, the red walls keeping them from blowing out into infinite space. 'You're late,' she said.

What's black and white and read all over?

'No-no, Sivvy,' her mother corrected, holding Sylvia back from the armchair where Aurelia nursed the new baby. Willful, passionate for her mother's lap, especially now that it was occupied by another child, Sylvia kept her bare leg hitched over her mother's knee, her leather

Mary Jane dangling at the armrest, waiting for her mother to relent. Her soft sandy hair neatly brushed to the side and tied in a floppy satin ribbon, Sylvia stared into her mother's face, her expression one of cherubic determination, a grave irreplicable oneness. 'No-no, Sivvy,' Aurelia repeated, pointing toward a convenient distraction. 'Bring Mummy the newspaper, darling. Let's play alphabet. Can you find me an "A"? That's a good girl!' Watching her mother's flat smile, her swift infant imagination seeking the pattern, the parting of the rustling curtain, Sylvia let her leg slide slowly back down.

The parting of the rustling curtain . . . *The broken wall, the burning roof and tower / And Agamemnon dead.*

The curtains glow and shimmer. Behind them the sun pushes bloody out of the chimney pots. Night's infinite blackness breaks into geometry, ceremonial planes of light and shape, a London etched by the palimpsest of centuries. The chorion of the dark sloughs off, every moment of the moments before become a shifting continuum of fragmentary clarity, a spectrum of light and dark, of blame and culpability, of hope and hopelessness – broken into facets, broken again: like memory, or a kaleidoscope churning, or the eye of a bee.

29
The Moon and the Yew Tree

October 22, 1961
Court Green

She stirs under the blue surveillance of the flood-light moon, the uncommon wakeful tempo of her husband's breathing the disharmony that wakes her. She is six months pregnant, restless with the heft of her growing baby, the skin of her belly itchy and taut. Ted, though, is mostly immune to her nocturnal shuffling, or has been, since Frieda's infancy – when he learned the time-honored husbandly art of feigning sleep through night feedings – until now. With effort she rolls onto her back and over, breasts and belly to his broad back.

'What's wrong?' she whispers into Ted's neck, sensing a peculiar fretting of his jaws.

'I dreamt my teeth had the texture of sugared cakes,' he whispers back.

'Pink frosting,' Sylvia offers knowingly.

Ted groans. 'Yes.'

'I know,' she adds, settling into the furrow formed by their nested bodies in the bedclothes, a warm bulwark against the bracing October predawn. She manages to protract her arm over his waist despite her increasing girth. 'I suspect these babies have sucked all the calcium from my very bones. If you find us a good dentist in

Exeter, then I'll go when you've tried him out.' She takes a deep breath, finding herself winded by the exertion of extended statement – the baby, it would seem, foundering in her lungs.

'So I'm the guinea pig,' Ted says, folding her hand into his own.

'Yes. I'm too ponderous to leave the house,' Sylvia confirms. They lay drowsing in the thin blue light, the black shapes of their bedroom arranging themselves along the walls.

'Are you too ponderous to work, then?' Ted asks, impulsively hoisting himself from the bed, turning to tenderly enclose her in the sheets and layers of comforters he's disturbed.

'Ha,' she scoffs. In the seven weeks since moving into Court Green, the work has been never ending. Though charming and only idiosyncratically neglected from a panoramic distance, the unflattering close-up of daily intimacy has revealed their house to be nothing short of falling apart. The backbreaking scullery sink, surely more prehistoric than Dido Merwin's at Lacan, had to be replaced right away, as did the house's only toilet. In those rooms not floored in quaint but treacherous, unmortared pitch cobbles or splintering softwood, the dry-rotted floor joists were resting directly on raw earth. Entire families of field mice skittered fearlessly to and fro under the stolid, carved back door, iron-clad and hewn of centuries-old, nearly petrified oak but gaping a good three inches up from the stone threshold. Ted scoured the local auctions and weekly market for carpentry tools and began building bookcases, cobbling together crude bits of furniture for the empty rooms, chopping firewood, digging beds for a vegetable garden, scything the chest-high grass tennis court. Sylvia worked beside him, painting the interior – pink plaster walls and glossy white wainscotting – while Ted whitewashed outside. She sewed curtains and corduroy draft stoppers, upholstered second-hand armchairs and cushions for window seats, supervised the endless stream of plumbers and carpet layers and miscellaneous tradesmen hired to repair whatever they couldn't manage themselves.

Even so, the Hugheses' housework has encompassed an institutionalized, imaginative dimension. They have renewed their day-splitting rota of child care, their arrangement since the arrival of eighteen-month-old Frieda. During his afternoons free of baby-minding, Ted has completed the radio script for his play *The Wound* and is finishing a second, meanwhile driving to remote Devonshire stations to make other motley recordings for the BBC. *Harper's Bazaar* has just published his short story 'Snow,' and with the story he's working on now, he's mulling his way toward completion of a collection awaited by his publisher. An invitation has just arrived asking him to serve as one of two judges for the annual Poetry Society book selection.

Sylvia, similarly, has written five good poems since the move, spending her mornings in her increasingly alluring study. While at Court Green she's sold her first article to one of the British women's weeklies and opened her London publisher's letter of acceptance for *The Bell Jar*. Remote as the Hugheses now are by design, the clairvoyant mail still finds them, bringing commendations, checks, sought-after commissions. For a fortnight Sylvia has been relishing the droves of new children's books arriving in oversized boxes from the *New Statesman,* more than she and Ted together can possibly review. This straightaway burst of literary fecundity seems portentous, a confirmation of their last two years' weightiest choices as a couple and expanding family – a ludicrously expanding family, Sylvia likes to joke, right out of her brassieres and underwear.

Ted steps into his shorts and ducks his head before their west-facing window, out of potential sight of the rector, who has told them, to their private amusement, that he can see all that goes on at Court Green from his house. Out of the way, also, of the moonlight shafting below the curtain hems and across their bed. Another plane of that same moonlight is most certainly staining Sylvia's study, the room next door to this, and the desktop Ted sanded for her from an oversized plank of elm last month.

'Why don't you come here? I think I have a subject to add to your list,' Ted says, looking out the window toward the churchyard that abuts and surmounts their front garden, held in place by a wall of stone-studded cob and a property-line embellishment of tombstones, moved purposely over the decades as wild storms originating over the otherworldly heaths of Dartmoor knocked the relics piecemeal into the grass, forever confusing the ownership of the ancient graves.

Grumbling theatrically, Sylvia extracts herself from the cozy bedclothes. 'Which list –' she asks, waddling loose-hipped in her nightgown around the wide bedstead to Ted's side, '– the "marvels of Court Green" list, or the "poem potential" list?'

'Both,' Ted answers, holding the thick corduroy curtains fully back from the mullioned glass.

Before them glows the full luminous moon, blue and silent, unloosing her griefs over the pointed arch of the church's Gothic yew. Blue clouds cross the moon's discon-

solate face like tissue flowers floated on water. The grave-
stone fence is up to its crenulated summit in a blue-gray
wash of curling mists. The churchyard, everything, is
otherwise lost in a netherworld of dry-ice fumes, pouring,
as they watch, over the embankment into their yard.
Motionless trees float blackly over their foggy property
and up the crop-stoned wall, dense as carbon and just as
unreadable.

This is their view. There is another view, toward
pastureland with a female countenance, fertile, curva-
ceous, and full; toward their apple-orchard hillside that
modulates, over the course of two miles, into the northern
boundaries of Dartmoor. But accessing that view is
somehow harder. On that easterly side of the house, the
Hugheses are mostly earthbound – protected from their
neighbors by their triple-trunked elm to weed, to plant,
to dig the last owner's forgotten potatoes, to lift dripping
laundry from a basket and pin it to the line, to follow
windfall apples as they drop with a crack from the trees
and roll away. On this side, the sober churchyard – the
granite church itself and its floors of primordial cold, its
eight-belled tower, the black supplicant arms of the yew
– commands their eyes. So elated over the house when
they found it and the succeeding month of elaborate home-
making fantasy prior to their move, Sylvia had hardly
remembered the church and its elevated grounds. Yet it
has followed her weirdly, like those ghastly rolling-eye
portraits of Jesus, as she composes her multifarious
domestic liturgy since they arrived. She has noticed how
heedful she's become of the ritual church bells tonguing
their carillons as she unpacks boxes of housewares and
books from the towers stacked in the parlor, or scrubs
years of ash from the fireplace, or cuts out play smocks

and baby nightgowns with her wedding scissors in the playroom. She has been torn between answering and shrinking from the bells' regular Sunday assault – the weekly rumor of her disinclusion. This morning, she feels her poles magnetized by the pull of that churchyard, that moon, and that yew.

'Put it at the top of the list or the bottom?' she asks, gazing.

'Why don't you put it at the top, while it's fresh,' Ted says.

Sylvia watches the moon throbbing white behind its vaporous garments and wringing its platinum hands. 'I may just try to write it this morning and dispense with custom,' she says.

'Not give it a day to gestate?' Ted asks.

'I'm already gestating,' she answers, with an exaggerated shrug. She turns from the window and rifles the foot of the bed for her robe.

'Is there any apple pie left?' Ted asks, scrabbling for his trousers in the shadows.

'Just enough, if you get to it before Frieda,' Sylvia says, striking a match to the candlestick on the bedside table, gentling the room's cold light to a mild glow. 'I'll warm it for you while I make my coffee.'

Ted climbs down from his study in the attic carrying the single dense page of her new poem, completed that morning. He stands in the stone entrance of the kitchen and watches his wife – for a fleeting, unsuspecting moment – icing cupcakes at their borrowed table. A stack of their sorted correspondence, letters and solicitations, waits for answer beyond the baking tins and the cooling racks. She's queued her sewing as well. Frieda potters in the background with a dustpan, muttering earnestly, lost in the last frantic moments of play before nap. The Bendix washer Aurelia has underwritten as a housewarming gift is chugging noisily in the larder, plumbed last week by no small effort through Elizabethan stone. The just-washed luncheon dishes glisten on the range top of the warm Aga, waiting to be arranged prettily along the plate rail. A spatula in Sylvia's hand drips thick, pink icing. She raises her eyebrows at him, pleased with herself, surrounded by the reassuring currency of young mother-hood.

'Cakes for the rector?' Ted asks.

Sylvia chuckles; they both recall the absurd episode of a fortnight ago, waiting for the Anglican rector's visit due to Sylvia's ambivalent, immediately regretted invitation, asking for an elucidation of evensong over tea. After three days of no-shows, Ted and Sylvia were fat and sick from the unoffered cakes they had gobbled. Finally the rector appeared with the Book of Common Prayer under his arm, his unassuming generosity succeeding only in making Sylvia feel even more unctuous about her desire to goggle, an infidel, during the most atmospheric services. But that misguided local debacle was not the genesis of these partic-ular cakes. 'You inspired me,' she answers Ted slyly, running the spatula over the top of the iced cupcake in her hand, finishing it with a swirled flourish.

Right on schedule, as Ted was preparing Frieda's lunch after their morning in the strawberry patch, Sylvia had emerged from her study with the poem, 'The Moon and the Yew Tree,' written in a matter of hours, her usual practice of spending a day and night in imaginative rumi-nation of a particular subject utterly forgone, this poem arriving in its complete state virtually unbidden, as if it had been waiting inside her, ready to be unloaded at her feet.

She waits, now, for his reaction. Uncomfortably he mouths the bit of his complicated assessment. It is a good poem. In its way, utterly new for her – unhesitant and unequivocal. It is a very good, perhaps a profound poem, and profoundly disturbing. The poem seems, to him, faithful: to her, about her. It is a thought he cannot manage without a precipitous sense of gusting loneliness.

'You don't need me to tell you,' he begins. 'You know.'

She frosts her cakes, smiling privately, knowing.

He watches her at the table: not merely a new mother, but seasoned. A book of poetry, a novel under contract, books to review, her opinions sought. Protected by the lares and penates of her stake in the world: child, pregnancy, words, garden, house. He does not know how to say more of what he feels about this poem, how he sees her within its mindscape, living, regardless of her children, her writing, her layered veils of happiness, in its minatory glare. He does not know what more, how much, to say. He stalls. Frieda is tasting infinitesimal, harmless fragments of lint in the cobbled hall.

'But tell me,' he asks, cautiously pulling a thread, 'what does it mean to you?'

'What do you mean?' she asks, outwardly concentrating on her baking, but her attention, as always, divided and acute, a mental calculus of all that requires her conscious engagement: Frieda – housekeeping – balancing these incoming checks against the remaining expenses of their move, and the expenses ahead – Ted's always desired, sagacious opinion.

He holds his breath, unassisted by the indifferent incense of fall, the season's patched midday light. His teeth hurt. She knows him too well – she is too shrewd – to permit his sloppy deflection. 'I only wonder,' he begins again, 'how close this might be to a statement of fact . . .'

Sylvia draws her spatula along the curved interior of the bowl, scraping together the last of the frosting. 'I don't know,' she says, equally cautious, trenchantly sensitive to any hesitation on Ted's part, suspicious of any hint of equivocation, any wavering enthusiasm, especially now, invested as she is, as they both are, in the advantageous-ness of their muse residing in Court Green. They are already, she has decided for them jointly, true believers. There is no better reason to have come here, removed from everything. Court Green's access of space, its expan-siveness, is even more spiritual, psychological in intent, than it is practical. Their life is a garden, nothing but light. She retreats under the expedient cover of kitchen routine. 'It's what you suggested,' she says, returning his volley. 'It was an exercise.' Her body is still but for her slender, delicate wrist dipping at the rim of the icing bowl. Her eyes are hooded, purposefully focused elsewhere, not meeting his discomfited gaze.

He listens to the room, their house, its sepulchral murmurings revealing nothing.

She places the last iced cake on its waiting plate. Resting her hands in her disappeared lap, dedicated, full of purpose, she surveys the stack of mail; the pattern pieces of a new flannel dress for Frieda; the mounded basket of yesterday's crisp, freshly dried laundry – her Magnificat. She decides on the sewing: a few straight seams, no lining, a task she can complete in toto before the Keys come to collect her at six for evensong, her first.

'Who knows?' she answers in reply to his unasked

question, toeing her Singer, which was moved out of harm's way, under the table, for lunch. 'It doesn't mean anything.' Ted steps forward to lift the sewing machine for her. The conversation closes, irredeemable, abruptly sheeted as her face.

30

A Birthday Present

December 22, 1962
London

Like another lifetime: she turns the packages, the cold mysteries, in her hands, like an amnesiac. Thick papered, irregular, tied with string. Purchased yesterday, and yet the butcher's wrap, the twine and waxed twists present themselves as unidentifiable, as if conjured from another lifetime. No great riddle, really – bones, buttons: her marketing, notions, baubles for Christmas. Several of the housewares she'd already opened and used: the yardage, the black floor paint. The rest languished a day on the kitchen table while she painted and sewed and took breaks only to make pancakes for Frieda and Nick, clearing goods then from the table to the drain board, leaving them heaped on the windowsill overnight. Utterly unlike her. She's exhausted, tired to her marrow; black eyed with another night beyond sleep, visionary with the glaze of insomnia, and the children would be waking soon. A can of coffee, a jar of molasses, cinnamon and cloves, a vial of anise oil. A packet of sugar shifting like sand. Eggs and butter—

—Irish brown bread, fresh butter and eggs. The previous night's milking skimmed that September morning, and the butter just churned. Breakfast waited on the table, a solid, handsome thing carpentered by a boatwright, like all the furniture in the cottage. Their host had stoked the hearth on his way out to check his boats at the pier, the blue smoke of the turf fire blowing inland over the cottage on its drumlin, away from the village and its few houses huddled about the harbor on Cleggan Bay. They were staying on the coast of Connemara, west of Galway, with a poet acquaintance from the London awards circuit, a fisherman who had invited them to sail in return for their good company. She had gone with Ted for a week without the children to part the dolorous veils of their recent life, for the transparent Atlantic air to sweep away the impurities that had poisoned their marriage. To renew it, if they could – or that was her hope.

Her string of flattening illnesses since July and the racking movement toward a trial separation had prompted the hastily organized trip; after their recuperative week in Ireland, Ted was of a mind to remand to Spain for six months. She had been too apprehensive to ask outright if he was going alone, and Ted had not offered details. Caught between resistance and crediting any kind of progress, she had imagined him in the landscape where they honeymooned, hoping, somehow, that the potency of those memories would reach him, even if Assia were there.

Meanwhile, she needed a bookend: a winter for herself in Ireland while Ted was gone, a plan she meant to compel during this trip. Ted would walk the baked roads of Andalusia with an image of her on this briny strand – a vision of their marriage in which Assia could take no part. Court Green had been corrupted, London as well; soon, possibly Spain. But Ireland was unblemished territory –

a place they had both imagined but never seen, a layer of their joint and private myth, as marriage, until this summer, had been.

Remote Cleggan, with its sand-edged views of the Western Isles, was an hour's drive through orchid bogs and salmon rivers to Thoor Ballylee, the tower home of William Butler Yeats, the poet loved independently by both of them before they met. Ted's first loyalty, the double helix about whom all literature, before and after, cycled, was always Shakespeare; she was more a reader of serial enthusiasms and legion jealousies. Yeats, though, was a shared passion, since their courtship a rallying point, a writer with whose works they were on equal footing – *equals* – whose mystical leanings and poetics seemed often to mirror their own. Ireland, then, had been reached with heavy freight – she, in particular, hectic with gushing appreciations, that old, mortifying fault reborn of desperation to rectify their marriage, the Roman candle of her trajected future suddenly snuffed, dropping to earth.

Thirty years ago, a freak storm blew up over Cleggan Bay while the entire fleet was at sea catching mackerel by hook and line. Forty-five fishermen drowned. Houses, farms still stood empty. Their host owned the last surviving fishing boat from the Cleggan disaster, a Galway hooker – the *True Light*, its triple-sailed rigging of brown calico stiffened with tar. 'Let's take the other one,' she had joked nervously, leaving nothing to chance, and for six miles of open sea and sky she lay on the sloping foredeck of the blessed *Ave Maria* gulping salt air with exaggerated pleasure, head down to avoid a crack in the skull from the jib, ballast groaning below the deck, the sinuous timbers of the hull slapping hard over whitecap swells as they sailed toward Inishbofin.

Not all of it was exaggeration. It *was* real, her sense of release away from Court Green – not merely a break from the numbing baby routine or the staggering blow of Ted's affair, its moment-by-moment reminders of their bond ringing hollow all around her in the house. Miles from shore on the muscular Atlantic, her lungs bursting from sea spray, icy-eyed diving gannets gliding high and watchful for herring, ribboned silhouettes of seals sleek beneath the surf on either side of the slicing hooker, her sense of strangulation faded back. That was the sea's gift, the legacy of her Winthrop childhood. But relief cut both ways, leaving her lashing for resolution, clear and final.

At Coole Park, with an insistent gaiety that she now cringes to remember, she goaded Ted to climb the forbidding iron fence and carve his initials next to Yeats's on the famous copper beech. Made her vague, panicked wish over the river rushing past Thoor Ballylee – screwing her eyes shut, flinging her coins, knowing the others were watching and counting on their audience. And from the top-floor window of the tower zeroed in, like a kamikaze, on the overburdened apple tree below, surely planted by Yeats himself. Shook red apples down out of the branches, gathering a hundred pounds or more in the nettled grass. They couldn't have possibly fit all those apples into Richard's van—

—The Court Green apples are nearly gone, a few rattling in the corner of the bin at the bottom of the electric fridge. She unloads the surplus of yesterday's produce she holds at her chest: carrots, onions, celery, all of it by rote, nothing she has an appetite for. Spaghetti tonight, beef stew on Christmas Eve. Moroccan tangerines hand-picked at Yeoman's on Regent's Park Road, the green-grocer wrapping them in crackling tissue and hiding them conspiratorially at the bottom of her basket when she whispered they would fill the toes of the children's stockings—

—Their ankles scraped and rashy, they pinched foxtails from their socks all the way back to Connemara. And Ted on automatic all the while, a replacement for himself, letting her lead, as usual, in public – indulgent, patient, but disengaged, his participation mechanized. He seemed to come to life only when the interrogatory spotlight she kept shining on their marital patch-up swung in an altogether different direction, the subject of pine martens or reel fishing or the founding of Dublin's Abbey Theatre dropping a coin into his mental operations. His tolerant unreachableness only made her more desperate to reach him—

—*How's this?* she recalls, *How's this?* A knot comes apart and the paper splays, streaked with blood. Involuntary flesh gleaming at the marrow, bone cut clean like a pipe. The agreeable butcher of Princess Road with his cleaver, the guillotine drop—

—Ted was up and dressed, wearing his raggy old sweater patched at the elbows. The new one of Irish wool she'd bought for him the day before, knitted by the widow next door who owned the cow, lay on top of the cupboard, untouched in its wrapping. The curtains were tied back, revealing crippled Cleggan's straggling army of chimney fires against the glass-bottle light of the sky, cotton smokes blowing up toward them, blotting the craggy hills sliding off on their damp mosses toward the mirrory inkling of bay. Ted was gathering his things, packing them in a knapsack torn open on the twin bed where he'd slept.

She widened the door, edged a step into the silent room, cranked her face into a wide, careless smile. 'I've put the kettle on,' she told him. 'There's breakfast ready.' She watched him rolling his socks and shirts into his kit. It was only Sunday morning; their tickets for the train were for Wednesday to Dublin, then the ferry to Wales and home. She didn't dare ask. But she couldn't bear the suspense; she never could.

'We're alone, you know,' she blurted, advancing into the room to stand facing him in the narrow passage between their two beds. She sat down on her own, watching for him to look up and meet her gaze, her weight on her wrists. Trying to look relaxed, brazen as she could manage, Cleopatra to the asp. 'Richard's gone to the pier. He won't be back for some time—'

Slowly, years of her life ticking past as she waited for his response, Ted stiffened, dropping the last of his folded clothing on the coverlet. He looked up at her, his shadowed face pallid with a sadness that was almost, but not quite, pitying. 'That's not what you need, Sylvia,' he said. 'You need something entirely different.'

She struggled to still her shoulders, her face kneading. She tried to hold her mouth steady, her chin collapsing as she fought back tears. '"We were the last romantics . . ."' she quoted, all she could think of, stupidly, the words beating without mercy in her ears.

'But we never were,' Ted answered, shaking his head slowly. 'It has always been much more real than that, or this –' he paused, tasting his thoughts before he spoke them, '– vacuous, premeditated sentimentality.'

After she left him, after the first night – the first of their sleepless nights – she crossed the channel from London in the car of Cambridge classmates, then drove on with them to Paris to meet a boyfriend from Yale. But Ted was already in her, had already entered her blood.

A Birthday Present

*It was serious; she felt the workings of the great machine.
Tried not to rest her head on the backseat's vibrating
window glass, but too tired not to. Niggled discreetly with
her head scarf for hours, making certain to cover the tell-
tale bruises that purpled her neck.*

'Of course it's real,' she argued, her emotions meta-
morphic, fear transforming under pressure into challenge.
'Look at all we've made.' Did she recite it, powerless to
stave off her mounting, dendritic anger, or merely think
it?

> *An ancient bridge, and more ancient tower,*
> *A farmhouse that is sheltered by its wall,*
> *An acre of stony ground,*
> *Where the symbolic rose can break in flower,*
> *Old ragged elms, old thorns innumerable,*
> *The sound of the rain or sound*
> *Of every wind that blows . . .*

'Our life has *not* been a dream, a romantic fantasy. We
were living it hard,' she told him, her voice adenoidally
furious. 'But you're throwing it away. *I* have been living it.'

'You give us both too little credit,' he said, looking at
her straight on, seeming entirely guileless and infuriating.

'I've given you far too much,' she answered, the spite
corrosive in her throat.

He was packing his things. He was speaking so softly
she almost didn't hear it: 'I think this is what you need
from me, whether or not you want it.'

'That's such self-justifying rubbish,' she answered,
sneering. And it was. But even then she wondered as she
watched him close the flap on his knapsack and tug the
straps tight – before she averted her eyes from the blood-
spot of truth—

—She averts her eyes from the bloody stains on the butcher's wrap, the sickening weight she holds in her hands. Even in September she wondered, ever so briefly, before she let her wondering slip, sleek and black, beneath the surface.

31
Letter in November

December 22, 1962
London

In November, a month after Sylvia's twenty-first birthday, the director of McLean wrote to her mother and Mrs. Prouty, making an assessment of Sylvia's condition after three unsuccessful months in the hospital. He recommended a course of action that they now considered their last hope. She needed another round of shock treatment, administered correctly a final time by the psychiatrist she had come to trust.

And it wasn't like the other ones – the shrieking, home-made missile of sizzling light that exploded at the center of the crowd in her mind, spitting Coke-bottle shrapnel, knocking everyone down, blackening the faces. Leaving everything killed but undead; leaving her desperate to die. No, the last shock treatment was more like a witless blink in time, a black holiday to oblivion from which she woke on a regular day, breathing. But it worked like a miracle. It was almost the concept of shock, the punishment, that she needed, and it soothed her. Enough, her doctor told her, to begin her recovery.

How does one know when something's done, when the cycle is complete—

The rise of the palpable dough, the flour-satined

surface; the hard rap of a knuckle on the crust of the hot loaf. The children distracted with slabs of warm bread and honey, the oven door wedged once more, her hand in a mitt: ginger heat wafting into the kitchen, the leavening and the deepening color, lebkuchen and gingerbread losing their raw sheen. A change in the air – the first sheeting rain of autumn washing the dregs of summer away; or the barometer's plunge, the pure iron descent of winter. Apples giving at the stem, unresistant to the grip of the branch, to the withered gold leaves. Words overtaking any possibility that they might mold themselves to some other shape, hardening to a form ineluctable and sure. The vein exhausted. The last man dead.

These poems, these pages she gathers up from the floor of the disarrayed parlor, slipping them into their files, their files into order, their edges squared – by November she had known what she had done. A second book of poems, a brilliant book, thirty poems written in roughly a month; not a projection for the future, one island in her archipelago of wishes, but incontrovertibly arrived. Yes, real: sharp as sudden pain. Not history but bodies piled where they fell in a mountain pass, bleeding still; not bodies piled in a mountain pass but her life, the wreckage and the spoils spread before her, the essential battle over. The truths fanning out a page at a time. No Greek drama but a life, a woman's life, her own, and her marriage the real and bloody sacrifice.

Flushed and spent, she picks up playthings strewn across the flat, rag dolls laid waste in the hall, pots and pans and wooden spoons the children banged on, the lurid skins of dead balloons. Frieda follows behind, mimicking her mother, trilling as she pads earnestly through the hushed rooms, pushing her doll buggy, pocketing trifles – spools of thread, remnants of wallpaper. Nicholas crawls to the restocked toy basket in the parlor and plumps down, pulls arms and legs from the brimming pile, kisses the cold mouths.

The hard, complicated truths – Sylvia sweeps flour and scraps of dough from the kitchen floor, sorts the dirty laundry, stacks the empty paint cans by the door, making her reparations in a clarified world. Bathes the children after supper, stroking her hand over their slick, arching backs, rinsing the wet silks of their hair. Lathering a washcloth, she bends to Frieda's whispered request: will she open the little blue door on her daughter's leg? Sylvia's forefinger and thumb turn the imaginary knob on Frieda's soapy thigh. Frieda gasps, raising her eyes – 'An owl!' They all watch, all three, lifting their faces to follow the invisible magic in its flight, Sylvia as willing as the children to believe, to trust the transforming act of a thought, a word, a transmission between bodies.

The children in bed, she puts away her sewing things and her Singer, her stock of curtain material exhausted. Reclaims her desk: moves her typewriter into place, her manuscript. Sets aside the files of the poems she's already assembled in her binder, stacking the rest on the desktop. Tugs the chain on her new desk lamp, describing an intimate circle of light against the black arctic night outside, the streetlight on the mews haloed in frost. There is no moon, or none that she can see. A memory of its aloof radiance hovers somewhere distant, beyond the scope of her windows. She sees without it.

The bodies of the Spartans lay in the pass at Thermopylae under the full moon, the light by which the Persians crossed into Greece. The oracle had warned: your city will lay in ruins, or your king dead. By the time the Medes were assembled along the cliffs of Mount Oeta, the Spartans knew they had been betrayed by one of their own. They waited, outnumbered, with their king at Thermopylae.

Under November's full moon, apples carpeted her orchard floor. She could smell the fallen fruit from the windows of her study as she wrote the last of these poems: their overripe pungence, winey and bee-sweet; apples softening in the grass, becoming something altogether different. She smells them now – the apples; the bodies stacked brown on the kitchen table, raisined and glazed; the honey cakes spicy and cooled. The small, perfect bodies in their beds, their hair rubbed dry beneath her fingertips, skin pinked by the vigor of the terrycloth towels; their sweet, powdered aroma of innocence, dumb, oh please, to the losses of the world.

The oracle had told her: *Get wine and food to give you strength and courage, and I will get the house ready.* Haggard, insomnolent, she stands at the center of the complicated truth of herself. She fingers her manuscript, this half-inch stack of vellum, her property, complete but not finished. Her eyes skim the pages. *What is the point of suffering but redemption* – that is the question she has posed, one of many that she could ask of her life, her poems the laurel leaf, not the prophecy. She knows what she has done. Alive within this clarity, this palliative flare, she prays to no one: *Please let me have this for a while.*

32

Amnesiac

February 5, 1961
3 Chalcot Square, London

How does one know when something's done, when the cycle is complete—

There is a shadow of green over everything. The shades are drawn. It is safer here, hugging her pillow, washed green by her bedroom curtains, cushioned by the torpid roses vining the wallpaper. The lie of it all, in here, while outside flushes red.

A day, a night, a day; and so on. Calling her doctor's panel, sighing and bleeding, tucked in. She listens to her young family's mild, faraway voices through the closed door, Ted humming, Frieda's talky, liquid chatter and occasional thumps, the sound of her rubber ball escaping across the flat's small space. Live and warm, her child; live and warm, nearly a year safe in the world, babbling in the front room with Ted—

Sylvia peels back the blankets and the sheet. Has it come? Is it over? There is only a little blood on the towel, and nothing to do.

Ted sits at his cramped hallway desk. He looks up when he hears Sylvia moving from the bed, traveling their bedroom floor to stand under its threshold. Frieda, too, sitting sturdily in the front room, looks up from the amusements that surround her. Arrayed across Ted's desk are a pot of glue and sheets of clean white bond, upon which tattered fragments of inked or typewritten paper are pasted in crooked horizontal trails, like inexpert ransom notes.

She opens the door. 'I can't bear to just lie there,' Sylvia announces flatly, her voice sudden and loud in the apartment's tense quiet.

Ted scrapes his chair back and begins to rise, getting out of her way in the narrow vestibule. 'Why don't I get you some tea, or a brandy—' he offers, enlisting his genuine compassion, ready to withdraw toward the kitchen behind them.

'No,' she answers, feeling suddenly abashed, resisting the impulse to wring her hands. 'I just need something to do.' The flat is miraculously orderly, as if nothing at all had happened. It seems to have already forgotten Friday's diplopic calamity – the ripped-up papers, the rags of paper all over the floor, apocalyptic against those red walls; and within hours, the real blood. While she has been in bed, doctor's orders, Ted has erased the evidence, a thought almost as mortifying as the evidence itself.

'Would you like me to call your doctor again?' Ted asks. 'Do you feel worse? How is—' he says, hesitating, avoiding the painful details, blanching himself at the horrific memory of her standing amid the debris of his life while he kneeled over the shredded book and manuscripts, salvaging handfuls, collecting scraps in a cardboard box, her face still a mask, fearsome, not of the stony, irrational rage he came home to, opening the door to a maelstrom, but of fear – of the unforgivable, of the very real pain that was draining her face of color. On his knees, in a blizzard of paper, a vision of his wife, newly pregnant: her face ghostly, a thin ribbon of bright red blood trickling down the inside of her calf.

'No,' she says, her voice catching. 'It's all the same. I need something to happen. I can't stand this waiting. It's killing me.' As she begins to tremble, her shoulders sinking, Ted steps forward to comfort her. He stands with her in the hall, his arms around her, rubbing her back, wrapping her up in what safety he can offer.

'Maybe it's not the baby,' he whispers gently. 'Maybe it's just the appendix, and this will quit.'

They stand in the hall, nothing to say, Ted running his hands over her back, her temple resting on his chest.

'Would you like me to read to you?' he offers. 'We can put Frieda on the bed and I'll read to you both.'

'No,' she says, her sigh muffled by his sweater. 'I can't simply *wait*. I need to do something.'

Ted rubs her back, deliberating, abstracted himself, trying to imagine some feasible distraction for her.

'Do you want to write?' he asks. 'Shall I give you an assignment?'

'No,' she says. 'I can't think to write.'

They stand together in the hallway, Sylvia leaning her weight into her husband's chest. Frieda is contentedly occupied on the rug in the front room, jabbering to herself, hugging her playthings and giving them noisy smacks. With her cheek against his heart, Sylvia senses as Ted's mind snags on an idea, as someone with their ear to a track can sense the vibration of a coming train. 'What is it?' she asks, subdued, gingerly comforted by his closeness.

Again, he hesitates, feeling reluctantly at risk. 'If you'd like,' he begins, proceeding with measured caution, hoping to shield himself as well as her, 'you could do some typing.'

'I don't have anything right now,' she answers, her voice, along with her latent panic, sparking.

Ted pauses, holding her, keeping her contained. 'I'll need to type up my drafts when I'm finished . . .' he says quietly, skirting a more graphic description of his work, all of his current poems and drafts and typescripts in their present state.

'But they told me to rest,' she equivocates, unsure of the right response, balancing two possibly contradictory impulses at once, both of them coupled to blamelessness.

'It's not doing you any good to simply wait,' Ted reminds her. 'We don't know how long . . .' he adds, his voice trailing off.

Tasting the breathable air, Sylvia registers her husband's sincere concern, a love, she prays, more powerful than her faulty self. Her instinct for self-preservation bubbles up from where it had sunk to the bottom. 'I could type,' she affirms.

'I could still make tea,' Ted adds, relieved. 'Shall I set you up at your typewriter?'

'Yes,' Sylvia answers, her attention foaming. She eases out of his embrace to inspect his desk. Six or eight pasted sheets, stacked in flaky layers, appear to be ready. 'Can I take these?' she asks.

'Yes,' Ted replies, his mind, as well, operating on two channels, 'but if you could keep them in reverse order for now, or number them—' He pats her arm as he passes by to enter the kitchen, Sylvia standing in concentrated attention before his unsteady table.

She picks up the first of the pasted sheets and begins to decipher. His inimitable handwriting leaps and splashes in blotty ink over the torn scraps. Spread across the desk, more of his handwriting maps the paper rags, her own typing evident on carbons and smudged bond. In the box at her feet, pushed aside toward the vermilion wall, reams and reams of rice paper settles, ripped from its signatures, the paper so transparent that the printing on one side shadows the other, the leather-covered boards and their Florentine endpapers utterly rent. Long before they ever met, the pages of his Shakespeare had thickened and buckled with the moisture of seasons on the Yorkshire moors while he waited out his National Service, fixing radios. Later, a bleaching summer in their sunny bedroom in Benidorm, his Shakespeare always on the table where they wrote side by side, newlyweds. It was what he read to her from while she cooked; what they memorized, slapping the book playfully shut to prevent cheating, when they were first lovers. The spine was chipped, the covers unintentionally warped in the crate they shipped to Massachusetts and back, two years later, to London. The fragile pages were dog-eared; the boards and their oxblood leather were stained with the trails of silverfish, the spine's glue reduced to powder. Still, it had not been easy—

'I've been meaning to toss this out,' Ted says, emerging suddenly out of the kitchen, slipping the box and its destroyed contents far under his table, his words steering sharklike through murkily deep water. Before she can speak, he returns to the stove, carrying the kettle back in his mitted hand.

She gathers the pages he has finished pasting and walks rigidly, like something breakable, to her desk by the window in the front room. Ted distracts himself in the background, flirting with little Frieda, lowering her uneventfully into her playpen, handing her toys, murmuring enthusiasm. Sylvia sits at her desk rolling fresh paper and carbon onto the typewriter platen, aware of the tart ache in her pelvis, its slow implacable failing. Frieda tiptoes the perimeter of her playpen, proud of herself and crowing, gripping the railing for support. Ted is in the kitchen putting the tea tray together; Sylvia hears the delicate clatter of porcelain. She types in spurts, studying the flayed fragments of Ted's handwriting, his rended words, piecing them back together. She wants to forget all this, the stain of blood touching everything, and she almost will.

33
The Rival

December 23, 1962
London

The temperature, near freezing, has chilled the color from the frosted sky. Along the arcing footpath that traces the boundary of Primrose Hill the trees have withdrawn, smoky colored and contracted with cold, their bare aloof limbs repelling the clouds.

She's had just enough sleep to brace her, coffee to start her heart, a warm breakfast. Frieda and Nick are dressed in their thickest wools, all but their rosy faces covered, enrobed together under a blanket she has tucked against the sides of the pram. In the pocket of her winter coat a scrap of paper rustles against the silky lining, talismanic scrolls of ink from Ted's pen: the telephone number of the flat on Montagu Square, Dido's mother's. He told Sylvia last week he would stay there through the holidays, moving elsewhere – he didn't know where, or he didn't say – when he returned from his Christmas in Yorkshire.

She guides the pram to a stop before the telephone kiosk at St. George's Terrace, presses the toe of her shoe to the brake. The shops are shuttered and locked, Regent's Park Road quiet and still as a mausoleum this early on a Sunday. Sylvia hands the children cookies she's brought to divert them, wipes spills from their covered cups of cocoa. She gathers the toys that have slipped out of reach, gathers her courage as she steps into the booth.

The coins throttle into their slots, the numbers on the circular dial tick and stutter. She holds the scrap of paper in her hand. As the ringing begins, she closes her eyes, breathing in the self so ready to fly off in a million pieces, not knowing what she will say, having no words at all – her sense of truth too enormous for words, an inchoate lexicon.

Planets pass between rings. The windows of the launderette and the newsagent's are lifeless; Yeoman's greengrocery is barred by a locked, metal grate. It's only the cold that makes her shudder, Sylvia tells herself; she steadies the receiver at her ear. There is a burr disrupted, and a swift black sweep of air as the line connects.

'Hello?' Dido wheezes into the phone.

Sylvia startles, unprepared, prepared only for the sonorous roll of Ted's voice. She had allowed herself to imagine only that: Ted's voice.

'Dido?' she responds, her own voice tinny and small.

'Oh,' Dido says, 'Sylvia. What are you doing up so inconveniently early on a Sunday morning?' Dido's question is thick with the haze of interrupted sleep.

'I'm calling for Ted. I thought you'd already gone to New York,' Sylvia blunders. It would never be easy for her, she thinks. Always the obstacle, the flaw; Cerberus always lunging at the gate.

'I'm leaving tomorrow,' Dido answers. 'I've barely just completed my rubbishing of this place and couldn't leave until I was done,' she adds in a tone of sleepy boredom. 'The agents start showing it next week.'

Veins throb at Sylvia's temples, purpling her meagerly

immured fears. 'Then Ted has already left for his mother's?'

Dido inhales deeply into the receiver, her voice becoming nasal as she lights her first cigarette. 'No,' she replies flatly. 'He's still here, camping out. I expect he's peacefully in bed, as I was.'

Feeling perilous, Sylvia takes a deep breath, fighting to keep her thoughts in check. She gets straight to the point, pushing her imagination aside. 'I need to speak with him, please,' she says to Dido.

Dido takes another deep drag of her cigarette. 'My dear Sylvia,' she says with withering coldness, 'I am still in bed. Ted is no doubt also still in bed, and, I would venture, given the hour, asleep. We had a very late evening last night, a last gathering – before my *banissement* to the States – of the literary set. You would have loved it, in fact. Lots of nasty gossip and clinking ice. Ted was the milkiest star in the galaxy, however, the model of generous wit. Or perhaps you wouldn't have loved it, after all.'

Sylvia is hanging, hanging by a thread. 'I really do need to speak to Ted, Dido. Please,' she says, knuckles ashen on the receiver.

'Why don't you let me relay a message and make it easier on all of us,' Dido answers, her voice contemptuous.

But Sylvia has no message: she doesn't know what to say. If she could hear his voice—

Her nerves begin to give completely away, welling into her throat. She is nearly speechless, unable to access the words. Truth and love and faith: signifiers only, only pyxes for the ineffable. 'I have been working so hard—' she chokes out, struggling to mouth the syllables.

'I thought you told me you couldn't work because your

wretched husband had left you high and dry, and without a nanny you were helpless,' Dido counters, cutting her Mayfair elocution with killing scorn. 'I thought you were sick. I thought the children were scraping their little knuckles on death's door. At least, that's the impression you gave Ted—' she continues.

Maybe it is Sylvia's speechlessness that gives Dido pause; maybe it is the notable absence of counterattack that causes Dido to hesitate, holding the phone in silence, the infinitesimal stoking of her cigarette's cinder the only sound, listening to the expansive quiet of Sylvia's humbled desperation. Nothing, for an endless, catalytic minute, is said.

'If you had told me you were ill, I could have brought you and the children something,' Dido says, steely, smoking her cigarette.

'I didn't know,' Sylvia answers with difficulty, the words like pebbles in her mouth. Beyond the encapsulated air of the kiosk the street is coming to quelled, Sunday life. The newsagent has opened his door and begun papering his racks. A woman with small children and a crocheted shopping bag stands patiently by, her back turned, at the empty wooden bins of Yeoman's fruit stand.

'How will you manage with the children for Christmas?' Dido inhales, her interest begrudging.

'We'll be all right,' Sylvia answers, her sense of endangerment idling, or at least less pressing than her need to draw Dido off. She glances through the kiosk glass at Frieda and Nick. Nicholas, holding a shard of cookie in his sticky mitten, watches his sister intently as she nibbles the edges of her own. Nicholas coughs and turns his head, gazing straight into his mother's face. Sylvia waves weakly. 'I've gotten some shopping done, and my mother has sent presents from the relatives,' she says. 'I managed to do some of my baking yesterday,' she adds, stirring a faint recollection of her familiar, sedulous efficiency.

'Not those tiny peppery German cakes?' Dido asks.

'Lebkuchen – honey cakes,' Sylvia says.

'They're a more devious weapon than the Luftwaffe,' Dido says, with bland drollery. 'I believe those biscuits and the rest of your hausfrau talents had a collateral involvement in my having to get my face done.'

'I just made a batch. I could bring you some,' Sylvia offers.

'I should say not!' Dido says. 'You might as well drive me straight to my surgeon. No, I think I'll allow Trans World Airlines to save me from the threat of your Christmas cakes.'

'So you are leaving tomorrow,' Sylvia says, the manifest threat of being ripped to shreds tempering into cagey conversation.

'Yes, Christmas in New York,' Dido says, in a tone of amused disparagement. 'And I believe Ted told me he would drive up to Yorkshire this afternoon as well. "Clearing out," as he put it.'

'He's leaving today,' Sylvia says, her alarm rising.

'Yes, taking someone or other's borrowed van,' Dido confirms, nursing her cigarette. 'I can see it from this window, parked on the square. Not elegant transportation, but I suppose it will get him to his mother's. Quite rusted away, in fact.'

'He's driving,' Sylvia begins, her mind straining at a pretense. 'Perhaps he can help me. I need some things I left behind at Court Green. I was hoping he could go there from Yorkshire and bring them to me—'

'It's hardly a detour—' Dido says tartly.

'But I can't go—' Sylvia says. 'The children are still recovering, and I have to be at the flat to wait for my phone,' she elaborates, her voice earnest. Churchgoers and early park strollers with dogs on leashes amble past her along the footpath. From the pram the children appeal to the glances of passersby, smiling winningly, their noses red and running in the cold. 'And I still don't have a nanny. It could be weeks,' she adds, sandbagging her argument.

'What do you need?' Dido asks. 'Perhaps I can save Ted the bother—'

She scrambles to think, her heart whitening. The truth of what she needs is inexpressible, not something Dido or anyone else, even Ted, can supply. 'Our apples, Dido,' Sylvia answers, trying to modulate her pleading tone. 'They'll go bad in the cellar if they're not used. I brought all I could manage in the car.'

'Oh yes, I heard about those apples,' Dido says, mildly sarcastic.

'—and my curtain material, my red corduroy. I need it – I can't finish the children's room without it. And a jar of my honey. I've used up the one that I brought with me.'

'Heaven protect the obstacle that prevents you from more lebkuchen,' Dido gently mocks. 'I'll struggle into my wrap and try to wake Ted,' she exhales. 'No doubt you know better than I the mayhem he stirs up while he's packing. It's good that you've told me your list. I'll be able to remind him.'

'Dido, thank you,' Sylvia says, genuinely grateful, suddenly – the feeling so remote she hardly knows it – even hopeful.

Dido lowers the phone and walks away to awaken Ted.

There is a click of the receiver meeting marble, a wash of wind crackling on the open line. There is the click of the clasp on Sylvia's pocketbook as she fishes nervously for a hankie for the children, and the magnifying sound of her own silent waiting – her blood beating, the quick rhythm of her beating heart.

34
Daddy

December 31, 1958
Boston

Through the sharp hawthorn blow the winds. Six floors above Beacon Hill maunders the sluggish hebetude post-teatime. Snow crusted on the banks of the Charles River below; sooty gables of neighboring brick limned with snow and wisping chimneys. The stark crowns of the trees of Boston Common strung with fairy lights blinking on as the afternoon fades. Businessmen streaming home down Riverside Drive on neon fantasy: kissing the boss's wife in the confetti dark, before the swells of 'Auld Lang Syne.' Ted articulated in the other room by the grave strains of Beethoven. Sonata Twenty-four. Twenty-five. Twenty-six.

Huddled inert beneath the quilt with *King Lear,* her knees flexed, on the messy bed. *Unhappy that I am, I cannot heave / My heart into my mouth.* Picking up where they left off, reading aloud together a few days ago over tea – ceremonial afternoon tea, the one reliable meter ticking over these unstructured days. Also Freud, also the *Story of a Soul* – the autobiography of St. Thérèse, the Little Flower, hauled up to welcoming heaven in a shower of roses – and the recent works of their Boston and Cambridge neighbors, whom she could practically trip over any day on the brick-paved streets of this literary enclave: Robert Frost, Robert Lowell, Elizabeth Hardwick, Adrienne Rich . . .

It is a test; a gauge of improvement after three weekly sessions with Dr. Beuscher, her old psychiatrist, who's taken her on as a private patient. In Boston since September, both she and Ted intentionally jobless, prudently monitoring savings from prizes and teaching that should hold them for a year with just enough remaining for ship fare back to England, timely escape from the bone-snap of this American rack. Living, meanwhile, in frugal refinement, reading and studying and thinking and writing, shopping at the cheap, fly-scrimmed open stalls of Haymarket; living like serious writers. That, anyway, is The Plan.

But after the first weeks of expansive ego, the grandiose stimulations of the new, pernicious self-doubt is back. The uncertainty crushing, dangling her over the edge of another fruitless depression. The fear? She'll never write anything to justify her rejection of the life she's been groomed for. So: Brooding over the sewing of buttons on Ted's shabby clothes. Morbid witness to the premature deaths of ill-fated goldfish in their bowl. Scanning Acorn Street from the window in her workroom, waiting glumly for the mailman to climb the steep cobbles. Listening for Ted's key in the lock, his daily return from steadfast concentration at the library. After all these years, no role in the outer world, by choice – taking sanctuary now in their insulated universe of two, a closed circuit of quotidian commerce, knowing her total dependence on Ted to be counterproductive, even if it is safe and comforting. The freedom she's wanted, and paralyzed to use it. *I am bound / Upon a wheel of fire, that mine own tears / Do scald like molten lead.* Maybe she should get a job; maybe she should get a Ph.D. in psychology. Panicked voices, those old familiars, needle her. How could she have been so foolish: throwing away a faculty appointment at Smith, disappointing her mother, Mrs. Prouty, her professors, to live – scrape by, really – among the rivalrous ghosts of the writers whom she has the temerity to think herself above. She'll fail; whatever made her think she could ever succeed? *Only one thing do I fear, and that is to follow my own will,* says the good Little Flower, *Accept then the offering I make of it, for I choose all that Thou willest!*

Life in the city of her birth, meant to dilate, instead constricts with history, tightening at the rime-edged windows. Floating heads block the view: holographic before the snow-bedded Charles, the ruddy shadows of Acorn Street. The real and current face of crew-cutted Lowell, wearily mumbling revelations of bleak inner grotesquery, of sordid familial failure – nothing short of electrifying. Frost's drawled, ramified monologues as unbreachable as his eminent countenance. Henry James, of whom she would be an apprentice to circuitous subtlety, to flawlessly weighted implication – though lost on the prep-school blondes she lectured through a Northampton spring. Her feverish father and his gangrenous toe, raving curses at his fate, in the slovenly beard he died with. (Was it red? Brown? White? She didn't know, she'd never asked; she had never seen him again after he left for the hospital.) Even childhood's Louisa May Alcott levitating over the lacework elms in Louisburg Square, scribing her earnest Jo; even Jo who broke down and gave up her literary dreams to marry a kind foreigner and save herself from a wizened garret life. History, poetry, fiction – everything contracts to level an accusing finger at the mediocre watershed of her avowed vocation, this, her arid life.

Hear, Nature, hear! Dear Goddess, hear: / Suspend thy purpose, if thou didst intend / To make this creature fruitful! / Into her womb convey sterility! / Dry up in her the organs of increase . . . How sharper than a serpent's tooth it is / To have a thankless child!

And her mother, making everything infinitely worse. (She sees this, at least she understands it now – indignant resentment blowing a glow on her cinder of health. The recognition alone is a step forward.) You would think a mother would be glad to have her children close by, happy for invitations to tea. But no – it was too hard to park on Beacon Hill, too long a climb up those brick streets from the subway. Pursing her wasted lips at their successes – Ted's Guinness Award, six of his poems read over the BBC; Sylvia's acceptances from the *Sewanee Review,* the *Nation,* and most laureled of all the *New Yorker,* at last, all this fall – but her mother's response one of barely veiled disappointment, as if every publication steered Sylvia farther and farther from ever succeeding in the way Aurelia had prescribed, floating her out into the open Atlantic on a tide of impecunious poetic hubris. Which, in fact, they just might.

There's a wolf at the door. A gray-furred face pieced from a moth-eaten sealskin. The flinty canine snout, ruffed ears alert to the cries of the meek, to the telling crush of leaves. Almond-shaped cutouts through which the sea of Ted's eyes, indeterminate blue-green, blue-gray, washes over her.

'What do you think?' he asks, his voice garbled under the stiff mask, though unmistakably pleased with himself.

The smile comes, involuntary; she must, despite herself, be getting better. 'Very wolfy,' she says.

'The newspaper itches,' he says, objectively critical, lifting the mask over his head and examining the rough inside edges of the papier mâché. His shirttail hangs loose, unironed, out of his trousers. 'I think it's going to make my face sweat.' His indelible voice returned, its reflective, resonant timbre. He glances up at her as he fiddles with his disguise, observing her encampment on their bed, bounded by thick volumes, including his Shakespeare. 'What have you got there?' he asks.

'The sainted,' she answers, matter of factly, tossing titles over the quilt, flourishing her library copy of Freud's essay 'Mourning and Melancholia' for Ted to see. 'The locals and not.'

'Have you assembled your costume?' Ted asks.

She shrugs.

'You still don't want to go?'

She sighs. 'I don't know. They'll all be there,' she says, waving a dismissive hand over the bed.

'Not Saint Thérèse,' Ted answers, reading the spine of one of her books as he motions for her to make room. She scoots across the mattress and Ted sits next to her, reclining on her quilt, his shoulders resting against the iron headboard.

'You've trapped me,' she complains, tugging the edge of the quilt with feigned aggravation.

'Sorry,' Ted says, lifting his hips as she yanks the quilt free. 'Let's go to the party, Puss. Once you're there, you'll have a good time.'

'I know,' she mumbles, without conviction.

'It's worse if you never get out.'

'I know.'

'For the most part, they're perfectly fine, you know.'

'I know,' she says, feeling sorry for the images of her public self that percolate in her mind: stilted, gloomily shadowed, or glib and foolish, and excruciated after.

'What sort of costume do you need? A red cloak?'

'That and a basket, I guess,' she answers.

'Let's walk down to Charles Street, then. Though we might have to hurry – the shops must be shutting soon.'

Having to hurry, having to put forth any supplementary effort, renews her sense of resistance. 'We don't have the money to buy costumes,' she mutters.

Ted rubs his fingertip over the smooth seal fur. 'You could wear your red shoes. You could wear your red shoes and nothing else.'

She cuts her eyes at him, ready to laugh.

'They would never forget you,' he adds, smiling slyly.

'That's just what Mother thinks,' she says. 'She keeps dreaming I'm a chorus girl or a hooker or some tart, and my father drives off a bridge in shame.'

'So she brings him back to life only to kill him,' Ted observes.

'No, *I* kill him,' she corrects.

'But that's *her* invention, not yours,' Ted says. 'You've been working at something else.'

'You mean with Beuscher,' she says.

'With Beuscher, but also in your writing.'

'Oh, "Full Fathom Five."' She rolls her eyes, the narcissistic pool of self-pity too attractive to allow herself to agree.

'Yes,' Ted answers emphatically, thumping the mask in his lap, his hair falling over his brow.

'But I haven't written anything really good since we've been here. My stories are just as glazed and static as they were in Northampton,' she argues.

Ted stretches his arm across the pillows behind him to reach the table on his side of the bed; he sets his mask down, avoiding the additional books and clock and water glasses there. He rests his other hand, radiating warmth, on her quilt-covered thigh. 'You've made the courageous leap, which was the first and most necessary step. Now you need to get past the intrusions.'

'Dr. Beuscher says I'm trying to accomplish two mutually canceling things this year. One is that I want to write. The other is that I want to free myself of Mother. But now I can't write because I'm afraid she'll take possession of everything I do, as she always has.' She slides the smooth soles of her wool-socked feet down the bed sheet to reach past her knees for the copy of 'Mourning and Melancholia' atop the quilt. 'It's all in here,' she says. 'Almost word for word my experience when I was twenty, eerily exact. In Freud's terms, Mother is a vampire draining my ego.'

'Then don't let her,' Ted says. 'While we're still here, simply do what you can to practice craft. Develop your daily discipline. But don't worry about producing anything, for yourself or for your mother. Just write. You have a wealth of words; they're there. They're your bank account. You needn't squander them frivolously or inauthentically.'

'Like Cordelia,' she says.

'Like Cordelia,' Ted answers. He rolls toward her, putting his arm around her, running his hand over the quilt, the weight of his arm at her waist. He stops, lifting the edge of the quilt in his fingers – a kind of masculine daintiness – and slips his hand under it, under the soft weave of her thin cashmere pullover, brushing her skin.

'So, shall we find your costume?' he asks, kissing the side of her neck, the ticklish spot under her ear. Fingers trace her ribcage.

'I don't want any costumes,' she whispers, his hand cupping her breast, turning toward him on her hip. '"She's mad that trusts in the tameness of a wolf,"' she whispers as she helps him with the zipper on her skirt.

The weakening sun sinks beneath the crest of Beacon Hill, drowning somewhere beyond the icy river on this last day of the year. Bits of ash caught in the last glint of light sweep up the window glass and spiral, clean and white, like snowflakes.

She *is* getting better. It's the shock of it all that is so painful: mourning, after all these years, the love, simply of herself – naked, not what she could make or be, merely warm and human, flawed, like the scar at her temple that he kisses now, lowering himself to her, entering her – the love that she had never, deep in her heart, felt to be truly hers.

'No – hold *me*—' he says when she reaches behind herself to grip the curving rail of the cast-iron headboard in both her hands. He lifts her, inside her still. His body fitting hers, seeming the one thing she has never had to struggle for. She lets go. She brings her arms forward, her long, bare, elegant arms, wrapping them around his neck, his muscled back, and he moves with her across the bed, carrying her, positioning her under himself so that her shoulders are off the edge of the mattress, off the bed; he cradles her head in his hands, supporting her. Holding her hair, loose and long, in his hands. 'Do you feel safe . . .' he whispers, moving inside her. She doesn't answer, watching him for a time in the dusky teal light, losing herself, his eyes, their deep and soundable sea, on nothing but her. Feeling herself nowhere but floating out beyond the edge of their bed. Their shed clothing, the quilt, the hard floor somewhere far below. Dark wood, blues, greens. Yes, she feels safe. Head and shoulders over a precipice. Her eyes closed.

35
You're

December 25, 1962
Christmas Day
London

The bells are tolling: Christmas, Christmas! A chance for salvation, an innocent hope. Incandescent as the slender candles on her tiny tree, the blown garlands of Bohemian glass so frail they shatter, a tinkling diminuendo, at a breath. Her mother's package arriving, miraculously, on Christmas Eve day, brought to the door by the postman, the blessed postman—

The long suffering, the brutal disappointments suddenly paled. Excited as a child, she stayed up into the night confecting Christmas for her children, the bitterness at the frosted windows – well below freezing outside, the lineaments of darkness stark in the cold – no matter, held at bay by the glow of hope, by the tinsel and spice-cake hearts she hung in secret, the silver birds taking flight among the branches. Frieda's new doll dressed in its ladybug gown, propped before a copy of *Make Way for Ducklings*. Red ribbons threaded deftly through gingerbread; Nick's miniature train on its track encircling the tree. The mantel strewn with greenery and foil-wrapped chocolates; a pyramid of leafy tangerines, dishes of ribbon candy and nuts and dates on the coffee table.

And the real miracle, the dazzle of their little faces!

303

Rapt before the candles' delicate flicker, the spectacle of the ornamented tree, bright packages gladsome in their ribbons, knit stockings bulging where she'd tacked them to the mantel. The Christmas carousel turning, its pinwheel fan catching the rising heat of the red tapers Sylvia lit before waking Frieda and Nick, its procession of hand-painted shepherds and gilt-edged Magi revolving in patient anticipation, following their fateful star as the candles burn down, leading lambs and laden camels toward the swaddled Child of Light. Her children, nothing but light – from her nightgowned lap, Nicholas reaching his fingers out to touch the brilliant shapes, the dangling stars of bent straw. Frieda still baby enough to be lost in wonder, squatting before the tree in amazement, simply marveling until a present is handed to her for opening; and then the oohing over every peppermint cane, every animal or whistle come free of its wrapping, the mystifying ritual revealed.

Lost in stunning wonder—

He said he would go; Ted was going to Court Green. He agreed to drive there on his way back from Yorkshire. He would collect their apples, their onions and potatoes. He would find her red corduroy. He would bring her a jar of honey, pure and sweet. They would meet, by agreement, on Saturday morning at the flat on Montagu Square.

It was a promise. How to keep this kindling prospect in check, this shimmer, finally, of tentative connection: a minor thing, a gesture; but no insignificant act in the climate of deadening chill between them. He said yes – the wonder of it, that she could ask for something and it would be all right; that on this one point, they could come to terms. But it is vague yet, not so clear as an olive branch, a declaration of peace. It is, perhaps, more like

304

the sight of the grove from a distance, over the knots of dark water.

Yet the bells of St. Mark's peal over Primrose Hill, calling the faithful, their mellifluous notes stirring the leafless willows that bow and sweep along the misty banks of Regent's Canal, a summons cutting the frozen air to carry past the old piano factories, the empty shops and terraced houses, the stilled swings of the schoolyard and playground. Cross-legged in the rugless parlor, feeling her bones, her whittled haunches against the unforgiving floorboards, she listens to the harkening toll of the bells, her fingernails paring the thin peel from a tangerine. Loosening the web of lacy tissues that binds the fruit, offering a section to Nicholas who refuses, muffling his cough into her flannel nightgown. Listening to the radio's soar and chant of medieval carols, their inebriate censer of mysterious faith. Watching Frieda's spellbound peeling of colored foil from every chocolate ball she unwraps, her beguiled gasp at the melting spheres. To keep it all in mind, to see it all: their onions, their potatoes, their apples and honey emblematic, the practical harvest of a complicated love, residue of their marriage and its betrayals – the myths of earth and air, the salt of tears, and sweetness. Yes, sweetness: these children, warm and alive, snuffling amid the litter of festoonery. Her poetry, finally – bled from her, but genuine for it, the one voice she had waited, needed, to hear. Out of the void, the meaningless black. How the mind, the heart, resist ambiguity, wanting to believe or not, yearning toward a single truth, edged and isolate, an Australia.

It is not just Ted. *The void, the terrible trapdoor of the world swinging loose.* She rubs her cheek against her baby's downy head. Huddled in her lap Nicholas holds one of his wooden train cars, turning it over in his fat little hands, conducting his examination with infantile gravity. Frieda is deep in the serious business of play, tenting the slick dust jackets of the new storybooks over her smeary chocolate balls, over her flocked zoo animals, ribbon candy pressed into service as fencing.

It is something else, fragile but understood. She touches the edge of it, like Nicholas this Christmas morning: the vulnerable nativity of faith in herself, naked as a baby, on which, despite herself, she relies.

36

Fever 103°

December 26, 1962
Boxing Day
London

'Now, blow—'
Delicately she pinches a tissue to Frieda's raw nose, manuscript balanced in her lap. Nicholas naps heavily beside her on the bed, a little hothouse convecting beneath the sheet, coughing in his sleep. Temporality lumbers: it is still only Wednesday afternoon, Boxing Day. Three more days, three nights—

Frieda takes a dramatic breath and puffs, blowing through her pursed lips. She prances with impatience at the interruption of her play, a tempest of arrested motion. Her face is flushed. The tissue flutters. Sylvia, too, feels the strobe of fever. Three days, three nights, the nights, if luck holds, as evanescent as the last, through which her mind flickered until morning, lit by a biochemical flare. All night she flew through the protean boundaries of time, alert to the crackling of stars. All day the low pearlescent sky has made its accounting, gathering itself operatic and close, frost contracting the windows of the flat.

'All right, sweetie,' Sylvia capitulates, giving up the futile exercise, digging a sharp elbow into the stack of loose pages as they begin to slide, dabbing her two-year-old's nose as Frieda squirms away.

Frieda squirms away, indignant, and the pages fall, blanketing the floor beside the bed. The damp tissue crumples in Sylvia's fist.

Easing herself off the mattress, careful not to wake Nicholas, she crouches over the promiscuous splay of paper. To see it all, to keep it all in mind – her poems lay in much the same turbulent way they came, all out of order, not the evolutionary sequence she knows now nearly by heart, almost done, her heart, too, a turbulent thing. She reaches for the sheets, picking them up page by page. It is her heart's story that she reassembles, its story built upon stories, its lingering ambiguities as authentic as anything else about her life, its ending as yet unsure.

Sylvia gathers the loose pages from the floor, inserting poems into their proper places, transposing others. She had told herself, told anyone who would listen: these poems saved her. She had thought she knew how, but how, like her heart, has changed. Frieda, engrossed by a toy piano, plinks her metallic, random scales. Sylvia's sinuses pound as she stoops, lightheaded; she sweeps the rest of the pages together indiscriminately with the flat of her hand and sits back with them on the edge of the bed, turning them over, turning them right side up, her unsettled title page appearing out of the drifts, a list, as yet, of possibilities. Frieda trundles by with her piano; behind her aerial laces fly spectral past the windows.

Sylvia raises her head. It has begun to snow. Before she quite thinks to coax Frieda from her toy, to lift her to the windowsill to witness the street diffuse and muted through the steady filter of snowfall's early delirium, stray flakes plinking at the panes; to see lamplight absinthine at the curb where the fragile, six-fold crystals blow weightless through the lamppost's brilliant cone; to see the gutters banking in a suspicion of white, snow scarving along the ornamental parapets of the houses across the street, the flanks of Primrose Hill smoldering in snow mist, the bare branches of the hawthorn trees tassled with scarlet berries; to see it before it melts away, a mirage—

—Before all this, in a moment that passes for a lifetime, past the pleats of honey-colored silk at Sylvia's windows, through the petticoats of unhurried snow, she glimpses a future she's already written, turned and shaken in its globe, the flakes falling calm as a blessing: apple leaves holding out their small, wrinkled palms to her, bees dusted gold and droning. Bulbs aching frozen in her garden beds, gladioli and daffodils and roses stoking spring beneath the soil. Her wintering's pure dissolve.

37

The Bee Meeting

October 4, 1962
Court Green

The taxi flashes past the wavy ancient glass of the scullery window set deep in Court Green's three feet of exterior stone. She almost doesn't see it, the taxi; doesn't hear it crunching over the cobbles into the back courtyard over the blast of the faucet, her bare arms soapy and wet to the elbows in dishes, steam rising from the sink. She shuts the water down, cranes her neck, apprehensive, to see.

The taxi, idling, ripples near the stable gate, the high russeting hedge, Ted's unmistakable silhouette black in the backseat.

Sylvia steps back, wipes her hands on her apron, disarmed. She's not seen him, not spoken to him since he left her in Connemara. Now, out of nowhere, no warning; he'd told her nothing—

A car door slams, augural. The trunk of the taxi croaks on its hinges.

Nicholas lies asleep in his playpen in the warm back kitchen, curled on his belly like a hedgehog. Frieda plays quietly on the linoleum, spooning air to her plush dog. An oblique sky hammers tin through the windows, threatening rain, smearing the magenta hills in mist. Reflexively

Sylvia tugs her apron strings, but hesitates. There is nowhere to hide. She can't run. She'd have to run for the rest of her life. She reties her apron, ties it tighter around her slender waist, smoothing the clean, damp cotton. Her six Mason jars of honey gleam from the thick, white-washed sill over the sink where she's kept them the last week to admire during her kitchen routines. Through the slumping window glass she sees Ted has his wallet out, his fare undulating toward the cabbie's undulating hand, his single, rawboned knapsack dumped on the cobble-stones, suspended in her honey's amber.

Without stopping to think she grabs the flashlight, hung on a nail by the studded back door, and slips it into the deep front pocket of her apron. She leans across the sink and takes her six honey jars, lining them up in both arms, jars clinking with mellow fullness, held tight at her bosom. She turns and with a finger flicks the cast-iron latch to the broom closet, walks through, quickly, past the mops and buckets, and flicks a second latch on the interior, iron-banded door to the wine cellar.

It is utterly black inside, musty, remnants of spider webs glazing the top of her head as she stands under the threshold. She steps into the engulfing dark, pulling the door tight behind herself. Feeling blindly with the fingers of one hand, hugging her precious jars, she finds the nearest shelf clear of stuff and sets her honey down. She clicks the flashlight, which hesitantly emits a weak yellow beam over the dank space, the small windowless cell at the heart of their house, the walls earthy, the color of dried blood.

The thin light slides over the dusty shelves peppered with mouse droppings. Ted thought it too cold to keep wine. Maybe mead, maybe cider – for eight hundred years it had never been warm. The cellar has stored only the last owner's rancid preserves in grimy jelly jars, necrotic heirloom jams, their paraffin tops grayed with age, and a few hoary, vinegared bottles. Since she's come back from Ireland, she's cleared two shelves, wall to wall, and lined them with straw, bedding her potatoes, her apples; her crop of onions soon, too, drying now under burlap in the shelter of the barn. Six years, for this: her meager harvest.

The back door sighs. Ted hums, nervous, as he steps inside. It's the end of everything. She stands very still in the dark skep of the cellar, listening, battery running down. She's grown so exhausted, so old in this patched and scabbed autumn, listening to the dark drone of the past, sealing off what little she has.

Now Frieda's joyous squeal, piping as she patters to keep up with Ted's distant movements through the house.

She can't bear the dumb tension. He's searching for her, quiet, not calling – his voice a mere drone as he mumbles to Frieda, as he climbs up and down the staircase. How would she ever make it; how would she ever manage alone? All she'd wanted was honey, pure and sweet; he hadn't wanted even that. Not the bees, not the hive – but it was hers now. Nectar to ward off the loveless death whose footfalls grow closer. She steps back against the shelf where she's placed her six jars, pinching her shoulder blades against the wooden planking, secreting her honey behind her back. Hoarding her honey, her potatoes, her six balsamic poems of this last burnt week, all her fetishes; her mantic pink paper from Smith, her apples, what was left of her heart. Her heart that kicks and throbs, urgent to get it over with, waiting for the confrontation.

The Bee Meeting

Darkness drops like a veil as the flashlight stalls. The sweet vapor of her honey wafts in the blackness; she breathes it in like air, a Delphic elixir against the terrible sick smell of her immobilizing fear. She is back in the dark, the deadly cellar. Is it really over, the end of everything? She takes a deep breath of her honey's euphoric scent, tonic to this free-flying peril, the maddening drone of silence and waiting.

She hears the dull scrape of Ted's black boot, the rustle past the brooms and aprons, and the cellar door's creak. An angle of light breaks through the opening door, across the shelves and bins, the straw. As he enters she turns to face him, sweeping the flashlight, which shines, for a fleet moment, across his real face; then, as she lowers its sputtering beam, shadows him, angular and weird, like a phantom.

Ted looks at her, mental contortions struggling forth.

The answer comes. She will risk nothing. She is ready to speak, the words clustering in the black hive of her mind; her ear, that flower, awaiting her own voice. It is hers now. She is the owner. She stands defensive, her winter stores gathered behind her. She will get through another year. She will live on, resourceful. She forecasts her authority on a lie she wills to truth. She won't flinch:

'I want a divorce.'

Whatever Ted had dressed himself in, whatever protection or disguise, falls away.

She shudders – it is so *cold* – before he nods and turns to pack.

38

The Arrival of the Bee Box

December 27, 1962
Court Green

Ted stumbles out of the van before the latched gate to the back courtyard, having fishtailed, the balding tires spinning in knee-high snow, up Court Green's unplowed lane. He unhooks the latch under the precise beam of the headlamps and struggles to tug the gate open against the resistance of the undisturbed, overnight drift. It is snowing still, though in a becalmed, leisurely sift, the fat flakes meandering into his coat collar, melting in his threadbare scarf; coating his uncovered head in white as if to warn of their true, decisive intent.

Back in the cab he eases the hand brake, grinding the reluctant gears uphill and into the blanketed back court. He kills the engine, shuts down the lights. Everything is blue. The silent, snow-packed old vicarage, the barn and outbuildings stand eerily still, the windows dark, the thatched roofs of the house and the empty cottage where he stores his tools coated thickly and glinting, as if in icing sugar. It hardly seems his house.

The journey itself has seemed his soul's trial, a cosmic return on his heedless investment in guilt. He said he would go to Court Green for her, his reasons for coming as errant as his emotions, as his current life. He has had

morning till night now to think about that alone, slog-
ging from the Pennines at a snail's pace down England's
whiteout spine, snow driving straight into the windshield
with no relent for three hundred miles. Having to stop
every quarter hour to clear the built-up slush from the
feeble wiper blades; almost as often – hunched over the
steering wheel to squint into the squall, like every other
underdressed pilgrim skidding benumbed over the nearly
impassable roads toward some necessary destiny, the
heater boxes groaning nonstop under the dash in every
vehicle – almost as often wondering what he was doing,
why he was doing this. He nearly thought better of it
yesterday, eating Boxing Day goose with his parents as
the snow began to fly, unworrisome flurries at first,
carried fast by the moor-top winds. By the time he'd raked
the coal fire in the tiny parlor hearth – the last one to
bed, sitting alone with his finger of brandy after the others
were asleep – the snow had begun to stick, a batting of
white running geometric over the tops of the hewn black-
stone fences patchworking the Calder Valley. When he
parted the curtain this dawn, it was snowing hard, the
derelict van caked to the wheel wells, the blizzard rearing
like a swan. Even so, he really never considered backing
out, of driving straight to London. He simply could not
disappoint her again, the reasons, though complex, clear
enough.

The children, first of all, had been ill, and so had Sylvia.
He didn't trust her to make the trip by herself, so phys-
ically spent; it was an all-day drive, one way, in ordinary
weather. He's come because he feels he owes her this
much – even so paltry a grant as this. His guilt, what he'd
done to them, to her, has made him as powerful as the
giant she'd imagined him to be: he could bring her the

treasures she wanted. In turn, he could justify his rationalization that this break, this end, as she would have it, was good for her. She had the things that were really important, what she wanted most – her children and her art. She was better off; he'd seen what she had been able to do, freed of their claustrophobic symbiosis, his eye upon her, her own, pitiless, upon herself.

And because, after all, this was how their relationship had always worked: she needed; he responded. He had moved to America because she so wanted to; it was a need, at the time, that he understood only in part. They came back to England, thank God, because she'd been ready to go, had needed to. There was no small relief, he could admit to himself, in fulfilling her limitless need with a mere trip through the snow, a few apples, some material.

And his need was to see his house, his home, to go back to the proof that it really existed, not a hallucination but a dream become nightmare. He needs that reminder: too easy, since summer, to slough away the unseen, unreminding losses, to reward oneself with the throb of the new, the heady, greedy, gloating ease of no history. To be forgetful when remembering holds such a razor to the throat. It was easy, he has discovered, to justify anything in a vacuum.

All he had ever wanted was to make his life simple; to make room for his soul's expansion. To write, only that. Instead, every decision – jointly made at her insistence, because of her need – despite how often practical, how often fruitful – complicated his imagination with distracting detail, like those intricate sketches she'd made during their honeymoon: melon carts heaped in the swarming market square at Benidorm; wreathed garlic, rope sandals, jugs of wine tethered against the swaying beads in shop doorways. The sardine fleet back with its silvered morning catch, the shimmer of jumbled scales and bald eyes glinting against the cerulean sheen of the ocean, under the critical blaze of sun; orange starfish and scarlet crabs caught in the bunched mesh nets. The more complicated the subject, the better she liked it. It gave her something to dissect, a problem she had the means to solve, something she could wrestle down by ingenious will.

Moving to Court Green: that, too, was complex. Sylvia's soulwork required motherhood and all that entailed; she needed, as well, to be freed from distraction, to give her mind rein: the combination a hazardous paradox. He, too, had wanted to retreat from distraction, the tug of a public literary life, increasingly interruptive in London. His was a dream of rooms, of landscapes, empty but of words, unburdened. They had isolated themselves purposely, and thereby created their own undoing. Life in exile had put them under the microscope of each other's incessant scrutiny, one mind become incendiary and suffocating, nothing left to breathe. It had been maddening, to strangle under such cultivated fecundity. This house, their joined life to be unfurled in it, had seemed so rare and fine a thing. The dream had seemed so real.

Dematerializing at dawn with his rod and tied flies, waiting silent in the shallows of the leaf-lit riverbed, otters bellying down the Taw's grassy bank beside him, unaware – he had waited for, looked for disruption, the bubbles escaping at the surface; had finally made it himself – unwittingly? Fatedly? It would be a relief to believe so. His one unilateral move: now he couldn't move at all.

Tied down like Gulliver, boxed up like their summer order of bees, huddling themselves alive in the snowy orchard. His every flinch, now, become something violent, as much a sting to himself as to everyone he'd become authorized to hurt. It had been insane. All of it? Not all, but some, certainly most of the last six months. So much lost now, historic regardless, to the finality of her fiat, which he dutifully, guiltily, obeys.

If not for the snow, he could have arrived at Court Green by early evening, gathered Sylvia's supplies, resecured the house, and made it to London late that same night, back for a few last days of incremental removal from Dido's place: a mattress, table and chair held back for his use – settling in their austerity – all that was left of her mother's Edwardian trove. The leasing agents had already taken possession, their full-barreled showcasing of the flat waiting only, at Dido's request, for Ted to turn in his key.

The sun is a memory, down hours past, set behind the dense, whitened crown of the churchyard yew, but the snow supplies its own light. He's made it. All that had kept him on edge, tense with concentration as he peered through the sweeping wiper blades, looking for the road through the blinding, driving snow, falters unceremoniously into a nearly disorienting exhaustion. Melting snow had long ago seeped through the seams of his boots, his wool socks; his feet sting with wet so cold it feels like burning. He climbs out of the cab, shutting the rusting door.

Her apples, her onions and potatoes, her red corduroy, her honey.

He heads first toward the apple shed, trudging stiff-legged through the snow after the first yard or two of passage proves the futility of lifting his feet. He hadn't asked where anything was; it seemed too provocative an

inquiry, an invitation for more disheartened fragmenta-
tion: a question that pointed with just accusation toward
his crime of abandonment. He'd seen the apples last, he
thought, in the wine cellar. Indeed, they were not in the
shed, its creaking door admitting a trapezoid of sapphire
light. Only bushel baskets stacked up, stout canvas
shoulder bags for apple picking, the old iron cider press
he'd had no chance to use, stored under a horsehair
blanket trafficked by mice. He gathers some burlap sacks
hanging by the door and turns back into his own path,
the churned snow phosphorescent, lightly powdered with
new-fallen flakes, and follows it as far as it takes him
toward the house until forced to trailblaze the last few
buried yards to the fortified back door. At the stone step
he stamps his stinging feet, trying to loosen the layer of
snow that has crusted to his trouser legs. The key orbits
smoothly in the lock, and he goes inside.

The interior of his house admits him, as if arrested,
frozen in time, a dim, closed museum of his life, the velvet
cordons transmogrified into crimson draft stoppers filled
with dried beans, sewn on her second-hand machine,
wedged against the chilling doorways. His eyes remember
the vaulting granite of the refloored hall, the immaculate
scullery, the orderly kitchen, the chairs squared at the
rounded perimeter of the dining table, all as if lit by the
glare of the moon. He remembers with a hitch in his
unsteady heart: climbing a staircase in Hampstead to
Assia's previous digs, there to collect that offered table on
their moving day – Assia's startling, penetrating eyes; his
stammering of Sylvia's invitation to visit once they'd settled
at Court Green as he tumbled out, that table on his back.

But the table was never theirs. In this house, now
condensed in the unfamiliar snow light, it is his marriage

that beats like a heart. He feels them everywhere, his wife and himself, more vivid than they'd ever felt while he was living here, their voices, their night sighs echoing off the creamy wainscotting, off the pink plaster walls, in the blue shadows, against the cold, contracted sides of the Aga, scrubbed and swept clear of ashes. He switches on the lights, retreating from the apparition he's caught in the shadows: the sharpness of his family, his grieving wife, the veracity of it all. He searches out the flashlight by the back door, taking the burlap sacks through the scullery and the broom closet and into the wine cellar to get what he came here for.

Apples, potatoes, onions on the shelves, layered in clean straw. Potatoes cold as river stones. The onions, even chilled, are freshly pungent under their papery skins, which he rubs his thumb against, smarting his eyes. He begins to fill the bags. A few yellow Early Victoria apples, still firm. The flat, hand-filling Bramley's Seedling: blushed, green cookers. His late Pig's Nose Pippins, streaked red over green. Though dull on the trees, the colors of the Bramleys and Pig's Noses have gone vibrant, ripening as they keep. The flavors of apples, he recalls, are said to reflect their season: summer apples refreshing, August apples tasting of strawberries. Early fall apples taste of melon and wine, those ripe in late fall of honey. He chooses one and bites into it, aromatic juice bursting against his tongue, melliferous.

The honey is there, before him, five translucent pints lined up, amber to the rim, their glass tops clamped. He picks up a jar, tilts it; the honey has not crystallized but it is too cold to budge. He sets the jar carefully inside one of the burlap sacks, resting it against the shoulders of apples, and leaves the cellar.

The house still waits, humming and patient. He walks the still corridors, hesitantly browsing, a visitor, intensely aware of each step on the staircase, the turn in the landing that leads to his closed study, Frieda's little room with its bright rug, the cribs both gone. The mirror that he passes in the hall, his silvered shadow sliding by; the guestroom, their bedroom (he does not enter either), and Sylvia's study: her thick elm desk that he made for her at its place under the window. He stands in the hall, looking in. His house, her house, is anything but silent, thrumming in basso profundo with their halted life, their marriage. He turns toward the stairs, the ache of her keening constricting in his chest – at her desk, those months alone, in blue light. The ground beneath the serried orchard covered with unharvested fruit, all those fallen apples reminding her, with their honeyed scent, of the waste. The beehive so slow now in the orchard's cold, suspended, all of it, in universal snow.

He needs her curtain material. In the playroom, in the cupboards he built, he finds stacks of washed, ironed, exactingly folded fabric, as neat as the linens in the closet upstairs, as the shelves in the meticulous larder. He pries her remaining red corduroy from the stack, fumbling with the other yardage as he lifts to keep them as straight as she has left them.

There had always been so much to be done. This idleness is perhaps the most strange, the most surreal, his standing helpless in his house, hapless, his task so quickly accomplished, the buildings and the rooms taken care of, efficiently defended, the fallow garden, the weathered trees under their custodial cushion of pristine, blue snow, self-contained.

There will be no moon tonight. The headlamps on his

borrowed van can't be trusted. His house, by all appearances, has every measure of warmth: the thick red carpet he installed on the stairs, the drawn curtains of red corduroy. Nicky's playpen loaded with toys in excess, the cocked heads of plush animals lined up on the cushioned window seat in the playroom. The crockery, the few copper pots she left behind, arranged artfully in the kitchen nooks, talismanic, to greet her on spring's return. Their books insulating his hand-built parlor shelves, dust jackets aged, colors deepened, like cellared wine or brandy or apples. All their smatterings of furniture from this auction, that neighbor's attic, the heat of her attention's love still kindled in their clean paint, their burnished, waxed finishes made new under her hopeful fingers. But in truth, it's cold to the bone, his breath a ghost hovering before his numb face. He'll have to live with it overnight.

A taxi smokes curbside at Montagu Square on the day after Boxing Day. The single passenger, a woman, has hurried to the front door to ring the bell and waits now on the step, hugging a heavy, rectangular parcel. A minute, two, pass; the snow continues to fall, silent, but loud, so loud it masks the dangerous sound, as yet unintelligible, of the parcel, hugged close against the damage of snowmelt. The snow falls, and a man appears in a dark suit: the agent from the estate company, present to show the leaseable flat. There follows a quick conversation, snow settling prettily onto the shoulders of the woman's coat, and then the man in the suit stands aside, nodding to the woman, holding the door open for her entrance. It closes behind her as she passes through.

39

Stings

December 28, 1962
Court Green

The snow has gone crystalline in the overnight freeze and pours like beads of shattered glass through his fingers. His carpentry tools – his chisel, his blade file, his mallet and square – are cleaned, honed, oiled, carefully lined up in the makeshift workshop he had marshaled in the cottage. In the loft the corms of the gladioli drowse under linen rags, dry in their frangible husks, snug with the tender dahlia tubers; all wintering over, all locked away.

The morning air against his skin, his face, is stitched with ice. He wipes his bare hands of dry, cold snow and turns from the cottage, his steps exaggerated and high, tramping up and through the crusted drifts, past the loaded van and its unsure battery, toward the thick oak door at the back of the house to lock it. He is leaving, his key in his hand.

When will he ever be back – the thought stings him more than the icy air. Another storm is expected by tomorrow, announced by the rector, who called a greeting over the holly hedge, his hat pulled low, plodding over the thickly banked footpath with his little aluminum garden spade to open the church for Innocents' Day service.

His hand on the back door's latch, the key in the lock – who knows when either of them, he or Sylvia, will come back. He leaves his key suspended in the lock, opens the door, and enters one last time, stomping his boots of snow, passing the scullery, the buckets, the brooms, the black latch sliding and in the dark of the cellar reaches for the remaining jars of her honey, the last of her harvest—

—Her face as she peered into the combs that first day of beekeeping, searching for the just-delivered queen, imagining the creamy wax cups full, the slow cascade of thick gold, the bellows of the bee man's smoker stoking her dream: her life in a cowslip's bell, under the blossom that hangs on the bough. The bees recognizing the unfaithful lover, climbing into his hair, the six sudden stings. Her fear as he ran through the orchard, pursued, her face transforming from sweet anticipation to helpless terror, throwing off her gloves, her cheesecloth veil, running after in the futile desire to protect him – the thought of it, so peculiar: Sylvia wanting to protect *him*—

—He loads the full jars against his jacket, safe under his crooked elbow. She might need all of this honey; there was no telling when she might get back. It was a kindness; he could still do that for her. He withdraws from the house and turns his key, leaving the cellar empty.

40

The Swarm

December 28, 1962

It is Innocents' Day, Childermas, the Feast of the Innocents: a day for reflection on ungovernable violence, and hope springing forth regardless. A day to reflect on the jealousy and greed of Herod, angered by the wisdom of the Magi, ordering the slaughter of the children of Bethlehem – all those black and bloodied roses. A day to remember the Magi, patient astrologers, those sacred Eastern scribes, priests to the heavens: they watched the fixed stars burning past Aries, past the sacrifice of fire and the ram, the laws of Abraham and Moses, toward Pisces: the fish, the waters, salvation through faith and the harvest of a virgin. They followed their stars, carrying gold and myrrh and frankincense; they joined the desert shepherds carrying fruit and honey and doves. A day to remember a dream of flight: both the Magi's, alerting them to bypass Herod's Jerusalem and slip unnoticed home, and Joseph's, sending him into Egypt's safety with the anointed Child of Light.

It is Innocents' Day and another storm is building, another chapter in the unfinished story of what will become the Big Freeze, the coldest winter in England since 1740. The winds spin clockwise from Iceland, from

Sweden, moving south, moving west. There will be snow-banks eight feet deep in Kent; there will be drifts of twenty-five feet on Dartmoor, freezing ponies in their steps, cattle and sheep, swans freezing to the ice of their lakes. The snow and the cold will stop the trains, the roads, the pipes, the telephones, the electricity, the Thames, London falling back on Dickensian candlelight, snow on the ground every day in England until the first week of March, the country ground to a halt, and spring an impossibility. Until the end of February 1963, the weather will remain incommensurate to the island it strands, the ungovernable heavens bringing out its big guns against so mild a target, the echoing report of snow slumping off rooftops seeming the voice of an unmoved God.

But on Innocents' Day the Napoleonic dimensions of the winter are yet unknown, the snow as yet a delight, an unusual wonder. London is a palace in ivory, tigers cavorting in their outdoor enclosures at the zoo, lions dragging their horsemeat into the snow to eat. And Sylvia, too, smiles up at the snow, like everybody, at the heaven-sent tabula rasa, at the sledders on their cardboards on Primrose Hill.

In the nearly undetectable warmth of two portable heaters running at once, Frieda rides the springing gee-up horse, her nose crusty, and slides off to give her babies rides. And Nicholas wriggles in Sylvia's lap, slapping her typewriter keys and squealing and grabbing, quick to imagine being unfairly thwarted, grumpy with his lingering cold. And before the view of a snow-marbled sky stilled under chimney smoke, Sylvia retypes the table of contents for her manuscript, her new book, her heart racing, her cheeks hot. Her book begins with 'love.' It ends with 'spring.' The bees will fly from their combs past winter, housekeeping at the door of the hive, sipping the roses. The hellebore, the snow rose, will bloom out of the darkest months – the legend of a simple faith. *The little shepherdess watched the wise men pass with their rich gifts, the shepherds with their fruit and honey and doves. The little shepherdess wept to have nothing, not even a flower. And seeing her tears, an angel swept away the snow. There was the Christmas rose: a single white bloom, its petals tipped pink.*

Rolling out Christmas cakes, lebkuchen and gingerbread and springerle, the anise-scented springerle dough imprinted with a thorny rose pattern, Sylvia's Catholic grandmother had told her the story, the cresting December waves of the Atlantic grinding ice on the beach outside. Her granny sang an old chorale in German and English, '*Est ist ein Ros' entsprungen,*' as she gathered scraps of dough to reroll:

> *Lo, how a Rose e'er blooming from tender stem hath*
> *   sprung!*
> *Of Jesse's lineage coming, as those of old have*
> *   sung.*
> *It came, a floweret bright, amid the cold of winter,*
> *When half spent was the night . . .*
>
> *This Flower, whose fragrance tender with sweetness*
> *   fills the air,*
> *Dispels with glorious splendor the darkness every-*
> *   where . . .*
> *Bring us at length we pray, to the bright courts of*
> *   heaven,*
> *And to the endless day.*

Bring us, we pray, Sylvia thinks, to spring, rolling the typed sheet off the platen, rescuing it from Nicky's quick hands. She aligns another sheet of paper in her Olivetti and types a new title page for the manuscript. The inscription she types reads 'For Frieda and Nicholas,' but the title is for herself only: *Ariel.* Her new book will not be *The Rabbit Catcher,* not *Daddy,* not *The Rival.* It is not for him, not for them – it is solely for herself, her words true in a slipstream of memory, desire, and flaw. True to herself. To keep faithful to that understanding, pure as this accreting sanction of snow: *Ariel.*

She reads her new pages over, held up and away from clutching Nicholas, struggling to focus beyond him as he bounces in her lap. She reads through the titles of her forty-one poems, their order as familiar and automatic as her every breath, until she gets to 'The Swarm.' What is it about this poem that alerts her dis-ease? She has caught the allegorical cycles of fruition and decay, has limned her satiric resistance to a single truth, a violent will to control. Yet something about it gnaws at her. She marks it with parentheses and leaves it, feeling queer, where it is.

And Ted is driving with his plunder, his progress tectonic in the lumbering van, the snow catching up to him early, blowing him back as he crawls up the arduous A30, the A303, the A30 again. He will drive day into night through snow, arriving, bone weary and cramped and cold, to dump his pirated goods in the chill corners of his eremitic room, to fall into bed at Montagu Square, not noticing the contents of the parcel brought to the empty flat in his absence, left unwrapped, squared in the center of the borrowed table he uses as a desk so that it would be the first thing he would see.

But he won't see. It will remain unnoticed, missed by
Ted, in its unmissable place through the next morning
until Sylvia arrives, slim and incandescent as a candle,
flushed, her cheeks bright with cold and fever, her skin
translucent with all her sleepless nights, like new and
gilded wax; her heart in the hands she keeps jammed in
her pockets, trying to imagine how to begin to speak of
faith. Not her faith in him, not an exterior faith, but her
faith, newborn, and tender still, in herself. Not a solution, yet, not an answer to the questions their spoiled
marriage has left unsettled, but something to hold on to.
Struggling at her dumbness, veiling her struggle with a
panicked critical eye, assessing the precise tone of the
green walls of the room, the provenance of the Della
Robbia crown moldings, his unmade bed, the burlap sacks
lumpy with the onions and potatoes and apples that had
gotten her here, her red corduroy in an unfolded heap, a
glint of glass and honey-gold out of the top of one of the
sacks, and on his desk the red leather binding of the
Oxford Shakespeare.

His *Oxford Shakespeare*: immediate, perfect, the
patina of its red leather deepened with age, like wine or
brandy or apples; unbelievably reincarnated, as if her
mistakes had truly, with the snow, been erased. And she
will step toward it, this miraculous recovery, and draw
her hands, empty, from her pockets, to touch it, to open
it, an act of faith, a confirmation. And as he looks on,
uncomprehending, and as she grasps the leather-bound
cover in her fingers and lifts it, revealing the scrolled
Florentine end papers and the new bookplate from a
shop on Regent Street and the inscription barely dry,
she will remember her days of playing the anagram game
with Mr. Crockett at McLean after her breakdown. It

was winter then, as well, at least in her mind, until she got the game. She will get it now, too, the letters swimming up from this replacement and its inscription. The anagram will read *you are ash*.

41

Wintering

December 29, 1962
London

She rose from her bath on the morning of their meeting. The children were still asleep, Millie hours from arrival. She had been able to linger, then, over her ablutions, her preparations seeming almost bridal in her anxious excitement. Soaking in the hot tub laced with lavender salts, supplementing the swiftly cooling water with a steaming teakettle. Shaving her legs, buffing her feet with pumice, washing her thick hair and binding it in a towel. Rubbing rosewater and glycerine into her pale skin. Before the full-length mirror in her bedroom, dropping her wool robe to dress; her long body leaner than ever, delicate boned and frail, but purified, milky and translucent, like a candle left long burning.

As she dressed, sorting through her closet, drying her hair before the courageous little heater, braiding the long plaits and pinning them up into a crown, her heart fluttered like a bird caught at a window, yearning at a freedom it could see beyond the glass. It was something between them, she and Ted, something inextinguishable – it was blood and more, not so simple as love – through the children (coming awake now, needing their own baths, needing breakfast and entertainment), through the intuitive, alchemical blending of their imaginations, of their lives. It's what has burned her down, burned through her, alembic to her heart.

What she does not know is how to say it. *What shall Cordelia speak? Love, and be silent.* How to say that whatever had combined them, really married them, had revealed her to herself. That the manuscript on her desk shows her progress in solving her problem – the problem of herself, a lifetime's work. That there must be something left for them, for each of them, that only the two of them could learn. *We two alone will sing like birds i' th' cage; / When thou dost ask me blessing, I'll kneel down / And ask of thee forgiveness.* That there is honey still, insulated and deep.

She knows she's grown thin, and she's shaky; not feeling heedless anymore, but admittedly vulnerable and resolved. Maybe that means brave. She pulls out blocks and children's books while the oatmeal burps on the stove, scribbles a list of emergency numbers for Millie. She was never good at being patient, at moving with grace through the seasons, at waiting. But she's going to try, to have patience for the cycling back. She's got her honey to get her through: this manuscript finished, *The Bell Jar* coming out in two weeks, the BBC still holding fire, news of a nursery school only a couple of blocks away.

Was it honey's immoderate sweetness, coming at such a bitter time, that made it so precious? Of the six jars that were her legacy, one she'd already used; Ted, if he's remembered it, should have one in his custody this minute at Montagu Square. The last four are in the wine cellar: the tangible promise of her return to springtime. Four more jars – four months left until she plans to go home. A jar for each of them: herself, Ted, Frieda, Nicholas. Her honey is waiting for her, for all of them, at Court Green. Her hive would make it through winter's dumb chill, enough honey to last until spring, hoarded, secreted away. A hope she can cling to, shimmering in the dark of the cellar.

She is getting ready to leave, giving instructions to Millie, newly arrived in her snowy wraps; pulling out more decoy toys, pulling out the lunch things and leaving them on the table. Giving a lipstick kiss to Frieda, busy with her buggyful of zoo animals, and to Nicholas, in Millie's arms. Putting on her coat, gathering her scarf and gloves and pocketbook. Millie agenting for Nicholas, perching on the edge of a wicker chair in the parlor, trying to jolly Frieda into sharing a zebra with her little brother. Palpable, beating, her life: the only life she'll ever have. Taking a deep breath, taking heart as she leaves, closing the door of the flat behind her, listening for its muted catch and click, heading down the stairs, she carries with her the soft, unknowing faces of her children, hot against her own hot cheek as she kissed them: the image of their mild little faces welling her eyes.

Snow, still, is sifting her world, the sky dense with it, and morning bruised and smoky. It falls steadily through the fooled lamppost's light, falls from somewhere so far away it can't be seen, from a heaven she can hardly imagine. She'll have to be patient.

She'd like to walk. Not the tube at Chalk Farm, or a bus or a taxi, nearly impossible anyway, she would guess, due to the weather – but to walk through the hush of falling snow, along the graceful sloping shoulders of Primrose Hill, past the zoo, through Regent's Park, the snow new and unblemished, only her own feet marking a trail of moonstone blue over the buried pathways, buried again behind her, in a moment, after she passes.

The snowflakes are falling on her face, melting in her hair, dusting the thick wool of her winter coat as she stands, ready, on the step outside her house on Fitzroy Road. She'll have to be patient. She can't expect miracles. Not like Cordelia: *love, and be silent.* But still she can close her eyes and see it all: the dripping feathered yellows of the laburnum brushing her skin. The daffodils waving, sturdy on their stems. The tulips and the lilacs and the poppies. Her cherry blossoms, pure and white. Her apple trees in bloom, their hypnotic spring perfume, the tender blossoms snowing down on her shoulders, in her hair. She can imagine her family on the sand near Appledore, at the northern mouth of the Taw, the Atlantic sun edging her daughter, her son, and Ted in gold – their shoulders, the crowns of their heads – and the loud pounding and sighing of the waves. If she could stand where the sun stands, would they be fronted entirely in gold, their souls exposed? Frieda runs and runs, chased by the waves and Ted, and little Nicholas drags a stick in the sand, her family's footprints, blue before the tide, so quickly erased. And when they turn to her, carrying shells and pebbles to her, running ahead of the foaming waves, they are still golden in the late light.

Snowflakes catch in her eyelashes at each step. There is no more waiting. It's here. Here, now, her moment of truth. And it falls like grace, only for her.

Postscript

On December 31, 1962, Sylvia Plath began writing poetry again, turning first to the revision of two poems left incomplete from the autumn: 'Eavesdropper' and 'Sheep in Fog.' During the next five weeks, she went on to write 'Totem,' 'Child,' 'Paralytic,' 'Mystic,' 'Kindness,' 'Words,' 'Contusion,' 'Balloons,' and finally 'Edge,' on February 5, 1963, which she composed on the back of a draft of 'Wintering.' On February 11, 1963, Sylvia Plath took her own life.

Author's Note

On December 10, 1962, Sylvia Plath left her home, Court Green, in rural Devonshire. Accompanied by her two small children and with the help of her temporary nanny, she moved to a flat at 23 Fitzroy Road, the former home of W. B. Yeats in the Primrose Hill district of London. Plath carried with her the poems she had written during the summer and fall of that year, inspired by the collapse of her marriage to Ted Hughes, and some of her earlier poems produced since the publication of her first book, *The Colossus*, in 1960. In his Introduction to Plath's *Collected Poems*, Hughes says that 'sometime around Christmas 1962' Plath made a careful selection of forty-one of those poems, arranged them in a specific sequence, and assembled the final manuscript in a black spring-bound binder. It was also around this time that Ted Hughes returned to Court Green to retrieve curtain material and apples at Plath's request. These actual events lie at the heart of *Wintering*.

Beyond the invention of the characters' thoughts and conversations and the fictional particulars attributed to real events otherwise known only in sketchy detail, the most significant departure from the known historical record is the account of the meeting between Plath and Hughes during which Plath saw a new copy of *The Oxford Shakespeare: the Complete Works* on Hughes's desk. In the novel this event takes place at the end of December, but it may have taken place about a month later, just days before Plath's death. It may also have occurred after Ted Hughes left Dido Merwin's flat on Montagu Square and moved to Soho in London; on these points the various sources conflict. The account of Hughes reading all of Plath's new poems in Chapter 22 also departs from what is positively known: Hughes did read some, probably most, of the *Ariel* period poems before Plath's death, but it is not known whether he read them all. There is also no record of Plath speaking on the phone with her mother on December 21, as she is presented doing here. A chronology detailing the correspondence between the facts of Sylvia Plath's life and the creation of her *Ariel* manuscript, and the fictional events depicted in *Wintering* can be found at the *Wintering* web site, www.katemoses.com.

I have relied on numerous sources in creating the characters in *Wintering* and their place in time. Among my primary published sources are *The Collected Poems* by Sylvia Plath, edited by Ted Hughes; *The Bell Jar* and *Johnny Panic and the Bible of Dreams* by Sylvia Plath; and *The Unabridged Journals of Sylvia Plath,* edited by Karen V. Kukil. I have also relied on biographies of Sylvia Plath by Anne Stevenson, Linda Wagner-Martin, Edward Butscher, Paul Alexander, and Ronald Hayman as well as Ted Hughes's essays on Plath collected in *Winter Pollen,* Hughes's *Shakespeare and the Goddess of Complete Being,* his early poetry collections, and *Birthday Letters*. I made extensive use of *Letters Home* by Sylvia Plath, edited by Aurelia Plath, as well as of Plath's unpublished correspondence, memorabilia, and prose archived at the Lilly Library at Indiana University and in the Neilson Library, Mortimer Rare Book Room, at Smith College. The unpublished manuscript and drafts of Plath's *Ariel* poems and her daily calendar for late 1962, collected at Smith, have been priceless resources. I have also relied on various audio recordings of Sylvia Plath, in particular those in the collection of the National Sound Archive at the British Library.

Among the critical works I have turned to are *Revising Life: Sylvia Plath's Ariel Poems* by Susan Van Dyne, *The Other Ariel* by Lynda K. Bundtzen, *Chapters in a Mythology: The Poetry of Sylvia Plath* by Judith Kroll, *The Other Sylvia Plath* by Tracy Brain, *Sylvia Plath: A Critical Study* by Tim Kendall, *Sylvia Plath: The Wound and the Cure of Words* by Stephen Gould Axelrod, *The Silent Woman* by Janet Malcolm, *The Haunting of Sylvia Plath* by Jacqueline Rose, and essay collections edited by Paul Alexander, Gary Lane, Charles Newman, Linda W. Wagner, and Edward Butscher. Two essays that have been key to my understanding of Sylvia Plath have been Marjorie Perloff's 'The Two Ariels: The (Re)Making of the Sylvia Plath Canon' and Catherine Thompson's uncollected 'Dawn Poems in Blood: Sylvia Plath's *Ariel* Poems.' Anita Helle's 'Family Matters: An Afterword on the Biography of Sylvia Plath' was my revelatory introduction to Sylvia Plath fifteen years ago and remained acutely relevant during the writing of this book. Access to Diane Middlebrook's work-in-progress and background research for her book *Her Husband* was invaluable.

Other secondary works and sources that have significantly informed the pages of *Wintering* include Robert Graves's *White Goddess*, Peter Davison's *Fading Smile: Poets in Boston 1955–1960, From Robert Frost to Robert Lowell to Sylvia Plath*, the poetry and autobiographical prose of W. S. Merwin, Kay Redfield Jamison's *Touched with Fire* and *Night Falls Fast*, A. Alvarez's *Savage God*, *Primrose Hill Remembered* by The Friends of the Chalk

Farm Library, the Dartmoor National Park Authority Web site, the archive of British Telecom, the Manuscripts Reading Room and Newspaper Library of the British Library, Emily Pollard's www.plathonline.com, *The Book of Apples* by Joan Morgan and Alison Richards, *The Beekeeper's Handbook, Third Edition,* by Diana Sammataro and Alphonse Avitabile, and *Bumblebees and Their Ways* by Otto E. Plath. Details of daily life with babies and small children were gleaned from my own family documents.

My most essential source was Sylvia Plath's table of contents for the manuscript of her second poetry collection, a list that was published in 1981 within the 'Notes' section in her *Collected Poems*. The structure of *Wintering* follows exactly Plath's original sequence for that manuscript, which was edited by Ted Hughes and published three years after Plath's death. Though Hughes reordered the poems into a more chronological arrangement and deleted several that Plath had intended for inclusion, he kept the title Plath had typed onto her final title page: *Ariel and Other Poems. Wintering*, then, takes its ultimate inspiration from the manuscript that Plath arranged with her customary meticulous attention, but a manuscript that has never been published in its intended form.

—KATE MOSES
San Francisco, California

July 2002

Acknowledgments and Permissions

I am enormously grateful to the following individuals and institutions for their assistance during the writing of *Wintering*:

Karen Kukil, Associate Curator of the Sylvia Plath Collection at the Mortimer Rare Book Room, Neilson Library, Smith College, provided hours of assistance – at a distance and in person – with painstaking grace. The Lilly Library, Indiana University, provided me with an Everett Helm Visiting Research Fellowship, and the librarians there, particularly Rebecca Cape, came to my timely aid on several occasions. Thanks are also due to the intrepid and generous curators of the National Sound Archive located at the British Library.

The scholars and critics Richard Larschan, Kathleen Connors, Marjorie Perloff, and Anita Helle kindly shared with me their expertise on Plath.

Rosemary Hooley of Skaigh Stables, Belstone, Devonshire, provided me with detailed information about riding practices in Britain and, in particular, northern Dartmoor and its environs.

For their unfailing support, their tireless curiosity and pride, and their myriad familial ministrations, I offer my appreciation to my extended family on every side – the various branches of Moses, Kamiya, and Alford clans, in particular David Alford, Bob Alford, Jonathan Alford, Season Jensen, Joe and Joanne Kamiya, Mark Kamiya, Adele Moses, Bill Moses and Tish Lee, Goldie Moses, John and Marina Moses, Nancy Moses, Ramona Pedersen, Dorothy Walker, and Kathleen and Fred Wagner.

More than thanks are due to the stalwart friends who shored me up as I wrote, offering me professional acuity, well-timed distraction, nourishment of every vital kind, and childcare:

Acknowledgments and Permissions

Alexandra Berven, Galia Baron, Tom Centolella, Karen Clark, Marni Corbett, Daphne de Marneffe, Jodi Douglass, Jaune Evans, Farhad Farzeneh, Robert Frumkin, Charo Gonzalez, Kelly Campbell Hinshaw, Stephen Hinshaw, Beth Kephart, Jeanie Kim, Yun Kim, Jean Hanff Korelitz, Sharron Lannan Korybut, Ed Lopez, Ruth Lopez, Christina Myers, Sultan Pepper, Camille Peri, Rahna Reiko Rizzuto, Susan Straight, and Katherine Whitney.

Diane Middlebrook's warm exuberance, camaraderie and scholarship have defied the notion of writing as a solitary endeavor. I am forever indebted to our unique partnership.

I thank Ellen Levine for her shrewd mind and her enormous heart, evident always, and her relentless belief in this book and in me. I am grateful for the work of the Ellen Levine Literary Agency on *Wintering*'s behalf; an unexpected phone call from Diana Finch or Allyson Giard or Louise Quayle has been better than Christmas.

I was immensely lucky to have a team of astute, intuitive champions behind the publication of *Wintering*. In addition to Ellen Levine and her staff, I want to offer my enduring appreciation to Diane Higgins of St. Martin's Press and Carole Welch of Sceptre, both perceptive, discerning editors with an amazing capacity for subtle and harmonious observations. Their wholehearted trust in me and complete faith in *Wintering* have been gratifying beyond words. Thank you, also, to Nichole Argyres and Amber Burlinson for their gracious, reliable and erudite stewardship of the vital details.

I'd like to acknowledge the generosity of my children, Zachary Paris Tomlinson and Celeste Erice Kamiya, not just for sharing me with Sylvia Plath through four school years but also for allowing me to plumb their babyhoods for material.

No one has done more in support of this book than my husband, Gary Kamiya: first among my editors, and unmatched as an insightful critic. My heartfelt thanks for his unwavering sustenance, his love, and his tender care.

Finally, I want to remember William John Moses (1936–1994), Arlen J. Hansen (1936–1993), and Wendy Alford Corpening (1940–2001) – my dad, my guide, my daffodil. Thank you for every minute.

A line from *Mother Goose* appears on page 23. The quotation from a children's chant on page 144 is from 'Little Cottage in the Wood', author unknown. A line from *The Hound of the Baskervilles* by Sir Arthur Conan Doyle appears on page 150. A line from Geoffrey Chaucer's *The Canterbury Tales*, 'The Squyre's Tale', appears on page 181. The New Testament, Matthew 8:12, inspired a line on page 183; on page 197 is a quotation from 1 Corinthians 13:9–13. Lady Caroline Lamb's description of Lord Byron is quoted on page 185. 'The bird flies itself to the hunter', from *The Double* by Fyodor Dostoevsky, was quoted by Sylvia Plath within the text of her senior honors thesis for Smith College; it appears here on pages 191 and 193. 'Sometimes one is so defenseless', which appears on page 203, is from Ingmar Bergman's film 'Through a Glass Darkly'. The quote 'Seek all the fame you will among mortal men . . . but yield place to the goddess . . .' on page 203 is from Ovid's myth of Arachne in his *Metamorphoses*, translated by Frank Justus Miller, Loeb Classical Library, first published in 1916. The quote by St. Thérèse on page 296 is from her autobiography, *Story of a Soul*, published in 1898. The passage on page 327 is from a 15th century German chorale, author and translator unknown, entitled *Est is ein Ros' Entsprungen*.

Sylvia parodies a line from *The Tempest* by William Shakespeare on page 165. *The Tempest* is also quoted on pages 178 and 324. *King Lear* is quoted on page 167 and opens chapter 34, through which appear four additional passages from the play. Two quotations from *King Lear* appear in chapter 41 as well.

A quotation from William Butler Yeats's *Unicorn from the Stars* appears on page 5 as well as on page 280. A line from 'Two Songs from a Play' appears on page 116. The poem 'My House' is quoted on page 127 and, in longer form, on page 275. Yeats's epitaph appears on page 160. The first three lines of the poem 'In Memory of Major Robert Gregory' appear on page 172. On page 210 is quoted an inscription on the wall at Yeats's home, Thoor Ballylee, in County Galway, Ireland. The quotation on page 274 is from 'Coole Park & Ballylee, 1931'. 'Leda and the Swan' is quoted on page 258. Passages from the works of William Butler Yeats are used by permission of A.P. Watt Ltd on behalf of Michael B. Yeats.